Ariel Quigley Mystery

The Lawyer Who Died Trying

Killer Cookbook #2
Recipes to Accompany The Lawyer Who Died Trying

The Chef Who Died Sautéing

A Killer Cookbook Volume #1
Recipes to Accompany The Chef Who Died Sautéing

All of a sudden, the Fat Man stepped between me and the other nun, grabbed my shoulders, handed me a duck, and ...

Artwork by Elizabeth Smily, FFCA, CIPA

The Lawyer Who Died Trying

Honora Finkelstein & Susan Smily

HILLIARD HARRIS

P.O. Box 275
Boonsboro, Maryland 21713-0275

This novel is a work of fiction. Names, characters, places and incidents either are the product of the author's imagination or are used fictitiously. Any resemblance to actual persons, living or dead, events, or locales is entirely coincidental.

The Lawyer Who Died Trying Copyright © 2007 by
Honora Finkelstein & Susan Smily

All rights reserved. No part of this book may be reproduced or transmitted in any form or by any means, electronic or mechanical, including photocopying, recording, or by any information storage and retrieval system, without the written permission of the Publisher, except where permitted by law.

First Edition-June 2007
ISBN 1-59133-191-9
978-1-59133-191-9

Book Design: S. A. Reilly
Cover Illustration © S. A. Reilly
Manufactured/Printed in the United States of America
2007

This book is dedicated to Honora's children, their spouses, and grandchildren (all of whom Susan has adopted as her "children in spirit"): Aileen and Gavin, plus Lionel and Tiernan; Kathleen and Dave, plus Kevin; Bridget, plus Robin and Ryan; and Mike and Amber.

Acknowledgements

Special thanks to Susan's mother, artist Elizabeth Smily, for another wonderful drawing of "The Fat Man" for our frontispiece.

Many thanks to Liadnan, whose knowledge about Channel Island Bank Accounts was so helpful in our resolving how embezzled funds would be treated.

Also, thanks to Kathryn Knight, who won our "Name the Nasty Lawyer" contest. Congratulations, Kathryn!

Thanks to Honora's nephew, Patrick Moore, whose Halloween parties are legendary (and possibly even internationally famous!) and who inspired the Halloween party in this novel. Also, many thanks to the crew at Patrick's party in 2004, who all came dressed as Princess Leia, for inspiring the Loo-Loo Ladies' costume selections at Halloween in this book.

Special thanks to all our readers and reviewers: Amy Bertsch, Public Information Officer with the Alexandria Police Department, who helps us get the police procedurals right; Amber Kent Wardwell, with the circulation department at the Beech Grove Public Library, for encouragement and some really great fashion suggestions; and to P. Arleen Charles, Randy Rawls, Marilyn Meredith, Jo Dereske, and Heather Webber, for their generous comments and support.

Also, thanks to Mike Finkelstein and Bridget Ingram for some terrific recipe suggestions; and Sergeant John Gregg, for being a good sport.

Prologue
Mexico City, 1991

He had hunkered in the shadows of some sweet-smelling jasmine bushes for nearly an hour, anticipating the arrival of his prey. As usual, he was wearing black clothing, and the skin on his face and hands was darkened with shoe polish. He kept his eyes focused only on the path that wound through the ornamental garden, priding himself on his ability to do the job at hand without emotional involvement.

He'd had a pleasant day. He'd wandered around the city soaking up local color and Hispanic culture. He'd seen a lot of Diego Rivera-style murals, had listened to mariachi music in several outdoor venues, had enjoyed a really superb lunch of chicken enchiladas with mole sauce, and had taken a city tour in English that had a surprising amount of really interesting historic information. Someday he'd like to come back to Mexico City on a real vacation. The only thing that bothered him was the somewhat smoggy air from the exhaust of too many autos with too few pollution controls.

But here, above the center of the city on an estate set on the slope of a higher hill, the air was relatively sweet and exhaust-fume free. And so he waited patiently, still savoring the pleasure of his day and enjoying the sweetness of the jasmine.

Hearing footsteps coming down the path, he shifted to a crouch and mentally prepared himself to spring. The one he'd been waiting for was finally returning home. Once the footsteps had just passed his hiding place, he silently rose and pounced, grabbing the small, dark-skinned man from behind, dragging him into the bushes, and forcing him to his knees.

"Please, Señor," the man whimpered. "Why are you doing this? I know nothing. I've *done* nothing."

"It's nothing personal," the killer said softly in a conversational tone. "It's an assignment. And why me? Because I have the stomach for these kinds of assignments. Besides," he said, pulling the little man's head backward to steady it against his body, "I have a spiritual purpose. I'm sure you can appreciate that." He fingered the crucifix on the chain around the man's neck. "So if you like, say a prayer." Drawing his knife, he pressed the blade to his victim's throat.

He waited only a few seconds, then with one swift movement he drew the knife across the man's throat, watched the blood spurt from his jugular, and lowered him gently to the ground.

The assassin straightened up and lifted the weapon. "There's more than one meaning to the term 'wet work'," he said. Slowly, he drew the knife toward his face and gently touched the tip of his tongue to the already congealing blood on the blade. Then he held it high in the air in front of him and chanted a few words of a strange incantation.

He wiped the blade on the little man's jacket and sheathed his knife. Then he placed his right hand over the Kali pendant that hung on a silver chain around his neck, resting on his heart.

Chapter 1
Friday, October 17th, Twelve Years Later

I was in the middle of my last class of the day, teaching the background of an early piece of feminist writing, Sor Juana Inés de la Cruz's *The Answer*, a letter written in Mexico in the 1690s.

"Sor Juana Inés was a scholar, a poet, and a very well-known author. In those days, women couldn't get the *brilliant* kind of education you people are getting." A couple of people tittered, and I grinned.

"Unlike most of the women of her day, she wanted to study instead of getting married. She'd even begged her mother to let her dress up like a man so she could go to the university in disguise."

One of the guys, looking around the room at all the female students in pants, said, "And this has changed *how?*"

Another fellow interjected, "None of *us* wants to get married. We'd all *much rather* study."

I grinned again. "Well, I have to tell you, as a feminist, a scholar, a poet, and a *not* very well-known author who joined the Army in order to get an education, I identify with Sor Juana Inés, who had to go into the convent to be able to study! And while I was in the Army during Desert Storm, I *did* dress up like a man—much more so than any of you ladies. I'll tell you, studying beats the heck out of guard duty in the desert."

There was another ripple of laughter from my students.

"Anyway, in the convent, Sor Juana got herself into a spot of trouble for mouthing off too much about a famous male writer's work, criticizing his arguments. For the benefit of her sisters at the convent, she wanted to point out his errors. But wouldn't you know it, the day she was delivering her criticism of the work, the local bishop decided to visit. He asked her for a copy of her disputation, so she had to write it up and send it to him, begging him as she did so that it be for his eyes only.

"The bishop, who decided Sister Juana Inés was a bit too arrogant, sent it to press and distributed it widely. Then, under the pretense of being another nun, he sent her a letter of advice—warning her to stop studying, stop writing poetry, and stop arguing with men or speaking in public. Sor

Juana Inés knew the letter was from the bishop and realized she might be in trouble with the Spanish Inquisition."

"What was that?" asked a student in the back of the room.

A girl on the front row answered, "It was a Roman Catholic police force mostly run by the Dominican order that sought out heretics and generally burned them at the stake in order to cleanse them of their sins."

Another girl added tartly, "Yeah, heretics like Jews, gypsies, women with brains, men with money—sinners like that!"

"Yes, exactly right! It was a pretty scary time," I said. "One historian estimates nine million women were burned at the stake for witchcraft over a four-hundred-year period. Mostly these women were midwives, herbal healers, and as you said, women with brains."

"Nine million women?" echoed a female voice, as the class lapsed into stunned silence.

"Yes," I said. "It was really mass legalized execution of anyone the Church disapproved of, and if they called someone a witch, nobody argued."

Just at that moment, there was a little tapping at the door.

"Excuse me," I said jokingly, "the Dominicans are here to take me into custody."

I opened the classroom door to a student assistant, who handed me a note. "Dr. Quigley, Dean Riordan would like to see you as soon as class is over."

"Thanks," I said, taking the note, looking at my watch, and nodding. "I'll be up at the end of the hour." Then I shut the door and turned back to the class. "You see, it *was* the Dominicans." And everybody laughed again.

If truth were known, being called to the dean's office did feel a little like being ordered to appear before the Spanish Inquisition. And the timing of the summons to my classroom discussion of the woes of Sister Juana Inés seemed eerily synchronistic. But that's a situation I'm used to.

My name is Ariel Quigley, and I'm an adjunct instructor of English at George Mason University in Fairfax, Virginia. That's about as low as a teacher can be on the academic totem pole—we do an equal amount of work per class as any other teacher, but we get paid about half what a full-timer would earn. And that means I get to do other things to fill in the financial gaps—like writing articles for local newspapers and magazines and teaching evening creative writing classes at a community center in Alexandria.

My sister, who's a real estate agent, has also been trying to talk me into doing a little ghost busting and house clearing for haunted houses that she's having trouble selling. See, I'm also psychic, and sometimes ghosts like to talk to me.

Actually, I believe everybody's somewhat psychic, but my talents are a little more out front and accessible than most people allow for themselves.

In fact, the whole topic of the Inquisition is of great interest to me because if I'd lived in that time period, I would doubtless have been burned at the stake for witchcraft.

However, as psychic as I usually am, I couldn't get any sense of what the meeting with the dean was to be about, partly because I have trouble accessing intuitive information about things pertaining to myself, and partly because I was nervous about being called to his office. I'd never met him before, though I'd seen him at a couple of meetings.

At one minute to the hour by my watch, I opened the door to his office and introduced myself to his secretary.

She smiled and hit an intercom button. "Dr. Quigley is here, sir."

"Good, good," I heard him respond. "Send her right in."

As she ushered me into the inner office, the dean stood and came around to shake hands with me. Clearly he was all politician.

"Dr. Quigley! So good of you to come!" he gushed, as if I was there of my own free will instead of by imperial summons. "Delighted to have you on the staff. So sorry we can't make you a full-timer yet, but budget cuts...you know. But I've just been reviewing your record. Very impressive scholarship. Oh, please, please, sit down, won't you?"

A little overwhelmed and still a bit puzzled, I put my briefcase on the floor and sat down in one of the chairs facing his desk. I raised my eyebrows, waiting for him to tell me the reason for this meeting, inwardly relieved that it didn't appear I was being fired—or anything else especially dire.

"Well, now, I suppose you're wondering why I asked to meet with you." He settled down in his own chair and paused as if composing his thoughts. "I've had a most unusual phone call this morning from a lawyer in Alexandria. She asked if we had anyone on the staff who had any scholarly background in the...um...the occult." I could sense he was both pleased to be asked by a prominent member of the community for assistance in a matter of scholarship and disquieted by the subject matter. "I remembered noting your dissertation topic when you joined the faculty last year—Yeats and the occult, wasn't it?"

I nodded.

"You appeared to be the most obvious candidate for this assignment." Then he chuckled. "Actually, you're the *only* person we have on staff at the moment with *any* background in the occult." He seemed artificially jovial.

I was intrigued by the situation. "Why would a lawyer need a scholar in occultism?"

"I asked her that and she said it was personal. But she did insist it was urgent. So I'd appreciate it if you'd be willing to give her a call right away." He handed me a slip of paper with a name and number on it.

I nodded and he immediately stood up, letting me know our interview—or was it an audience?—was over. "Good, good, good!" he said, stepping around his desk to shake my hand again and conduct me to the door with many thanks for taking the burden from him and bearing it away to my own office cubicle and telephone.

As I made my way down the hall I was still in a bit of a daze. I'd heard rumors and gossip that the dean wasn't a very good teacher, but I could now vouch personally for his prowess as a politician.

Once I was in my cubicle, I dropped my briefcase on the floor, then simultaneously hit the computer's ON button and started dialing the number on the paper the dean had given me. I was no slouch at multi-tasking!

On the third ring, a deep, rich, female voice answered with, "Jessamine Steele here."

"Ms. Steele, this is Dr. Quigley from George Mason University. Dean Riordan asked me to call you." I was amazed with the formality in my voice since I very seldom had to identify myself with my academic credentials outside the classroom.

"Oh, Dr. Quigley, thank you so much for calling," said the woman. She sounded relieved. "Dean Riordan said you had some knowledge of occultism. Do you think your background might be sufficient for you to act as an expert witness in a court case?"

"I guess that would depend. What branch of occultism are you talking about? My real expertise is in the occultism of William Butler Yeats, but I've studied a variety of schools of magic, alchemy, Theosophy, mystery religions, and Eastern philosophy. What in particular do you need me to have a background in?"

"How about black magic?" she asked tentatively.

"Again, it depends. Are you talking about African, Asian, Caribbean Island Voodoo—or Aleister Crowley's version of just being beastly?" At the turn of the previous century, Crowley had made quite a reputation for himself by telling people he was an incarnation of The Beast of 666.

There was a long pause at the other end of the line, as if she was loathe to put a name to her poison. Finally she said softly, "What do you know about Kali worship?"

I thought for a moment and then answered, "Enough to know it can be distorted and abused like anything else. But I've read quite a bit about it as part of a course I took in Eastern religions. The dualism of Shiva and Kali as simultaneous life bringers and destroyers is just part of the cycle of life. But if you're talking about a negative form of Kali worship, it probably focuses, as some 19th-century cults did, on calling upon Kali's destructive powers for personal gain or retribution."

"Oh, that's exactly what I need!" said the woman, and I felt as if I'd passed muster. "Would you be willing to meet with me, perhaps tomorrow? I'll be happy to buy you lunch, and we can talk about the details of what I need."

"Where are you located?"

"My office is in Old Town Alexandria. On St. Asaph. Do you know where that is?"

The Lawyer Who Died Trying

I smiled to myself and answered, "Yes. I live in Alexandria myself, quite near Old Town. I'd be happy to meet with you tomorrow."

"Wonderful! Please come to my office around noon, and we'll talk a bit and then do lunch." She gave me her address and said, "I'm on the second floor. You'll have to take the stairs up—there's no elevator, I'm sorry to say—it's a very old building. My office is at the end of the hall on the left—my name's on the door. Ring the buzzer and I'll let you in."

I wrote down the details and said goodbye, and she responded earnestly, "Thank you *so* much."

I checked my school email account and was grateful to see no students had any pressing emergency needs. I logged out, switched off the computer, and packed up my things. As I walked to my car, I thought about the joke I'd made to my students in class about being summoned by the Dominicans of the Inquisition. And here I was, being summoned to go to court in what appeared might be an actual witch hunt. Fortunately, I wasn't the witch who was being hunted!

For the past few weeks I'd been living in a self-contained apartment in the "splendiferous" colonial mansion of my friend Bernice Wise, a fifty-something hippie wannabe psychotherapist. Bernice was a perpetual student in my evening poetry classes at the Alexandria Community Arts Center, and she gave me a break on the rent for my apartment because I'd also helped her clear the house of a long-time live-in ghost, Annie Grace, a pre-Civil War slave who'd often disrupted her cooking preparations. Bernice and her twins Mike and Michelle, who were also students at George Mason University, young TV producer/directors at a local cable station in Fairfax County, and entrepreneurs with their own website business, had become part of my extended family. Not being much of a cook myself, I often joined Bernice for a meal in her mess-hall size kitchen, and it had become *de rigueur* for me to share weekend breakfasts with the three of them.

This weekend should prove to be interesting for all of us, since Mike and Michelle were working as crew at the cable station on a talk show that had invited us to be guests. The subject was ghosts and house hauntings, always a popular topic in the month of October, and Bernice was going to join me to talk about her experiences with Annie Grace.

As usual when I walked through the front door, Bernice's voice greeted me with a cheery, "Hello, Ariel! I've got the kettle on and cookies already on the table."

I'd had to double my exercise efforts since I'd been here just to offset the effects of Bernice's goodies and snacks.

"Be with you in a jiffy," I called back. "I just want to change clothes. I have a date with Greg and his son this evening."

I dashed upstairs and shucked my semi-professional outfit, which consisted of a wool pantsuit and pumps, exchanging it for jeans, a blouse and my favorite angora sweater, and running shoes. I preferred to wear sexy, slinky, silky clothes when Greg and I were going out alone. But this weekend he had his son with him, and we were all going for fast food and a movie.

Greg is a sergeant with the Alexandria Police, and we'd met less than a week after I'd started staying at Bernice's. I'd helped bring a murderer to justice, partially thanks to my psychic abilities and partially due to just dumb luck, and in the process, I'd encountered the sergeant several times, during which I'd noticed he had extraordinarily gorgeous gray eyes. He'd been intrigued by the whole concept of how psychic talents work, and when the dust had settled at the end of that case, he'd asked me out for pizza. We'd been dating for just about a month now, and our relationship had rapidly moved into a more personal and steamier stage, with regular dinners out and occasional sleepovers.

Greg was divorced with an 11-year-old son, Brandon, whom he had for weekends as often as his unusual work schedule would allow. Greg had told me his relationship with his wife was amicable and that she was very flexible in sharing custody of their son. When Greg had a weekend off and his son was visiting, I didn't stay over because Brandon's mother had a live-in boyfriend, and Greg wanted to keep his relationship with his son uncluttered. Moreover, I didn't want to be a live-in woman unless I could be a wife and mother, and I wasn't ready to make that kind of commitment yet, nor had Greg asked me to. We were taking the relationship slowly, spending as much time together as we could, but leaving plenty of personal space.

When I got downstairs, Bernice had already settled at the table with a big pot of tea and a heaping plate of oatmeal-raisin cookies. I always enjoyed my little chats with Bernice, especially after a day of trying to push intellectual information into teenage minds mostly occupied with non-intellectual thoughts like relationships, social events, money, jobs, cars, clothes—and hormones. Bernice was intelligent and witty with a wide range of general information in many areas—she was, in fact, a Renaissance woman—and I appreciated being able to use her as a sounding board. She'd helped me analyze many things, from concepts I wanted to present to my students to the clues on the murder case I'd been involved in the previous month.

Bernice poured a cup of tea for me and pushed the cookie plate in my direction.

"Just one cookie, Bernice," I said, "since Brandon's taking me and Greg out for fast food and a movie, and I don't want to spoil my appetite for popcorn."

As soon as I'd settled onto a chair, Bernice's fluffy Tabby-point Siamese, Freud, jumped onto my lap, looked me in the eye, and turned round so she could tickle my nose with her tail before settling down for a nap.

"You're always the epicure, I see," said Bernice. "What kind of fast food will it be this time?"

"I don't know. I think we're going over to the theater area in Shirlington where they have a bunch of different eateries. That may mean I can choose something a little upscale from hotdogs and pizza. Or it may not. I'm easy." I munched the cookie, enjoying the homey atmosphere of Bernice's kitchen. She was always ready to listen to my adventures in the classroom or discuss philosophy or simply trade jokes and anecdotes. In fact, a lot of her psychotherapy clients had shared tea and cookies with her at this very table, receiving healing and wisdom in the process. Food for the soul as well as the body.

"Do you know a lawyer here in Alexandria by the name of Jessamine Steele?" I asked. Bernice had been in practice for over twenty years with her office in this house, and with many clients from all walks of life from Virginia, D.C., and Maryland.

Bernice cocked her head. "I've heard the name, I think, but I don't know her personally."

"Well, I had something kind of strange happen today. The dean called me in to tell me Ms. Steele was looking for a 'credentialed' authority on occultism to act as an expert witness in some kind of legal case, and he told me I was 'it.' I'm meeting with her tomorrow for lunch. And when I spoke to her, she said I'd need some scholarly background in black magic and Kali worship. What do you think of that?"

"Do you mean 'cauli' as in the floweret vegetable I sometimes cook as a side with dinner—although I can't understand why anybody would worship it—or is this a dog worshipping cult?" As I grinned appreciatively at her puns, she continued, "Or do you perhaps mean Kali, who is a mother goddess in one aspect, while in another she's a bug-eyed demon with long claws and her tongue sticking out about half a foot?"

I laughed. "The last option," I said. "Of course, with respect to food, people say *I* have the ability to perform black magic in the kitchen—I can take just about any food and turn it black by trying to cook it."

This time it was Bernice's turn to laugh, but then she got back to the subject of Kali. "Sometimes when I'm working with a particularly uptight and angry female client, I'll show her a picture of Mother Kali in her demon-goddess pose and tell her to think of the man she's angry with and make a face to match Kali's—and *aim* it at him! It's really very therapeutic."

"I'll have to try that in class sometime," I said. "There are one or two arrogant young men I might be able to put in their proper places with the fear of Kali."

"If you do that in class, my dear, I might have to bring your cookies to you at the Braddock Road Home for the Bewildered."

"Given that Ms. Steele was talking about black magic, I don't think it's the worship of Kali as mother, but rather as demon-goddess—the taker of life rather than the giver of life."

Bernice took another cookie for herself and nudged the plate toward me.

"All right, one more," I said. "But *just* one more."

"I know you," she said. "You're easy."

"Now you're making me eat my words as well as your cookies."

Bernice nibbled her own cookie pensively. "There are always two sides to everything, aren't there? Even with goddesses. The life giver is also the death bringer, quite naturally since the minute you come bawling and mewling into this world, you're already in the process of dying."

"Yes," I agreed. "And since women are the givers of life, they set up the whole process in the first place—and get blamed for everything. Oh, well, nothing like a little entropy to set you on your way in life. The Kabbalistic Tree of Life, like the one Michelle constructed in the back yard last month, also displays this dichotomy of life, you know. The left side of the tree is controlled by Binah, the Dark Mother, and is called the Pillar of Severity. The masculine side of the tree, on the other hand, which is headed up by Chokmah, the energy of the Great Father, is referred to as the Pillar of Mercy."

Bernice snorted. "Just sounds like a patriarchal religion taking out all its woes on the females in the society."

"I can't deny it sounds that way," I laughed.

"Of course," Bernice continued, "you know the right side of the brain is considered the 'feminine' side. It's our non-verbal, intuitive, visual, imagistic, artistic side. And it controls the left side of the body, which has also been associated with the feminine, and words that simply mean 'left'—like 'sinister' in Latin and 'gauche' in French—have taken on negative connotations over time. That's why in earlier times it was considered bad to be left-handed."

"*Earlier* doesn't go too far back!" I countered. "When I was in the Middle East, I learned that many of the people consider the right hand to be good and use it for eating, while the left hand is the one used for cleaning up after—how can I put this delicately?—taking a dump. So the worst punishment for someone caught stealing would be to cut off his right hand, leaving him forever outcast—and unclean!"

Bernice put down her cup and her cookie and examined her hands. "I'm glad we live in a culture where we have soap and water readily available and don't have to make that kind of distinction."

"Yeah...and where we don't have to drink goat urine or blood to keep up our own precious bodily fluids!"

Just then the doorbell rang and I got up. "That must be Greg and Brandon, come to take me away to dinner."

"Well, don't drink anything I wouldn't drink," said Bernice by way of goodbye.

As I'd mentioned to Bernice, Brandon had already decided the evening would consist of hamburgers and the latest family-rated action movie. Fortunately, there were enough eclectic restaurants near the Shirlington theater that we found one with a food bar where we could all be satisfied. It

The Lawyer Who Died Trying

had faux New Orleans cuisine—oyster and clam Po' Boys—as well as subs, burgers, dogs, and fries. Greg got a plate of fried clam strips, I treated myself to an oyster Po' Boy, and Brandon got a burger with all the fixings that was slightly larger than himself.

I looked at his plate somewhat aghast as he proudly carried the giant burger and mountain of fries to a table. I turned to Greg and asked, "Are there government grants available to help defray the cost of feeding boys through their growth spurt years?"

Greg grinned and said to Brandon, "I've heard it said you should never eat anything bigger than your own head."

"Well," answered Brandon, "Mom always says I have a really big head." He paused to settle more comfortably in his chair, then continued, "And that I get it from you." He stuffed a fistful of French fries into his mouth.

I took a mouthful of the Po' Boy, then gazed at the two guys sitting across from me. Brandon had Greg's sandy hair, gray eyes, and casual, laid-back attitude. Some of their actions and gestures were so similar they almost seemed choreographed. I looked at Greg fondly and thought what an excellent role model Brandon had in his dad and how strong the bond was between them.

Greg had just swallowed one of his clams and speared another onto his plastic fork when Brandon looked at him and asked, "Hey, Dad, how do you make a clam strip?"

"All right, I'll bite," said Greg, doing so on an unoffending clam strip.

Brandon grinned, "You offer it a role in a nudie film."

We both looked at him in shock.

"Brandon!" exclaimed Greg. "You're only 11. What do you know about that sort of thing?"

"I'm almost 12!" Brandon proclaimed haughtily. "Anyway, they talked about nudie movies on one of the cop shows last week."

I said thoughtfully, "Hmm, a professional clam stripper. I wonder if she keeps her occupation a secret from her family."

The guys looked at me questioningly, and Brandon said, "If her mom's like mine, she's not gonna talk about it."

"You mean," I said, pausing to emphasize the punch line, "she clams up?"

"Aargh!" said Greg. "What have I done to deserve this? Enough already."

After we'd finished dinner, we wandered toward the theater. Brandon kept about two shops ahead of us, gazing in windows and occasionally pausing if something caught his eye. Greg took the opportunity to hold my hand as we sauntered along.

I smiled up at him. "It doesn't take a psychic to see you have a really good relationship with your son."

He smiled back. "Thanks," he said. "I've tried to stay sane since the divorce." He gave my hand a little squeeze. "But you know I could actually use a psychic at work. We've had two more grand theft auto cases just this week. Can you tune in on a Hummer or a Mercedes? Oh, well, they're probably hundreds of miles from here by now or dismantled for parts."

"I don't know if I'm up to taking on this kind of case right now. I'd have to brush up my dowsing skills and really spend time focusing on it. Looking for a piece of property is like looking for an individual—the psychic would need the owner's name or license number or a lot of distinguishing features that would make it unique. And as you say, it might be hundreds of miles away. But I'll bet a good dowser, like the ones who use maps to dowse successfully for oil, or precious metals, or buried treasure, could train himself to dowse for stolen cars."

"Well," Greg said, "if you get any sudden hits about cars that are in the wrong places, let me know."

Then I had another thought. "You know, you have all the details about the stolen cars. Why don't you see if you can get your own psyche involved in trying to find them? All you need to do is when you go to sleep at night, just before you drop off, give yourself a suggestion that you're going to dream about where one of these stolen cars can be located. Then write down whatever it is you dream about, see if it makes any kind of symbolic sense, and follow up on it."

He glanced at me with one of his eyebrows raised.

"Really, I'll bet you can get something if you try."

He smiled an enigmatic little smile at me. "Trying to teach an old dog a new trick?"

"Well," I said, giving his hand a little squeeze, "he's not such an old dog, and he's a pretty smart dog. And if he succeeds, I'll give him a doggy biscuit!"

We caught up with Brandon in front of the multiplex, bought our tickets, and went in.

"Can I get some Starbursts, Dad, for dessert?" asked Brandon, and Greg acquiesced.

"Want anything?" he asked me. I just smiled, rubbed his hand, and raised an eyebrow slightly. He had the grace to blush a little. As we entered the theater where our show would play, Brandon asked if he could sit up front.

"You'll be by yourself, buddy," said Greg. "I can't sit that close anymore."

Brandon said that was okay and chose a seat in the middle of the first row. We wandered down to about the center of the theater and settled into seats on the end of the row, saving a seat for Brandon in case he were to change his mind and decide to join us after all. As the theater darkened, Greg took my hand and gently began to stroke my palm and the webbing between my fingers.

Interesting, I thought as I began to feel a little warmth creep down my body. This film had just changed from a family-rated feature to an X-rated one!

The Lawyer Who Died Trying

Chapter 2
Saturday, October 18th

Jessamine Steele's office was in an old three-story brick building on the northern edge of Old Town, Alexandria, not too many minutes from where I lived at Bernice's glorious old colonial. The front door, as in many buildings that didn't have permanent security guards, had a system requiring that a visitor ring the office he or she was intending to visit and then wait while someone in that office pushed a button allowing the front door to be opened. I saw the name "Steele" next to one of the buttons, so I pushed it, after which I waited about twenty seconds before I heard the buzz indicating the front door was now accessible.

As soon as I stepped into the building's foyer, I was aware that like much of Old Town, this building had been lovingly restored—highly polished hardwood floors and woodwork, antique brass knobs and fittings, stained glass in geometric diamonds in two front windows—and all of it gleaming in the light from tastefully elegant chandeliers.

On the wall opposite the stairwell was a glass-fronted name board with each office's occupant and suite number in gold lettering. I paused long enough to check for Jessamine's office number, noting also the variety of services one could receive in this historic place—three other lawyers, a chiropractor, a massage therapist, a few odd consultants, and a couple of names that left me speculating as to their actual business. Was RDO Communications involved in editing, or publishing, or installing car radios? And did Aquavest, Inc. sell water purification systems or safety vests?

With these thoughts in my head, I climbed the stairs to the second floor and made my way to the office at the end of the hall where I found the correct number and a tastefully lettered name plate that read *Jessamine Steele, Attorney at Law*. I pressed the doorbell and in seconds another buzzer sounded. I let myself in.

As I closed the door behind me I heard a voice call, "Back here!" from an open door on the inner wall. I followed the call, crossing a waiting room comfortably fitted with leather chairs and oak tables for clients and a small secretarial area to the right of the open inner office door.

As I walked through the door, a dark-haired woman elegantly attired in a gray wool dress with a shirt collar and abalone shell buttons was just making her goodbyes into the desk phone. She smiled and waved me in, then hung up the phone and came around the desk to take my hand in a strong, friendly, two-handed handshake. She was approximately my height and age, or perhaps a couple of years older. She had an air of authority, and I suspected she was accustomed to getting her way. And when she spoke, her voice was modulated and commanding, seemingly trained the way actors—and trial lawyers—often are.

"Dr. Quigley, thank you so much for coming! I really appreciate your giving me time on the weekend!" She looked me squarely in the eyes and with one hand still on mine and the other on my shoulder, she half guided and half directed me toward a roomy sitting area, where she deposited me in a huge leather chair. "Would it be all right with you if we chatted a bit here before we go to lunch? There are some things about this situation that are probably best discussed in private."

"Certainly."

"Then can I get you something to drink, Dr. Quigley—coffee, tea, a soda?"

"A cup of tea would be nice, thanks. And please, call me Ariel."

She smiled before turning to a little bar area. "Ariel! What a lovely name. Something out of Shakespeare. And you must call me Jessamine." I watched while she made two cups of tea with water from an instant hot tap.

"I was wondering about your name. Does it come from jasmine, perhaps?"

"Probably. That's the state flower of South Carolina. I think my mother was hoping for a daughter who'd be a little more the Southern belle type. She was a romantic. You know, I think she was yearning more for the 1860s than the 1960s when I was born—while other people were being hippies, she was building a sort of myth about planning barbecues on the mansion lawn under oak trees *dripping* with Spanish moss. Oh, well, do we ever live up to our parents' expectations?" She paused to set the tea in front of me along with sugar, cream, and a little dish of lemon slices.

"We were actually a very ordinary family, and from the Midwest, at that, not from the South." She settled down in the chair nearest the one I was in and picked up her cup. "But I was taught to have high expectations for myself, and they turned out not to be the same expectations my mother had for me. I was probably a British barrister in a former life—like Rumpole of the Bailey. So here I am, a lady lawyer practicing corporate law of a kind, on the fringe of Washington, D.C. Truth to tell, I really wanted to be a trial lawyer when I started out—not a trial to my mother. But I'm still trying—trying to be a good daughter, trying to be a good mother...and that's why I've asked you here."

I smiled at her while thinking how often people will tell their whole life histories in the first couple of minutes with a stranger—almost as if they're afraid they'll never get another chance to present themselves as they'd like to be seen and remembered. I nodded encouragingly, sure she'd continue without my having to ask her to.

"But before I give you the background of what it is I need, let me just say that Dean Riordan assured me yesterday you have the necessary academic credentials to function as an *amicus curiae*—a friend of the court— or to be an expert witness for me, and that you could deliver an opinion articulately in court. And from our conversation yesterday on the phone, I realize you do have the pertinent background to deliver such an opinion, or could at least do the research necessary in short order. But I need to know that if you're called upon by the court to provide authentication of your credentials, is the necessary paperwork readily available?"

"Yes, it's all on file at the university. And if you need documentation of the legitimacy of my Ph.D. and scholarly research, I graduated from the University of Maryland, so I could probably get a transcript for you within 24 hours."

"I'm sure that will suffice," said Jessamine, and again there was a faint note of relief in her voice. "So now to particulars." She crossed her legs and took a deep breath. "The case I need your expert testimony for is a custody case. I won't be the lawyer involved, because it's my own son Jeffrey who is under dispute. I've had sole custody of him ever since my divorce five years ago, when he was just a year old. And now my ex has come back into the picture and wants to share custody with me." She paused and just looked at me.

"So how does black magic enter into a custody case?"

She took a deep breath, let it out, and said, "I believe my husband is a black magician."

I saw she was studying me to see whether or not I believed her. "And what makes you think that?" I asked.

"When Jordan—that's my ex-husband—came back to the D.C. area three months ago, he contacted me about seeing Jeffrey and taking him for a weekend occasionally at his apartment or for trips to the zoo and museums. I was a little apprehensive because Jeffrey didn't really know his father at all and because of the circumstances of our separation. But Jordan assured me he'd take good care of Jeffrey, and we had a couple of dinners all together so they could get to know each other. And Jordan is quite a charmer when he wants to be. I felt it might actually be good to get them together. Jordan is, after all, Jeffrey's father. And Jeffrey has lacked male role models. So he soothed my fears, and I agreed. And the first couple of weekends when Jeffrey went off with Jordan everything seemed fine. Jeffrey would come home full of excitement and stories about what they'd done, and usually with some sort of present—a CD player, video games, that sort of thing.

"But the last time Jordan had him, which was a couple of months ago, Jeffrey came home with some pictures he'd drawn on the back of some of Jordan's scrap computer paper. And when I was tidying up this mound of artwork, I noticed some information on the back that startled me. I asked Jeffrey where the paper had come from, and he'd said out of the trash at his dad's apartment. So after I put him to bed that evening, I got on my computer and searched some of the words that were on the pages. And in pretty short order, I discovered Jordan has a web site where he's advertising a correspondence course he's selling. For developing personal power."

Her face was grim, but I wasn't quite getting the picture, so I said, "I don't yet see what there is to be concerned about. Where's the threat?"

"He mentions advanced levels of training on the site. And, from things he's told me and some of the stuff on the papers Jeffrey brought home, I believe the higher levels of the course are based on Kali worship," she said, as if that should explain it all.

"Well, as I mentioned on the phone yesterday, there's a good side and a possible bad side to Kali worship. And almost any kind of worship can be used for enhancing personal power. So what gives you the idea Jordan is into the negative side of it?"

"Because he's a murderer!" she said shortly.

I blinked and shook my head, startled by the vehemence of her words. "Excuse me?"

Jessamine collected herself and sighed. "When I met Jordan he was in the Marines with a desk assignment in D.C. He hinted to me he'd been in some kind of hush-hush job with Force Recon in various locations outside the country before being posted to Washington, but he wouldn't give me any details. He said I didn't want any.

"For a while, I let it go at that, thinking that probably I really *didn't* want any more details. But eventually, his hints became a bit broader, and finally he told me all kinds of things about what he'd done in those years in special ops that he hadn't been willing to discuss at the beginning of our relationship. The Marines trained him to be a killer! And this is a mark of his powerful charm—I decided I didn't really *care* what he'd done. I figured people could change, and that he certainly wasn't killing people now."

"But that's what the military is all about," I said, as one who'd been up close and personal with military weaponry myself. "We learn how to kill when we have to." Though if pressed, I'd have to admit that I wasn't sure I'd actually ever killed anybody—firing big guns long distances doesn't carry quite the same emotional impact as killing people one-on-one with a gun or a bayonet in close combat—something I'd always been grateful I hadn't been required to do.

"Oh, but this was different. It seems Jordan had killed dozens of people, without even batting an eye! Shortly after Jeffrey was born, which was about a year after we'd married—I was about 30—he announced he was putting in for a posting as a special ops instructor that had become available at Camp LeJeune in North Carolina. I didn't want to go to North Carolina, but he was adamant. Things escalated and tempers flared. And that's when he told me even more about his ability to kill people without it phasing his conscience one bit. I admit he may have been trying to frighten me into doing what he wanted, but I also got the sense he really was finally telling me all of the truth. He said he was not only good at killing, he'd enjoyed it. And he said for him, the assassinations had even had a spiritual quality. And as he was talking, I saw that he was very different from the

The Lawyer Who Died Trying

man I thought I'd married. He was cold and distant, and he might just as easily have been talking about building a bookcase.

"But I don't want you to think I'm overreacting." She paused for a moment. "I think I'd better give you some of his background.

"Like other people born in the '60s, Jordan grew up with Clint Eastwood and Superman movie characters as his role models—you know, a combination of the man of steel and the good, the bad, and the ugly. In addition, his maternal grandmother is Spanish, and he seemed to feel an obligation to be a matador or something equally exotic. He realized early on, however, that people don't necessarily have super powers, but he was very interested in what power really is. It was startling to me that you mentioned Aleister Crowley yesterday on the phone, because that was someone whose writings he told me were influential when he was growing up."

I nodded. "That's a little scary, considering how many people went insane from being under Crowley's influence. And he didn't end up very well himself."

"Anyway," she went on, "Jordan also did a lot of sports—but not the team kind. He was into the ones that develop individual coordination and timing, like wrestling, swimming, and long-distance running. He also took training in karate and tae kwon do. By the time he got out of high school, he already had black belts in both of those skills. And that training in the Asian martial arts led to an interest in Eastern philosophies. Well, somewhere in this timeframe, he also came to realize that his ability to understand and influence people was beyond the normal. And so he started looking at psychic abilities, and how to enhance *them*.

"Just before he graduated high school, his tae kwon do teacher, an ex-Marine, sort of recruited him. He told him he could make use of the skills and the powers he'd already developed if he went into the armed services and in particular into the Marines. His family wasn't going to be able to afford much funding for college anyway, so he decided to join up.

"Within a short time, he'd proved himself and volunteered for an elite corps of Force Recon special ops personnel. A contingent of this group was what he later told me was really an elite corps of trained assassins. And somewhere along the way he made the connection with the 19th-century *hassassins* and with the murderers associated with Kali worship. And he started dedicating all his kills to Kali."

She got up from her chair, went to her desk, and brought back what I took to be a very fancy letter opener. "This," she said, "was a little gift he gave me very early in our relationship. It was only after that fight near the end of our marriage where he seemed to be trying to frighten me with his stories that I realized it was the knife he'd used in many of his kills. I don't know why I kept it. I should have gotten rid of it. Still, it reminds me now of why I don't want Jordan to have any influence over our son."

She handed me the knife to examine. I saw it was silver, highly polished and elaborately engraved with what I thought to be Hindu figures.

As I took it into my hands, I suddenly had a strange, coppery, metallic taste on the tip of my tongue, as if I were tasting blood. And to my distress, I was enjoying it, and that realization made me feel ill. I quickly put the knife down on the table.

Jessamine had been watching me. "May I ask you something personal?"

I raised my eyebrows and nodded, figuring I'd answer if it wasn't *too* personal.

"You reacted to it, didn't you? You're psychic, too, aren't you?"

I smiled and nodded again. "Yes. Just touching the knife was enough to give me a clear impression of what it was associated with. I feel better not touching it."

"Is your psychic ability why you've studied occultism? To understand yourself better?"

"Probably," I agreed. "But unlike what you're telling me about Jordan, I was curious about what humans are really capable of. I knew there were things I could do that other people didn't seem to be able to do, but I wasn't really interested in enhancing my personal power—just understanding what my gifts were all about."

I paused. "There's a question I need to ask you. If you see Jordan as such a dangerous figure, why did you allow the visits with Jeffrey?"

"He told me he'd given up the attachment to Kali. And as I said, he's very persuasive. But clearly, if he's selling a correspondence course on Kali worship, that was a lie. So I don't want my son anywhere near him."

"Obviously I can't talk about your fears in court as that would be considered hearsay. So what do you see as my role if I agree to testify?"

"I'd want you to make the connection as an expert witness between the worship of Kali and human sacrifice."

I nodded. "There *are* many negative associations, not the least of which is that 19th-century Kali worshippers in India were said to have sacrificed children. On the other side, Kali was also seen as the great mother, patroness of women, children, and childbirth. But if what you're saying about Jordan is true, and he dedicated his kills to Kali, it's highly unlikely that he's focusing on the gentle, feminine aspect of Kali's nature."

"Of course, I'd get my lawyer together with you. Oh, and I'd better get your address and phone number for him," said Jessamine. I explained my living arrangements to Jessamine and gave her Bernice's address as well as both my home phone number and my cell.

"You'll probably have to give a deposition, and then the judge will decide if you need to be called to testify. If so, we'll issue a subpoena, so that you can be released from class. Does this work for you? Will you help me?" There was a tinge of panic in her voice.

"I think I can, given what you've told me."

"Oh, thank you," she said, and there were tears in her eyes. She'd obviously been holding herself together very well, waiting to see what my response would be. "I've asked everyone I can, people who knew him, and nobody is willing to testify. Everybody's afraid of him."

"I'm not," I said. "But tell me what's happened since the last time he saw Jeffrey...when you discovered the papers."

"I confronted Jordan with his lies and told him I didn't want him anywhere near Jeffrey. He threatened me, not in so many words, but he said it would be in my best interest to allow him visitation rights. I said that wasn't going to happen and then I received notification of the suit. I'm worried. I think he has...powers. He's dangerous, Ariel, and I'm scared."

"I'm not," I repeated. "I believe I'm totally protected from him. I don't think there's anything he can do to me. And I can probably teach you some techniques you can use to protect yourself and lend you a couple of books on psychic self-defense."

Jessamine paused to collect herself. "I'd appreciate that. And by the way, you'll be paid as an expert witness for your testimony. But I'm a little cash poor at the moment—I was hoping you might be willing to accept some shares in a venture I'm connected with. Come, let's go to lunch. We can talk about this aspect of it over salad and sandwiches!"

She got up and took a black leather coat and slouch hat off her coat rack. It was really classy and very expensive looking. She might be cash poor, but she certainly did dress well. But anyone who'd had to deal with a husband like hers probably deserved a little pampering!

Chapter 3

What I learned at lunch with Jessamine was almost as mind-boggling as what she'd told me in the privacy of her office, though it was information on a totally different subject. I came away yearning to talk to someone about it, but Greg and Brandon were having a father-son afternoon and evening, and Bernice was out when I got back to the house. I found a little note on my door saying dinner would be at 7 p.m. if I didn't have other plans, and it would consist of "A Little Chicken Something."

I decided to take a short run around the block in preparation for eating one of Bernice's "little" dinners. Her meals were always ample, and it was a constant battle not to become ample myself. So I changed into some jeans and a sweater, put on my runners, and because the weather had turned quite cool that morning, I also put on a jacket, a knitted cap, and some matching gloves and went out for a jog around the neighborhood. While I was jogging, I kept thinking about Jessamine Steele and her extraordinary situation. When I got back from the run, I settled down to do some grading of student compositions so the dinner could be my reward for good behavior.

At just about 6 p.m. I finished recording the last grade, packed the papers away in my briefcase, and headed downstairs to bend Bernice's ear while she was cooking dinner. As I walked into the kitchen, I found her at the central island preparation area, surrounded by bowls filled with coconut milk, pineapple chunks, diced mango and kiwi, chopped onions, and what appeared to be chicken broth, plus assorted spices, a big tin of imported curry powder, and a jar of chili sauce. Also, she seemed to be deep in conversation with someone. As there was no one else in the kitchen, I was mystified.

"Are you talking to yourself, the chicken carcasses, or a new ghostly tenant?" I asked.

"I'm talking to Freud the Cat who's been sitting on my feet ever since I started this process, and I was just giving her a gentle warning. I said, 'Back off, baby, or I'll make you a Manx cat!'"

Being half Manx myself, I knew this meant Freud might lose her lovely, fluffy tail, so I went around and picked her up to keep her out of

Bernice's way. Then I gestured toward the array of dishes. "Are Mike and Michelle coming to dinner and bringing the entire senior class from George Mason?"

Actually, I knew better. For Bernice, this was just a simple, little home-cooked meal. But in preparing a simple meal, Bernice could cook up a storm big enough to carry the house to Oz and provide enough leftovers for a gathering of late-night Munchkins.

It was pretty much guaranteed Mike would stop in for snacks on whatever was left in his mom's kitchen before retiring to the apartment suite out back in the remodeled carriage house that he shared with his twin. Bernice had joked once that they'd decided to assert their independence and move away from home at the age of 21, so they'd packed up and gone to the guest house out back. "The great emancipation!" Bernice had laughed. But I was just as glad they'd moved at least that far, as it had left their old "playroom" upstairs—an area about the size of a small cottage—available for me.

"Dinner will be just the two of us," said Bernice. "There's a bottle of Chardonnay in the fridge, so pour yourself a glass, have a seat, and tell all the news. What did you learn today from Ms. Jessamine Steele, Attorney at Law? I know that's where you were going when you headed out this morning. As you know, I listen very well when I'm slicing, dicing, chopping, pouring, mixing, stirring, and sautéing."

Tucking a droopy Freud over one arm, I got a couple of glasses from the cupboard and the Chardonnay bottle from the fridge and pulled up a stool on the far side of the island where I settled Freud on my lap. Then I poured half a glass of wine into one of the glasses. "Do you want any yet?" I asked.

"Not yet. I'll wait until we're a little closer to serving." She was still tangling with a chicken carcass.

As I savored the tart, smoky flavor of the Chardonnay, I began to fill Bernice in on my visit to Jessamine's office and on what would be expected of me as an expert witness on black magic and Kali worship. I also told her about my reaction to the knife Jessamine used as a letter opener. Bernice was intrigued by that and by the story Jessamine had told about Jordan Steele's background in special ops, since Bernice's own ex-husband Alan had been an FBI operative for nearly twenty years.

"It's difficult enough," she mused, "having a husband in one of the clandestine government services without knowing for sure that he's also involved in officially sanctioned assassinations...and ritual murder! Thank God Alan's religious fervor extends only to lighting candles at Hanukkah and doing a Seder at Passover. And a very short one at that. He likes to say all Jewish holidays can be encapsulated into three phrases: 'They tried to kill us. We won. Let's eat!'"

I laughed and thought of Alan, whose presence in the house, though he hadn't actually lived there for nearly two decades, was still very prevalent. He liked to show up for Friday night dinners that extended into Saturday morning breakfasts. Bernice joked he still had visiting privileges—with his ex-spouse—and that their relationship was a lot better than it had ever been when they were married. "All very civilized—and quite sexy!" she'd said more than once.

"So what's Jessamine like?" Bernice asked, since I'd stopped talking and drifted off into thought.

"She's physically a very attractive woman. Probably about thirty-five and very self assured. But there was an undertone of barely controlled...what? Panic? Hysteria? I did get the impression she's really afraid of her husband. She says she is. And she actually seems to think he has power to do her harm."

"And you don't think so?"

"She warned me I should also be afraid, but I'm not picking up anything personally threatening yet. Still, I ring myself with light every morning and night. I've been doing that for years. Gives me a sense of security."

"And you think that really helps?"

"I'm still alive, am I not? And until I'm not, I'd have to say it works. But getting back to Jessamine and Jordan, I don't know if there really is a threat or if it's all in her head. I'll admit the knife she showed me spooked me. On the other hand, I haven't yet looked up Jordan's website and tried to get any other vibes. He may have been a ritual murderer in the past when called upon to do wet work for the military but not be recommending any such thing in the present. I just don't know yet what to think."

"Will you have to confront him in court?"

"I don't know. I may not even have to go to court. I may just have to give a deposition."

"I know your good heart," said Bernice. "You really like to help people who are in trouble. But I hope there's some kind of compensation involved. I've been called as an expert witness before, and the standard fee used to be in the range of $1000 plus."

"Well, that's the strange part of this. Jessamine said she was a little cash poor at the moment but was expecting to come into a lot of money very soon. She's in some kind of investment program—actually, she's the lawyer for the corporation—its name is Aquavest, Inc. It seems the company is currently negotiating with the Japanese and with several European countries for the sale of an energy device that makes use of tidal power. The current investors are providing the capital to keep the company going with the testing and patenting procedures.

"Anyway, Jessamine's being paid in shares to do the corporate law stuff for this company, and she's offered to sign over $2500 worth of her shares to me if I'm willing to speculate instead of taking a straightforward cash fee. So I wanted to sort of pick your brains about that kind of thing. I know you have a lot of investments. What do you think about this arrangement?"

The Lawyer Who Died Trying

Bernice did the math in her head. "A thousand dollars now, versus a quarter of a million later. Well, since you aren't breaking the piggy bank to get involved, you aren't really speculating with anything except your time. However, it would be a good idea if, before you accept this arrangement, you were to learn a lot more about the company."

I nodded. "That was my feeling, and I said essentially the same thing to Jessamine. She invited me to a dinner this Monday night with a group of three of her women friends who are investors, and there's also a corporate meeting of all local investors with the inventor next Thursday evening. I mentioned my living arrangements with you, and she said I was welcome to bring you to either or both meetings. Actually, when I told her you owned a colonial house on King St. near Old Town, I almost saw dollar signs in her eyes. I think she's hoping you'll want to invest. But also her women friends are all writers, so it should be fun."

"I think I'm free both evenings, and as much as I love cooking, I also enjoy eating out."

At that point, Bernice moved to the gas stove and began cooking up the chicken and combining the many ingredients she'd been preparing for dinner. I put Freud on the floor, got cutlery, placemats, and napkins, and set two places at the table.

"The dinner on Monday will be at the Bon Appétit Café in Tyson's Corner at about six. One of the women is in real estate and has an afternoon showing near there, so that's why we're going that far away for dinner. I'll probably go there straight from work."

"I don't much like driving by myself at night," said Bernice. "Maybe I'll take the Metro to Dunn Loring station and get a bus into Tyson's Corner. I love shopping at the malls there because they have everything everybody else has, times two. They even have a Bloomingdale's and a Saks 5th Avenue. It's almost like going to New York to shop. So I'll thoroughly exhaust myself and then grab a cab to the restaurant."

"Bernice, you live in psychedelic muumuu's and Birkenstock sandals. Your kitchen has every conceivable appliance, and some that I'd judge inconceivable, and your house is decorated to the nines. What on earth could you possibly want to shop for?"

She threw a hand to her forehead in mock hurt. "You malign me! And anyway, I think they have a Birkenstock's outlet there, and these really do need resoling," she added, looking down at her dainty size elevens. "I presume you won't mind driving me home?"

"As long as you don't mind riding in my Jeep instead of in your BMW."

"Oh, my dear," she said, grinning, "you know I'm always up for adventure. And on that note, it's time for adventures in eating. Pour me a glass of that Chardonnay, and then get the lazy Susan from the fridge—I've prepared a few cooling side dishes to go with the hot Madras curried chicken I'm feeding you."

The *few* side dishes turned out to be sliced bananas, cucumber, and cold sweet potatoes, plus peanuts, yogurt, shredded coconut, crystallized ginger, and chutney. "Bernice," I said, "there are enough different dishes on this lazy Susan to make up a meal in themselves."

"Well, yes, it's an eight-boy curry." When I flashed her a look of curiosity, she explained, "Each side dish is called a 'boy.' It's a term from British Imperialist India, probably because it took a different servant to carry out each side dish."

"Oh, boy," I exclaimed as Bernice set a large dish of her curry on the table. "Where's the senior class from George Mason University when you need them?" But I didn't mean it.

In the dream I was at a wedding, or rather in the foyer of the church where a wedding was about to take place. I was watching three women in bridesmaid dresses giving the bride items of apparel—something old, something new, something borrowed.

"Don't bother with the last item," said the bride gaily from behind her veil, "I'm already blue!"

The women were very excited, giggling and laughing and jumping up and down. Then the wedding march started, and I got the distinct impression it was one of the variations of Handel's Water Music. *I was thinking to myself I should be in my seat in the church before the wedding started, but instead I seemed glued to the spot, watching the whole thing from the door in the foyer. Then another late guest came into the foyer to stand beside me. I turned to see who it was and found myself eye to eye with the Fat Man, a guardian spirit who had been meeting me in dreams—and sometimes in waking visions—for many years. He handed me a program for the ceremony with stylized wedding bells on the cover tied together with a big bow. But when I opened the program, there was only one word printed inside: Finis.*

Then the wedding was over, and all the guests were partying in a function room. A band was playing a fanfare, and a caller on the dais with the band said, "Grab your partners, ladies and gents! It's time for a good, old fashioned square dance!" I glanced at him and saw he was wearing a white jacket with a cotton hospital mask hanging around his neck.

But oddly, there were only women who formed the square in front of me—four women from four different ethnic groups—Asian, Black, Caucasian, and Native American. Three of them were the bridesmaids I'd seen earlier, and the Caucasian woman was the bride, still wearing her veil down, covering her face. They all joined hands, but unlike the earlier dream scene where they'd been so happy and excited, they seemed to be angry. They were yanking at each other and scowling.

Then the music started and the caller began his patter: "Allemande left with your left hand, give a right to your partner, and a right and a left grand; right over left, left over right, hold your partner and squeeze her tight; swing your partner through and through, till you don't know who is who." The multi-racial women began to wind themselves together and I got the impression of an elaborate and convoluted Celtic knot.

The Lawyer Who Died Trying

  I was still just watching from the sidelines when the music stopped abruptly and someone shouted, "She's going to throw the bouquet!"

  With her back to me, the bride threw her bouquet and it came sailing directly toward my face. I automatically put up my hands and caught it. To my surprise it was a huge, beribboned head of cauliflower. The wedding party began to pelt the bride with birdseed—"For the crows," said someone beside me—and I turned to see the minister standing there, waving goodbye to the bride. I noticed he had a silver knife tucked into his belt. Then the bride climbed into a Mercedes decorated with ribbons, tin cans, and a sign that read, Just buried. *I was startled, and then I saw the bride roll down the window, turn to look at me, and lift her veil—and I was staring into the face of a corpse.*

  As I was recoiling in shock, the Fat Man tapped me on the shoulder and showed me a picture of a duck.

  I woke in a sweat and reached for my dream journal to write it all down. Then I lay awake for a while, trying unsuccessfully to go back to sleep. My Fat Man dreams were usually warnings of impending danger, and this one had been particularly scary. Finally, I got up and had some warm milk, telling myself Bernice would have a field day in the morning helping me work through these symbols. I thanked the deity that I lived with a Jungian psychotherapist!

Chapter 4
Sunday, October 19th

The hot milk put me back so solidly asleep I didn't wake again until almost 10 a.m. "Too late to run this morning," I said to my running shoes as I nudged them out of sight under the bed. "I'll make it up to you later." I zipped through a shower, blew my mop of hair dry, and put on a clean sweat suit as attire for breakfast. Then, picking up my dream journal, I went downstairs.

When I got to the kitchen, Mike and Michelle were sitting at the table sipping cappuccino out of enormous mugs, their plates covered with crumbs. Bernice was also at the table, also sipping coffee and reading the Sunday edition of the *Washington Post*. On the center island were assorted bagels, tubs of various flavors of cream cheese, a mound of butter, and a plate of lox, plus capers, chopped hard-boiled eggs, very thinly sliced red onion rings, and somewhat thicker slices of tomato.

"Yo!" said Mike, getting up when I entered the room. "Single or double espresso?"

"A cappuccino, please. And you'd better make it a double—I'm running late and I need to wake up fast." I put an "everything" bagel in the toaster and leaned back to wait for it to brown. "What time do we need to be at the studio?"

"You and Mom don't need to show up until about 1:15, but Mike and I have to be there at noon to start getting the equipment warmed up and run all the tests," said Michelle.

"Any tips on what to wear?"

"Any colors except black, white, or red. And don't wear any busy patterns that the cameras will have trouble tracking on—hound's tooth runs off in all directions! The interviewer for this show, Mac Jacobs, who's also the producer, always wears the same navy blue suit. Why don't you coordinate with Mom on different shades of blue or green so you don't clash with each other?"

"So this isn't the show you and Mike do that we're going to be on?" I asked just as my bagel popped up and I began to dress it as elegantly as I could.

The Lawyer Who Died Trying

"No, it's something called *Driving Force*. It's been running for years. Mac is a taxi driver for his real job, and he hands out his business card about the show to everybody who gets into his cab and asks them lots of questions while he's driving them around to get a sense of whether they'd be good subjects for interviews. And he's built up quite an audience, so he says. He's a really zany guy who does all kinds of off-the-wall stuff. Like last Christmas when he interviewed a couple of blowup Christmas decorations—Santa and Frosty—in a silly ventriloquist act. But then sometimes he just does a really straight sort of show. That's the joy of doing community access cable television—you can do just about anything you can think up as long as it's clean and doesn't name a price for a product or service."

"I gotta disagree with you, Michelle, on one thing," Mike interjected. "Mac's shows are never really straight. Usually they're a little bit bent. But they're always entertaining. And we suggested to him he might want to interview you and Mom about the ghost who used to live here and how you contact ghosts. He's promised not to make fun of the idea. In fact, he said his grandma's house was haunted, or at least that's what she told him when he was a little kid to make him behave himself. Besides the two of you, I think there's going to be another woman on the show who has a haunted townhouse. Just try to be entertaining."

Bernice put her newspaper down and looked at her offspring. "I'm sure we'll be at least as entertaining as Santa and Frosty."

Michelle nudged Mike in the ribs and said, "Let's go, bro. We need to tidy up the habitat before we head for the station."

Mike stretched all 6'2" of his lanky frame and got up. "Exeunt the twins, stage left. *Adios, Madre,* Ariel. See you in the funny papers. Uh, I mean, on TV."

We both waved as they exited the back door. I continued munching my bagel sandwich as I watched Bernice take the TV guide out of the newspaper Sunday supplements and set it aside.

"Before we start matching up our apparel for the show, do you have time to give me feedback on some dream symbols? I had one of my Fat Man dreams last night, and I'm wondering if I might be getting into something deeper than I'd anticipated with Jessamine Steele."

"Certainly," said Bernice. "There's nothing I like better than analyzing a few symbols after breakfast on a Sunday morning."

"You know, from anyone else, I might think that statement was facetious. But I realize that coming from you, it's probably the truth."

I read off the dream verbatim. When I finished, I looked at Bernice. "Okay, what do you think?"

"The ending is a little bit creepy. No, come to think of it, it's all a little bit creepy. A wedding is usually a new beginning. But when your Fat Man's program says, '*Finis*,' it's clearly aborting that meaning of a new start. But there's one deficiency in this wedding scene. There's no groom."

"No, there isn't. And except for the Fat Man, the square dance caller, and the minister, there aren't any males in the dream."

"Then should we examine each of the symbols one at a time and see what substance they might have?" suggested Bernice.

"Okay. I'm guessing the bride is Jessamine because she's the key figure in these two new situations I'm going to be dealing with. So the bridesmaids are probably the three women we'll be meeting tomorrow night at dinner. But I don't have any idea what the something old, something new, something borrowed might be referring to."

"If this dream is prophetic, we may find the answer to that question at dinner tomorrow."

"And what about Jessamine being 'blue'?" I asked. "I imagine she's a little depressed, though actually she seems more scared than sad."

"There's also 'blue' blooded, 'blue' movies, and 'Blue's clues,' and we know dreams often joke with us."

"I hadn't thought of that last association. But I guess all the symbols are really clues to something, aren't they?"

"Now, Handel's *Water Music* is really interesting," said Bernice thoughtfully, "since you told me the name of the company Jessamine is working for is Aquavest, Inc. And that gives another meaning to 'blue' since you'll turn blue if you're over your head in water."

I nodded, then added, "The next symbol seems pretty straightforward to me. Jessamine said the person who introduced her to the company is actually a dentist. He's the one calling the shots locally, so it makes sense for him to be the square dance caller. And what he's wearing could suggest a dentist's work wear. I mean, it was a sort of formal dinner jacket, but with a medical neck, and he had the protective mask, which most dentists use nowadays to protect themselves as well as their clients."

"Sounds probable," agreed Bernice. "So do you think the three women are Asian, Black, and Native American?"

"I guess we'll just have to wait and see. But according to Jessamine, they're all good friends, though in my dream, they're pulling at each other and scowling. That doesn't bode well for the company, I would guess."

"Well, they weave themselves into a Celtic knot, with a convoluted design. That suggests something very pretty and at the same time difficult to unravel."

Again I nodded, then said, "Bernice, I think you put the cauliflower in my dream with your suggestion of Kali-flower Friday afternoon at tea. And Greg was talking at dinner that night about a Mercedes that had been stolen that day. Of course, I'm not sure having it show up in my dream will be of any benefit to *him*."

"Are you sure your catching of the bridal bouquet doesn't suggest you'd like to be the next one to marry, as the old tradition is supposed to show?"

"Possibly," I agreed thoughtfully. "But it was a whopping big head of cauliflower and very heavy. And the flowerets are quite convoluted, similar to the Celtic knot. I think I've been invited into a situation with a heavy and convoluted responsibility."

Bernice nodded. Then she suggested, "I imagine from what you've told me the minister in your dream is Jessamine's husband, Jordan, because of the silver knife in his belt."

"And also," I added, "because he's a religious leader, of sorts. The Kali worship and all that. But I don't understand the birdseed for the crows reference at all."

"People have taken to throwing birdseed at weddings instead of rice since studies show rice can be deadly to birds. But the specific mention of crows, which are black and the opposite of the doves one usually sees associated with weddings, is another creepy sort of symbol. Makes me think of Edgar Allan Poe!"

"And that brings us to the final images. The *Just Buried* sign on the back of the car and the bride finally lifting the veil and showing the face of a corpse. *Very* creepy! I still shiver when I think of it. And then the Fat Man and the picture of a duck."

"Well," said Bernice, "I hope for Jessamine's sake your dream is suggesting neither the end of the business nor the end of *her*. But your Fat Man is definitely warning you to be careful and thoughtful in your dealings with her."

I finished making a few notes in my journal and looked at my watch. "Okay, we've frivoled away enough time. Let's get serious and go raid our closets for what we're going to wear on the air. Our public awaits us!"

The studio was in a small industrial park office area in Merrifield. There was plenty of parking because virtually all the other businesses around the site were closed on Sundays. We went to the side entrance as Michelle had directed us to do. We rang the doorbell and waited for an attendant to buzz the lock and let us in.

"We're here for the Mac Jacobs show," said Bernice.

"Sign the book, please," said the fellow behind the desk of what looked like an equipment room. When we'd registered the pertinent information, he handed us visitor badges and said, "You'll need to wear these in a conspicuous place except when you're on camera. Please turn them in when you leave, and be sure you log out. If you go down this hall to the end and turn left, you'll come to the studio areas. Mac's show will be in..." he paused to consult a schedule sheet, "looks like it's in Studio B this afternoon."

We followed his directions, going past one glassed-in, soundproofed room on the right that appeared to be a radio station with a big red light over the door that said *On the Air*. I noticed a DJ sitting at a console talking into a microphone with a stack of CDs on the desk beside him. As we progressed down the hall, we saw rows of lockers on the right and several more glassed-in, soundproofed rooms on the left, all marked *Edit Suite* followed by a number. Three of the rooms had people in them looking at multiple television screens.

Honora Finkelstein & Susan Smily

When we passed through the door at the end of the hall, we found ourselves in the main lobby. Obviously during the week a receptionist manned the desk near the front door to our right. There also seemed to be a lot of administrative offices in that area of the building, all of which were closed at the moment.

We turned left and made our way into the rear of the building. Almost immediately there was another glassed-in, soundproofed room with monitor screens and large numbers of tapes on shelves and another person manning the area. Again, there was a red light over the door that said *On the Air*—clearly this was the TV broadcasting studio.

Just beyond it was another foyer with couches and easy chairs. On the left wall were doors marked *Studio A* and *Studio B*, and on the back wall was a door with a sign that said *Studio C*.

We poked our heads into the open door of Studio B where we saw five wooden armchairs with somewhat tattered seat cushions set up on a carpeted platform in a semicircle, with a large, round coffee table in front of them. Michelle had warned us that community access cable operates on a low budget and that the furniture got used by countless shows and was sometimes pretty worn. Nevertheless, she had said the chairs would be comfortable enough to sit on for the show's duration, and that the scratches and wear wouldn't show on camera. Then we spotted Michelle, coming through a curtain at the rear of the set, with a large, fake potted plant. She turned to a young woman who was dollying a camera into position and asked for input on the placement of the plant. The girl pointed to a location at the left of the set, and Michelle moved the plant to that spot. Then the girl looked through her camera lens and said, "Good! Homey, not threatening." Michelle thanked her; then she glanced our way and came toward us.

"Hi, Ariel. Hi, Mom! Wow, do you look professional today!" Bernice was wearing a very elegant teal blue business suit.

"Well, you said no hound's tooth, and most of my muumuus are in patterns that have a bite far more serious than your ordinary hound."

"It'll also be a lot easier to pin a mike on you in this outfit," said Michelle, patting her mother on the shoulder. "And you look great, too, Ariel," she said, looking me up and down. "Very sophisticated."

I smiled and thanked her. I'd chosen a soft green wool suit, one I'd bought the previous year to go to the dean's wife's Christmas faculty tea. Since I couldn't really afford it, I was probably going to have to wear it for at least another five years' worth of special events.

Michelle motioned us to follow her. "Mac's in the dressing room getting into his blue suit, so come into the control room with me and be impressed by Mike's technological prowess in getting all the cameras and stuff ready for the show. We've almost got the set ready for the taping, but now I need to key in the credit roll information on the graphics equipment. I'll be doing graphics, and Mike will be directing."

We went into the control room and said our hellos to Mike, who whistled at our outfits and then pointed us to some folding chairs. We watched for a few minutes while he worked back and forth with the crew members who were manning the three cameras on the studio floor, each of which he was following with a monitor in the control room, doing color balances and giving instructions for angle shots.

Meanwhile, Michelle sat down at another monitor and began keying information into a program she had pulled up on the screen. I watched the work of both these young people with interest and realized I was getting a little bit excited. I was actually going to be on television!

"Ariel," said Michelle, "do you want viewers to be able to get in touch with you after the show?"

"Umm, for what reason?"

"Oh, I don't know. Like maybe if they have ghosts they want you to talk to or clear out of their houses? I remember you telling me your sister—the one who's a real estate agent—wanted you to help her clear haunted properties to make them more saleable. So might you want viewers to call you or email you after the show? Or would you want them to call her, maybe?"

"I guess they could email me at my personal address." I gave it to her, then watched as she typed it in.

Mac Jacobs, all spruced up in his blue suit and a conservative matching tie, came into the control room and shook hands with us. "My other guests have arrived, and it's pretty crowded in here, so why don't we go out to the set while they give Michelle their names and contact information."

We followed him out to the studio, while a middle-aged woman—I thought she must be the one with the haunted townhouse—and a young man with a somewhat tight mouth went into the control room. I accidentally brushed his shoulder as I went past and got a picture of a 4-year-old boy talking to the faint image of a very elderly woman. I murmured, "Pardon me," and flashed him a smile, but all I got in return was an even tighter set to his mouth. I wondered whether he was also here to talk about his ghost and solicit my advice or had some other agenda altogether.

Someone had placed a jug of water and some plastic cups on the coffee table. Mac gestured toward the two chairs on the left and said, "Why don't you two sit over there? Dr. Quigley, you take the outside seat so you can get a clear view of everyone else. I'll be opposite you on the right."

At this point the other two guests came out to the studio, and Mac made introductions all around. The woman's name was Joan Emerson, and the young man was Bryan Corcoran. He sat down beside Mac with Joan in the center, and although I glanced at him several times, he never met my eyes. A thin young man with very curly hair came scurrying in with several small antenna boxes that had to go on our belts or waistbands and tiny lapel microphones, which he began attaching to our jackets or collars.

Once our microphones had been tested for sound, Mac addressed us all, saying, "Okay, folks, we're just about to start. Now, we're doing what's called a 'live to tape' show. We aren't going on the air right now, but we'll tape the show straight through with no stops, unless there's some kind of emergency. And if somebody makes a major flub, I'll either edit it out later, or leave it in for added humor! But don't be nervous," he laughed, "I only have a viewership of about 40,000 people."

I noticed Bryan glance at me and give a little smirk, and I thought to myself, "He's planning to discredit me if he can." I was really puzzled because I knew he'd had an experience with a ghost as a child. So what was up with this guy? I realized right then that Mac had set up the show for controversy—and I was glad I was prepared.

I glanced at Bernice and she nodded, indicating that she, too, had picked up on Bryan's body language. She inclined her head slightly toward me and whispered, "Let the games begin!"

Just then the voice of the sound tech blared out over the public address system, "No talking in the studio, please. We're about to start." We all straightened up on our chairs, and his voice came again, "Five-four-three-two-one—show time!"

Music began to play, presumably as background for the opening credits, and as it tapered off, a person with earphones on pointed to Mac, who smiled brightly and said, "Hello, and welcome to *Driving Force*. I'm Mac Jacobs, and my guests this week are here to tell us everything they know about...ghosts! On the far left is Dr. Ariel Quigley, who teaches at George Mason University, and who says she talks to ghosts, one of whom until recently was supposed to be haunting the house of our second guest, Bernice Wise, who is a psychotherapist in Alexandria. In the center of our group is Joan Emerson, who also believes she has a ghost in her townhouse. And finally, seated next to me is Bryan Corcoran, who is currently at the Air and Space Museum here in Northern Virginia. Welcome to the show, folks!"

We all nodded in his direction as we were introduced. But I'd noticed that Mac hadn't commented on Bryan's association with ghosts, which confirmed my suspicion that his presence wasn't necessarily friendly.

"Dr. Quigley," Mac said, "let me start with you since you're supposed to be a 'ghost conversationalist.' At what age did you have your first encounter with what you believe was a ghost?"

"Call me Ariel, please," I smiled. "I had my first experience with a ghost at age four, very much like Bryan here, who was only four when his dead grandmother came into his bedroom the night after her funeral and told him to tell his mother how much she loved her."

Bryan, who was taking a sip of water just at that point, nearly choked, and I got the psychic impression that when he had tried to deliver that message to his mother, she had screamed at him and hit him, yelling there were no such things as ghosts—that if he thought he was seeing ghosts, he was really seeing demons.

When Bryan stopped coughing and finally caught his breath, he stared at me bug-eyed. Locking eyes with him, I continued, "She hit you, didn't she? Your mother hit you when you tried to give her the message. She said what you saw was demonic, and that scared you, didn't it?"

Bryan's eyes filled with tears and he nodded slowly, saying, "Yes...yes, but how did you know that? I didn't...I didn't even remember all of that myself until just now."

Bernice smiled at Bryan. "In my profession, Bryan, I see a lot of people who have repressed unpleasant childhood memories. These are usually associated with some kind of punishment or perhaps abuse by an adult whom we trust. In your case, it seems that you were excited by your grandmother's visit, and you thought you were giving a present to your mother. Her response was so extreme and contradictory to what you expected that you repressed the memory. And I would venture to guess that you either embraced her opinion as your own, or you went the scientific route instead and totally denied that ghosts exist because their existence can't be proved in the lab."

Mac shook his head in astonishment. "It seems you've debunked my debunker. How did you know this about Bryan, Ariel?"

"Because I'm also a little bit psychic, Mac. And I think that as Bryan was preparing his arguments for the show today, the memory of his own childhood experience came bobbing up from the subconscious, making itself more available for me to access. When we bumped into each other before the show, I just got a visual image of him as a small child, talking to his ghostly grandmother. The rest of it I got when my question to him triggered his memory. I'm sorry, Bryan, I don't usually read people without their permission, but it just jumped out at me."

He nodded, looking down at the floor, and I could see he was trying to pull himself together. Then he turned to Mac with a wry smile and said, "I guess my role in this discussion has just been cut from the script. I'm glad my mother lives far enough away that she isn't likely to be one of your 40,000 viewers."

After this admission on Bryan's part there were no more surprises. I talked about the ghost of the Fat Man, who had first visited me in person when I was four, then had begun coming in dreams and waking visions as I got older. Bernice gave the particulars about Annie Grace, the ghost of the pre-Civil War slave who until the previous fall had lived in her colonial house in Alexandria and the circumstances of whose death she had learned about with my assistance. And Joan talked about the amorous Civil War captain who seemed to be living in the basement laundry room of her townhouse in Manassas, and who would try to hug and kiss her every time she went down to do the laundry. Bryan, bless him, got to talk about the scientific view of ghosts—that they really don't exist or at least cannot be proved to exist—after which he agreed that viewpoint is too exclusive because it denies personal experience.

When the floor director held up the three minute sign to indicate it was about time to wind up the show, Mac asked, "Ariel, what would you do if one of our viewers got in touch with you about a ghost? Would you be open to doing a little 'ghost busting'?"

"I would certainly consider it, Mac. But the first thing I'd have to do would be find out if the phenomenon was really a restless ghost or just noisy plumbing or creaky floors. If I actually got vibes about an entity in the house, I'd try to tune in to it to find out what it wants. Usually, once a ghost has satisfied its needs, it becomes willing to move on to higher dimensions."

"And you, Bernice, would you be open to doing a little psychology on any ghosts?" asked Mac.

"I'd be open to that, but only if Ariel feels it's necessary—and only if she were acting as the medium. I don't do ghost interventions myself."

"But for example, what would you do if you had an amorous ghost like Joan's in your basement laundry room?"

Bernice got a wicked little smile as she replied, "I'd probably do a lot of laundry." We all laughed, but then she turned to me and said, "Seriously, though, do you get any hits on Joan's ghost, Ariel?"

"I think," I said, trying to tune in to Joan, "that he's caught in a loop in time and space. This seems to happen a lot with people who haven't accomplished what they set out to accomplish. From what I'm picking up from you, he probably was on his way home from battle, looking forward to seeing his wife and taking her in his arms again. And he probably died with her on his mind. Now, I'm being logical here, but I think he may have been buried right there where your townhouse is since you're close to the battlefields of Manassas. And he may have transferred his yearning to see his wife to you, Joan, because you're there and available. I suggest you try to talk with him and see if you can convince him to go to the other side where his real wife from that life is probably waiting for him. If you stop getting hugged and kissed, then you can bet he's heard the message and moved on. And if that doesn't work, send me an email and I'll come talk to him! I can always use a hug!"

Mac wrapped up the show by giving particulars for each of us again, and in my case he asked me to spell out my email address in the event any viewers wanted to contact me after the show. We all continued to smile brightly for the cameras as Mac made his goodbyes to his audience and invited them to tune in next week for another edition of *Driving Force*. As the show's theme music came back up, Mac asked us all to remain seated. "Our microphones are off now, but let's wait until the crew comes in to remove them before we stand up."

When we'd been divested of our sound equipment and were shaking hands all around, Bryan asked for Bernice's card. "Now that I know I have some issues, I'd like to work on them." Then turning to me he said, "I feel a little unstrung, but I thank you nevertheless. And the person I feel sorry for is my mom, who literally didn't get the message."

I flashed him a megawatt smile and gave him a hug. "All things considered, that's very generous of you."

Mac's crew members were racing around, dollying cameras out of the way and locking them down, removing the furniture, plant, carpet, and platform, and taking back all the microphones to the equipment room.

We poked our heads into the control room, where Mike and Michelle were still working at their respective monitors. When we got their attention, Mike said, "Way to go, Mom and Ariel!"

Michelle jumped up and came to hug us. "It was a good show and I'm awfully glad that Bryan fellow didn't turn out to be a jackass. I realized when he came in to give me his info for the credits he was Mac's ringer. There was no way I could warn you, but you caught him off guard right away, and he had the grace to admit defeat. I'm glad 'cause he's kinda cute."

"Well, sweetie," said Bernice, "you may be seeing him again. He's taken my card and may be calling me for tea and psychotherapy."

Michelle got a mischievous smile on her face. "Good. I'll have to work up a scenario about how to block his car when he comes for a session, and then how I appear—dressed in a fetching frock or designer jeans or maybe a skimpy pair of shorts—ready to save the day by unblocking his car. But first, I engage him in conversation..."

"Spare us the movie script," mumbled Mike.

As Bernice and I walked out of the studio I thought about how, less than an hour before, we'd been girding our loins for a battle, but the foe had been disarmed without a fight. Sometimes things simply weren't what they seemed to be.

"Thank goodness Bryan was open to change," I said to Bernice.

"I'd say thank goodness you're psychic!" she replied.

Chapter 5
Monday, October 20th

At 5:58 by my car clock I pulled my Jeep into a parking space in front of the Bon Appétit Café in Tyson's Corner. Jessamine was waiting for me just inside the door and motioned me down the hall toward the ladies' room. Her face was drawn and pale.

"Before we sit down with my friends, I wanted to tell you that I think Jordan is increasing the negative energy against me."

"What makes you think so?"

She gave a shiver. "When I got up this morning, my balcony was covered with a flock of crows. Is that what they're called, a *flock*?"

"Actually, I believe they're called a *murder* of crows," I said, experiencing an internal quiver of my own.

Jessamine shuddered. "Knowing that makes this even creepier than I thought! There must have been over a hundred of them, all facing in toward my living room. They were rising and settling, over and over, and flying at the window, and all the time they were cawing madly. It was really scary. I felt like I was in that old Alfred Hitchcock movie about the birds! It had Jeffrey in tears."

My skin crawled, especially since I remembered the crows in my dream. "And you think this is a message from Jordan?"

She nodded. "What else could it be?"

"I don't know. Maybe there's a logical explanation. What else would attract them? Meat, seed, newly budding plants, any sort of decaying garbage? Might there have been anything like that out on your balcony?"

"No, it's really sterile. I have nothing but a patio table and chairs. No plants and certainly no garbage. The balcony safety railing is sort of rusty so we don't go out there much—I keep meaning to call the building superintendent to have it repaired. But the crows weren't interested in the deck anyway. All they seemed focused on was trying to get in my windows. It has me really scared, enough that I'm thinking of sending Jeffrey to stay with his grandmother."

"Well, there are some things you can do for protection. Traditional magic suggests that you put down a ring of common table salt on all your door and window sills. And surround yourself, Jeffrey, and your entire

The Lawyer Who Died Trying

living space with white light—do it every time you remember it. Do the same whenever you get into your car. I'll do a little research and copy out some rituals you can do for self-protection. If nothing else, they'll help you feel you're doing everything you can to counter anything Jordan may be sending your way."

"Thank you, Ariel. I feel better just talking to you about it." She gave me a wan smile. "And there are a couple more things. Is there any way you can come to my lawyer's office tomorrow at three o'clock? I asked him to get you in to take that deposition as soon as possible, and he's holding that spot until I let him know otherwise."

"That'll be no problem. I have Tuesdays and Thursdays off since I work only part time. Just give me the address and I'll be there."

She reached into her purse and handed me a card for her lawyer's office. "And also, did you have a chance to think about letting me pay you in stock in Aquavest? If so, I can bring the share certificates tomorrow when I meet you for your deposition."

"Well, I'm a little bit of a gambler. Plus, your offer is very generous, and the potential for it's being worth more in the future seems good. So, yes, I'm willing to do this for stock."

"Thanks so much! It takes a load off my mind. And there's a meeting this Thursday of general stockholders, and the inventor of the Aquavest device will make a presentation. Bring your friend Bernice if you like."

"Okay, I'll check with her about it."

"Good. Now let's get back to the party. My friends are dying to meet you. Oh, and by the way, I've told only one of them that you're going to be an expert witness in my custody case. I've just told the others that you're going to be an expert witness in one of my cases. So we won't talk about that tonight, okay?"

I nodded and she flashed me a brilliant smile, then led me to the table where her friends were waiting.

Bernice arrived at the table just as we did, so there were introductions, handshakes, and hugs all around. It was a long table with three chairs on each side, so Jessamine placed Bernice and me opposite each other in the middle seats so everybody could talk to us. There were already two bottles of wine on the table that Jessamine had ordered plus ample glasses of water, so we applied our attention to the menu selections and gave our dinner orders to our waitress as soon as she came over.

"Okay, Ariel and Bernice, meet the Loo-Loo Ladies. We're all writers of a sort and have been friends for years. In fact, we all went to Mary Washington College together, class of 1990."

She gestured to the woman on my right, a statuesque blonde in a red dress. "In the red corner, we have Lorelei Warren, a juvenile court lawyer, soon to be judge, we hope. She's written articles about family court law for journals and magazines. Don't let her hair color fool you—she knows how to close the Velcro strips on her runners. Actually, I'm maligning her with faint praise—she's the sharpest stiletto in the shoe box. She's a whole lot smarter than I am because she's never gotten married. Over to you Lorelei, you do the next introduction."

"Ah thank you for those kind words, my *deah*," said Lorelei in a rich Southern drawl. "To use your terminology, in the blue corna' on Bernice's right is Patricia Barnes." I looked at the woman next to Bernice, an attractive woman in a blue suit with shoulder-length auburn hair.

Lorelei continued, "Now, Patricia is what you might call a 'natalist,' by which Ah mean she has a flock of children that she raises as a stay-at-home motha'. She can afford this 'cause her sweet husband makes boodles of money as a beltway bandit suckin' up government contracts doin' somethin' or other with computers. Now she hasn't always been a lazy, stay-at-home, good for nothin'—she was once the leader of a UN political action committee, an' she still serves on the board. Her book is about changin' from career track to parenting track by choice an' not because of religion. Patricia, over to you."

"Well, thank you, Lorelei." As Patricia began to speak, I thought I detected a slight, upper-crust Boston accent. "To your left, Ariel, is Maggie Leigh—that's Leigh like Janet, not like Robert E. She's a real estate agent, and she's the 'serious' writer in our group—she's published bunches of short stories and is working on a novel right now." Patricia raised her eyebrows pointedly as if there was something she didn't want to say but thought Maggie might want to add.

And Maggie did. "What Patricia isn't telling you, because she's much too discreet, is that I'm gay—and I write mostly Lesbian fiction." Maggie was more rounded than her friends with very long dark hair pulled back in a clip. Her accent was what one might term six o'clock evening news—very precise and not giving away any particular regional origin. "And I do have a long-term partner—we've been together for nearly seven years—but she's quite shy and doesn't like to come out to these Loo-Loo Lady gatherings."

Bernice asked, "Why do you call yourselves the Loo-Loo Ladies? That seems a strange name for a writers' group."

They all laughed and Jessamine answered, "It's because while we were in college we published a little chapbook of limericks—suitable only for the loo."

"Oh, I love limericks," I said. "Recite a few for us, please."

"Well, then, you asked for it," said Jessamine. "Here are some *Loo-Loo Ladies' Lavatory Limericks*."

Maggie started with this ditty:

> "An Australian lady named Sue
> Made a pass at her pet kangaroo.
> It really out-foxed her...
> It wrapped, stamped, and boxed her
> And sent her to Kalamazoo."

Next, Lorelei cleared her throat and intoned solemnly:

> "A resilient lady named Dot
> Could tie herself into a knot,
> But then her friend Davy,
> Learned knots in the navy,
> And he really showed her what's what."

Then Patricia, with a deliciously mischievous smile, quoted the following:

> "I once met a man on the stair,
> Who made me an outrageous dare...
> If I'd done what he said,
> I'd have wound up in bed
> With tortilla chips stuck in my hair."

Finally, Jessamine grinned and recited:

> "A buxom young lady named Claire
> Climbed a ladder to get some fresh air.
> But she fell off—kerplop!
> And came to a stop
> On her well-cushioned, soft derriere."

"Those are very funny," laughed Bernice, "but they're not nearly as naughty as some I've heard."

"Oh, we have some much naughtier than these in our book," said Maggie. "But we usually don't recite them in public places—in case somebody calls the poetry police."

We were all still laughing when our server and two other waiters showed up with our dinners. Jessamine poured out wine for each of us: then we set about consuming our meals. The food was simpler fare than some of the very fancy restaurants in Alexandria but still offered a good range of appetizers and entrées. Maggie had decided to make a meal of the ever-popular spinach dip, some twice-baked potatoes, and a side salad. Bernice and I shared a shellfish and rice dish that offered clams, mussels, shrimp, and scallops, and the others all had an assortment of chicken dishes: *Chicken Spinach Alfredo* for Patricia, *Honey-Dijon Smothered Chicken* for Jessamine, and *Chicken Stuffed with Brie with a Pecan Crust* for Lorelei. Everything sounded delicious, and everything was served with a side dish of fresh steamed vegetables.

"Ah can't resist anything made with pecans," said Lorelei, "even if the calorie count exceeds mah monthly limit!"

As we began to eat, Bernice asked about Aquavest, and all four of the ladies offered excited comments.

Patricia said, "It's going to be *really* good for the environment—less necessity for burning fossil fuels, and I'm all for that."

"And there's the potential that it can become a major energy source. We'll be able to store the energy for later use as is done with wind energy out in California and other places that have tried similar alternatives," said Maggie. "And cheaper energy means lower costs for homeowners. Always a plus in my business."

Lorelei put down her fork to add, "Y'all need to know it's already bein' looked at by someone on the senate energy committee, and Ah understand there are already foreign investors lined up."

"And as a matter of fact, Bernice, there's the potential for it to go up in price very soon because of foreign investment, which will help us generate prototypes and bring it to the markets where it can start being used. Our company CEO thinks it could easily go up to $100.00 a share very soon," said Jessamine. "But you can buy in right now for just a dollar a share if you buy a thousand or more shares."

Bernice smiled and said, "Well, it certainly sounds good, but I always do investments with my ex-husband, Alan, so I'll have to discuss it with him first. But thanks for the offer."

"Well," said Jessamine, "why don't you come with Ariel to the general stockholders meeting on Thursday evening at 8:30 at the Hyatt in Crystal City? And bring Alan if you like."

Lorelei shook her head. "Oh, Jessamine, you're always tryin' to sell ever'body ya meet on this heah project. But Ah didn't come to this dinner to listen to all y'all. Ah came 'cause Ah wanted to meet a real live psychic who knows all about magic. That's right, Ariel, Jessamine has told us you teach at George Mason University, an' you do psychic readings. So, can ya look into your crystal ball and tell me somethin' about these gals Ah don't already know? Preferably somethin' juicy?"

I laughed. "Well, I don't use a crystal ball—I use Tarot cards, and I generally only read people if they give me permission." Naturally, I immediately got a chorus of permission from all the Loo-Loo Ladies—there's nothing people like better than hearing about themselves or gossip about their closest friends.

While dinner was cleared away, Jessamine asked for dessert and coffee preferences and placed the order with the server for us. It arrived fairly quickly and I took a long sip of my cappuccino and set my apple crumble to the side to nibble while I read the cards, keeping the space in front of me clear. I dug into my purse for my mini-Tarot deck and said, "I'll let each of you draw one card now, what we call a significator. And I'd be willing to do full readings for you at a later date—for only a few hundred shares each."

The ladies laughed and Maggie said, "Ariel, you're beginning to sound just like one of us! But I for one would be happy to pay your normal fee, whatever it might be, for a full reading." The other ladies nodded assent.

I sifted through the deck rapidly and pulled out the queens of the four suits, explaining that they were all powerful women, so I was going to use

The Lawyer Who Died Trying

the powerful females in the deck. Then I mixed them up face down and invited them to decide who should go first.

"Well, that would be me!" said Lorelei. "After all, Ah'm the one who asked for this, and Ah'm also probably the nosiest one of all of us—Ah mean, the most interested in other people. It's mah Southern blood." She reached out and tapped one of the cards. "This one is me, Ah'm sure."

It was the Queen of Swords, so I said, "This card shows that you're a very strong business woman, very accomplished at everything you do. And you believe in power through planning. You're more intellectual than emotional in making decisions. And you like to cut through—how shall I phrase this delicately?—the crap of life. And when you're in a situation where you aren't sure how to act, you'll nevertheless take action—do *something*, even if it's wrong—rather than not do anything at all. But remember that the sword of intellect is double edged and can cut both ways."

"Well, gracious me," drawled Lorelei, "this gal is good! Ah'm glad Ah don't have any dark secrets Ah'm hidin'."

As Lorelei said these last words, I got the definite impression that there *was* something she wasn't telling the rest of the group, but I couldn't pick up on what it might relate to.

I mixed up the cards again and said, "Okay, who's next?"

"Pick me, pick me," said Maggie in a little girl sing-song voice, waving her hand in front of my face. She reached over, picked up a card, and handed it to me.

"You're the Queen of Pentacles which means money, money, money."

"I like *that*," said Maggie with a grin.

"You're a good money manager and good at making ends meet. And you don't take risks unless you really trust the project you're investing in. You trust yourself most of all because you truly know your strengths. So since you're investing in Aquavest, I have to think you truly trust Jessamine."

"I do indeed," confirmed Maggie. "She's never steered me wrong."

As she said that, I suddenly had an image of the card turning upside down, and I wondered if the investment really was all that sound.

Again I put the card back in the pile and mixed all of them up.

Patricia reached out and said, "I've got to be next because the cutest can't be last." She touched a card with a well-manicured, glossy nail tipped with sparkles, and I picked it up.

"Well, Patricia, you're not only the cutest, you're the sexiest, if we're to believe this card."

The other ladies hooted at this. "She's like a brood mare, for sure," agreed Lorelei. "Ah always knew with all those kids she was a slutty sexpot!"

"Well, the Queen of Cups is more than just sexy. Patricia, you're a dreamer of big dreams and motivated to achieve them. But you're not out for power or money or even intellectual success. Your drive is for emotional fulfillment—you want to do things you can feel good about when you've accomplished them. Feeling is the key. And unlike the Queen of Pentacles, you *are* willing to take risks—which is very attractive to the opposite sex, by the way. You're the lady a pirate would choose to kidnap, and you'd go with him willingly if he turned you on."

Patricia made a prim little mouth and looked at the ceiling in a gesture of feigned innocence, again making all the ladies hoot.

"Well, that leaves me," said Jessamine. "And what do the cards have to say?" She didn't wait for me to put the Queen of Cups back in the pile but chose one of the other three.

"It seems you really are the four musketeers," I said when I saw the one she'd drawn, "because you've each chosen a different queen from the deck. Yours is the Queen of Wands, suggesting you've found your true purpose in life, and your primary motivation is to do good in the world. You have a strong sense of righteousness."

"So woe betide any transgressors, for Jessamine will surely turn them into toads with her magic wand," intoned Maggie.

"Thank you for those upliftin' words, sistah Maggie. This woman is not out for money, sex, or power the way the rest of us are, but is *truly* a saint."

As I started to put my cards away, Bernice said, "Why don't you let me draw a card for the investment, Ariel? Give everybody a chance to see how it may go."

I shrugged, said, "Okay," and handed her the deck. She drew a card and laid it on the table for everyone to see. It was the Sun card, which I'd generally read as positive. But then I saw that another card was stuck to the bottom of it. When I lifted the Sun, I saw that its accompanying card was the Two of Swords. My first reaction was that my immediate reward for helping Jessamine was going to be in experience, not in cash.

"I'd say there's a lot of potential for a positive outcome because that's what the Sun means, but there's another card that came along with it that's striking me as problematic. The Two of Swords suggests there are some decisions to be made, and the principals involved in the investment may not have all the facts yet. I'm not sure what it is, but I'll definitely come to the general meeting on Thursday to see if I can pick up any vibes. And please, don't worry. I don't want to be a wet blanket because the Sun generally suggests positive auspices. I'll do a full reading on the investment and all the people involved later, if you like."

Patricia piped up, "This is all so exciting and so much fun. When can we get together for these readings?"

Bernice patted her hand. "That's my cue. Whenever anybody wants a get-together, my fridge calls out to be involved. Why don't you all come over to my house for dinner next Monday night? I'll do something simple."

"Bernice," I scoffed, "you don't know the meaning of that word in the kitchen."

Everyone consulted pocket calendars and agreed tentatively.

The Lawyer Who Died Trying

As I put away my cards I picked up my coffee cup for one last sip and said, "My goodness! While I was reading the cards, somebody ate my dessert and drank my coffee!"

On the way home, Bernice noted humorously, "Those four women would seem to be the four women from your dream. They're not a politically correct *racial* mix, but they are a diversified relational mix—one divorced, one single, one married, and one lesbian. Four different persuasions. And the three of them do seem to be bridesmaids to Jessamine's bride in this situation."

"Well, she's certainly the center of the action. And I'm a little worried because the crows in my dream have turned up, too. Jessamine took me aside tonight before you arrived and told me her balcony was covered with crows this morning. She thinks her husband, Jordan, is sending them with his spooky black magical powers. I think maybe I should talk to her about the dream tomorrow. What do you think?"

"It couldn't hurt," Bernice agreed. "And I know from reading your body language that you got some kind of hit from the Sun card linked with the Two of Swords. What was that all about?"

I sighed. "Much as I don't want to admit it, I don't think I'll be getting rich from Aquavest any time soon. My gut feeling from seeing the Sun card plus the Two of Swords is that solar power would be a better investment!"

Chapter 6
Tuesday, October 21st

Being an expert witness in a court case is nothing like the TV shows would suggest , especially if what one is doing is giving a deposition to be read in court, as opposed to actually appearing in a courtroom. I sat across the table from Frederick Dowling, Jessamine's lawyer, in his conference room, answering his questions while a court reporter took down my exact words with her little stenographic machine.

First I had to give my name and my credentials and tell a little bit about my scholarship in the field of Yeats and occultism. Then the lawyer asked me about Kali worship, and I told him about the nature of this important goddess, and how some of her worshippers had corrupted it in the 19th century by engaging in human sacrifice. I also had the opportunity to talk about Aleister Crowley's teachings, his bid for power as a supposed incarnation of the Beast of Revelation associated with the infamous number 666, and a listing of the people he was credited with having driven mad.

Though I couldn't claim any personal knowledge of Jessamine's husband, Jordan, I noted that on the papers Jessamine had shown me from his course were references to both Kali and Crowley.

I concluded by saying, "The relevance of this information has little to do with whether ritual magic of the dark kind actually works—what's important is whether its practitioners *believe* it works. And in my opinion, given the historic precedent of Crowley, someone who actively seeks dark power and teaches dark magic can potentially cause emotional harm to those with whom he or she comes into contact."

"Would you think such a person should have custody of a young child?"

"Given the potential for collateral damage, I'd have to say no."

After that, the lawyer asked me if I'd mind waiting for about fifteen minutes while the court reporter transcribed the deposition so I could sign it. I went out to his waiting room where I'd left Jessamine reading *People* magazine, which she'd commented was totally suitable for a Loo-Loo Lady. "Definitely good, gossipy potty reading."

"Just in time," she said as I sat down on the couch next to her. "The only article left that I haven't read is on hip-hop, and the only kind of that I really know anything about is the kind bunnies do. I'm hopelessly mired in the past when it comes to popular music." She dropped the magazine on the end table and turned to me. "How did it go?"

"Well, I told him pretty much what I've already told you. It was very scholarly and kind of boring."

"Yes, depositions *are* pretty boring, which is why expert witnesses get paid the big bucks. And on that note," she said, taking an envelope from her purse, "here are the shares I promised you. I really do think they will eventually make you rich."

Just then, the outer door to the waiting room opened and a voice said, "Well, hello, Jessamine. He sounded like Anthony Hopkins in *Silence of the Lambs.*"

Jessamine's face changed from relaxed to tense and slightly angry. "What are *you* doing here?" she demanded, and I looked around to see a stunningly handsome man standing just inside the door, looking at us. He had an almost cat-like grace and a great deal of magnetic charm. He was clearly charismatic, and I could see how people would be attracted to him personally.

"Temper, temper, Jessamine. *My* lawyer asked me to deliver these papers to *your* lawyer," he said. He strode over to the receptionist and handed her a large envelope. Then he came toward us. Looking at me, he extended his hand. "You must be Jessamine's expert witness. I'm Jordan Steele, Jessamine's expert ex."

I raised my hand to shake his. "Ariel Quigley," I said. As our hands touched, I immediately felt an energy drain and regretted having acted automatically. He created the same tension in me as I'd felt when I'd been called to Dean Riordan's office—as if the Dominicans of the Spanish Inquisition were knocking at my door once again. At the same time I felt totally walled off as if my psychic ability had been put in a box and couldn't get out. I couldn't put my finger on anything specific, but I knew he was trying to look into my head. Immediately, I went inside my mind, collected my energy, and surrounded myself—and Jessamine—with white light. Within a couple of milliseconds, I could breathe again. I pulled my hand away from his and watched as he visibly reacted to the shift in my energy. Then he gave me a little wink and a Machiavellian smile.

"Ah," he said with a sensuous undertone in his voice, "I see you're a reader. And a good one, too. Well, my dear, feel free to try to read *me* anytime." Then he turned back to Jessamine. "I'll see you in court, my sweet. That is, if I can't change your mind before then." He turned on his heel and disappeared through the door.

I looked at Jessamine, let out a long breath, and opened my eyes wide. "He's a very powerful magician—and very creepy."

"But you blocked his energy, didn't you? You protected yourself—and me! I could feel it. I've never felt that way in his presence before. As if I have...a soul of my own."

"I know what you mean," I agreed. "He's got the power of a psychic vampire. That combined with his sensual good looks makes it easy to see how a woman could be caught and held by him. I'm amazed you were able to divorce him."

"I was only able to do it because he went away. At that time, it's what he wanted. And now he wants Jeffrey and I don't really know why. But now you can understand why I can't let that happen."

Just then, Jessamine's lawyer came out with my deposition on a clipboard, ready for signing. I quickly read through it, initialed all the pages as he instructed, and signed it at the bottom of the final page. Then he took it to his receptionist to have it notarized.

On an impulse, I stood up and went over to him. "I just met Jordan Steele and I want you to consider seriously actually putting me on the stand. I realize that if my testimony is just read into the court record it may not be as influential. So please don't hesitate to call on me."

He nodded and thanked me. What I hadn't said was that Jordan Steele was powerful enough to put a glamour over the eyes of the judge, and that if I were there, I might be able to do what I had just done here in the office—deflect his power.

I recounted the events of the afternoon to Bernice while she put together a light supper of blackened tilapia and pasta primavera. During the meal, by mutual consent, we always stayed away from any topic that might affect our appreciation of the food, so the closest we got to my involvement with Jessamine's soap opera was a review of the previous night's dinner with the Loo-Loo Ladies.

Sitting with Bernice later over cappuccinos, I said, "Tell me, oh wise one, what's your take on all of this?"

"By 'all of this,' do you mean sexy black magicians, Aquavest, child custody cases, or bawdy limericks?"

"Yes," I said, "all of the above. Especially the bawdy limericks. 'There was a young girl from Nantucket...'"

"They really were an amazing group of ladies. I'm always impressed by groups of people who were friends in high school or college and manage to remain close friends later in life. I'd guess one of the ties that bind must be living near each other in the same part of the country. That didn't happen for me because I went to school in Canada."

"It didn't happen for me, either," I said, "since I went to school on my G.I. bill after four years in the Army. I was four years out of sync with most of my classmates."

"But I was just thinking that all of Jessamine's friends, even though they're very different from each other, are bonded by virtue of their naughty creativity more than a dozen years ago when they wrote and published a little book of limericks. There's something bizarre—and sweet—about that."

The Lawyer Who Died Trying

Then she added, "The point you made about trust is also worth considering. They all obviously trust Jessamine and she trusts Aquavest. Now, all investment is based on trust at some level. But when you put your money into venture capital, you really need to be prepared to lose it all. I wonder how many of these women could afford that. And what would happen to this group if Aquavest does indeed prove to be an 'inverted Sun'? Might they turn on Jessamine the way the bridesmaids in your dream began to fight with the bride?"

I shivered a little. "Way too much of that dream has proved to be prophetic already. And I can't see any way to avert the disaster it seemed to predict. I was so totally diverted by Jordan Steele's appearance at Jessamine's lawyer's office today that I forgot to mention my dream to her. But I almost feel I should give her a call right now."

"Go ahead if you think you need to. Though it might scare the socks off her."

I looked at my watch and saw it wasn't yet nine, so I went and got the phone book to look up her home number. Unfortunately, only her office number was listed. I called it and left a message asking her to call me on my cell, though I was sure she wouldn't get back to me before the next day.

"Well, I imagine you'll pick up more information when we go to the corporate meeting on Thursday. And remember that all the ladies are coming over next Monday evening for dinner and Tarot readings. We'll learn a lot more about them then. So you'll have plenty more opportunities to tell Jessamine about your dream, and you might have more insights about it by then."

"I guess I'm really involved in Aquavest now that Jessamine has paid me in stocks. She gave me 2,500 shares this afternoon when I went to give my deposition." I looked at her with a little twinkle in my eye. "Uh, could I pay you the rent for the next couple of months' in stocks?"

Bernice was still for a moment, pondering the possibility. Then she said evenly, "You know, your card reading has probably saved me and Alan from becoming involved in this investment. But it's an interesting idea. I trust you, and if you had said you thought it was a viable investment, I probably would have gone with it. But you didn't. So by some weird kind of logic, I feel as if you've probably saved me, oh, maybe ten thousand dollars. And I told you that you could expect at least a thousand dollars for appearing as an expert witness. So I guess you could give me half your shares in lieu of the next couple of months rent, and we'll call it even."

"Bernice, you are just too kindhearted for your own good. I *was* joking because I can't imagine this company's having any viability. It would be like paying you with Monopoly money. I think it would be positively *evil* for me to take you up on this offer."

She took a sip of her coffee and looked at me pensively, her head cocked to one side. "You know, there's a fine line between good and evil. Elisabeth Kübler-Ross once said inside each of us is a little Mother Teresa—and inside each of us is a little Adolph Hitler. So each of us has the potential, given the right circumstances, to become either a saint or a sociopath. Now only about four percent of the population actually becomes sociopathic. Most of us just want to live our lives without having to give up our selfish desires so completely that we have to become totally altruistic. We don't want to be saints. But most of us have at least had a conscience inculcated in us somewhere along the line that keeps us from doing actual harm to other people. And what is guilt but the uncomfortable feeling a good person with a conscience has when he's done something he thinks is going to be judged as bad, or indeed, something he has already judged as bad? When a person doesn't feel that guilt or doesn't have that conscience, and acts in a totally antisocial manner, we generally call him a sociopath."

"Are you suggesting Jordan Steele may be a sociopath?"

"If, as his wife says, he was a trained assassin and both enjoyed his kills and dedicated them to some dark god in a ritualistic way, then yes. I don't know the man myself."

I thought about this for a moment before asking, "Do you think this could be the difference between those who practice black magic and those who practice white magic? Black magicians are sociopaths?"

"Could you clarify what you mean by 'black magic' and 'white magic'?"

"Traditionally, black magic calls up dark forces—demons, dark gods, negative astral beings—in order to enhance personal power. White magic, on the other hand, calls on angelic beings and forces for good to do healing of all kinds, spiritual as well as physical. I guess that people traditionally have felt God wouldn't allow angelic forces to assist in the development of their own personal power, so if that was their goal, they had to go to the other end of the spectrum and call on the demons. Does that make sense?"

"Given that definition, then yes, people who practice black magic are sociopaths because if one is calling on 'demons,' then one is calling on that which is meant to bring us down, to entrap us, to destroy us. But do you actually believe in demons?"

"Not necessarily. But I believe that everybody has some level of psychic ability. And those who use their power to control and manipulate other people for their own personal ends are really practicing something we could call dark magic. So I guess Jordan and people like him are sociopaths. I hadn't really thought of that before."

Then I realized I'd been sidetracked. "Oh, but we were talking about my paying you in stock and how it might be evil for me to do so, especially if I think the stock is worthless."

Bernice grinned. "Do you really think the stock is worthless? I mean, are you actually doing *pro bono* work for a lawyer?"

I laughed. "Well, maybe it's not totally worthless. But I don't think it's going to be as good an investment in the short term as the ladies were suggesting last night. So if you were to accept stock for rent, it might be a few years before you'd actually get next month's money."

Bernice raised an eyebrow. "Tell you what. Let's do it for one month's worth of rent—that way I have a stake in the company, and if it makes a lot of money, I won't be sorry I didn't invest. And if it turns out to be worthless, there are all kinds of little things I can ask you to do to make up for it."

Knowing Bernice and the workings of her mind, I had no clue as to what kind of indentured servitude I might be getting into!

Wednesday, October 22nd

The next day was one of my teaching days, but I knew Greg was "home alone" for a couple of days mid-week and wouldn't have Brandon with him. So out of the kindness of my heart, I decided to relieve his boredom. On my lunch break, I called him on my cell.

As soon as he picked up, I said, "How about pepperoni, sausage, green peppers, mushrooms, and onions?"

"Don't forget the black olives," he said. Then he added in a husky voice, "And what do I get for dessert?"

I loosened my collar a bit to let out the steam and panted into the phone.

"That'll do," he said.

Since I was watching my figure, I ate only three slices of pizza, plus five or six of the pepperoni slices off the fourth piece.

"You've very nearly denuded that slice of pizza," Greg commented, raising an eyebrow.

"And your point is?" I asked, reaching for a piece of pepperoni from his plate.

"Have you no shame?" he laughed.

I cocked my head and looked at him semi-seriously. "Bernice and I were discussing that very thing last night after dinner."

"You and Bernice were discussing the fact that you have no shame?"

"No, we were discussing sociopaths—people who really have no shame. And I think Jessamine Steele's husband, Jordan, may be one of those people."

I filled him in on the events at Jessamine's lawyer's office and my encounter with Jordan. When I got to the part about his draining power from me until I put up my shield, he gave a low whistle.

"I don't like the sound of that," he said. "I want you to keep that energy shield of yours up at all times—except when you're with me, of course. I kinda like you, and I don't want you to get hurt."

Chapter 7
Thursday, October 23rd

When I checked my email on Greg's computer the next morning, I found I had 42 messages in my new "ghost account." The gist of most of them was, "I saw the show tonight. Can you come and check out my ghost?"

I'd forgotten the show was to air on Wednesday night—since Greg lives in Alexandria we couldn't tune in on Fairfax cable, and I hadn't expected this kind of feedback so quickly. As I was contemplating how to handle this turn of events, an arm slid around my shoulder and Greg started nuzzling my neck. "Is today a *Law and Order* day or do you want to tackle an art gallery?"

The options he was offering harked back to our second date. The first date had been a pizza getting-to-know-you evening.

The second was a dress-up evening at Giorgio's, a small Italian bistro, where we listened to romantic Italian love songs as we dined on a simple but delicious meal of Pinzimonio—fresh vegetables dipped in olive oil—and Eggplant Parmesan. You are never rushed at Giorgio's—he subscribes to the Italian philosophy that mealtime is an occasion to relax with friends and family. We were cozily ensconced side by side in a candle-lit booth, and I could feel the warmth of his thigh next to mine. Over the after-dinner coffee, Greg had finally asked the question that can make or break a relationship.

"So, ah, you teach at George Mason University. I guess this means you have more than a high school education?"

I had laughed. "A bit more. But I won't force you to call me Dr. Quigley, although my students do."

He'd looked stricken. "Oh," was all he could say, and he'd looked down into his coffee cup. "I'm a really smart guy, but I'm not terribly cultured."

I'd put my hand on his cheek and turned his face toward me so I could look into his eyes. "Culture is a matter of choice. I'm an Army brat who just happened to be very good at reading and writing, and I didn't know when to stop. If somebody wants to become cultured, there are about 1,500 museums and galleries in this area, in addition to symphony, opera, and theater. I'd love to experience all of this with you. Then we can get cultured together."

The Lawyer Who Died Trying

His face had softened, and I'd leaned even closer. We'd started a kiss that just didn't want to stop. The waiter broke in with, "Can I get anything else for you?" At that we'd broken apart and started to laugh.

"Just the check," said Greg, and as the waiter walked away, he leaned toward me and said, "I think I can provide everything else the lady needs."

The next day TNT was running one of their 12-hour marathons, with back to back episodes of *Law and Order*, a show that doesn't necessarily require one's full attention. We'd spent the entire day in bed, watching shows as they attracted us, and doing other things as we drew each other away from the TV.

That was the basis of Greg's *Law and Order* reference. And I had to admit, there was nothing like a healthy sexual relationship to give a girl confidence. It made me feel wanted, needed, cherished, desired—tasty! Greg had let me know I was the pastry of choice on his dessert tray of life.

"I have to answer this ghost mail before I do anything else. I have a newsletter I set up for my students—I'll do the same thing for these and send out a quick message to all of them, then contact them individually later."

"How many emails do you have there?"

"I've counted 42. Most of them are from people who want me to come talk to their ghosts."

"You can't just give away your time. You probably can't charge for your services without a license of some kind—although I don't know what kind of license you'd need for ghost hunting. But you could tell people you take donations to defray the cost of your time and travel."

"Maybe at first I shouldn't go anywhere that's more than a 30-minute drive—although that won't get me very far in this area!"

"You might consider setting up a website just for your ghost consulting. And you could also set up a PayPal account with no trouble, and people could make a donation to you online."

"Slow down! The 42 emails may be the entirety of the business—though Mike and Michelle will be pleased to find that at least 42 people are watching. Also, I'll have to make appointments to coincide with your goofy schedule. It's hard keeping up with what days you're on or off."

"I know you English lit types like poetry. I know a little poem about that." He came and stood behind my chair. I leaned back against him and looked up.

With a mock British accent, he intoned, "She offered her honor, he honored her offer...and all night long it was on her and off her."

"You're terrible," I said emphatically and dismissively returned my gaze to the keyboard.

"Wait a minute—last night you told me I was really good!" His hand started to move south from my neck, and the letters on the keyboard blurred.

I returned to my email an hour or so later. Once I'd deleted the new crop of spam and taken care of personal messages, I realized the ghost email count had risen to 54.

"I'd better set up that newsletter right now," I said, "and forward all these email addresses to the newsletter sign-up page. Otherwise, I won't have a ghost of a chance of connecting with all these people before they pass away and turn into ghosts themselves! And if I pay him, Mike would probably be happy to build me another small website where people can come and post their stories on a form. I'm sure he'd appreciate another paid commission."

"Well, you could call the website 'A Chance of a Ghost'—you know, www.chanceofaghost.com," he suggested.

"I like it!" I said enthusiastically.

Once I had set up the newsletter, I went back and began reading through some of the messages. One of them was from a woman in Franconia, who said she'd seen the show at her sister's house the night before and was hoping I could give her family some help.

"My grandfather lived with us for the last five years of his life after my grandmother died. His favorite time of the day was breakfast. There was too much going on in our children's lives for us to have a set dinner time, and Grandpa liked to have his supper by six p.m., so breakfast was the only meal the family ate together.

"Every morning, Grandpa would come downstairs, get a cup of coffee, take a seat at the table, and regale all of us with stories from his childhood, or his time in the Pacific during World War II, or what life was like when my father and my aunt were growing up. The kids enjoyed it, and they always ate a good breakfast because the family time was fun. Often they'd even pitch in with little tidbits of their own about what had happened at school or with their friends. Then about six months ago, Grandpa passed away very peacefully in his sleep in his room upstairs.

"We were really shocked the day after the funeral when we sat down for breakfast. My ten-year-old son, Billy, had said he wanted to sit in Grandpa's chair, and we let him do it. Then we heard footsteps coming downstairs, and Billy said, 'Uh-oh, here comes Grandpa,' and he got up and moved back to his former place.

"The footsteps continued into the room, pausing first at the coffeepot, and then stopping at Grandpa's chair. This has happened every morning since Grandpa died. Nobody but Billy sees anything, although he does insist *he* sees Grandpa, but we all feel a kind of coldness and hear the footsteps. And it's put a bit of a damper on breakfast. We don't have Grandpa telling his stories anymore, but with our sense that he's there, we're a little subdued. I had thought we'd eventually pick up the slack and continue to have a sharing time in the morning, but that isn't happening.

"When I saw you on the show the other night, I realized how much better it would probably be for Grandpa if he moved on to wherever it is he's supposed to go. Do you think you could help him to do that? It would probably be best if you were able to come for breakfast as that's the only time we have impressions of him."

The letter was signed Mary Prescott and gave a phone number, so I called her. She was very grateful to hear from me and asked if I had a fee schedule. Following Greg's suggestion, I told her I'd be willing to accept a donation for a successful outcome. She told me her family usually had breakfast at about nine a.m. on weekends, so we made an appointment for Saturday morning at 8:30.

When Greg wandered back into the room a few minutes later, I said, "Okay, I'm in business. I have a breakfast meeting on Saturday—with a ghost!"

Since we'd already had an episode of *Law and Order*, we checked the *Washington Post* to see what was going on in the D.C. art scene and found an exhibition of French Impressionism, "on loan from the Louvre."

Greg looked at the address for the gallery and commented, "Good. That's near a restaurant I know that does a pretty fair impression of French food. How would you feel towards a dinner of a superb garlic and tomato soup followed by a serving of Caqhuse?"

"It sounds interesting. Although I do understand 'garlic' and 'tomato,' my French doesn't extend to whatever that other thing was!"

"Caqhuse—it's a pork and onion casserole, from Picardie, I'm told."

"You're on," I replied. "And I hope they also have a truly French and sinfully delicious dessert!"

Five hours later, full of misty impressions and French cuisine, we arrived back at Greg's house so I could pick up my Jeep and go learn all about Aquavest.

As I started walking toward my car, Greg reached for my arm and gently pulled me back, saying, "I like the French. They came up with some really good stuff—French toast, French fries, French kisses..." He pulled me close and demonstrated.

When I could breathe again, he asked, "Are you sure you don't want to come back inside for another episode of *Law and Order*?"

"It's pretty tempting," I sighed as I regretfully pushed him away. "But I really have to go to this meeting. I promised Jessamine. And Bernice is going to be there, thanks to my invitation, so I'd better show up. Besides, you have to go to work at five tomorrow morning, so you need some sleep."

"Spoil sport," he grumbled. "I won't see you again until Sunday."

"Well, think of me until then," I whispered and gave him one more kiss.

"If I do, I won't get *any* sleep."

Honora Finkelstein & Susan Smily

When I arrived at the Hyatt, I consulted the board in the front lobby and made my way to the Aquavest meeting room. I was running a little late, and Bernice was already waiting for me at the door.

"We've got seats up front, and since Lorelei and Patricia were fighting over you, I've told them you can sit between them."

"Gee, thanks, Mom," I said.

No sooner had I greeted all the Loo-Loo Ladies and taken my seat than a young woman came to the podium and introduced the CEO of Aquavest, Dr. Ernie Redmond. The man who stepped up to the podium was about 55 years old, with thinning sandy hair, a mustache, and glasses. He was dressed casually but well, in dark gray slacks and a tweedy sport jacket, with a burgundy shirt and light gray tie. He wasn't a commanding presence, standing only about 5'7", but he had an air of success and affluence that can be quite attractive and inspirational, even charismatic. If I didn't know better, I'd have pegged him as a TV evangelist.

"Good evening, everybody. I'm delighted to see all of you here tonight, and I notice a lot of new faces in the crowd, so I want to let you know we'll be having a reception after the meeting where I hope I'll get to shake everybody's hand.

"Now, I'm not much of one for fancy speeches. I spend most of my time wiring the mouths of the rich and famous—and their offspring. So I won't lie to you—I like making money—hey, that's why I went into dentistry! And I like having my money make money. Is there anybody in the room who doesn't like making money and having their money make money for them?"

There was a ripple of laughter while he paused and scanned the room. "I didn't think so. But I'm not here to raise money for cutting down the Venezuelan rain forests so we can have more gold. No! And I'm not here to ask you to invest in a new weapons system that will let the Colombian drug lords protect their crops. No! The invention you're going to see demonstrated here tonight is intended to have only positive effects on the economy, the environment, and the lives of people everywhere. It will provide cheap renewable energy for this country that will reduce our need to rape the earth for fossil fuels, reduce the toxins in the air, and reduce the cost of electric power for every man, woman, and child in this country. And it will eventually do the same for people around the world. Now, from my conversations with many of you, I know these things are pretty important for you guys, too. So with no more ado, let me introduce to you the inventor of the Aquavest device, Dr. Cristien Frandsen."

There was enthusiastic applause as a slightly rumpled, bearded man of about 40 wheeled out a cart with a long basin of water that had small models of three oil rigs evenly spaced along its length. All of the rigs had a metal sleeve around each leg, with several donut-shaped devices fitted over the sleeves. There was a paddle attachment at one end of the basin and a pump sitting on the lower shelf of the cart. Frandsen plugged the pump into a wall outlet and stepped forward to the table with a little robot. He connected some wires from the third in the series of oil rigs to a small box, and he ran the wires from the box to the robot.

"'Ello, everybody. I am French Canadian, so if you will excuse my accent, please, I will try to explain to you what you are seeing here."

He sounded very much like what I had experienced of English spoken by the Cajun French in Louisiana, with a pleasant sing-song quality.

"The thing what we are dealing with here," he explained, "is that the ocean, she traps *magnifique* stores of energy from the sun. And right now, there are happening all over the world projects to draw out this thermal energy stored in the water, projects to dam the fjords in Scandinavia for to catch the incoming tide, projects to use the force of ocean currents and ocean winds. There are even projects that attempt to generate electricity from what they call the salinity gradients—the difference in how much salt you find from this part of the ocean to that. These will cost millions to develop because they start from the beginning and have to build what you call the infrastructure. Hydro power is cheap—as long as you use the dam built in the 1930s. It would be *très expensive,* how you say, prohibitive, to try to build your Hoover dam now, because the increased labor cost, she has gone up so much.

"What we are planning to do is make use of an infrastructure what is already there—the *magnifique* lines of oil rigs in the Gulf of Mexico down there near Texas. We then use what is called the diurnal flux of tidal power. The tides, they come and go every twelve hours or so, pulled along by the moon, and they will move my little devices up and down. See how each of these slides up and down this sleeve, which is placed, like so, around the leg of the oil rig. The upward trip and the downward trip, each one, will generate electricity, through a system of dynamos, creating an electromagnetic effect. All these devices, they are connected together, so the power in cumulative. And *finalement*, it is delivered to the power plant at the shore, *et alors*, and then, delivered to your house the same way any other electric power is delivered...like this."

He flipped a switch, and the pump started the paddle moving up and down, creating a small wave that pushed through the basin. The devices on the legs moved up and down in sequence as the wave passed them, and within just a few minutes, the robot began moving across the table. We all watched with the pleasure and excitement of school children being let in on some new and marvelous idea, and I was reminded of a song by Tom Paxton I had learned as a child, "The Marvelous Toy": *"It went 'zip' when it moved and 'bop' when it stopped, and 'whirr' when it stood still. I never knew just what it was, and I guess I never will."*

"So you see, using this Aquavest device, it takes not so much motion to generate electricity. Which is a good thing, I think, because we are going to fit these donuts to oil rigs in the Gulf of Mexico, and there are *beaucoup*, many, of those, so the result should be *très magnifique*. There are some brochures in the back of the room that explain the science behind this little invention of mine. Later, when you have read the brochures, I will answer your questions during the reception after this meeting."

Ernie came back up, leading a round of applause. "Thanks very much, Cristien," he said, shaking the inventor's hand and patting him on the shoulder. As Frandsen sat down again, Ernie continued, "Ladies and gentlemen, Aquavest, and that means *you* if you're already an investor, owns the patent on the structure of this device. As those of you who've been with us from the beginning of this venture know, we've been working to pull together $500,000 to cover the cost of setting up the corporation, developing and testing the actual prototypes of the device, paying for legal services, and what might possibly be the most important step, hiring a lobbyist to represent us in the U.S. Congress.

"And you fine people here tonight are what is known as Angel Investors—you are the angels of this operation."

I looked around at the group and noticed head-nodding and smiles. They all seemed to be pretty proud of this designation.

"For those of you who don't know the term, an Angel Investment is what can take us from merely having a concept to being a multi-million-dollar enterprise! You are providing us with the capital we need to get started, and you receive ownership equity in return for your investment. And so far, more than $200,000 has been invested by our angels, people who want their money to make money for them.

"And you're smack dab in the middle—right after we hit up all our friends and relatives for everything they could spare—which was in the neighborhood of $14.93," he paused, and received the anticipated chuckles from his audience, "and before we reach the big players—the venture investment boys, with their multi-million-dollar funds. And what's more, you are the backbone of investment in this country, providing tens of billions of dollars annually, even more than all those venture capital funds combined."

I noticed a few people take in this fact with a bit of amazement.

"Not that I'm asking any single one of you for a billion dollars!" And again he paused for the laugh. "But I *am* asking you to take the plunge with us. And in return, we will pay you back very handsomely. Now usually, angel investors are in for a three- to five-year period, anticipating a return of ten to twenty times their investment, with a company that has prepared for a public offering or is looking at potential acquisition. But we're already ahead of the curve, and we suspect you'll reap your profits much sooner than that.

"Up until now, we've allowed people to buy in for as little as a thousand dollars, and that would get you a thousand shares. But now we have to dial up a notch or two, so after tonight we're going to be asking new investors for a minimum purchase of five thousand shares, at $2 per share.

"Now, I have an important announcement. We have a venture capital investment potential for two million dollars, giving us the opportunity to go forward. And we will, folks, we will!" There was much applause at this announcement.

"I'm not telling any secrets when I say we expect some important foreign investors to join us before the end of the year, and they're willing to pay as much as $50 a share. So those of you who have already bought shares can multiply what you've got by fifty in just three weeks, and our experts tell us that amount per share is likely to rise to $75 or $100 once Aquavest is in full operation."

I could feel the room becoming charged with the electric energy of excitement as people in the audience began totting up their potential wealth. Ernie capitalized on this surge with an invitation to all potential investors, whether they were new or already involved in the company, to meet with the company accountant at a table at the back of the room. Then he signaled for two attendants to open some sliding room dividers, displaying a second room with two bars and several tables of hors d'oeuvres and desserts.

"It's an open bar for the next hour, folks, so enjoy yourselves."

Patricia and Lorelei both vied for my attention immediately.

"Now that you've seen the device at work, what to you think?" asked Patricia.

"It's just amazin' how so much energy seems to be generated from somethin' so simple," said Lorelei. "And don't you just love the idea of bein' an angel?"

"Well, it looked interesting," I admitted, "but I'm not an engineer. However, I can certainly see there's a lot of excitement about it from those who've already invested."

"Why don't we go have some of the party goodies?" said Patricia. "Maybe we can introduce you to Ernie and Cristien and see what vibes you pick up."

Like well-trained sheep, we began making our way into the party room with the majority of the crowd. But I also noticed several people eagerly surrounding the accountant at the back of the meeting room.

"Have to feed and water the potential investors," murmured Bernice, coming up behind me. "One of the necessities of this kind of event."

As we followed Patricia and Lorelei to the closest bar, intending to get glasses of wine, Jessamine's excited voice rang out behind us. "Ariel, Bernice, I want you to meet Dr. Ernie Redmond."

Patricia and Lorelei went on to the bar.

Bernice extended her hand. "I know Dr. Redmond already. He reshaped the teeth of my daughter Michelle when she was 12, and she's been happily biting ever since. Hello, Ernie."

"Bernice!" he responded enthusiastically. "What a pleasure! I haven't seen you in years. But," he added as an aside to Jessamine and me, "she was always a favorite in our waiting room. Do tell me you and your husband are considering investing, Bernice."

"We're considering it, Ernie. But Alan wasn't able to make the meeting tonight," she smiled.

"Don't wait too long," he said jovially. "Time's a-wastin'!"

Then he focused his bright blue eyes on me. "And you must be Dr. Quigley!" he said, grabbing my hand in both of his. "I understand you're one of our newest shareholders. I can't tell you how much we all appreciate what you're doing for Jessamine. She's been like a new person since you came on the scene—so stressful, these custody disputes."

"Sh-h-h," said Jessamine, putting a restraining hand on Ernie's arm. "I haven't told my friends the real reason I contacted Dr. Quigley."

Ernie's raised his eyebrows a bit and nodded. "I understand," he said. "Mum's the word."

Just then Patricia wandered over with a martini in hand. "Two olives, and shaken, not stirred," she said with satisfaction, "just the way James Bond likes his drinks. Ernie, my dear, I see you've met our Ariel. Did Jessamine tell you," she asked conspiratorially, "that this lady reads Tarot cards? Would you like to have her read yours?"

Ernie smiled benignly at Patricia and replied, "I have no idea what that means, but I'm happy to have her read me anything but the riot act. But right now, duty calls, and Jessamine and I have to go talk to some of the potential investors and allay any fears they might have. Ladies!"

He nodded to us and took Jessamine's arm, and together they moved away. I wondered if I'd get a chance to speak to Jessamine about my dream this evening. She hadn't called me back on my cell, so I assumed she'd been very busy the past couple of days making arrangements for tonight's meeting.

Bernice and I each got a glass of wine, then turned toward the more substantial treats. Piped music began playing into the room, and I stood back and people-watched for a few seconds before joining the line behind Bernice at one of the hors d'oeuvres tables. I saw Lorelei chatting with a tall, good-looking man in the crowd. So far this evening I hadn't seen Maggie at all, and I wondered if she was even here. But among those who were present, the excitement was palpable. People were clearly buoyant, congratulating themselves on being in on the ground floor of this marvelous opportunity. Then suddenly I was reminded of my dream and the words of the square dance caller. I closed my eyes, and he was in my vision shouting, "With a left to your partner and a right and left *scam*..."

Startled by this rephrasing, I knew I needed to share the dream with Jessamine as soon as possible!

Chapter 8
Friday, October 24th

As soon as I got to campus the next morning, I put in a call to Jessamine's office again, but the message on her machine indicated she was going to New York and would be out of the office all day. I tried to reach her on her cell phone between classes, but she must have had her phone turned off—all I got was a robotic voice saying in a monotone, "Please-leave-a-message." I asked her to call and hung up. I wondered what might have come up the night before that had required her to go to New York on such short notice.

When I walked into my noon class a few minutes later, one of the more enterprising students had closed the blinds, turned on the TV in the room, and tuned it to Channel 10. And the opening credits of the Mac Jacobs show were just beginning.

"Hey, Doc, you're on TV!" he said. "I caught this show on Wednesday night, and I figured everybody else should have a chance to see our famous ghost-busting prof."

A chorus of voices that sounded more like a group of eight-year-olds than a college class chimed in with, "Can we watch, please?" and "I don't get TV at my place, so you hafta let us," and "Rockin'! Ghost-buster III!" and "We can do Locke and Hobbes on Monday, can't we?"

"Simmer down," I said. "I suppose it fits into the curriculum in a very loose way—ghosts have appeared in literature since the beginning of written records. Okay, shhh!" And I turned out the lights for better viewing.

I looked better on TV than I'd expected to—maybe a little bit stiff since I'd been very nervous, but I was glad it didn't show. I knew the show stopper was within the first minute—and when I told Bryan about the visit of his grandmother's ghost when he was age four, I was somewhat prepared for the momentary stunned silence in the classroom. Then one student broke the silence with a long, drawn-out, "Coo-ool!"

This was greeted with a sharp, "Hush!" from one of the girls, after which I experienced one of the most attentive classes I'd ever had. It was a bit like an out-of-body experience, watching myself from a distance, and watching the students watch me. Yeah, I thought, really coo-ool! It doesn't matter that it's community cable TV—their seeing me on screen gives me as much credibility for them as if it were network television.

When the show was over, I flicked on the lights and grabbed the remote to turn off the TV. And again I was greeted by a chorus of voices.

"What's that email again?" and, "My aunt Joan's got a ghost in her root cellar," and, "So all this psychic BS is for real?" and, "Can I have your autograph, Doc?"

I moved to the desk at the front of the room where I perched myself and said, "One at a time, please. We've still got fifteen minutes."

From the discussion during the rest of the period, I realized an interest in ghosts is pretty universal. Some people may not believe in them in our scientific age, but that didn't stop people from encountering them or being interested in them, and these kids were no exception.

Then one of the girls asked a question I would remember later.

"Does everybody become a ghost when they die?"

"Dead is dead," scoffed one of the guys.

"Maybe," I said, "but it's my understanding we only hang around after death if we've left something unfinished. Or if death is sudden and traumatic. Or if we don't actually know we're dead."

"How could you not know?" asked the scoffer. "Not that I'm agreeing there's an afterlife, but if there is, I don't see how you could not know when you're dead. I mean, if nobody can see you, and you can't move objects anymore, wouldn't that be a clue?"

"Well, suppose your perception when you get to the other side isn't the same—maybe you aren't aware that you're not in a real body. Or maybe you *can* move objects—there are lots of cases where people have experienced poltergeist activity. Consider a situation where you're studying late into the night and you doze for a second. And then you wake up somewhat disoriented—it might be like that for some people's spirits when they're dead. They wake up disoriented and don't know where they are or what they were doing before they 'dozed off.'"

Another one of the girls then asked, "What do you do in that case, like if you're ghost busting? How do you handle somebody who doesn't know he's a ghost?"

"I generally tell him or her the straight scoop: 'You're dead, and you need to move on to the other side.' And when they get the message, they either move on, or they tell me why they're still hanging around."

Then one of the boys asked, "What exactly is the other side? Heaven...hell...Akron?"

There was a general laugh, and I noticed we were out of time. "Time's up, so we'll have to save that metaphysical discussion for another day. You have papers due on Locke and Hobbes on Monday, even though we frivoled away the time today."

That night Michelle was waiting for me, glowing with excitement, when I got back to Bernice's.

The Lawyer Who Died Trying

"I got two calls today about your TV appearance," she enthused. "The first was from the studio 'cause they've been getting *beaucoup* calls from people who saw the show on Wednesday night and today at noon, and they think Mike and I should produce a show with you as the talent, talking to people about their ghosts. I don't think we'll have any trouble getting guests 'cause there's already a pool of people you could consider interviewing. And maybe we could get a field camera or even the studio's three-camera van and go out to the haunted site and do the interviews and some real ghost hunting. What do you think of that?"

"I think it sounds like a lot of fun, but I'm not sure I could work in a TV career just now."

"Well, we wouldn't be able to get it approved and on the schedule before the spring anyway, but it would be a really good credit for our resumes. So please, please think about it. Oh, and the other call I got was from Mac Jacobs. He wants to do two more shows with you—one in November and one in December—until we can set up your show. He said he jokes about having 40,000 people watching his show 'cause the only people he can guarantee do it are his mom and dad—except when his dad is off playing golf somewhere. But anyway, he says with all the calls he's had and all the calls the studio has had, maybe there are more people watching than anybody thinks!" She suddenly did a little dance and started singing, "I'm so excited—yah, yah, yah, I'm so excited!"

I laughed and gave her a hug. "Okay, I'll definitely think about it."

"Oh, and while I have your attention," said Michelle, "Mike wanted me to let you know we're having a Halloween party on Friday. You're new to the family, so you don't know about Mike's Halloween parties, but he's been throwing them since we were 14, and they get more elaborate every year. So this year, the theme is a ghostly graveyard. We're gonna set it up in the backyard, which is where Mom used to let us set up tents with haunted house effects. And this year Mike has a bunch of his buddies from the art department at George Mason working on some elaborate moving spooks with Disney-like animatronics. So it should be a much more professional show than we've ever had before. Anyway, we'd like you to participate if you have time, and at the very least come to the party with Greg and his son."

"That sounds like fun, too. But what would I have to do?"

"Well, Mike assigned me to make some headstones out of wood and paint them and put names on them. Then we'll put them in one part of the backyard like a little grave plot. And the other thing he assigned is for me to write up a sort of story to go with each of the big displays—these will need to be edited before they go in light boxes. If you could help me with either one of these projects, I'd really appreciate it."

"Maybe I could help you with getting the stories ready for the light boxes." I had no idea what she meant by light boxes, but I figured I could handle the story editing part.

"That would be great!" she said and bounced happily out the back door.

When I got up to my room, I turned on my computer to check my personal emails and found the ghost mails had risen to 64. And I knew the Mac Jacobs show would air at least one more time on Saturday afternoon. I was definitely going to have to learn to schedule my time a little better since I now had a job, papers to grade, friends to pal around with, a graveyard to build, a sexy boyfriend—and fan mail to answer!

Chapter 9
Saturday, October 25th

I was up with the birds the next morning, showered, and made a promise to my jogging shoes I'd have a more intimate relationship with them as soon as I got back from the Prescott house. Nobody else had made it to the kitchen, so I foraged for some coffee and as soon as it was ready, I filled the largest travel mug I could find and headed for the beltway. I figured my destination was only about twenty minutes away, and since it was Saturday, I wouldn't have to deal with frenetic rush-hour traffic this morning.

I followed Mary Prescott's directions and found the house with no problem, arriving at 8:25 by my car clock. When I rang the bell, a teenage girl of about 14 answered the door, looked me up and down, and yelled out over her shoulder, "Mom, the ghost buster's here." Then she turned back to me, smiled, and said, "Hi, I'm Sara. My mom's in the kitchen. C'mon in."

I followed her into a large country kitchen, where her mother was already making breakfast preparations. Mary came over and grabbed my hand. "Thank you so much for coming. Is there anything special we need to do?"

"Well, you know, I was thinking while I was driving over here about your letter. Your grandfather died in his sleep and it's quite possible that he doesn't yet know he's dead. Since what he used to do when he'd wake up in the morning was come down to breakfast, he seems to be caught in a loop and keeps repeating this pattern. So I'm going to suggest that the first thing we try is to disrupt the pattern. Would it be possible to move the table about three feet back from where it is now?"

"Let me call my husband," she said, and she went to the door and called up the stairs, "Jim, can you come down now?"

Moments later Jim Prescott came into the kitchen with Sara and a young boy I assumed was Billy peering in the doorway from the hall.

"Ms. Quigley wants us to move the table further back," she said.

"Which way?" he asked, and I pointed to where I thought it should go. We moved the chairs out of the way, and Jim and I each took an end of the table and gentled it across the floor to a new position. Then we repositioned the chairs around it. Meanwhile, Mary went back to her breakfast preparations.

I explained to Jim my sense that their grandfather might be repeating a pattern, and that to get his attention I was going to try to disrupt the pattern. He nodded and sat down in one of the chairs at the table, and I sat down, too.

"Still feels funny to me, having the old man hanging around like this."

"Well, maybe we can send him on his way, provided he gets the message it's really time for him to leave. Oh, and what was his name? Just in case I need to use it."

"His name was Carter," said Mary. "Carter Wells."

"And what about his wife's name?"

"Her name was Anna."

I noticed Billy hanging into the room by the doorframe, so I addressed him. "Are you Billy?"

He nodded and gave me a tentative smile, still swinging on the doorframe.

"Why don't you come in and sit down and tell me about your grandfather?"

He came tiptoeing over and took a seat across from me.

"Do you still see your grandfather when he comes down to breakfast every day?"

He nodded.

"And are you able to hear him?"

"No," he answered, shaking his head. "He comes down every morning and sits down in his chair just like always, and I can see his lips are moving, but I can't hear anything he's saying. It makes me kinda sad."

"I'm sure it does. Have you ever tried to talk to him, even though you can't hear what he's saying?"

Billy looked puzzled and shook his head.

"Well, I'm going to ask you to help me when I try to talk to him. I'm going to tell him that he's no longer living, and that as much as everybody here loves him, it's time for him to move on to where his wife and other friends and family are waiting for him. And I'm going to call on you to speak to him, too. When I do, I want you to say, 'Grandpa, I love you.' And if I ask you for more help, just say, 'What this lady is telling you is true.' Do you think you can do that?"

Billy nodded.

"Sara?" I called. "Come, in Sara."

The teen, who had been waiting quietly in the hall, came into the kitchen. "Jim, Mary, and Sara, I know you don't see Grandpa Wells, but can you speak to him if I ask you to?"

They all agreed.

"Well, then, let's give it a try and see if we can help Grandpa move on now that he's gone. Now, Mary, can we give you a hand with breakfast?"

"Sara will help me put everything on the table," Mary said.

We continued to chat until it got closer to nine o'clock. Then suddenly we heard footsteps at the top of the stairs. I motioned to Mary and Sara to sit at the table with us. The footsteps continued, becoming louder as they moved closer. They entered the kitchen and moved toward the coffee maker, paused there, then came toward the table.

Billy watched the progress of the ghost, but I wasn't actually seeing Carter Wells any more than Mary, Jim, or Sara were, though I could certainly hear his progress. I closed my eyes and tried to focus on my inner vision. And then I saw him, a tall, stately, white-haired man who moved toward the table, then into the very middle of it, and sat down in his usual place, which in this case—since we'd moved the table—was in the middle of the salt, pepper, and butter.

"Grandpa's in the middle of the table," said Billy softly.

In my mind's eye, the ghost of Mr. Wells looked a little disoriented.

"Mr. Wells," I said, and he turned to look at me. "I'm Ariel Quigley. How are you this morning?"

"Why, I'm quite fine, young lady," he answered cheerily. But he still seemed a little disoriented. Then, as if he'd figured out what the problem was, he stood up again, moved out of the middle of the table, and walked around to what must have been his usual chair. I opened my eyes and glanced at Billy, who was now looking at the chair I'd seen Mr. Wells move to.

"Grandpa moved," he said, sounding relieved that his grandfather was no longer in the middle of the condiments.

I closed my eyes again. "Mr. Wells," I said, "your family asked me here this morning to talk to you."

"Well, that was mighty nice of them," he said smiling. "They know I love company."

I smiled back. "And I'm very glad to be here, too. But Mr. Wells, I need to tell you something you don't seem to be aware of, sir. Mr. Wells, about six months ago, you passed away. You died in your sleep one night, sir. And your family thinks you'd be happier if you moved on to the other side."

"Oh," he said, and again he looked a little disoriented. Then he laughed. "Well, that does explain some things. Like why when I talk nobody seems to listen to me anymore. And why I can't get my sock drawer open!"

"Mostly," I said, "people don't listen because they can't hear you anymore. But they still love you, and they want you to be happy. Jim, Sara, Billy, Mary, tell Grandpa how you feel."

The family members all said in chorus, "We love you, Grandpa."

"And if you look around you," I continued, "I think you'll see there's a light beckoning you, and perhaps even friends and family members waiting for you."

Mr. Wells gave me a little half smile and looked around. Then his eyes widened. "Why, look over there—there's my Anna!" And he stood up. "Thank you, ma'am," he said to me without turning back to look at me. "Tell my kiddos goodbye for me." And he began walking toward the other end of the kitchen, as his audible footsteps attested. Then, almost as an afterthought, he stopped and looked back at me. "Oh," he said, "there's a Fat Man here who says for me to tell you that the dance is almost over, but it's not your fault." And then he was gone.

The Prescotts had asked me to stay for breakfast, and I'd thought it would be impolite not to do so, especially since everybody wanted to know exactly what I'd seen, what Billy had seen, and what Carter Wells had said. So it was nearly 11 o'clock by the time I got back home to Bernice's. There were no cars in the driveway as I pulled in, so I assumed the whole Wise family was out running Saturday morning errands.

I hate talking on my cell phone while driving, but the minute I was inside the house, I pulled it out and dialed Jessamine's office. The message about her trip to New York was still on her machine, but I left a message anyway, just in case she came in over the weekend, ending it with the words, "It's urgent!" Then I tried her cell number. And this time I heard the robotic voice say in a monotone, "Mail-box-full."

I was more than a little bit disquieted by the Fat Man's message that Carter Wells had delivered to me, and I was frustrated at not being able to connect to Jessamine. So I went upstairs and decided to keep my promise to my jogging shoes. I got into my sweats, socks, and shoes, did a little stretching, and went out for a half-hour run. As I jogged through the neighborhood, I thought about the symbols of the dream again. All the characters of the dream seemed to be representatives of what I was currently experiencing with Jessamine's circle of friends. By the time I got back home, I'd decided to try calling the Loo-Loo Ladies to see if any of them had a clue about where Jessamine was.

I'd gotten cards on Monday night from the two career women, Lorelei and Maggie, so I called them first, asking if either of them had any idea why Jessamine had gone to New York. Maggie's line went directly to a machine associated with her real estate company, but I left a message anyway. Lorelei's phone rang four times, and I was expecting to hear another disembodied voice on an answer machine, but just as I was preparing my spiel with my name, number, and reason for my call, she answered.

"No, dahlin," she drawled, in answer to my question about Jessamine's trip. "Ah don't know why she went to New Yawk, but she did leave me her key so Ah could go feed her cat. She left her son with his grandmother, or at least that's what she said she was gonna do. Now, the only person I know she knows in New Yawk is that inventor, Cristien. But Ah don't think she's havin' an affair with him, or anythin' like that. Ah do know he was talkin' at the meetin' on Thursday about some high-powered people from a former administration who were interested in Aquavest, so maybe she went up there to talk with them. But Ah'm sure she'll be back by Monday."

"I don't have Patricia or Ernie's personal numbers, but I'd like to try calling them to see if either of them knows how I can get in touch with Jessamine. Can you give me their numbers?"

"Ah surely can. Y'all just sit tight for a minute." And a few moments later I had the numbers. "Now don't worry," she said. "Ah'm sure Jessamine's jus' fine."

At Patricia's number a little girl answered. She sounded about six years old, and her telephone skills included a rundown of family history. "My mom's not here right now. She had to take my brother Charlie shopping 'cause his feet are too big for his shoes, and his toes are poking out the ends."

"Well, is your daddy at home?"

"No. He went out, too."

"Do you have an older brother or sister there with you?"

"Well, my other brother's upstairs working on the computer, and he doesn't want me to bother him 'cause he's studying 'cause he's going to take the tests to go to college. And when I get bigger, I'm going to go to college, too. And my brother Charlie was going to college, too, except my mom says he's not going to have any college money left because she has to buy him too many pairs of shoes."

I laughed to myself. "Um, do you think you could take a message to give to your mom?"

"Yeah, I'm good at taking messages. I do that all the time," she said, then added proudly, "I know *all* my letters."

"Then can you ask her to call Ariel Quigley? Can you remember that name?" Then I thought to myself, "Can you say Quigley? I *know* you can."

"Just a minute. I have to find a pencil to write it down."

I heard the phone clunk on the table at the other end, and I waited nearly a full minute before she came back.

"Okay, now you have to spell your name for me."

I spelled it slowly and followed it with my phone number. With luck, Patricia might get it before I heard from Jessamine.

Finally, I called the number for Ernie the dentist and got yet another answer machine. I left yet another message.

I was pretty frustrated and no closer to finding Jessamine than I had been before. So with a sigh I pulled out my briefcase. When in doubt, grade papers!

Chapter 10
Sunday, October 26th

The next morning I went out for a 30-minute run, then hit the shower. When I came out wrapped in my robe with a towel around my head, I checked my cell phone for messages. To my frustration, Jessamine had finally called me back. Unfortunately, the message she left was a little disconcerting.

"Something has happened with Aquavest, and it doesn't look good. It's too long and involved a story for me to put it on your phone, so I'm going to send it to you as an email. As soon as you've read it, give me a call."

I sat down at my computer and booted it up to check my email messages. Sure enough, there was one from Jessamine addressed to me, Ernie, and all the Loo-Loo Ladies with a document attachment. I opened it and read the following:

"I hate to be the bearer of bad tidings, and I hope you won't kill the messenger. Something has happened to Aquavest, and I have the responsibility of sharing it with all of you, and at the earliest opportunity with the rest of the investors in the company.

"Shortly after Ernie first came to me with the Aquavest project, he introduced me to Cristien's attorney, William Love, who was down from New York. And I checked on the law firm he was supposed to be with, and it was highly respected. And I even checked to be sure he was with the law firm, and they confirmed he was. He was the one who kept telling us the good news about people from Congress being interested in the device, and the New York politicos, and the dealings with the oil companies in the Gulf of Mexico, and all about foreign investors from Japan and Europe being ready to invest in the near future. And he was the one who was handling all the paperwork for the foreign investors' offering. And I've called him on a private line he gave me dozens of times and talked to him myself about questions I've had. And he's the one who showed us copies of Cristien's patent and drew up the paperwork that allowed the company to buy the patent.

"But at the meeting on Thursday, I overheard two of the potential investors talking. And one of them said to the other that he couldn't believe the invention would work in the Gulf of Mexico because the tidal action

The Lawyer Who Died Trying

doesn't work there the way Cristien described it. Cristien was still around, so I jokingly asked him about this, and his reaction made me uncomfortable. In fact, he seemed almost evasive. So on Friday morning first thing, I called a person I know who has a friend on the congressional energy committee, and I tried to trace what we'd been led to believe was interest in the device. And I couldn't find anybody who'd heard about it.

"Then I called our accountant and got him to check the bank balance for the Aquavest fund. And a lot of the money that had been in the account on Thursday morning was no longer there. So I asked him to have the bank trace where it had gone. He got back to me about an hour later and said it had somehow been shifted to accounts in the Cayman Islands and on the Isle of Jersey. When I asked him who had signing rights on the company accounts, he explained that he did, Ernie did so that he could pay for special operations, and that Cristien did, for the purpose of paying for the technical development of the device's prototype, for travel, and for entertainment of foreign investors, but that any transaction needed two of the three signatures.

"I called the Hyatt in Arlington, where Cristien had been staying for the meeting, and the desk clerk told me he'd checked out Thursday night, just after the meeting. I tried to call him on his cell phone but got no answer. And I tried his home number in New York but again got only an answer machine. I also tried his lawyer's private number but got no answer there, so I called the firm's number and was told he'd be in at 11 o'clock. Through his secretary, I made an appointment with him for two o'clock and took a shuttle to New York. I was also going to try to confront Cristien at his residence, figuring if something was amiss, he might not be answering his phone, but that I could probably force him to talk to me if I showed up in person.

"The last thing I did before I left town was to call Ernie and tell him about the remark I'd heard at the meeting Thursday night about the tidal behavior in the Gulf of Mexico being too limited for the device to work properly, and how when I mentioned this to Cristien, it had apparently spooked him. Ernie said he'd do his best to look into the business about the tides.

"When I got into New York City, I took a taxi to the firm where William Love worked, and I met the lawyer by that name, but he wasn't the same man as the one Cristien had introduced me and Ernie to months ago. This lawyer said it seemed he'd been the victim of identity theft. And by this time, you probably won't be surprised to learn that when I went looking for Cristien, he wasn't home.

"I've copied this to all of you to let you know the status of the company and of your investments. I'm planning to call an emergency general meeting of the local investors as soon as possible, so please check your email again throughout the day so you'll know when and where we'll be holding the meeting."

I tried to call Jessamine back right away, but her cell number was still giving me the robotic message that her mail box was full, and her office line was busy and not giving me the option of leaving a message.

I was due at Greg's at about noon, but it was only a little after 10 a.m. and I really needed to talk to someone before that, so I got dressed and went downstairs to see if Bernice was up yet. Sure enough, she was sipping coffee and reading the Sunday *Washington Post*.

When I had shared the gist of Jessamine's message with her, Bernice shook her head with a wry look. "Your friend Jessamine seems to have a penchant for drawing sociopathic people to her," she said. "Jordan sounds like an ice man, and Cristien would appear to be a scam artist."

"It does seem that way. I'll still go to court for her, if necessary, but I'm glad I didn't put any of my own money into Aquavest. I just wonder how this is going to affect the other investors. Especially the Loo-Loo Ladies. I like them, and I'd hate to see them get hurt."

I was still mulling over the problems with Aquavest as I drove to Greg's, but when he opened the door for me he was looking so utterly hunky in a blue cambric shirt and jeans, that I dropped my purse and decided to kiss first, talk later.

When we came up for air, he looked at me with a grin and said, "I like that! Dessert before dinner!"

"I just needed a little reality check," I countered, "and you're the reality I want to check in with. Things have been pretty intense since I left you on Thursday. I'll share *all* over lunch if you like. But right now I'm starving!"

We decided to get some take-out Chinese food, so we put in a call for our order, and Greg went off to pick it up. While he was gone, I checked my email again on his computer to see if there was anything further from Jessamine, but there wasn't. I did, however, have another 11 messages from people with ghosts who had seen the show on Channel 10 on Saturday. I replied to all of them with a response intended to buy some time and hoped the deluge would recede now that the show from the previous week had aired the final time.

As I was turning off the screen, my cell phone rang, and I dashed to get my purse from where I'd dropped it when I'd gotten into the clinch with Greg. It stopped ringing before I got there, so I waited a moment to give whoever was calling time to leave a message. Sure enough, when I checked it moments later, it was from Jessamine. Her voice sounded distant and a little disoriented, and she said, *"Something is very wrong. I need help. Can you come over and do your psychic thing?"*

I tried to call her back immediately, but she didn't pick up, and both the numbers still gave me the same messages as they had earlier.

The Lawyer Who Died Trying

I paced for a few minutes, feeling increasingly disquieted. When Greg got back, I told him about the message and asked if we could go right over to her office.

"Hey," he said, "you're hungry and I've got hot food here, so let's take a few minutes to eat, and you can fill me in on why the big urgency."

Over sips of hot and sour soup and bites of General Tso's chicken and Buddha's feast, I told Greg everything that had happened since I'd seen him on Thursday night. I even included a quick rundown on my visit to the Prescott family and Carter Wells' message from the Fat Man about the dance being almost over.

"Okay," he said. "I understand why you're upset. Let's put the leftovers away and head over to her office now."

We took Greg's car. When I described to him the building on St. Asaph the office was in he said he knew which one I meant. Twenty minutes later he pulled up in front of the building and parked. I started to buzz Jessamine's office, but then I noticed that the door was standing slightly open.

As I led him up the stairs to Jessamine's office, Greg commented, "I would have expected the outer doors to be locked on a Sunday."

"I guess she left it open for me. That way she wouldn't have to come down and let me in."

When we got upstairs, the outer door to Jessamine's office was also ajar, but I knocked anyway as I pushed it further open. "Jessamine?" I called. "It's Ariel. And I've brought my friend Greg with me. Jessamine?"

There was no answer, but the inner door to her private office was standing wide open, so we crossed the waiting room and went in as I called again, "Jessamine? Are you here?"

She was lying sprawled beside her filing cabinet, the top drawer of which stood open. The handle of the knife she'd used as a letter opener—the one she'd shown me the day I visited her—was protruding from the middle of her back. It almost seemed to be glowing, and I suddenly got a mental image from my dream of all the people dancing, then fighting.

The dance was definitely over.

I stumbled backward, feeling as if the breath had been knocked out of me, and bumped into Greg, who had stopped right behind me.

"Easy, Tiger," he said softly. He held me by the shoulders for a moment until I had a chance to recover my balance. Then taking in the scene, he went to Jessamine's body, hunkered down beside her, and checked her vital signs. He looked up at me and shook his head grimly. Then he stood up, took out his cell, and called 9-1-1.

"This is Sergeant Greg Mason. I have a DOA, probable homicide." He gave the address and suite number, then explained that he was off duty.

In answer to a question from the other end, he said, "No, we don't need paramedics—rigor has already begun to set in." Then another pause, and he said, "No, no witnesses." And again a pause before he said, "Since I'm on the scene, I've secured the office, though not the building. Here's my cell number." And he gave the number, then paused again. "Yes, I'll be waiting here."

When he'd finished, he closed his phone and came back toward me. I'd been standing stock still in a state of semi-shock, a multitude of things running through my head. What if we hadn't taken the time to eat—would Jessamine still be alive? Thanks to my Fat Man dream, I'd known there was the possibility of danger. Why hadn't I taken action? My lunch felt like a brick in my stomach.

"Let's step out to the waiting room," said Greg, taking me by the shoulder and turning me around toward the door.

As he led me out of the room, I whispered almost despairingly under my breath, "Jessamine, what happened to you?" And I felt the faintest brush of air stir against my cheek.

The knife in Jessamine's back had seemed to be glowing when I'd first seen her body lying on the floor. As Greg guided me out of the room, I glanced back over my shoulder at the knife handle. The glow was gone.

I let Greg lead me to a couch in the outer office where we sat down side by side. He left me in my reverie for a few moments; then he put his hand gently on my knee and said, "Earth to Ariel. Come in, Ariel."

I looked at him with a sad smile.

Reading my face, he squeezed my knee sympathetically and softly commented—with what to me seemed an echo of Carter Wells' message from the Fat Man—"It's not your fault. There was nothing you could do. Rigor has started to set in, so she'd been dead at least two hours."

I glanced at my watch and gave him a puzzled frown. "But that's not possible. She called me while you were out getting our food. I mean, I didn't actually talk to her when she called. The phone was in my purse, and I heard it ring but missed answering it by a few seconds. But she left a message asking us to come over here. And you came back with the food only about five minutes later. So it's only been about forty-five minutes tops since she called me. She can't have been dead that long. And I can't stop thinking...maybe we could have prevented it."

Greg shook his head almost imperceptibly. "You're the expert," he said. "Do ghosts leave telephone messages?"

The question took me aback. "Oh," I breathed softly and thought about what he was asking. I replayed Jessamine's message in my head, remembering my own reaction to it—she had seemed distant and perhaps a bit disoriented.

"Maybe," I said, "maybe. I've never experienced electronic voice phenomena before, but there are lots of cases on record of people who have. I even read one report that suggested if you get a phone call with dead air space on the other end, just hang on for at least thirty seconds and see if

The Lawyer Who Died Trying

you're getting a call from the other side. It might be your departed loved ones trying to get in touch!"

Greg grinned. "You're full of..." he paused for a couple of beats, then finished, "surprises. I never know what I'm going to learn in a conversation with you. But before you beat up on yourself anymore, let's wait and see what the ME says about your friend's time of death. And let's check the time your phone call actually came in before we chalk this up to...what did you call it?"

"Electronic voice phenomena. In the ghost biz they call it EVP."

Just then his cell phone rang. He answered with, "This is Sergeant Mason." And again I got to listen in to half of a conversation.

"Yes, ma'am, no witnesses. We're in an office building that appears to be empty, though it would be worthwhile checking all three floors. The patrol officers can do that when they arrive...no, nobody on the street when we got here...I'm off duty, so we'll need another sergeant. Yes, ma'am. Thank you." And he closed his phone.

"That was the 'Violent Crimes Unit' supervisor. She deals with homicide, rape, and suicide cases and dispatches the appropriate personnel. She says she'll be sending Detective Flanagan—you remember him from that case last fall—plus another detective named Harris, and she'll get in touch with the medical examiner's office and the commonwealth attorney's office. She said the ME may not come here—she'll have to locate him—but either he or the medics will have to declare Jessamine dead. And he'll likely send Metropolitan to pick up the body and take it to the morgue. Also, she said the CA—that's the commonwealth's attorney—will want to see the office to get a look at the crime scene while it's still intact."

Just then we heard footsteps coming down the hall. Greg stood up as two patrol officers appeared at the outer office door. I heard him say, "From the looks of the body, the vic seems to have been surprised from behind. This office door was standing open when we got here. So it wouldn't hurt to secure the whole building, at least temporarily, to ensure it's all clear and that there are no other possible witnesses."

"We'll go do that if you don't mind waiting here," said one of the officers. "Sergeant Bennett is on his way and should be here in a couple of minutes."

Sure enough, the patrol officers had no sooner gone down the hall than we heard more footsteps coming our way.

Sergeant Bennett, whom I'd met briefly when I'd stopped by the police station with Greg a couple of weeks before, walked in and said, "Hi, Greg. Hello, Ariel. What have we got here? Heck of a way to be spending your Sunday off."

"Hey, Paul," Greg responded. "Looks like we've got a dead lawyer in the inner office. And no lawyer jokes, please. She was a friend of Ariel's."

I acknowledged Paul's greeting with a little finger wave and a wan smile.

The two men turned to look through the door of the inner office. "Did anybody touch or move anything?" Bennett asked.

"I took her pulse before calling 9-1-1. Ariel was standing at least five feet away the whole time, and we left the office as soon as I'd completed my call. So everything is as it was when we arrived."

Bennett made a few notes, and Greg repeated some of the things he'd said before on the phone to the 9-1-1 dispatcher and the violent crimes supervisor.

While they were talking to each other, I drifted back into my reverie. I couldn't shake off the burden of guilt I'd been feeling ever since I'd heard Jessamine's message. I pulled my cell phone out to listen to it again, but there were no stored messages. I was sure I hadn't deleted it, but it just wasn't there.

"What were you trying to tell me, Jessamine?" I asked softly, and I suddenly felt a touch on my cheek and a presence beside me where Greg had been sitting a few minutes earlier. I centered myself and tried to tune in to the energy of the presence.

What I got was a strong sense of confusion. As I kept repeating in my mind, "What happened? What happened?" all I got back was an echo, "What happened? What happened?"

Then I got another sense of what the questions meant. I was asking Jessamine to tell me what had happened to her, but she was asking me to tell her what had happened with Aquavest. And then I actually heard her saying, *"I'm trying to piece it all together. I've got to get this ready for the meeting. Help me! You can see things. Please help me!"*

Startled as I was by her voice, I tried to maintain a calm exterior. "Jessamine, do you know what happened to you?" I whispered. "You were stabbed from behind, and you were killed. You're dead, Jessamine."

There was a space where she seemed to be taking in that piece of information. Then she said, *"But I'm still here."*

"I know. But this isn't where you belong now. You're dead, and you need to go to the other side."

"The other side of what? I'm not going anywhere until I know what happened!" she said adamantly. *"Help me find out what happened!"*

"Do you know who stabbed you, Jessamine?"

Again there was a sort of blank space where she seemed to be trying to understand her situation. Then she said, still with confusion, *"Stabbed me? Who stabbed me? I don't know what happened. I don't know what happened to the company. I don't know what happened to me. I don't know. You have to help me."*

Just then I heard Greg explaining some further details to Paul about why we were on the scene.

Paul came over to me and said, "I'm very sorry for the loss of your friend, Ariel."

"Thank you, Paul."

At that point one of the patrolmen returned. Addressing Paul, he said, "We've checked the whole building, sir, including basement and roof.

Nobody else is in the building. The only back entrance is locked, and Tazewell has set up tape and will maintain the front door."

"Thanks, Mecklenburg. Did you check the stairwells for cameras, or did you see any other electronic security devices?"

"No, sir, we didn't notice any."

"Then go do a survey up and down the street and see if there are any potential witnesses who might have seen anything these last few hours."

Over the next several minutes, the outer office became very crowded. Detective Flanagan arrived along with Detective Harris, whom I hadn't met before. Moments later, a full team of crime investigators arrived. I noticed one of the female investigators starting to take pictures of the scene. First she went to the door of Jessamine's inner office and began taking pictures from the doorway, making notes on a pad after each shot. Then she stepped into the office, and I could hear her clicking away.

Greg noticed me watching her while she was working from the office door. "First long shots, then close ups," he explained. "It's her job to record the homicide scene exactly as it was before anybody entered the room—and to keep a very accurate record of each photo taken."

"*We* entered the room."

"True, but we didn't touch or move anything. Crime scene photography may be the most important aspect of a case like this. Remember how important the photos were that you took of that case last fall?"

I smiled, remembering how I'd used the photos I'd taken as if they were Tarot cards, and how we'd figured out what was wrong with the crime scene from the photos. "Yeah, the pictures really helped me recognize what was bothering me about the scene."

"Right," said Greg. "We think of pictures being used to show a jury what the crime scene looked like, but they also can help the investigator recall important details or figure out discrepancies, and sometimes they even provide a new slant on a case."

While all the crime professionals were working between the outer and inner office doors, Flanagan led me and Greg to chairs near the windows, away from the doors, and began asking me questions.

"How did you come to be in Ms. Steele's office today?"

"I got a call from her around 12:30 this afternoon. Sergeant Mason and I were about to have lunch, and he was out picking up our food when the call came in. I missed actually talking to Ms. Steele directly because I couldn't get to the phone in time. But she left a message asking me to come to the office this afternoon. And it sounded urgent. When I tried to call her back, I couldn't get her. So after Greg and I had a quick lunch, we came over."

"And how were you acquainted with Ms. Steele?"

"I'd met her just a week ago. She'd called George Mason University, where I teach, about needing an expert witness in her own custody suit, and they recommended me. I met her for the first time on Saturday a week ago.

But she sort of adopted me, so I've seen her three more times since then. She was working as the legal counsel for an investment company called Aquavest, and last Monday night she invited me and my friend Bernice Wise to have dinner with her and some of her close friends who were investors in that company. Then on Tuesday I gave a deposition of my expert witness testimony to her lawyer in the custody case, and I met her ex-husband, Jordan, who had come to the office to deliver some papers. And finally, on Thursday my friend, Bernice, and I went to an actual meeting of the general stockholders of the investment company, where I met the company's CEO and heard a presentation made by the engineer who had designed the device everybody is investing in. Jessamine wanted to pay me for my court testimony in stock rather than in cash, and I'd agreed. I went to the stockholders' meeting to find out what it was all about."

"So do you know of anyone who might have wanted to do Ms. Steele harm?" asked Flanagan.

I thought a moment before answering. There were probably several people I'd met in the past week who might be upset with Jessamine, but not all of them for the same reasons.

"I guess the first person would be her ex-husband, Jordan Steele. I believe the murder weapon is the knife Ms. Steele used as a letter opener, and if so, it used to belong to him. Or at least, that's what she told me when I was in this office last week. What I'm going to tell you is hearsay because it came from Jessamine in my first meeting with her, but nevertheless, while I was visiting her last week, she actually handed me the knife, which she said she sometimes used as a letter opener. She told me it had belonged to her ex-husband, that he used to be a Force Recon operative with the Marines, and that when he gave it to her, he claimed he'd formerly used it in some...assassinations."

"So Jordan Steele could be a prime suspect?"

"Well," I said, thinking further, "the knife was in her office, on her desk, so anybody could have used it on her. And..." I paused, because what I wanted to say next was a psychic impression, not hard evidence. Then I remembered that Flanagan already knew about my psychic hits, so I finished the thought aloud. "And when I was holding the letter opener, I got the distinct impression Jordan Steele had used it for some of his kills, but that his usual method of operation was to slash their throats. He didn't stab people in the back. Cutting their throats was a quicker and surer means of dispatching them." I left out the part about it also being a more likely mode of ritual murder and about my impression of tasting blood in my mouth while I was holding the knife.

"And his motive for killing his wife would have to do with the custody suit?"

"That would be my assumption. Ms. Steele wasn't at all sure she could block him from having joint custody. Hence her desire to have me as an expert witness."

"And what was the substance of your deposition?"

The Lawyer Who Died Trying

"Ms. Steele had some materials indicating her husband has been teaching a form of personal empowerment with cultic associations. The cult was connected with the goddess Kali, and at least in the late 19th and early 20th centuries, there was a form of it that was heavily based in dark magic and ritual murder, sometimes of children. My testimony, as an historian of occultism during that period, had nothing to do with Jordan Steele personally. But by implication, it was supposed to bring his ethics and morals into question as well as his suitability for being a custodial parent. My testimony was supposed to make it less likely he would win the custody suit."

Flanagan raised an eyebrow. "Clearly we'll need to see if Mr. Steele has an alibi for this afternoon." He made some notes, then continued, "Is there anyone else you've met in the past week who might have wanted Ms. Steele out of the way?"

I nodded. "Possibly. I have an email from her that she sent this morning to some of her closest friends indicating she had discovered some discrepancy in the Aquavest books and also a possible flaw in the device itself. And she went to New York on Friday to check these things out and discovered some hanky-panky going on with the inventor's lawyer. I can send you a copy of the email if you think it would help. But to answer your specific question, it's possible that the inventor, the company CEO, and just about anybody who had a significant stake in the company might want Jessamine out of the way, especially if what she was about to reveal to the membership at large ended up blowing the whistle on either a faulty invention or on wrongdoing with company funds."

Flanagan pursed his lips and gave a rueful shake of his head. Glancing at Greg, he mused, "Have you ever had a crime scene on a Sunday that was *easy* to figure out?" Then to me he said, "You'll need to come to the station later and record your statement for us. But I can let you and Sergeant Mason leave now and come by later. And in the meantime, see if you can come up with a full list of people we might want to talk to."

As Flanagan was finishing with us, the commonwealth attorney, Jules Rivard, arrived. He was a tall, elegant, and well-dressed black man in his early forties. He shook hands all around, and the impression I got was a sense of immediacy—his presence conveyed the idea that with this man in charge, things would get done.

"I knew Jessamine Steele," he said. "She was a very fine lawyer. I'll handle this case myself. I want to be sure whoever did this is brought to justice. I don't take it kindly when someone harms a fellow officer of the court."

Just at that point the ME arrived to pronounce the body dead. He had also called a full contingent from Metropolitan to bag and move the body to the morgue as soon as the crime scene investigators were finished with the scene.

Greg and I conferred briefly and decided we could use some strong coffee, so we told Flanagan we'd meet him in about an hour. We decided to head over to my apartment, which was closer than Greg's to the police station.

A few minutes later we were down at street level and climbing into Greg's car. As I reached for my seatbelt, I again felt the tickling sensation against my cheek that I'd felt up in Jessamine's office right after we'd found her body and again while I was sitting on the couch in her outer office.

"We aren't alone," I said to Greg. "Jessamine is coming with us for our coffee break!"

I was just a little weirded out by having Jessamine literally in my lap on the way back to Bernice's, so I asked Greg if he'd mind if Bernice joined us for coffee so I could fill her in on what had happened. He was happy to have the extra insight into the situation, so I called her on my cell.

"Good heavens!" she said when she heard the news about Jessamine and that we needed some therapeutic input. "I'll put the coffee on right now!"

I was still definitely feeling Jessamine's presence when we got to Bernice's house. She was right behind me when I unlocked the front door and practically treading on my heels as we went through the house to the kitchen. Bernice already had cups and a plate of her special maple pecan coffee cake on the table waiting for us. When I told her Jessamine was with us, too, she asked wryly as she began pouring coffee into the cups on the table, "Should we set another place for her?"

"I don't know. I've never had a ghost lock on so tenaciously before. I mean, I know the Fat Man's around most of the time, sending me messages. But he's not intrusive in my day-to-day affairs unless there's trouble coming. I'm not sure Jessamine has left my side since we found her body."

"Well, then," said Bernice, like a true psychologist, "we'll just have to find out what her needs are and provide acceptable ways of satisfying them. Then maybe she'll be able to heal and move on. What do you think is her reason for focusing on you in particular?"

I explained that Jessamine had called me—presumably through some form of EVP after she had died, if her time of death was really as early as Greg had suggested—because she wanted me to help her figure out what was going on with Aquavest.

"She seems to have been caught in the activity she was focused on at the time she was killed. I don't know if she fully accepts yet that she's dead. But from what I'm picking up, she's still trying to straighten out the situation with Aquavest."

"And if she doesn't know she's dead, then is it safe to say she probably doesn't know who killed her?"

"So far I haven't picked up anything about her murderer or even whether she knew there was anybody else in the office when she was attacked. She's agitated and disoriented, but not about having been murdered.

The Lawyer Who Died Trying

"Now, Detective Flanagan asked me to come up with a list of potential suspects," I continued, "based on the people I've met in the past week who might have wanted to do her harm. We have to go meet him at the station in a little while, so I was hoping you could help me come up with a list. Oh, and Jordan is already at the top of the list, but we don't have a motive for him."

Bernice looked serious and pensive as she stirred her coffee. Finally, she said, "If our analysis of Jordan is correct, and he is indeed a classic sociopath, then his primary reason for doing whatever he does is to win. Sociopathic people want to win—arguments, fights, court cases, whatever. If he really is teaching a form of black magic, then he's doing it for the power trip it gives him, not for the benefit it might bring to anyone else. But what would be his motive for killing Jessamine? Does he think he's going to lose the court case? Or would her death in some way enhance his power over others? I suppose if he wants control of his son, and he thinks he might not win it in court, he could be pushed to kill—especially if he truly has done it before in the line of military duty."

"That's the reasoning the police will probably take," said Greg. "But there will have to be substantial evidence to support his guilt as well."

"And we don't know anything about evidence yet," I added, "except that Jessamine wound up with a knife in her back that was on her desk a week ago when I met her and that she told me her ex had used as a weapon before he gave it to her. But I guess what I need right now is some help coming up with a list of possible suspects."

"Or at least," countered Greg, "a list of other people who knew Jessamine and whom the police could contact for more information about her."

"Right!" I said. "I've been really uncomfortable thinking I was going to need to put the Loo-Loo Ladies on the list as suspects. But the police could contact them just for more information, couldn't they? I mean, I did dream of three women dancing with Jessamine and then fighting with her, but the fighting doesn't necessarily make them potential killers."

"No," said Greg with a little smile, "nor does the dancing exonerate them. But if you think they might know something you *don't* about Jessamine, you should probably put them down to be contacted."

"And," suggested Bernice, "if, as they all insisted last Monday night, they got into Aquavest because they trusted Jessamine, and if they saw her email yesterday and panicked and lost confidence in the investment, there's no telling what any one of them might do. Especially if they had invested money they couldn't afford to lose."

"Good point," I agreed. "Of course, we have no clue about any of that, but it does make it worthwhile for the police to at least check them out. And of course, I should also put Ernie on the list, as the CEO of the company. And Cristien also, since he seems to have been milking the company's funds for what may very well be a fake invention. And most definitely his lawyer, William Love, should go on the list, given what Jessamine learned about him. Though from what Jessamine said in her email, I wouldn't be surprised if they're both already out of the country."

"Mention that in your statement, too," suggested Greg, "so the police can check him out early on in the investigation."

"Would it be a good idea for me to take a copy of the email with me? Just so Flanagan has the background of Aquavest and how it might be involved in what's happened to Jessamine?"

"It couldn't hurt."

"Then I'll go print off a copy. And I'll get the contact information for all the ladies, too."

I got up from the table and went upstairs. I'd forgotten Jessamine's presence for a little while though she'd apparently been sitting quietly next to me while we were talking. But as soon as I was up and moving, I got the distinct impression she was following me again—up the stairs, into my apartment, over to the computer where I found the email, waiting with me by the printer, to my satchel where I kept my address book, back to the desk to find a pen and pad for the ladies' contact information, then back to the satchel to put the address book away, and back down the stairs again. She dogged me the whole way.

"I'm not sure what I'm gonna do!" I said when I got back into the kitchen. "Jessamine is following me around like a puppy. I feel as if she's so close that I don't even know how to contact her by myself. She's too much in my space."

"We could try a little therapy," suggested Bernice. "As I said when you came in, if we can figure out what she needs to help her feel complete and solve that problem, perhaps she'll move on, and that could solve *your* problem."

"How much time do we have left before we have to leave for the station?" I asked Greg.

He glanced at his watch. "About fifteen more minutes."

"Then what do you suggest?" I asked Bernice.

"Try altering out, the way you do in meditation. Get relaxed, go to your alpha level, and see if you can tune in to Jessamine. And if it's appropriate, I'll ask questions as if I'm talking directly to her, the way we did with Annie Grace."

I did as Bernice suggested, relaxing and going into a slightly altered state. And sure enough, as my ego stepped out of the way, Jessamine was there, ready to talk. So I nodded to Bernice.

"Jessamine," said Bernice, addressing her through me, "can you tell us what's wrong? What can we do to help you?"

"I don't know what to think," she said, through me. *"I don't know what to do. I can't figure out how it all fits together. I don't know who's at fault, or whether we were all just duped by Cristien and his lawyer friend, the fake William Love. Help me figure this out. Ernie doesn't want me to do anything. He doesn't want me to call a general meeting until we have more information. But I don't want to be blamed by all the people who trusted me for the company going under."*

The Lawyer Who Died Trying

"How can we do that, Jessamine?" asked Bernice.

"Ariel sees things," said Jessamine urgently. *"She can find out the truth. I need for her to help find out the truth. Maybe she'll know how to get the money back so people won't lose everything they've invested."*

"I'm sure Ariel will do everything she can," said Bernice. "But she needs for you to back away a bit and give her some space to take action. Can you do that? Can you give her some space?"

Jessamine was reluctant, and I could sense her frustration.

When Bernice realized Jessamine wasn't being placated, she added, "Ariel is going to the police in just a little while, and she's going to get some help in finding out what's happened. But you need to give her some space and some time to work things out. She can't just drop everything else in her life and dedicate herself to this pursuit. But she *is* going to get some help for you, and so am I. So do you think you can just give her a little space in which to do that?"

Very reluctantly, Jessamine agreed. Then she added, *"But I'm not going away."*

I sensed Greg giving a sign to Bernice, who said to Jessamine, "Ariel needs to go to the police station now. So she's going to have to go with Greg. Please try to give her some space and some time to work things out for you." And Jessamine pulled aside, allowing my ego personality to move back into control.

As I came back to normal consciousness, I said, "That was a little bit strange. It's as if she really doesn't want to give me room to operate, though she knows she has to if I'm going to succeed and find out what she needs to know. But she hasn't moved very far away."

"Well, maybe we can work with her more later," said Bernice as I was getting up and preparing to go with Greg. "And in the meantime, I'm going to call all the Loo-Loo Ladies. They were supposed to be coming here tomorrow night, as I'm sure you remember. I'll let them know about Jessamine, and I'm going to ask them to come tomorrow night anyway. It might be an opportunity for you to get more insight into the who, what, where, when, and why of her murder."

Giving my statement took up about another hour of our afternoon. Flanagan taped it, then asked if I wanted to come back the next day to sign the transcript. Since I had to teach the next morning and didn't expect to get back to Alexandria until around supper time, I opted to wait until the transcript was ready before leaving. Greg had his own paperwork to fill out for the day's events, so it was time for supper when we finally got away from the station.

And though she wasn't exactly in my pocket, I could tell Jessamine wasn't very far away.

"Would you like to come back to my place instead of going out?" asked Greg. "I have some Chinese take-out just waiting to be warmed up.

Oh, and I taped a brand new episode of *Law and Order* the other night that's just begging for us to watch it." This last was added with a sly little grin. Then, when I didn't answer right away, he added, "And we could actually *watch* it, if you're not in the mood to just have it on as background."

I looked at him fondly. Then I hooted with laughter. "I can't tell you, sir, just how very much in the mood I am. I think there's something about experiencing death that makes the whole body anxious for sex. Bernice would probably say it's all about denial of the reality of death—or the desire to affirm life. But be assured, if I weren't held in by this seatbelt, I'd probably fling myself upon you right here and now!"

He started laughing, too, and his laughter inspired me to laugh more, and we laughed and laughed, letting go of much of the negative emotion the events of the day had aroused.

When I sobered up, though, I had a realization. "I don't know how having Jessamine hovering around me is going to affect my libido. I mean I've never made love before with an audience!"

I looked at him to see how he was going to react to this idea. It took a couple of seconds, but then he said with a wicked grin, "Just try to think of it as a really outrageous *ménage a trois*."

I was still laughing when we got to his house.

Chapter 11
Monday, October 27th

I reluctantly left Greg's sometime after midnight and made my way back to my apartment at Bernice's. I used the back stairs entrance so I wouldn't wake her and brushed my teeth but skipped the flossing. "Tomorrow morning, I promise," I said to my teeth. Setting the clock for six a.m., I fell into bed.

Jessamine hadn't bothered us much at Greg's, especially after all the *Law and Order* action got going, but now I was aware of her presence right behind me. "I have to sleep fast!" I said aloud, "'cause I have to get up in about four and a half hours and go to work. I'll do more on your case tomorrow. G'night, Jessamine."

In my final dream cycle before the alarm went off, I was back in the military again. My assignment was to act as a courier with a briefcase full of secrets. The case was locked to my wrist with a kind of single handcuff, but I couldn't get it off or open it because I didn't have the right keys. So I had to keep lugging the case around until somebody found the right set of keys for me. And then the Fat Man showed up and handed me a duck!

By the time I'd showered, dressed, gathered up my purse, jacket, cell phone, and school briefcase, and got downstairs, Bernice was in the kitchen making breakfast for herself, and Freud the cat was standing with paws up the side of the counter, begging for table scraps.

"What's the buzz for tonight?" I asked. "Are the Loo-Loo Ladies still coming over?"

"Yes, they are. When I talked to them last evening, they all seemed badly shaken by the news of Jessamine's death, but they were still willing to come over. Given the circumstances, I redefined our get-together as a sort of 'group therapy' dinner during which they'd have a chance to mourn their friend and perhaps express some of their other fears—like maybe about Aquavest. So they all agreed to come. And by the way, I didn't tell any of the ladies that you were the one who found the body. I thought you could drop that little tidbit yourself tonight, if and when you think it's appropriate."

"That's a good plan. We might be able to use that piece of information strategically. If one of these ladies was involved, it would be best not to show all our cards up front."

"Too bad we can't get Ernie over here at the same time. When I talked to Lorelei, she mentioned she'd tried to call him but that he was incommunicado all day yesterday."

"Well, I know the police were planning to track him down for questioning. I imagine they'll be checking with all the ladies as well. Greg's on duty today, so I'll give him a call this afternoon and see if they've pulled any information together yet."

"Would you like anything before you go off to school?" she asked.

"Just some coffee. I'm not ready for food yet, but I've got some nutrition bars in my desk at school, so I'll probably have one of those before my first class."

"I hate to ask, but is Jessamine still hanging out?"

"O-o-o-h, yes!" I replied while I poured a travel mug full of coffee and doctored it with half-and-half. "I feel like I'm carrying baggage I can't put down. She did give us a little bit of a breather last evening while I was with Greg, but she's right behind me this morning."

"Well," said Bernice, "I hope you two have a nice day." She sounded sincere and I thought she might actually be a little sorry for me because she added, "Maybe we can do some more therapy for Jessamine after the ladies leave tonight."

"I'd appreciate any help you can give me. But right now, I'm off to be the wizard." I slipped on my jacket, and juggling coffee, briefcase, and purse, I headed out the back door to my car.

The discussion of Locke and Hobbes wasn't too disappointing since my students had needed to grapple with both the cynical Hobbesian viewpoint and Locke's idealism without having any input from me before writing their papers. When I asked for a vote on who they sided with, about three quarters of the class had decided to reject Hobbes' idea that men in their natural state would be more self-interested than social, and that without a strong force to govern them, they would live a life that is "solitary, poor, nasty, brutish, and short." But one of the guys, a young man named Joe Simpson, who usually sat near the windows so he could look out in case he got bored with the class discussion, had chosen to align himself with Hobbes' cynicism.

"I don't think people are naturally good *or* bad," he said. "But I *do* think most humans are more self interested than they are altruistic. Now, when Hobbes says most men think they have as much wit as the next person, that has to be true, because we're stuck in our own skins, and we can't really see things from somebody else's perspective. And most of us think we're probably at least as good and as smart and as talented as the next person. And whether we're going to behave well—and I'm speaking here in relative terms, meaning 'well' according to the ideas of society—rather than behaving badly is really determined by what's in it for *us*—can we get what we need to fulfill our own desires without fighting for it, or do we need to wield some kind of power over others to achieve it? Hobbes is just looking at the world the way a modern behavioral scientist would—I'm a psych major, and I lean toward the behaviorists. So I believe we behave well if it's in our best interest to do so, but if it's in our best interest to behave badly, we'll do that, too. It all boils down to motivation and self interest."

"Can you give me a concrete example?" I asked.

"Sure," he replied. "It was in my best interest to read Hobbes and Locke and write my paper for this class this weekend because I'm on scholarship and I need to keep my grades up. And if I were paying for my tuition and books myself, I'd still want to keep my grades up in order to graduate from school with a high GPA and thus stand a better chance of finding decent employment when I get out. That's the motivational carrot most of us follow that gets us to do our course work in college. But I'll have to admit, I'm not especially interested in knowledge for its own sake. So if I didn't have that carrot being dangled out in front of me, do you think I'd have read Locke and Hobbes this weekend? Don't bet on it."

I grinned, and there was a ripple of laughter from the rest of the class at his frankness. But then my own experiences of the past week intruded on my consciousness, and I said, "Okay, let's make the example a little more extreme. What do you think would motivate someone to *kill* another person?"

"Are you talking about killing in wartime, or killing as in committing a homicide?"

"You can answer either possibility or both."

"Well, then, I think in war, people are largely motivated to kill because they're required to do so. I have a buddy who was in the National Guard when the Iraq thing started. And he didn't want to go over there. I mean, he'd joined the National Guard, for Pete's sake, not the Army, so he hadn't expected to have to fight a foreign war. But he went, and he fought, because he had joined up and agreed to do what he was ordered to do for a certain period of time. So any killing he may have done was mandated by someone else. And his motivation in that case would have been to 'go along to get along,' as the saying goes."

He straightened up in his chair a bit before continuing, "Now homicide is a different matter. I think to commit a murder would require a really strong motivation on the part of most people—I think the carrot would have to be a pretty big one. What are the most consistent motives for murder?"

"Usually, money, sex, and power."

"Okay," he said. "Hobbes has those covered in his saying men will fight over what they desire and his idea that we all want to look good to other people—we want them to hold us as valuable. So I think the money and sex motives are a part of what we all desire. And the power motive is an ego thing—we want people to think well of us whether we deserve it or not, and we try to make them believe we're deserving because we want them to do what we tell them to do. But even if they don't think well of us, we nevertheless still want them to do what we think they should do. And having the power to *make* them do it, even if they don't want to, is important. So, if somebody wants somebody else to do something, but that person refuses to do it, then the first person might need to resort to force, or even murder. It may seem extreme, but in our history, murder is said to be the oldest crime of all—the crime of Cain was that he killed his brother over an ego issue. And that story suggests that we have it in us as human beings to kill anybody, even relatives and friends, if the motivation is strong enough."

I glanced around the room and saw a lot of nods from other students. But one girl named Bethany Scott decided to take the challenge.

"What about conscience?" she asked. "You're assuming that conscience isn't a motivating factor. But for most people I think conscience is what keeps them from doing cruel or evil things on a daily basis. And I think conscience—whether it's socially engrained or biologically inherited—is what keeps most of us from picking up a rock and killing our neighbor when we can't make him do what we want."

"Oh, well, if we're discussing Hobbes, he certainly doesn't suggest that conscience is a factor for most of us," said Joe.

"Maybe we've evolved since his time," countered Bethany. "Or maybe we're under more social pressures to behave in a positive way."

"M-m-m, I don't think so," said Joe. "If you look at all the white-collar crime in this country, I'd say we're just about as good as we have to be on the surface to get away with whatever we can under the table."

"Clearly," I said, by way of being a moderator, "you're solidly in the Hobbes camp, Joe. And we've spent a lot of time on Hobbes. But Bethany, are you in the Locke camp? Do you think the majority of people are sufficiently able to judge good government versus bad government? And do you think we really focus from an enlightened conscience, as Locke would like us to, on 'the good of mankind' when we vote for our elected officials?"

"I don't know," she admitted. "I think fear plays a big role in why we do what we do. I mean, we're in a war right now that our current government tells us is necessary in order to fight terrorism. And people are going along with it because the majority of people in this country really are terrified of losing what they have. I mean, I've heard other students say that the world changed when 9/11 happened, and that we have to understand it will never be the same again. But I think what they mean is that they aren't as comfortable that things will just go on being the way they've always been in their lifetime. So while people are scared, I guess they really are going to vote based not on the good of mankind as a whole but on who they think will make them feel safe."

"Ha!" said Joe. "The motivation is self interest!"

"Not entirely," said Bethany. "I think you're oversimplifying human nature. People are just conflicted. It's part of human nature to be conflicted.

But I'd like to think the majority of us, if we don't feel personally threatened, will act for a higher good than just our own self interest. And part of the reason for that is conscience."

"Then let me throw out one more idea," I said. "I have a friend who's a psychotherapist who just this past week suggested to me that the thing that separates the vast majority of people from those who are sociopaths is this thing you call conscience. She says the majority of people have a conscience, but sociopaths don't. Can you factor this idea into your discussion?"

Both Bethany and Joe pondered this question for a few moments.

Then Joe said, "I guess being a sociopath would make it a lot easier to control people. You'd never be hampered with any nasty remorse."

And Bethany added, "I would just hope that we don't have too many sociopaths in public office. It would make it a whole lot harder to provide checks and balances for the abuse of power if the people who have the power don't really care who gets hurt."

"Well, that's what Locke's argument is all about," I said. "He wants his readers to recognize that the people who are under the governance of a tyrant have the right to rebel. It's the same argument the American revolutionaries who founded our current system used when they opposed the rule of King George III." And I asked the class to actually flip forward in their texts another thirty pages and read Jefferson's famous *Declaration of Independence* and try to jot down at least five ideas that matched those of Locke.

While they were doing this assignment, I thought that both Joe and Bethany had made points that applied to society at all levels, and I wondered to myself how they would ultimately apply to the situation with Aquavest or Jessamine's murder. It didn't matter much whether the person or persons responsible were operating out of strong self interest or total lack of conscience. Jessamine was dead either way, and the company was probably going under. And if I didn't find out why, I might never get Jessamine to move on.

I put in a call to Greg on my first break between classes. He was out on patrol when I called, so I left a message for him to call me back as close to 3:15 as he could because by then my last class would be over, and I'd be back in my office area.

When he got back to me, he said, "I asked Flanagan about what's happening so far in the case, and he said they've checked Jessamine's computer for email contacts for yesterday morning, and also her phone records for the time period up to her death, and she had made calls to all the same people to whom she sent the email, with one exception. She doesn't seem to have called you on either her office phone or her cell, and certainly not at the time you say you got the call. By then, she was already dead."

"What are they giving as the time of death?"

"Between 10 and 10:30 yesterday morning."

I was quiet for a moment, thinking. "Okay, it doesn't make sense. But somehow she got through to me, even if this does sound like some kind of psychic voodoo." I wasn't going to back down—she *had* called me, even if I couldn't explain how.

"Oh, and there's another thing. Some woman from an apartment building across the street from Jessamine's office building was out walking her dog at about 10 o'clock yesterday morning, and she saw a person of about 5'8" unlocking the front door to the office. The person was wearing black slacks and a black leather trench coat and matching slouch hat. She was pretty sure the person was female, but she didn't get a look at her face. However, the time is right for this person to have been in the building when Jessamine was murdered."

"Jessamine had a black leather coat and matching slouch hat," I said. "She wore it the day she took me to lunch after our first meeting."

"Well, I suppose it could have been Jessamine herself, but if she got to the office at 10 a.m. and was murdered no later than 10:30, that might not have given her quite enough time to make all the phone calls and send the emails before she was murdered. I'll have to check the details of when the calls were made and emails were sent. But there was no leather coat in her office when the police got there."

"That's a puzzle I can possibly check on tonight. Bernice says all of Jessamine's friends that I met last Monday night are coming over this evening to sort of have a 'group therapy session' about their feelings over Jessamine's death and their fears about what may happen to the company. I'm hoping we'll find out something that will help us placate Jessamine. And I'll see if I can find out anything about who wears what kind of coat."

"If you do, just pass it directly to Flanagan. Oh, and there's one more thing. I know *you* don't own a black leather coat and matching hat, or I'm sure I'd have seen them by now. But there were only two sets of fingerprints found in Jessamine's office—hers and yours."

"What?" I squeaked.

"I know you were in Jessamine's office eight days before the murder, so that's the explanation of how your fingerprints got on a cup and table in her inner office."

"But how did the police identify my fingerprints? I haven't ever been fingerprinted here in Alexandria."

"No, but you were fingerprinted in the Army, and you're permanently in the DOD files."

"Oh, of course," I said, feeling silly. "Military records follow you forever. I did mention to Flanagan in my statement to him that I was in her office on Saturday a week ago. So I hope I'm not a suspect."

He paused. "You won't be a suspect so long as you have an alibi for where you were between 10 and 10:30 yesterday morning. Remember, you got an email that was sent out yesterday, but you didn't get a phone call, at least according to Jessamine's phone records. So somebody has already posited that perhaps you didn't get the phone call because you were in her office when she was making the calls."

I gulped. "But I wasn't in her office yesterday until I went there with you."

"I'm sure you weren't, but do you have anybody who can verify you weren't?"

"Bernice, I guess. Let's see, I got up yesterday and went out for a run around the neighborhood. Then I went back home and showered and logged on to my email. That's when I found Jessamine's letter. So I got dressed and went downstairs to see if Bernice was around. And she was, so I chatted with her until it was just about time for me to come meet you. I think I'm covered for an alibi."

"Good," he said in mock relief, and I finally realized he'd been pulling my leg about my being a suspect. "I was afraid I'd have to go back to watching *Law and Order* by myself!"

I had a faculty meeting late that afternoon, so I didn't manage to get home until just after seven p.m. I saw a silver BMW in the driveway and figured at least one of the Loo-Loo Ladies had already arrived. When I entered the foyer and poked my head around the corner of the living room, I saw Lorelei and Patricia ensconced on one side of Bernice's huge, U-shaped sofa. Each had a glass of wine, and there were plates of canapés in front of them, but neither seemed to be eating. Both looked subdued, and Lorelei seemed to be patting Patricia's hand. I waved a hello to them.

"Hello, ladies. I need to take my things upstairs, but I'll be back with you in a minute."

They looked up, Lorelei nodded, and Patricia gave a wan smile of acknowledgement.

Bernice was nowhere in sight, so I assumed she was in the kitchen putting final touches on dinner. I took my school paraphernalia upstairs, brushed my teeth, ran a comb through my hair, and put on a fresh touch of lipstick. Just as I was coming downstairs again, I heard the doorbell ring.

"That must be Maggie. I'll get it," I called out, reaching the door in a few steps. I opened it and did a double take, for there stood Maggie dressed in black slacks, a black leather coat, and a matching slouch hat.

I pulled myself together, put a big smile on my face, and did my best to act like a gracious hostess. "Hello, Maggie. Let me take your coat for you." I helped her out of her coat and put it and her hat on the hall rack, then ushered her into the living room. She leaned over the couch and gave each of the other two a supportive hug. Then she settled near them on the couch. I poured two glasses of wine from the decanter on the table and handed one to her.

"Did I surprise you for some reason at the door?" asked Maggie. "You looked as if you'd seen a ghost."

"It was your outfit," I said. "It looks exactly like one Jessamine was wearing the day I first met her."

"That's because it is exactly like it," she said, somewhat ruefully. "A couple of winters ago, we'd all been talking about how much we wanted real black leather coats, and Jessamine found a sale at Nordstrom's. She bought the coat and hat and wore them to one of our dinners, and when we saw her in them, we nagged her until she told us where she'd bought them. Then we all went to the mall at Tyson's Corner and bought our own."

"Except for me," countered Lorelei. "Ah don't do black—Ah'm a summer. So Ah got my outfit in white instead."

"We all...back in college, we all used to try to dress alike," said Maggie. "It was kind of a mark of our friendship and our little personal clique, I guess."

"Oh, God, Ah am so much goin' to miss Jessamine," said Lorelei. "She was the very heart of our group."

Patricia's eyes filled with tears, and I reached for a box of tissues and handed one to her.

Just then, Bernice came in from the kitchen in her most glamorous muu-muu, a gray-green silk one with Oriental figures and flowers on it. She'd once told me she thought she looked like a Rose Medallion vase in it.

"Ladies," she said, "I know this evening is going to be difficult for you. You've all lost a very good friend, which is reason enough for allowing the grieving process to take place. But to add to the problem, you've also had an unpleasant turn of events with respect to the investment company. So I just want to let you know that you don't have to stand on social etiquette this evening and put up a pretense of happiness you aren't feeling. And if there's anything you'd like to discuss this evening, please remember that I *am* a psychotherapist, and I'll be happy to help you in any way I can."

I could feel the energy shift in the room as the mood lightened a bit and as each of the ladies looked at the others and then back at Bernice.

"That having been said, dinner is served, ladies," she said and bustled us all into the dining room.

I'd never dined in the formal dining room before since Bernice preferred to lounge with family and close friends at the long wooden table in the kitchen. Her dining room was elegantly furnished with beautiful Oriental black laquer furniture—table, eight chairs, two curio cabinets, and a huge breakfront, all with hand-painted designs. Five places at the table were set with pale pink placemats and napkins and beautiful square black stoneware that had a scroll pattern around the edges.

"Oh, I love this stoneware set!" said Patricia, with the first note of pleasure I'd heard in her voice this evening. "It's Mikasa, isn't it?"

"Yes," responded Bernice. "It's beautiful, but practical—dishwasher, microwave, oven, and freezer safe. And I got it on sale at Macy's."

We seated ourselves at the table, with Bernice at the head. She had already placed four covered serving dishes and a salad bowl on the table, with filled water glasses and empty wine glasses at each place.

The Lawyer Who Died Trying

"Please serve yourselves," she said as she began moving around the table, filling the wine glasses with a California Chardonnay.

The salad bowl contained baby spinach, walnuts, and mandarin orange slices in an orange-flavored vinaigrette. The covered dishes held stuffed Rock Cornish game hen halves, wild rice, root vegetables, and long green pole beans. There was also a basket of assorted dinner rolls.

When Bernice had seated herself, the dishes had been passed, and all our plates were filled, Lorelei lifted her glass and said, "Ah'd like to propose a toast to our dear, departed friend, Jessamine. Ah know that some of us are anxious now that we no longer have her as a consultant and a buffer with the Aquavest company, and now that things are clearly not going right with our investments. But we need to remembah that she was our friend for many years and nevah intended to steer us wrong. So here's to Jessamine."

We all took a sip of wine, and I glanced at Bernice to see if she and I were thinking along the same lines. Jessamine wasn't all that departed; in fact, she was hovering right behind me at the table, and I could feel her anxiety. But I wasn't yet ready to tell the ladies she was still alive in spirit. Bernice and I locked eyes, and I gave a tiny shake of my head.

"Lorelei and I were talking before you got here, Maggie, about having been grilled today by the police," Patricia said. "Did they track you down?"

"Yes, they did. I was in between showings when I got a call from my office that I was 'wanted.' It wasn't a comfortable feeling."

"Ah actually had that Detective Flanagan in mah office first thing this mornin'," said Lorelei. "He's a right good looker, and I wish I could have met him undah other circumstances."

"Do you think the police suspect one of us?" asked Maggie.

"Well, of course, dahlin'. We all had money in this Aquavest project. And as Jessamine told us in her email yesterday mornin', she was gonna have to pull the plug. Money is a big motivatin' factor for murder. So the police are gonna suspect anybody who had money in the project and knew it had gone south. From the list of people she sent her email to, that would be the three of us, Ernie, and you, Ariel."

All the ladies turned their heads to look at me.

"Well, fortunately for me, I didn't have any of my own money invested. Jessamine had given me some stock in payment for my being willing to act as an expert witness. So all I'm out is a couple of hours of time."

"But it seems like the police do think we might be suspects," said Patricia anxiously.

"Right now they do," I replied, "principally because of the calls they found she'd made on her cell and office phones and because of the names of people she emailed. But they also know the gist of the email, with all the information about Cristien and his phony lawyer. And they know about Jordan."

"How do you know what the police know?" asked Maggie.

"Because I date a cop on the Alexandria force," I said, and I glanced at Bernice. "And because he was with me when I found Jessamine's body yesterday."

"You found the body?" all the ladies exclaimed in chorus.

"That must have been awful for you!" said Lorelei.

"It wasn't exactly pleasant."

"How...how was she killed?" asked Patricia.

"She was knifed in the back."

There was an audible gasp from all of the ladies.

"If you've been to her office, then you've probably seen the letter opener she had on her desk. The one with the extremely thin blade."

"That's the knife she said Jordan had given her," said Patricia. "When she was divorcing Jordan, she told us about how he was supposed to have used that knife to...to kill people when he was in Force Recon work. But I think he may have just told her that to give her a little scare."

"I asked her why she'd stayed with him if she knew something so awful about him," said Maggie. "And she said that he'd done what he'd done because it was part of his job. And that for a very long time, she didn't believe he'd have done anything like that if it weren't a part of his job. Later, though, she wasn't so sure."

"Why do you say that?" asked Bernice.

"Because he could be kind of scary sometimes," said Maggie. "He could be very cold if she didn't do exactly what he wanted her to do. She didn't want to go with him to Camp LeJeune because she had a very good law practice starting to bloom here. He tried to manipulate her, and when he couldn't, he turned really cold on her."

Bernice nodded, and I knew she was adding this to her theory about Jordan's sociopathic tendencies. Then she asked, "Do all of you ladies know Jordan Steele? I mean, have you all actually met him?"

"Of course, we have," answered Patricia. "We all took a couple of courses from him while Jessamine and he were still married."

"What kind of courses?" I asked.

"Oh, some personal empowerment stuff. Kind of like Tony Robbins teaches. You know, positive thinking, positive self talk, neurolinguistic programming to release negative habits—that kind of thing."

"Do you still have the materials from those classes?"

"Ah cleared all of mah things out when I moved a couple of years ago," said Lorelei.

"I think mine are up in the attic somewhere," said Patricia. "I put all that stuff away when I turned my office into a nursery a few years ago."

"I *do* still have my work sheets and the notebook he made up for each of the courses," said Maggie. "I review that stuff all the time because I use it in my work. I could drop the notebooks off here on Wednesday, if you like. I have a showing over in this part of town that evening. Just remind me again before I leave tonight, and I'll make a note to bring them by—that way I won't forget."

The Lawyer Who Died Trying

Lorelei looked pensive. "Do ya really think the police suspect Jordan? Ah mean, the husband is always a suspect in a case like this, isn't he? Ah've just been thinkin' about poor little Jeffrey. Ah know he was with his grandma this past weekend, but with his mama gone, the most logical person to take over his care is his daddy. Most any family court in the country would award Jordan custody now that Jessamine is dead. So what's gonna happen to that dear little boy if Jordan gets arrested?"

Patricia shifted a bit in her chair and looked uncomfortable. "I think I may know a little bit more than either of you about that," she said, nodding to Maggie and Lorelei. "Jessamine said she wasn't going to spread this around, but she was having Ariel testify as an expert witness in her custody case because of some recent changes Jordan had made to his coursework. And she was trying to make sure he never got his hands on Jeffrey."

Both Maggie and Lorelei looked confused. "What are you talking about?" asked Maggie. "When Jessamine said she was having Ariel testify as an expert witness, I had no idea it had anything to do with her own custody case." She paused, shaking her head a little. "But I guess I didn't really think much about it, because Jessamine also said Ariel was going to do a kind of psychic overview of Aquavest. So I didn't link her up to Jessamine's own lawsuit."

"Ariel isn't just a psychic that Jessamine called in to give us a clean bill of health about Aquavest," said Patricia. "She's an expert in black magic. And it was black magic that Jordan had added to his course work."

"Oh, my goodness," exclaimed Maggie.

"Ah don't believe that!" said Lorelei.

Then they both stared at me until Patricia finally said, "It's true, isn't it, Ariel? Weren't you testifying in the custody case because Jordan was teaching black magic?"

"As to what Jordan was teaching, I don't have a clue," I said. "That's why I want to see what kind of materials he provided back when the three of you took his course. But, yes, Jessamine did ask me to testify about the nature of something Jordan was allegedly teaching, and yes, I was asked to do so because I'm a scholar in some of the permutations of the magic that was taught by certain secret societies during the late 19th and early 20th centuries. And although my role was strictly to discuss the ramifications of what Jessamine was alleging Jordan was teaching, I did meet him last week, and I'm reasonably certain he *is* a very powerful channeler of energy—which is the same thing as being a magician."

There was a silence for several moments. Then Lorelei said, "Oh, mah dear, really—when you say Jessamine was 'alleging' Jordan was teaching black magic, what do you mean? Did she not have proof?"

"She thought she had proof," I answered. "And it was up to her to present that proof in court. My role was simply to explain the ramifications of what she was proving."

"And what were those ramifications?" asked Maggie. "Can you tell us now?"

I waited a few moments, thinking before I answered. Jessamine had told only Patricia about the details of Jordan's coursework. For some reason, she hadn't shared them with Maggie and Lorelei. I wondered why not.

As if echoing my thoughts, Lorelei turned and asked Patricia, "And why would Jessamine tell you about this and not us? Ah, mean, Ah am, after all, Jeffrey's godmother, and Maggie loves little Jeffrey just as much as the rest of us do."

A voice in my head said, *"Children,"* just as Patricia answered. "It was because like Jessamine, I have children. She wanted to talk to me as one mother to another mother."

"Yes, I think that's really it," I said. "Jessamine said Jordan was teaching the worship of the goddess Kali. Now in its straightforward practice, Kali worship simply represents the dualism of life. Kali is called the 'Dark Goddess,' because she is both the giver of life and the destroyer. She represents the energy of manifestation into material form, as well as the inevitable destruction of that material form. However, in the late 19th century, there was a cult of Kali worship that sought to placate this Dark Goddess by making human sacrifice—allegedly often of children. Jessamine was determined to protect her child from his father."

There was a stunned silence, which was finally broken in my head by the voice of Jessamine. *"My child!"* she urged anxiously. *"You've got to save my child!"*

I nodded rather than answering verbally and thought to myself that we might be making progress. Jessamine was no longer simply stuck on the endless loop about Aquavest failing, and she was communicating with me directly. Perhaps I could start a meaningful conversation with her once I was alone again.

Lorelei broke the silence around the table. "Jeffrey stays with Jordan all the time. You can't be suggesting Jordan would harm his own child."

"I'm not suggesting it. All I was asked to do in the case was provide the historical background Jessamine needed to give her own testimony in court."

Bernice broke in with a comment of her own. "A parent need not physically harm a child in order to do harm. Parents who are on power trips of any kind whatsoever will affect their children psychologically and often negatively. You're a family court lawyer, Lorelei, and I'm sure you've seen plenty of cases where even well-meaning parents have been so overbearing that they've damaged their own children."

Lorelei nodded, though I thought it was a little grudgingly. "Ah admit that's true. But what Ah can't see is Jordan actually considering killing his own little boy."

"Aleister Crowley did a lot of psychological damage to the people around him," I said. "His practice of black magic can't be discounted as a factor in the insanity, depression, and physical ill health others who were near to him suffered. So if there *is* proof that Jordan was teaching a form of dark magic, then he may not be the best choice as either a role model or a custodial parent for his son."

Maggie gave a decisive thump on the table with her empty wine glass. "All of this talk is very disturbing, I'll admit. And I'd rather Jordan be a suspect than one of us. But even if he is, I don't think that lets any of us off the hook as possible suspects, too. And if we are, then any dirty laundry we might be hiding is going to be hung out for airing, particularly anything having to do with how we financed our investment in Aquavest. So I for one think it would be good right here and now to confess that part of our personal situation." She looked around the table to see if the others were willing to share, and when she got their nods, she continued. "Okay, now also, we need to know that what we may spill here stays here."

"I'm a psychotherapist," said Bernice. "I have to maintain therapist-client privilege. And I invited you here for therapy."

"And what about you, Ariel? Are you going to tell your boyfriend if I say something that's going to compromise me or make me more a suspect than I already am?"

I looked at her and considered my options. If I didn't give her assurance that I'd keep her secret, she wouldn't tell it. On the other hand, I'd feel bound to try in every way possible to get her to own up to the truth publicly if what she was going to share warranted it. I decided to get the information and then encourage her to confess it to the police if the situation called for it, so I said, "If what you're going to tell me isn't about your having murdered Jessamine, then I can probably keep my silence for at least a limited period of time."

Maggie nodded. "Okay, then. I confess. I was so sure Aquavest was going to be my ticket to the upper income brackets that I did a bit of 'creative borrowing' from one of the accounts at my brokerage house. I tapped into a couple of property management accounts. So even if I'm not arrested for Jessamine's murder, there's a chance I could be arrested for fraud if I can't make good on those accounts in the next sixty days. But I swear I didn't murder Jessamine."

Patricia looked stricken at Maggie's confession, and when I glanced at Lorelei, she was looking grim.

"Ah see why you might be feelin' anxious," she said. "You truly could be in big trouble if that information comes out."

"Well, I told Andrea what I'd done immediately after Jessamine threatened to pull the plug yesterday. Andrea's my partner," she added for Bernice's and my benefit, "and she's going to talk to her parents to see if they can help bail me out. So I might have a solution before the week is up."

"It still doesn't excuse what you did," said Lorelei. "And as an officer of the court, Ah'm not supposed to know anything like this unless you retain me."

"Okay, then, I retain you, Miss Priss," countered Maggie with a mock glare. "I'll give you a nice, crisp, green dollar bill as soon as I can get to my purse."

"Ah accept your case," said Lorelei.

"Well, fortunately," said Patricia, "I won't have to retain your services or pay your exorbitant fee. The only people I'll end up being in trouble with are in my family. I financed my investment in Aquavest with money from my kids' college funds." She looked as if she might start crying again, and Maggie patted her on the shoulder. "I'll probably have to go back to work to make up the deficit. But I won't have to go to jail." Then she did start to cry. "The hardest part for me is that I'll have to give up being a stay-at-home mom. I put in $50,000.00, so it'll take me at least three years to make up what I'll have lost, especially considering the interest on the high-yield accounts. Not to mention how angry my husband is going to be with me."

"Ah feel for you, Ah really do," said Lorelei. "The only person who's gonna be mad at me is me. Ah maxed out a couple a' credit cards, so if it's all down the drain, so be it, an' I'll jus' have to pay 'em off over time. An' if Ah'm not more careful than usual about getting' mah bills paid on time, Ah don't imagine the interest rate is gonna be pretty."

Patricia blew her nose and smiled grimly. "A fine bunch we are, aren't we? Tops in our class, excellent status white-collar jobs, and all of us good looking to boot—and here we got ourselves in a bunch of trouble over the prospect of quick riches. We all had blinders on—even Jessamine."

"It happens," said Bernice soothingly. "Everybody wants to be in on the ground floor of an investment opportunity. Who wouldn't like to have bought Google or Yahoo or Microsoft when they were start-up companies?"

I found this statement amusing, since Bernice's husband Alan actually *had* bought some stock in Google and Yahoo and Microsoft when they were start up companies. But I kept my amusement to myself, covering my mouth with my napkin so the grin I was suppressing wouldn't slip onto my face.

"But nobody knows what will be successful until it actually *is* successful," Bernice continued. "So when you make this kind of error in judgment, figure out what you can learn from the experience and go on. And grieve the loss if you need to, but don't keep beating up on yourself."

"And maybe next time," said Patricia, "I guess we should follow the old adage not to invest any more than we can afford to lose."

"In that case," quipped Maggie, "all my investments will be in the $5.00 range. Unless, of course, they're in real estate—in which case I'll be investing in myself!"

Chapter 12

There had been many revelations at dinner that might have made the actual repast difficult to digest, but when Bernice had finished her own serving and looked at what was left on her guest's plates, she seemed gratified—they all appeared to have eaten most of what they had served themselves. Then she glanced at her watch, nodded in a satisfied way, and made an unexpected announcement.

"Ladies, I didn't want to interrupt our dinner with any outside intrusion. But I took the liberty of inviting one more person over this evening for dessert."

We all looked at her expectantly.

"I wanted you all to be able to speak freely among yourselves about Jessamine and Aquavest. But I also thought you might appreciate getting an additional viewpoint on the investment from one of the people who was responsible for the situation in which you now find yourselves. So I was able to reach Ernie Redmond this afternoon, and I invited him to join us for this portion of the evening. He promised he'd be here at exactly 8 p.m., which will be in about five minutes. So Ariel, if you'd be so kind as to help me clear the table, I'll go put the finishing touches on the Grand Marnier chocolate mousse. Ladies, there's a liquor cabinet next to the piano in the living room, so please feel free to help yourself to a liquer. Or if you prefer, you're welcome to have more wine."

As the ladies retired to the living room, Bernice and I stacked the dinner dishes and glassware on a tray she magically provided from one of the curio cabinets, and I carried it into the kitchen. As I set it down on the central preparation island, Bernice whispered, "I have some thoughts to share with you after this little *soirée* is finished. But in the meantime, go mingle, and get the door when Ernie gets here, if you don't mind. We'll deal with dishes later."

True to his agreement, Ernie arrived just as Bernice's grandfather clock was striking 8:00. I smiled at his boisterous greeting, shook his proffered hand, and offered to take his overcoat and hat. The hat was one of those little Alpine felt hats with a jaunty brush of feathers on one side of the band, and I thought how appropriate it was for his upbeat personality.

Ernie saw me examining the hat before putting it on the coat rack, and he said jokingly, *"Ich bin ein Berliner."*

"Oh, I hope not, Ernie," responded Bernice, who was bustling in with a tray full of dessert plates and coffee cups. "We need you right here in the USA for a while yet."

Ernie and I followed Bernice into the living room, where she set the tray on the large table centered in front of all three sides of the U-shaped couch.

As soon as they caught sight of Ernie, Lorelei, Patricia, and Maggie leaned toward him as if on cue and started asking questions, many of which were also on my mind.

"Is it true, Ernie? Is the money all gone?"

"Was the whole thing a fraud, as Jessamine said?"

"What are we going to do now? Ah mean, what reparation is the company going to make?"

And Jessamine, standing directly behind me in my auric field, became quite agitated and started shouting, *"Ernie, what happened? What happened?"*

I was overcome with her energy and found myself blurting out, "Ernie, what happened?" in an exceptionally loud voice with inflections amazingly like Jessamine's.

Hearing those inflections, everybody was somewhat startled and turned to look at me. I glanced at Bernice, who raised her eyebrows and took everyone's focus off of me by saying, "Yes, Ernie, what *did* happen?"

Ernie sat down on the couch and swiveled his head to look at each of us in turn. "Well, as you know if you read Jessamine's email message yesterday, there was someone at the meeting on Thursday night who indicated within Jessamine's hearing that there was something faulty with the tidal projections we were being presented with. And while she didn't believe it at first, Jessamine did send the information to me right away. So even before I knew anything about Cristien's possibly absconding with company funds, I started doing some research on the tides and how they would affect the workings of the device."

He paused and looked at each of us in turn to be sure we were following before he continued. "Like most people in our culture, my understanding of the tides has come from visits to the seashore. For example, on Cape Cod, the tide comes in, the tide goes out, and it does this pretty regularly twice a day—approximately every 12 and a quarter to 12 and a half hours—and there's as much as a 10-foot differential between low tide and high tide. I used to check the tides before going for a morning swim just to know whether I could jump right in or would have to walk a fair distance before getting to the water. And Cristien, who was the inventor of the device, seemed to be operating with the same understanding of the tides that I had. Now, he's French Canadian, and I remember him saying once that he got the idea for the device by watching the tides coming up a river near the Bay of Fundy. It was as if someone was pulling a blanket up the river from the bay. He said he was so enthralled he wanted to keep watching even though he realized it would take nearly 12 hours for the cycle to complete itself. Anyway, the tide from the Bay of Fundy is an Atlantic tide. But when he was thinking of where he might use his device, he got the idea of the oil rigs in the Gulf of Mexico near Galveston, because it would be so easy to attach the device and collect the energy. So *that* part of the whole equation might be forgiven as simply an error in judgment on both our parts."

"It was a pretty expensive error," interjected Maggie.

"Might it be considered an actionable error?" asked Patricia. "I mean, could you be sued for not having done all your homework, Ernie?"

Ernie looked a little discomfited, but he recovered and said, "I suppose you're right. As the chief officer in a limited liability company, I guess I could be sued. Although since the majority of the money is gone, and the accountancy firm we use is working its way through what's left of the operating budget, if the investors were to initiate a class-action suit, we might as well just write a check for what we have left and hand it over to whatever law firm you might hire. It would only be in the thousands rather than the millions, so you might have trouble finding a lawyer who'd be willing to take it, and I guarantee the plaintiffs wouldn't be getting more than pennies on the dollar out of a suit."

Lorelei said, "It's not mah field, but Ah think investments in start-up businesses might be handled differently from Wall Street investments. Ah mean, it *is* called 'venture' capital, and that implies there is risk involved. Ernie, when Ah invested, Ah considered what you were offering. Cristien had a patent, which means the device worked *somewhere, somehow.* Furthermore, your company was set up properly and bought the patent, which means the company owns the technology. And Ah was given an opportunity to buy a piece of it. Now, if Ah'd been given an opportunity to buy into Edison's light bulb venture, Ah'd have had to wait through 20,000 experiments before Ah saw any return on mah money. But that return would have been *very* good once it paid off."

I still had Jessamine's confusion about what had happened with the company casting a heavy shadow on me, so I decided to ask for more clarification. "I'm still not clear about this problem with the tides. Just why is it that the device actually works in the Atlantic Ocean but not in the Gulf of Mexico?"

Ernie nodded thoughtfully. "Then let me clarify. With respect to the mechanics of the device, it works well if there are normal oceanic tides with a high-low frequency of approximately 12 hours. But high tide in the Gulf of Mexico is erratic. Usually it's only once in 24 hours, with a smaller increase in between the high tides. This can be anywhere from 4-16 hours after the high tide. But then, the high tide may be once in 24 hours for three days, and then the fourth day it'll be once in 16 hours. That's what I mean by erratic. In addition, the tides in the Gulf aren't high enough for this device to work at its optimal capability. So I realize now that the way Cristien was describing the device's operation in the meeting was the way it would work if it were out in the Atlantic. But that isn't the way it would work if it were in the Gulf."

He looked appropriately chagrinned. "I probably should have done more homework on the tides in the Gulf of Mexico. But the way I understood the tides to work is the way they work all over the world, except, as it turns out, in the Gulf of Mexico and on our own Pacific Coast. Now, whether Cristien knew before the meeting last Thursday that he was perpetrating an untruth on the investors isn't clear yet. The demo has always been based on tidal patterns in the ocean, whereas the device was being sold as something that could be put on all the oil rigs in the gulf."

"But exactly why won't it work?" I asked again. "I'm very right-brained, and I'm just not getting the picture."

"Because," he said patiently, "the tides in the gulf are not two high and two low tides daily, as they are in the Atlantic. Rather, they're mixed, and not high enough to produce the necessary constant pattern of wave strength. A good analogy would be the difference between mountains and rolling foothills—the Atlantic has tides that produce a rise equivalent to mountains, while the Gulf of Mexico produces a rise more like the rolling foothills." Ernie announced this with some chagrin.

"Now, this doesn't mean that the device doesn't work," he continued, "or that it couldn't work in a revised context. It may still be viable. We just have to figure out how to change the context."

"I think your glasses have a slight rose tinge to them, Ernie," said Maggie. I could tell she was barely controlling her anger. I think that given the opportunity, she would have enthusiastically taken a bite out of him.

"Well, I'm just hoping Ernie's right," said Patricia. "I mean, I don't want to think we've lost everything we put into this project."

"It won't matter if the device is viable if it's going to take years to make it pay," said Maggie. "I mean, some of us were expecting the turn-around to be almost immediate. That's what I thought we were promised." She huffed peevishly and added, "And it sounds as if Cristien has run off with our investment money. Isn't that really more important than whether the device works or doesn't work? Let's get to the bottom line here."

Ernie held up his hands and tried to calm Maggie down. "We're all in the same boat, my dear. Yes, *somebody* does seem to have flown the coop with some of the money, but there's still some operating capital in another company account, as I suggested earlier. It's not a lot, but we're not entirely dead in the water either."

"Well, what I'd like to know is why Cristien and his lawyer had access to the accounts in the first place. Who allowed that to happen?" Maggie glared at Ernie.

"Originally, I, as the company founder and CEO, Cristien as the inventor, and the company accountant/treasurer were the three names on the bank accounts, and it took two signatures to write a check or draw money out of the main account. Then, it was decided at the general meeting at the first of this year to set up a second account that would allow the business manager to make expenditures for running the business without having to come to the three of us. At the same time, Cristien was given a business credit card with a fairly high limit so that he could purchase the necessary hardware to create the prototypes of the device as well as have money for travel and entertainment of foreign investors. Cristien brought his lawyer, the so-called William Love, on board because he supposedly had a lot of contacts both abroad and with members of Congress. And we gave his lawyer a business credit card as well because of all his contacts—though his limit was considerably less than Cristien's. And we were all fairly confident of success, as well as of all the participants' honesty, because usually after one of the jaunts to foreign countries, we would find that money had been invested and deposited. And of course, we would pay Love his fees for services rendered."

Behind me, Jessamine was practically jumping up and down, and I got the impression she was saying, *"Cristien knew what he was doing. His lawyer, William Love, got fees, and I got worthless stock."*

"Why was Cristien's lawyer given fees when Jessamine was paid in stock?" I asked just to placate her. "I mean, I know she was being paid in stock because that's what she paid me for being her expert witness."

Ernie coughed into his hand, and I thought he looked a little embarrassed. "Well," he said finally, "it was ultimately her choice to receive stock instead of a salary. Cristien convinced her it would be to her advantage in the long run. And she had a thriving private practice, so it wasn't essential that she receive regular pay from the company. "

Maggie looked unconvinced. "Hindsight is always 20-20. But this seems strange to me. How come if Cristien was able to convince Jessamine to take shares of stock in lieu of pay, he couldn't convince his own lawyer to do so as well?"

Ernie shrugged. "When Cristien's lawyer came into the mix, he said he wanted to keep a distance from the company personally as it would look better to foreign investors. I don't know if that's true, but it's what he said."

Lorelei looked pensive. "Well, the way Ah put this together is that Cristien was on the up-an'-up initially. But somewhere along the line, Ah think he learned about the problem with the tides in the Gulf of Mexico and decided to build himself an escape hatch from this leaky boat you keep referrin' to that we're all stuck in, Ernie. So instead of comin' clean about the faults of the whole plan, he just kept on lullin' us all with promises of a rosy future while he's been layin' plans to abscond with our money. And it seems as if he was in cahoots with his lawyer, and they were tryin' to get all they could from the company."

Again, I was sensing Jessamine's agitation, this time about the status of the person who was supposed to have been Cristien's lawyer, William Love. I said, "Jessamine clearly indicated in her email to us all on Sunday that the person who was supposed to have been Cristien's lawyer was playing a role. He wasn't really the lawyer he was pretending to be. Is anyone doing anything about finding out who he actually is?"

Ernie cleared his throat and shook his head. "When I spoke to Jessamine on Friday, I asked her not to panic and promised to try to find out when the company account had been drained. Our accountant had told her the bulk of the money had been traced to offshore accounts. But in order for it to have been removed to a new bank account, another person besides Cristien would have had to sign off on the transfer—and that other person would have to have been me or our company accountant. I'm confident our accountant wasn't involved. And I certainly wasn't. So the only other simple alternative is that someone may have forged one of our signatures.

"Now, I tried to contact Jessamine several times over the weekend. I couldn't get through to her, so all I could do was email her. But at the same time, I was following up on more details about the tides, consulting some people I know in engineering firms, trying to get more input on what might be done with the device, and just generally trying to figure out how to put out the fires that this situation was bound to cause. When I got Jessamine's email on Sunday, I got back to her and asked her not to try to set up a general meeting until we had more to report, because until we have more facts, it just doesn't seem like a good idea to make any kind of announcement to the company at large. I don't want to panic anyone yet without having a course of action planned. Meanwhile, I contacted our accountant and started him working through the appropriate channels to see what else he can find out. Some of the money has been moved electronically, but that doesn't mean it can't be moved back again. And I called a fellow I know who's a private detective and had him start seeing what he could track down about Cristien and his lawyer. In fact, I spent several hours yesterday gathering info for him so he'd have some leads that might tell us just who was working with Cristien."

He shrugged. "But so far, none of the bread I've cast on the waters has come back. When it does, I'll give you all a shout." Then he heaved a sigh. "And of course, complicating everything is the murder of our company lawyer. With Jessamine dead, there are pieces of information I won't be able to access until the police release the crime scene, though I *have* hired another lawyer to help us get access as soon as possible. But her murder has come at a very inconvenient time, since some of our corporate documents weren't computerized, and Jessamine had the only copies in her office files." He shook his head and added, "Wouldn't surprise me if Cristien had a hand in killing her, just to muddy the waters of his embezzlement of funds."

"What do the police think?" asked Patricia.

"Darned if I know," Ernie responded. "They've asked me a lot of questions, but they haven't given me any answers yet. But I want to assure you I'm doing the best I can."

"You know," said Bernice, who had been quietly waiting to pass out the coffee cups, "this is all first year psychology."

We all looked at her and waited for an explanation of what she was thinking.

The Lawyer Who Died Trying

She continued, "Studies have shown that when people invest in something of considerable monetary value, such as a car, then they become emotionally committed to that purchase, and the car becomes the best possible purchase from the marketplace, whether it's a Volkswagen or a BMW. Ernie, my dear, you got taken for a ride, though the vehicle didn't look like a standard automobile. To be sure, Cristien had a patent, and there may very well be validity to his claims of how the device works. However, we medical professionals are notorious for jumping into venture capital opportunities that are high risk. Hey, we're smart, we've got degrees—we should be able to understand what's going on in the world, right?

"And Ernie, you've got a magnificent personality. You're friendly, charismatic, and very cute. And once you were hooked on this venture, you did everything in your power to share it with your friends—because you believed in it. That's who you are. And Jessamine was exactly the same. She came in because of you, trusted your enthusiasm, and brought in her friends. That's how it goes. And nobody knows whether a mine actually has gold or just pyrites until it's been mined. So while you're all trying to recoup your losses, don't beat up on yourselves or each other for poor judgment. You might even find that some good will come out of the situation after all."

She said this last as she leaned toward Maggie and patted her shoulder.

Maggie, though still looking rueful, said, "Maybe you're right. You know, when my partner Andrea and I got together, her parents wouldn't even speak to me. They thought I was responsible for corrupting their daughter. But over time they came to realize that we really love each other, and now they like me well enough to take out a second mortgage on their house to help me out of this situation I've gotten myself into."

Ernie looked at Bernice and nodded. "Thanks for your words of wisdom," he said, sounding as if he really meant it. Then he looked around the room at the Loo-Loo Ladies, and I watched as a detached observer since the only emotions I was feeling at the moment were Jessamine's.

Finally he said, "Look, ladies, as I said before, we're all in the same boat. I've probably lost my shirt, but the creditors just haven't come to collect it yet. Instead of retiring to my own South Sea island, I may be fixing teeth until I'm 85! But oddly, and I guess this ties in to what Bernice just said about commitment, I believe the device is really viable, though it's pretty clear we were being scammed by Cristien, at least toward the end, as to how effective it would be in the Gulf of Mexico. However, we may figure out how to make it work in the Atlantic. I've got feelers out already with some engineering companies to look at it and tell us what they think, and its technology might be applicable not just for our own country but for many countries worldwide. And we do own that technology. So let's not despair yet. We don't have enough money left to pay back all our investors, but with the infusion of a little more money, we might make this company viable after all. And in the meantime, keep hoeing whatever row you're standing on."

I was astounded at Ernie's mixture of metaphors, but Bernice, who was finally pouring the coffee and passing out portions of the Grand Marnier mousse, said, "Eloquently put, Ernie. Now please, everybody, put down your gardening tools and indulge in this dessert. I promise it will get your endorphins charging a little bit, and you *will* feel better!"

Though the original reason for the dinner this evening had been for me to do Tarot readings for the ladies and to get a better sense of where the Aquavest company was going, everyone seemed to have forgotten about it. I figured their concern over the implications of Jessamine's death and their loss of investment monies was overriding any desire to play with the paranormal. So the subject didn't even come up until they were all putting on their coats.

As she was giving me a goodbye hug, Patricia suddenly said, "Oh, we forgot! You were going to do readings for us tonight!"

"That's right," said Maggie with a little disappointment. "And now we've missed our chance."

"Could you do it in absentia?" asked Patricia. "I mean, is it possible to read us while we're not physically here?"

I smiled and nodded. "Sure. Thoughts aren't restricted by time or space."

"Then please do it when you have the time, and let us know what you get," said Patricia. "You don't mind if she reads you, do you Ernie?"

He looked a little confused, but then he shrugged and put his little alpine cap on his head. "No, though I really have no idea what you're talking about."

"Ariel's a card-carrying psychic, Ernie. So she's going to do a reading for each of us."

He gave a little lopsided smile, looked at Bernice as if her harboring me was a surprise to him, then said, "Okay. Can't see how it could hurt." Then he shifted gears and gave us all assurances he would try to have answers for us and put together a general meeting before the end of the week.

Once we had cleared away the dinner debris and put all the dishes in the dishwasher, Bernice said, "Well, my dear, do you want to debrief the evening?"

"Yes, I do. Especially since the ladies forgot about wanting a Tarot reading until they were practically out the door."

"That isn't surprising, for several possible reasons. They're in grief and shock over Jessamine's death and in fear over the loss of their money, so having you read cards might have seemed a little frivolous. *We* know reading Tarot is not a game but a way of tapping the subconscious through looking at symbols, but a lot of people think of it as a frivolous party game. However, I'm still wired, so do you have the energy to do a little peeking into subconscious motivations? I'm asking because I *did* invite the ladies over this evening for dinner and counseling, and part of that counseling was to have been having their cards read. And as their semi-official counselor, it would certainly help me understand their motivations and fears. I'm also asking because I think I was responsible for disrupting the counseling by inviting Ernie here for dessert. That sort of took the evening along an alternate path, and it might benefit them to have you do a reading and then send them the results."

I did a little inner attunement for a moment about whether I had enough energy to do a reading, or whether it would be more appropriate to do a little psychotherapy with Jessamine, as Bernice and I had earlier considered. As I tapped Jessamine's energy, she seemed more interested in looking at her friends' cards than in being the subject of a session herself, and that's really what helped me make my decision.

"Surprisingly, I'm still kind of wired, too, so I guess we could give it a try, especially since they've all just given me permission again. Well, Lorelei didn't actually say anything, but she smiled when the subject came up. And even Ernie said yes to it again, though I doubt he understood it meant I would be tapping into his subconscious mind. For that matter, even Jessamine's husband Jordan gave me permission to try to read him, though he seemed pretty confident I wouldn't be able to."

Behind me, Jessamine was urging me on. *"Do it! Do it! Do it!"*

"Okay, be calm," I said, twisting my head and giving a shrug over my right shoulder. "Jessamine wants me to do it."

"Well, then, I think you should put your cards on the table, so to speak, and let's see what kinds of psychic hits you get. And I'll make some tea."

I went to my room to get my cards and my tape recorder, so that I could tape the reading and transcribe it to send to each of the ladies, and when I came back a few minutes later, Bernice already had some tea cups steaming at one end of her long kitchen table with something spicy steeping in them and had seated herself in a chair, with Freud the cat on her lap, waving a tail under her nose. I eased down in the chair across from her and began sorting through the cards.

"While I was upstairs, I looked through a couple of books for suggested spreads when reading a number of people at once, and I hit upon doing four cards each for all the principals involved in this case. For the ladies, we already know their significators—they each pulled a queen a week ago. So the new information we want to know most is their motivations, their hopes, and their fears. I'm going to start by pulling the queens out of the deck and then taking a look at what comes up for each of them in turn."

I hadn't used my cards since the previous Monday night, so the four queens, the Sun card, and the Two of Swords were all still sitting right on top of the deck.

"I'd be curious to know what was, or is, motivating Jessamine," said Bernice once I'd laid the four queens out in a row.

I nodded. "I established early on that she didn't know who killed her. But I'll start with her cards just to see what comes up."

At that point I relaxed, went into a slightly altered state, and pulled three cards from the deck—one for Jessamine's motivations, one for her hopes, and the final one for her fears.

"Jessamine's significator is the Queen of Wands, so she's charismatic, a real people person, with a strong desire to do good in the world. But her overriding motivation is represented by the Hierophant. So she's also very concerned about following the rules of the prevailing social order. Society's approval is very important to her, as is truthfulness and honesty in all her dealings with others. Her hopes are represented by the World card, which means she wants it all—success of all her dreams and expression of all her talents. Her ultimate power trip would have been the completion of her image of herself, especially if she could have said, 'I helped save the world.' Her fears, on the other hand, are represented by the Five of Wands, which to me suggests she was so ready to move forward that any strife would cause her great distress. That, I think, is why she was pressuring Ernie to call a general meeting right away on Sunday. She wanted everything resolved, and of course, she didn't want any of her friends or any of the people she'd brought into Aquavest to feel she was responsible for their losses. That would have been the ultimate challenge to her self image."

"How's she taking this reading of her inner drives?" asked Bernice.

I tuned in, and for the moment Jessamine was quiet. "Not too badly," I said.

"Then why don't you move on to Lorelei?"

I put the cards I'd drawn for Jessamine back in the pile, mixed it up, and drew three cards for Lorelei.

"Okay, then, Lorelei is the Queen of Swords, meaning she's into increasing her personal power through planning. She's a woman with a lot of mental ability—remember, Jessamine called her the sharpest stiletto in the shoe box. So she uses her intellect to enhance her strength in business and accomplishment. She's determined, organized, dynamic—and a risk taker. On the negative side, though, if someone crosses her, she could become a back stabber."

"An interesting choice of words, given the weapon used in Jessamine's murder."

"But of the three friends, she's the one who seems least perturbed about losing money in Aquavest. And look, here's the Seven of Cups as her motivation card. She has many, many talents—so many she can't pursue them all. What she really wants is time to focus. And she has some unfulfilled dreams and fantasies with respect to her emotional life. Since she isn't in relationship with anyone, I think her drive to become a family court judge may be a sublimation of her sexual and emotional desires. And then there's the card for her hopes, which is the Ace of Pentacles. The judgeship would give her a renewed sense of self worth, as well as more prosperity. And the card for her fears is the Three of Wands. Usually that's a really positive card, showing that her creativity can finally emerge in her career. Since we're reading the cards as expressive of her fears, perhaps she's

The Lawyer Who Died Trying

reached a point where she fears that career move won't be possible. But I don't see any of these cards as being related to the Aquavest failure."

Bernice nodded and gave a little smile. "So as Jessamine suggested last week, Lorelei's blonde Southern belle exterior is just a façade she wears to disarm people. She's really strong, intelligent, talented, and a real whiz-bang powerhouse. But somewhere along the line she's missing the sexual connection to a male counterpart."

"That may be because the Queen of Swords is the masculine intellectual actualized in the female. It would be hard for her to find a male counterpart as strong and dominant as she is herself."

Again Bernice nodded. "Okay, then, what about Patricia?"

I put the cards for Lorelei back in the pile, stirred it up, and pulled three for Patricia.

"As you probably remember when I read this card last week, Patricia is the Queen of Cups—dreamy, sexually attractive to the male, and strongly sexually motivated. Though she may not be especially good with business matters, I can certainly see her giving herself wholeheartedly to nonprofit work. She wants the world to be a better place, so of all the Loo-Loo Ladies, I think she'd be the one most interested in the environmental, planetary healing aspects of Aquavest. Her motivation card is the Ten of Wands, which says she wants to see a job well done. But this card also indicates that perhaps she's been feeling a bit overburdened by her lifestyle—she can carry the weight, but she's happy to be coming to the end of the cycle, as suggested by the number ten, because she's ready for a change of pace so she can put down some of the burden she's been carrying."

The next card I turned over was the Chariot reversed. "Patricia isn't as strong as Lorelei or Jessamine. This card suggests to me she needs to stay very balanced physically and emotionally or she's likely to end up going to war—and this would be out of keeping with her loving façade. It would make her like Alice in Wonderland's Queen of Hearts, shouting, 'Off with their heads!' And look, this is her fears—the Five of Pentacles. Her biggest fear lies in not having enough money. She's afraid that without the income, she and her family may end up 'out in the snow,' always on the outside, looking in but unable to participate fully in life."

"Well, she and Maggie did indicate their huge investment in Aquavest was going to cause a lot of upheaval in their lives," said Bernice. "She indicated she might have to go back to work to repay her children's college fund. And for someone for whom being loved and admired by an adoring partner is so important, it will be very difficult for her to tell her husband about her error in judgment."

"You know, I wondered about that. I think it was Lorelei who said last week that Patricia's husband makes lots of money as a government contractor. So I'm wondering just how bad the loss of $50,000 could be. Would that overwhelm her so gravely?"

Bernice shrugged. "You know, I've learned that most of my clients and their families live right on the edge of a financial precipice. It doesn't matter how much money they make, they often are extended right up to that limit, if not beyond it. So losing a big chunk of money, especially when you may need to start paying it out for a child's schooling, could be devastating. She probably would need to go back to work for a while to make up the difference."

"Okay, then, I get it. Not that I'm in any position to cast aspersions since I'm living here under your patronage."

"You pay your rent on time."

"True, but you've set it a lot lower than a room the size of mine should go for in this area. And besides, between you and Greg, I have almost no food expenses."

"Well, we feed you because we like to keep you around. I think you're interesting, and at the very least, Greg thinks your cute. But let's get back to this reading. What do you get for Maggie?"

Once more, I put the cards I had drawn for Patricia back into the pile and mixed them in. Then I drew three cards for Maggie.

"Maggie is the Queen of Pentacles, meaning she's a good money manager. I get that she took the risk with Aquavest primarily because she really trusted Jessamine, but otherwise she's good at making ends meet when she doesn't have much income, though she's also entrepreneurial enough that whatever she attempts will probably succeed. And if something doesn't work, she's quite willing to walk away from it and not keep banging her head against brick walls trying to make it work.

"For her motivation, I've drawn the Eight of Cups. This suggests she's far more motivated by her relationship than she is by money. And she actually said she wanted the Aquavest investment to succeed so she could move somewhere out of Virginia that would be more open to her relationship with her partner. Her relationship is crucial to her happiness.

"Also," I added, turning over the next card, "for her hopes I've drawn the Moon, which is sometimes considered a somewhat sinister symbol for bringing the shadow side out of the subconscious. But this is actually her strongest desire right now—to be able to live in the open, out of the closet, with her lover, while receiving the blessings of heaven—that's what is represented here with the 'dew' falling from the sky as the moon looks down. As for her fears, this last card is the Four of Pentacles. This isn't a weak card, and it feeds back to Maggie's being a good money manager but not a greedy person. She just wants to stay balanced and financially secure. She's not really interested in wealth per se, since her relationship is more important than anything money could buy."

"Then," said Bernice thoughtfully, "it doesn't sound to me as if any of the Loo-Loo Ladies would have been motivated to murder Jessamine over the failure of Aquavest."

"You know, I was worried that Maggie might have been at fault earlier this evening. She showed up in a black leather coat and slouch hat. And Greg told me someone who lives in the block where Jessamine had her office saw a woman in a black leather coat and slouch hat entering her office

The Lawyer Who Died Trying

building at just about the time Jessamine was supposed to have been murdered. Of course, Jessamine herself had a hat and coat like that, too, although it wasn't in her office when we found the body. Anyway, I must admit I thought for a while that Maggie might have been the woman the neighbor saw. But this reading makes it unlikely she would have murdered Jessamine over the failed investment."

"It *is* very curious," agreed Bernice, as she stroked Freud, who was purring like a steam engine. "I frankly find it hard to believe any of the Loo-Loo Ladies would have killed Jessamine over the money issue."

I heaved a sigh. "Well, then, maybe it was one of the men in her life."

"Since you have the cards out, and you have permission, you might as well read Ernie, too. And Jordan Steele as well, if it's possible."

I nodded and began sorting through the cards to find the kings of the various suits. When I'd located them, I turned them upside down and pushed them in her direction. "Here, your subconscious is a pretty good judge of character. Pick one for Ernie and a second one for Jordan Steele."

She slowly ran her hand over the cards about an inch above them, finally settling on one that she tapped with her forefinger. "This one for Ernie," she said. It was the King of Swords.

"Well, then, Ernie is into power through mental achievement. He's a good planner, and very proud of his ability to think things through. I get a feeling he's really surprised at having been conned by Cristien because he's so proud of himself for his ability to follow a logical process and accomplish things through reason and analysis."

I reached into the pile of cards and pulled three more out for Ernie. The first was the Page of Swords. "Usually this card is about someone in the first stages of learning how to use the intellect. So perhaps with respect to Aquavest, which was a new venture, Ernie was just learning to use his intellectual power in business. And this next card is also the Knight of Swords, so what he was hoping to do was move quickly to a higher level of achievement. He just wanted to rush right in and be an intellectual mover and shaker in the environmental field. But it also suggests he was operating with a bit of impatience. He didn't want to wait for things to simply play out."

"I'd say that's correct," said Bernice. "Ernie has always been really action oriented in a lot of ways. I thought when he was doing orthodontics with Michelle that her teeth would just move into place on demand because he wanted them to!"

"And finally, here's his fear card, the Four of Swords, which is usually a card indicating having moved beyond pain and failure. And so he must fear failure. Actually, I'm getting that he fears that he might die before he's made a mark that he himself can feel is a success."

"Well, you heard him tonight," agreed Bernice. "He voiced the fear that he might have to continue working until he's 85 to make up for what he's lost in Aquavest."

"But recognize it isn't money he's working for—it's intellectual achievement. It must be really hard for him to admit he's been duped because he takes such pride in his mental abilities. And look at all these cards—they're all swords! Mind is the one thing—maybe the only thing—that matters to him."

Again Bernice nodded thoughtfully. "Okay, then, it looks as if none of Jessamine's woman friends would have killed her over the money lost in Aquavest. And neither would Ernie."

"But," I asked, "is it possible that if he saw Jessamine pushing to make known the bad news he might have 'killed the messenger'?"

"Well, I suppose that *is* possible," she mused softly. "He *is* driven to succeed. I guess he might have taken action to stop her if he thought his path to success was out of his control. But if he did do it, or by the same token if any of the ladies who were here tonight did it, they were all able to mask their actions well."

I nodded. Jessamine was quiet, and I thought perhaps we were finished. Then Bernice asked, "So...do you want to try to read Jordan Steele?"

"I can try," I said, "if you'll pick one of those other cards to represent his significator."

"I'm drawn to this one," she said, pushing one of the three remaining kings I had pulled out of the deck toward me.

Turning it over, I saw it was the King of Cups. This was a card of the romantic man, who could be a great lover and fulfill every woman's sexual fantasies, a spontaneous and creative dreamer. But it was important to watch out for those times when he showed his negative side. Then he could be filled with fantasies and deceptions. I'd known a few con artists who fit the model of the King of Cups. Their power lay in their ability to manipulate people. I shared all of this with Bernice as I pulled three more cards to help round out the picture.

"This card sort of surprises me." I waited for a few seconds to see if any insight would come, then said, "It's the Hanged Man, so I'd have to say Jordan Steele has a martyr or Christ complex. Actually, I guess that fits, though it would be an inverted Messiah he's playing out if he's into Kali worship and ritual murder. But this card does suggest he's willing to look at things from unusual perspectives—probably because he really believes he has the answers to everything."

Next I turned over the Eight of Pentacles. "This card suggests he's willing to put his artistry to work to fulfill his dreams, which he's hoping will be exceptionally successful. He doesn't mind the nitty-gritty work that's necessary to make things happen—he doesn't mind getting his hands dirty. He'll do anything he has to in order to accomplish his goals."

"Including murder?"

I grimaced. "It's what he was trained to do in the military. That's his artistry."

The Lawyer Who Died Trying

Finally, I turned over the Six of Cups reversed. "This card generally has to do with finding love from the past. But since it's what he fears, then I think it has to do with something he has loved in the past that he fears will come back to do him harm. Perhaps it was an emotional weakness he had in the past. In any case, I'm getting that he fears something from the past will cause him problems."

"Well," said Bernice, "there's not much there that's definitive, but if he's the King of Cups, and it's the Six of Cups that's causing him fear, then maybe it has to do with one of the cons or jobs he pulled off in the past that's going to come back and bite him."

"We can only hope!" I said.

And behind me I felt Jessamine nodding and saying, *"You'd better believe it!"*

"But you know, for some reason, I'm drawn to pull just one more card for Jordan." And I went to the middle of the deck and drew out one more card. It was the Nine of Swords. "Oh," I breathed softly, looking up at Bernice. "It's what some people call the true death card in the deck!"

Suddenly I felt an energetic thud on the top of my head. It was as if someone had dropped a brick on me. My body went cold, and my mind went blank for a few seconds, and I had a terrible ringing in my ears.

"Ariel!" said Bernice. "What's happened?"

"I ... I don't know," I whispered. "Suddenly I got walloped on the top of the head by something." Then I saw the face of Jordan Steele, smiling in a smarmy way. "It's Jordan," I said. He's put up an energy block."

"Are you okay, my dear?" asked Bernice. "Is there anything I can do?"

"Just put up your own energy shield," I said, sending up a swirling of protective energy around myself. "Surround yourself with light, as I'm doing right now, and don't let down your defenses, awake or asleep."

As I moved to stand up from the table, my protective shield began to take effect, and I felt the pain of the energy blow begin to recede. "There, that's better," I said, by way of reassuring Bernice that I was okay. "But I'm very glad I recorded this reading because all of a sudden none of it makes any sense to me. I'll have to transcribe it and review it tomorrow after I sleep!"

Chapter 13
Tuesday, October 28th

The next morning my head seemed a little clearer when I woke up. I'd had a dreamless night so far as I remembered, but as soon as I got up and started moving around, Jessamine was there, piggy-backing in my energy field.

"I'd like to go for a run this morning," I said, as I tied the laces of my runners. "You may come along if you like or you can stay here. I'll be gone about 30 minutes." And pulling on a hooded sweatshirt, I charged down the back stairs, out the door, and into the driveway on my way out to King Street.

As I jogged, I realized Jessamine had decided to stay behind. I wondered if ghosts were antithetical to exercise. Then, with a little giggle, I thought, "Jessamine's not ready to be exorcised yet!"

The energetic whomping I'd received from Jordan the night before had stunned me and left me with a blank mind, but I realized as I jogged that the cobwebs had totally cleared and I was feeling sharp and bright-eyed again. Unfortunately, that didn't help much in my figuring out the puzzle of the case. Unlike my previous experience of chancing upon a murder victim, where I'd been able to take photos of the crime scene and look at all the potential clues later, there seemed nothing to go on at the scene of Jessamine's murder except the knife itself and the file cabinet she'd been searching through when she'd been stabbed. Oh, and the report the police had that a woman in a black leather coat and matching slouch hat had been seen entering Jessamine's office building at about the time of the murder.

As I jogged along, I considered what I did know. It seemed likely Jessamine's death was related either to the disintegration of Aquavest or to the custody case over her son that she was embroiled in with her ex. To be sure, though Jordan Steele was handsome and charismatic, he seemed to me to be a very creepy character. He had been an assassin for the government, and as I'd learned the night before, he was a really powerful magician, who could control energy from a distance. The question was, would he need to murder Jessamine in order to achieve his goal of winning the custody case?

With respect to Aquavest, it seemed that the people most closely related to Jessamine within that company had been in Bernice's living room the previous night, and though all of them had a similar motive for murder, not one of them seemed especially likely as a suspect. Nevertheless, I went over them one by one in my mind, bringing in the few hints I'd learned from the card reading I'd done with Bernice.

Ernie seemed to be the prime candidate. He had invested his life savings to establish Aquavest and had wanted Jessamine to wait to blow the whistle before disclosing what she knew. Could his genial attitude be a cover-up? As Bernice had pointed out last night, he as the King of Swords and Lorelei as the Queen of Swords both might have possessed the negative tendency to stab someone in the back if they felt they'd been crossed. Might he have been so stressed by Jessamine's discoveries that he'd have resorted to violence? Was it possible he was part of the fraud? And if so, might he have decided to eliminate Jessamine before she uncovered his role in the deception?

Looking at the Loo-Loo Ladies, Lorelei seemed unlikely as a suspect. Of the three of Jessamine's friends, she had the highest income and seemed the least concerned about the money she'd lost. Or was her ho-hum attitude simply a fine bit of acting on her part? If she was to be believed, she was more concerned about Jessamine's son Jeffrey and his safety than she was about the money. This was, of course, a natural response, since she was Jeffrey's godmother. And she apparently didn't own a black leather coat and matching slouch hat.

Maggie, on the other hand, did own such an outfit, and so did Patricia. Of the two of them, Maggie stood to lose the most if she couldn't replace the money into her real estate company's accounts that she'd it borrowed from. But she seemed to have that financial problem covered. Nevertheless, could she have committed the murder out of panic before her partner's family stepped in to bail her out?

Patricia appeared to have found a method to recoup her losses, and even though she was disappointed at the prospect of having to go back to work, I was hard pressed to find a motive for her to have killed Jessamine. But in order not to eliminate her precipitously, I ran over in my mind the key motives for murder—money, sex, power, and revenge—to see if any might apply.

Okay, top of the list was money—she would lose her investment. But that wasn't Jessamine's fault. Would she have killed out of panic, as I saw Maggie possibly doing? It seemed unlikely. Okay, scratch that. And there didn't appear to be any sexual motive involved either, unless Jessamine had been having an affair with Patricia's husband, and that seemed pretty farfetched. And Patricia wasn't power-driven except with respect to the power of an enticing female over her male partner. Finally, so far as I could see with what I knew, none of the people in this close circle of friends appeared to have any sort of revenge motive.

Then I remembered Cristien. He'd checked out of the Hyatt early on Friday morning and disappeared. Had he gone back to New York, to the Cayman Islands, or elsewhere? Or had he found out about Jessamine's investigation of his fraud from her messages to his cell phone and that of his pseudo-lawyer and decided to come back and eliminate a pesky troublemaker? And then there was the lawyer himself, who wasn't who he had pretended to be. If he wasn't William Love, then who was he? He might actually have had the best motive of all for murder. Might he have come looking for her? Did he even know she'd been to New York?

I wasn't getting any hits on any of these possibilities, however. Was I looking at the wrong people or just the wrong motives?

As I rounded the final corner of my jogging route and came in sight of the driveway to Bernice's stately colonial house, I decided I needed to get in touch with Greg as soon as possible to see what the police might have turned up. And I was hoping with his help to have an opportunity to visit Jessamine's office again. If I could go back there with her in tow, maybe we could get some more clues out of her about how, when, and why she'd been killed.

When I got up to my apartment, I started up my computer and began to download emails. Then I stripped and hopped in the shower. Fortunately, Jessamine had the decency not to join me in the shower, so I was reveling in having had a full 45 minutes that I'd enjoyed just to myself. But she was right behind me when I came out of the bathroom, seemingly agitated over having been left alone for so long.

"We're progressing!" I said to placate her. "I'm calling Greg today to find out what the police know, and I'm going to ask him if it's possible for me to go back to the crime scene if somebody from the police department accompanies me. So be patient with me."

That seemed to calm her down, so I took a few minutes to look at email. There were a few more messages from people who wanted me to investigate their ghosts. There were a couple from students who'd been absent from class the day before and had sent me their Locke vs. Hobbes papers as attachments. And there was one from Michelle saying, "Meet me and Mike down in Mom's kitchen for breakfast at 9 a.m. this morning before we leave for the campus. We've hacked into Jordan Steele's personal power course!!!!"

I glanced around at the clock and realized it was already 9:05, so I punched off the computer screen, pulled on jeans and a clean sweatshirt, slipped on some moccasins, and ran downstairs.

Bernice, having been informed that everybody on the grounds would be congregating for breakfast, was standing at the center island making waffles. "Blueberry or peach?" she asked as I entered the kitchen. "And maple syrup or sour cream topping?"

Mike, sitting at the end of the long kitchen table, his lanky frame stretched out into the middle of the floor, said, "Take both, Ariel, just to confound her. I've been agitating for kumquat and boysenberry, but Mom keeps ignoring me."

"Kumquats and boysenberries don't share the same season, you twit," said Michelle, who was busy at the espresso machine.

"That's very true, Michelle," countered Bernice placidly, "but the real reason I'm ignoring Mike is that boysenberries aren't easy to come by in the frozen fruit case at the supermarket, and I'll only put kumquats in a waffle if somebody else is willing to peel and seed them ahead of time. However, if you feel you're citrus deprived, Mike, I can toss you an orange."

"Make it a grapefruit," said Mike, "and I'll consider your debt paid."

"You are far too gracious for words," said Bernice.

"I've got a blueberry waffle," said Michelle, handing me a freshly made cappuccino, "so if you get a peach, we can split 50-50."

"Sounds workable," I nodded. "And I'd like maple syrup with a dollop of sour cream topping in the middle." I was feeling righteous about having already done my daily jog.

"I'll let you put the toppings on yourself," said Bernice. "They're on the table."

The scent of both the cappuccino and the freshly baked waffles was heavenly, and I breathed it in just for the pleasure of the smell before I even took a sip of the hot drink. Then I felt a surge of wistfulness from Jessamine about her not being able to enjoy food anymore, and considering her closeness to my shoulder, I was grateful that ghosts don't drool.

Bernice handed me a waffle that had bits of peach in it and her own preserved peaches from the summer piled on top, and I went to sit across from Michelle at the table. "Here, you do the splitting," I suggested to her, thinking I'd probably make a mess of the piles of peaches and blueberries.

"Coward," said Michelle, recognizing the reason for my reluctance. "Hey, Mike," since you've already inhaled your breakfast, would you get me a fresh plate so I can perform this delicate surgery without harming the two patients?"

"Oh, yeah, a minute ago I was a twit, but now that you need help, I'm your operating room assistant." But he hauled himself out of the chair and went to get a plate.

While she was carving the waffles into two parts, I asked, "So what's the news you have to tell me about Jordan Steele's website? I didn't know you knew anything about that."

"Well, Mom asked us yesterday if we could do some research for you."

"I hope you don't mind, Ariel," interjected Bernice. "Yesterday while the kids were here, I thought about what you'd told me concerning Jordan Steele's website course, and I know how proficient they are at doing web research. So I just asked them to see what they could find. That was before Maggie volunteered to bring us her hard copy of Jordan's basic personal empowerment course."

"Was it difficult to find it?" I asked the twins.

Mike gave a little snort of a laugh. "It wouldn't have been if Michelle weren't dyslexic. But we were all pretty confused for a minute because Michelle Googled KLAI instead of KALI."

"It was just a simple typing error," said Michelle righteously. "It had nothing to do with my dyslexia!"

"What did you get with KLAI?" asked Bernice.

Mike laughed with a little snort again. "Oh, lots of really interesting things. First was the Kappa Lambda American Institute that runs summer camps in the Ozarks. Then we found out about the Klai: Juba architects, who specialize in gaming, hospitality, and entertainment architecture. They even have a lecture series on their architecture—actually some of my buddies would think that was pretty interesting. And finally there's the Klai Kang Won Palace in Hua Hin, Thailand. But by the time we got that far in the list, we'd figured out from what Michelle was reading that she'd typed in the wrong word."

"Are you going to give me a plate or not?" asked Michelle. "These waffles are getting cold."

Mike put the plate he'd been sent for next to the waffle plates Michelle was operating on, and said, "But just so you know how hard we had to work, there were a whole lot more items that turned up when we Googled KALI—nearly 23 million hits!"

I made an appropriately shocked noise, to which Mike responded, "Well, that's when all you type in is the word KALI. Really, it took us at *least* thirty seconds to find the website Jordan Steele has up once we narrowed the field by adding his name to the search. After that is was a breeze. And we were working with a buddy of mine who's very good at hacking into supposedly secure web addresses. Once he took over at the computer, he got right up to the third level course. It wasn't really very secure."

"Oh, dear," said Bernice, "I'm not sure I want to hear anything about hacking. I don't want my twins locked up for breaking and entering."

"Okay, Mom, we won't talk about hacking. We'll just tell Ariel what we found. Although I'm sure Dad could get me a job with the FBI if I get really good at this skill myself."

Michelle finished splitting the two waffles with barely a blueberry out of place, and she pushed one plate toward me. Mike passed the maple syrup and sour cream topping in my direction, and I was set.

"So what did you find out?" I asked as I took the first bite.

"It's a pretty cool website," said Mike. "Good graphics, nicely laid out, easy to navigate from page to page. The freebie section—those pages you can get to from the home page without a subscription—talks about pretty mundane things like learning to feel good about yourself, discovering your gifts and talents, overcoming resistance to change. All the positive thinking stuff Mom taught us when we were kids to be sure our little psyches were secure and we could grow up feeling good about ourselves. It's good stuff, but very basic.

"Then there's a course that people have to pay for. It's twenty lessons for $500.00. And again, it seems pretty straightforward. It has a lot of really good exercises for changing your behavior, overcoming emotional and psychological blocks to claiming your power, some NLP suggestions, a lot of stuff about enhancing your energy field...that kind of stuff."

The Lawyer Who Died Trying

"That sounds like the course the Loo-Loo Ladies were talking about last night—the one they all took when Jessamine first married Jordan," I said.

"Maggie is supposed to bring her notes and workbook over tomorrow afternoon," said Bernice, "so you'll be able to compare it to what's on the website when you get home from school tomorrow evening."

I nodded. "It sounded like a pretty benign self-improvement course from the way they talked about it."

"Well, what's on the website is benign at that first level," agreed Michelle. "It's only when you get to higher levels of coursework that it gets dicey."

Mike nodded. "What it looks like is that people can pay for all the lessons up front, or $25.00 for each lesson. But either way, they can't download a new lesson until they've completed a test on the previous lesson satisfactorily." Mike made a wry face at this point before he continued. "And after finishing the twentieth lesson's exam, there's a little personality test. It's a pretty sophisticated matrix, and you get directed to one of two websites depending on your answers. For people whose answers show that they've taken the course to feel better about themselves and are now ready to use what they've learned in the workplace and in social interactions, there's a section with a few pages on applying the skills they've learned and a page of congratulations on completing the course. And they're told if they type in a mailing address, they'll receive a graduation certificate by USPS. But if their answers indicate a desire for more power and a willingness to be a bit more cutthroat in acquiring it, they get sent to another page that offers a second level course that guarantees enhanced personal power in all aspects of life.

"This course starts with a full-year of study on Hindu mysticism. It costs $1,500.00, and it's the first stage of the full meal deal, which apparently involves a lot of one-on-one stuff with the instructor. The Hindu mysticism is a pretty elaborate course, though I couldn't see anything in it that would warp somebody's soul, although it does talk a lot about tantra and sex magic. But the exams are sent by email, apparently, so exactly what a person needs to get out of it isn't absolutely clear. And while we were able to get into the front page of the rest of the course, its topics are just teasers, as apparently the lessons for the rest of the course are also done by email or in personal workshops with the instructor. But the rest of the course is another $8,500.00."

I whistled. "Guess I won't be signing up anytime soon. But do you have the teaser topics from this third level?"

"I can probably show you how to access it. Or maybe easier would be if I'd get my friend who helped me hack it to download everything that we're able to access. Would that be helpful?"

"It certainly would," I said. "And thanks, you two. I'm mighty glad to know you!"

"Oh, you're welcome," said Mike. "And in return...?" He raised an eyebrow.

"What do you need?" I asked resignedly. "I only have a zillion Locke and Hobbes papers to grade today, plus an appointment I'm trying to make with the Alexandria Police."

"Well, it has to do with the Halloween party this Friday night. I've had all my friends make up descriptions of what their contributions to the haunted yard are going to be. I think Michelle already talked to you about them, and you offered to help with the light boxes. Anyway, I have all the descriptions on a disk, and I was hoping you'd sort of edit them for us, then print them and tape them into the light boxes we have out in the garage. We put the boxes on eye-level stakes so people can read them as they navigate the haunted yard."

"Every year the theme for the party is different, and this year it's famous ghosts," said Michelle, "like I told you the other day. And I just thought we'd need you to edit the writing and maybe print it out for us. But Mike thought maybe you wouldn't mind helping with the light boxes themselves. We put up lighted boxes at each station, with a description of what the station represents, so people know what they're looking at, just in case it isn't intuitively obvious. If you'll come out with me to the garage under the carriage house, I'll show you what they look like. The size of the writing needs to be no bigger than six and a half inches by ten inches in order to fit in the window of the box. Oh, please, oh, please can you do this for us?"

Her pleading was so comical as she cocked her head and batted her eyes that I had to laugh. "Okay, I said. "I'll squeeze that project in sometime today."

"I can show Ariel where the boxes are in the garage," said Bernice, "so you don't have to bother with that now, Michelle. And I can help you with putting the boxes together, Ariel. I don't have any clients today until early afternoon."

"Okay, that sounds fair," I agreed.

"And Ariel," added Michelle, "please feel free to invite anyone you like to the Halloween party. I know Mom wants to meet your family—at least all those she hasn't already met—and if Greg and his son can come that would be really super. You can invite anybody else you like, even those with lots of kids. We'll have cupcakes, party favors, plenty of kinds of candy for their trick-or-treat bags, games just for kids, and a magician. All of this will be in the garage that's under our carriage house apartment."

"Where did you find a magician?" asked Bernice.

Michelle grinned and put on an innocent face. "I hadn't told you about this, Mom, but remember that guy we met at the TV station who was going to try to discredit you, Ariel?"

"You mean Bryan Corcoran?"

"Yup! Well, he called me the other night and asked me out for ice cream."

The Lawyer Who Died Trying

"Interesting," mused Bernice. "He actually called me the other night also."

"Did he ask you out for ice cream?" asked Mike.

"No, he made an appointment with me for a session."

"I think ice cream would be more fun," said Mike.

"So do I," agreed Bernice, "but your sister beat me out. So, am I right in assuming Bryan is the magician you mentioned?"

"Yes," said Michelle enthusiastically. "I was telling him about how we always do the Halloween party, and he volunteered. Then he said it was also a part of what he was going to discuss with you, Mom. He's had a need for years to debunk the so-called 'mystical' side of life. He wanted to show how a lot of what we think of as 'magical' or 'supernormal' is really just misdirection and sleight of hand, so he practiced doing a lot of magic tricks—and he got good at the sleight-of-hand stuff. Anyway, like I said, he offered to perform for the kids at the party."

"And speaking of people doing things at the party, would you also be willing to perform, Ariel?"

"You want me to sing and dance perhaps? Maybe I could sing Mrs. Lovett's meat pie song from *Sweeney Todd*—that's appropriately grisly for a Halloween party. But no, that would require full orchestra accompaniment. Well, I used to be able to do Irish ceili dancing when I was a little kid, but that's about all I can think of that would fit the description of performance art."

"That sounds like it would be fun to watch," said Mike dubiously, "but what we had in mind was asking you to read Tarot cards. You know, dress up like a Gypsy fortune-teller and do one-card readings for people. It would be easy for you, and I know it would be fun for everybody who comes to the party."

"And I have some nifty Gypsy costume stuff you could get tricked out in, if you don't have anything of your own," offered Michelle.

"Okay," I agreed. "And I'll invite my family and Greg and Brandon, and maybe the Loo-Loo Ladies. I'm sure anybody with kids would like to bring them to a place where there's wholesome entertainment and no fear of the kids getting poisoned by trick-or-treat candy."

"Yay," said Mike, "we sucked her in! Okay, Madre and Ariel, we must depart for campus. Put the rest of your waffle on a plastic plate, Sis, and let's make an exit before anybody backs out of her agreements."

Michelle scurried to get a travel plate and plastic fork, then the twins got on their jackets, hoisted their backpacks, and made an exit, with Michelle blowing kisses to both me and her mother.

Still working on my own waffle, I asked Bernice, "What's this about Michelle being dyslexic?"

"Oh, she had some problems with it when she was a little girl. She seemed to be doing fine from first through third grades. But when she was in the fourth grade, her marks plummeted. I asked her what the problem was, and she said she really didn't understand what she was looking at when she saw a page of writing or something written on the blackboard. So I questioned how she'd managed to get by up to that point, and she said it was because she listened very carefully to what other kids were saying or reading in class, and she memorized that and spouted it back. But by the fourth year of doing this, things had become too complicated for her to get by with that tactic."

"That suggests she was pretty smart, though, to be able to compensate in that way."

"Well, it was pretty hard to convince the school we had her in that she was smart enough to benefit from classes for the learning disabled. They decided because of her low grades in math and reading that she probably didn't have a high enough I.Q. to merit giving her those classes. And then they refused to have her I.Q. tested, saying it would be pointless."

"You're kidding!" I was really shocked.

"No, that's actually what some fool of a principal said to me. So Alan and I hired a tutor for her, and by the time she was 11 we had her up to grade level, and she was testing at around 100 I.Q. We had the testing done privately."

"Well, at least that's a nice average number."

"Yes, but you know I.Q. tests are based on left-brained skills—reading, writing, and mathematical computation. As it turned out, Michelle was mostly right-brained—her real talents are in visualization, imagery, color, design, body movement in space, and making music. She couldn't actually read musical notations at first, but she had a grand ear for music and could play almost any tune on the piano nevertheless.

"Anyway, when we finally got her into various arts classes, she really began to blossom. In fact, one of her art teachers said she was a genius with spatial design. That was when she was 15. And that's when we really began to see a difference in her learning skills, because she started bridging what she was really good at—all the right-brained art and sound and movement skills—with the left-brained reading, writing, math computation skills, and the reading of musical scores. And last year, as a part of her social sciences classes at George Mason, she took another I.Q. test and scored 138."

"So she really is a genius," I nodded.

"I think probably a lot of kids are who get lost in the school systems. We were lucky to find ways to help Michelle compensate with her lack of left-brained understanding, and then when we learned how very talented she was at right-brained skills, the final bridging took place. But the schools don't focus on whole-brained thinking, you know. That's why so many school systems minimize and marginalize the arts as 'trivial' and 'unnecessary' and only have them in the curriculum for recreation."

"Maybe you should go on the Mac Jacobs show and talk about brain-hemisphere bridging," I suggested.

"Maybe I should," she said. "But today I have other fish that need frying, like getting the menu together for the Halloween party, and making sure our yard man has the backyard in good shape for the party. And you need to make some phone calls to potential guests."

I popped the last succulent bite of waffle into my mouth at this point, and my mind returned to thoughts of Jordan Steele and his coursework. I could only speculate what was in the more advanced classes on his website, but some of the pages Jeffrey had found must have been components of the advanced third level. As I thought this, I felt Jessamine tuning into my thinking.

"*Jordan is scum!*" she said. "*He must be stopped!*"

"We'll see what we can do," I promised.

As soon as I got up to my apartment, I called Greg.

"Hey, sweet stuff," he said when he heard my voice, so I knew he was alone in his office. "What's up?"

"A couple of things. Bernice's twins are having a Halloween party on Friday night, and people with kids are invited. So do you think Brandon would like to come? There'll be lots of things for kids to do, as well as a 'haunted backyard' with scary displays to walk through. Do you think he'd like that?"

"Well, I do have him this weekend, and he was asking if we could do a haunted house somewhere around town before trick-or-treat time. So I imagine he can be talked into it. And it's certainly fine with me, especially if I get to walk through the scary displays with you to hold my hand."

"Okay, tough guy, I'll protect you," I grinned. "Now the other thing I have to ask is about business rather than pleasure. Has the crime scene at Jessamine's office been released yet?"

"Um," he said, and it sounded like he was hedging a little. "Well, I know it was about to be released last evening, but something else happened that caused Flanagan to hold on to it for a little longer. So I think we still have it cordoned off with crime scene tape."

"Well, the reason I'm asking is this. Do you think Flanagan would approve my going back to the crime scene for another look? Jessamine's still hanging around, and I'd like to take her back to her office and see if she remembers anything else that happened just before she was stabbed. So far I've managed to get nothing out of her about who might have done it—she says she doesn't know. But maybe if I can stand in her office and get her to replay what she was doing before it happened, she'll get some clarity about it. Or at least give us some more clues."

"Hey, why don't you call Flanagan up and ask? I know there was a request from a Dr. Ernie Redmond for us to clear the space from its crime scene status so he could get papers associated with the Aquavest company, but as of this morning, Flanagan hadn't done that yet. I think there was a question as to whether we might need copies of all papers associated with Aquavest for police files. But give Flanagan a call. He knows about your slightly...bizarre talents. If you tell him Jessamine's still hanging around, and you're hoping to jog her memory, he'll probably let you go in there with an officer, as long as you promise not to touch anything. He's not likely to send me with you because I have one of my school lectures to do today. But whoever goes with you will be able to guarantee you don't touch anything."

"Right. Okay, I'll call him. And, um, are you free after work tonight? I want to hash over what we learned at the Loo-Loo Ladies' dinner last night. I'll bring steaks if you say yes."

"Are you actually offering to cook?" he said in mock disbelief.

"Not unless you like your steaks grossly overdone. I think what I said was, 'I'll bring steaks.' Did that imply I intended to actually cook them?"

"No, I guess not," he laughed. "Okay, my place at 7:00?"

"Yes, please. And here's a kiss to hold you until then," I said, making a lip-smacking, wet "Mmwa!" sound.

"Be careful!" he laughed. "Don't short out your cell phone."

As soon as I'd clicked off with Greg, I looked up Flanagan's number at the police department and dialed it. When he answered, I identified myself and told him about Jessamine's still being with me, and I asked whether her office was still a crime scene and if so, whether I could visit it just to see what she might remember.

He was quiet for a couple of beats, then said, "I don't get calls like yours very often. In point of fact, I don't think I've ever had a call like yours. But hey, we're open minded. When did you want to go over there? We're probably going to release the site by this evening, as we've had both the building owner and the CEO of one of the companies Ms. Steele worked for petitioning for access. We haven't quite finished with the crime scene yet, so if you can go today, I'll contact a patrol officer to meet you there and let you take a look, but if you wait, you might need to talk to the building owner about getting in."

"I work tomorrow, so it would be better if I could come today."

"How about 2 p.m.?"

"That would work," I agreed.

"Then when you get outside on St. Asaph, either there'll be an officer waiting for you downstairs, or if the patrol car is empty, just punch the buzzer on the front door, and the officer will let you into the building and the office."

"Thanks so much," I said.

"And be sure to call me if your...haunt...reacts to anything."

"I certainly will. The sooner this case is solved, the sooner I can expect her to move on."

After I'd hung up with Flanagan, I called the members of my family who were in the vicinity to invite them to the twins' party. Deirdre, my youngest sister, was the one who really liked dressing up for costume parties, but she was at High Point College in North Carolina earning her bachelor's degree in theater and wasn't due home again until Thanksgiving.

The Lawyer Who Died Trying

I called my sister Catherine at her savings and loan office to see if she and her husband Mark wanted to come, but she said they already had tickets to the Kennedy Center for Friday night.

"Wouldn't you know it?" she said. "This is the only time we've been planning a night out in the past month, and now there's a party at the same time! And I really wanted to meet this cop you're dating, but now I won't have a chance. Boo, hiss!"

"Well, don't worry too much about it," I soothed. "I know you'll get to meet my new guy sooner or later, 'cause I'm hoping to keep him around for a while."

When I hung up, I pondered what I'd just said and thought that my relationship with Greg was becoming more and more meaningful to me as time went on. I liked talking things over with Bernice because she seemed so much wiser than most of the people I knew. And in spite of the fact that she was a healthcare professional, she didn't think my paranormal abilities made me a candidate for the loony bin. In fact, far from it. But I also loved talking things over with Greg because he always gave attention to everything I said and was a good sounding board when I had problems to solve, letting me think things through rather than taking over and telling me what I *ought* to think. I really appreciated that in a man I was dating.

I sighed, thinking about how much I enjoyed just being with him. Then I gave myself a mental nudge.

"There you go getting all moony—and it doesn't pay to be loony *and* moony! Besides, you'll get to titillate your libido tonight when you take him some steaks. So get back to work!"

I dialed my sister Bibi, who lived out in the country near Leesburg. She had three little kids that I thought would love to come to a Halloween party, and sure enough, she accepted the invitation.

"I was dreading the trick-or-treat routine," she said, "because, as you remember from last year when you were living here, we have to go into Leesburg in order to take the kids door to door. We were thinking about driving door to door to visit our nearest neighbors out here in the country, but that's such a drag, and it takes so long. I mean, I've made all the kids costumes like a good mother should, but I was so dreading the thought of actually doing anything on Halloween night! So you've saved my sanity! And it sounds like there'll be plenty of people they can show their costumes off to."

Next I called my mom to see if she and my dad might want to come to the party.

"Oh, sweetheart," my mom gushed, "I'd LOVE to come to the party and meet this fascinating group of people you're now living with, and especially get a look at your new beau! But since your father retired from the Army and started working for beltway bandits, he's joined practically every service organization known to man! So there's a Kiwanis event—or maybe I'm confused and it's a Knights of Columbus event—anyway, whatever it is, he's volunteered us, and we're going to help run a Halloween carnival and potluck supper at one of the schools in Laurel. So we can't come this time. But do bring this police friend of yours up for dinner sometime. Just call me a couple of days in advance—you know I'm good for a special dinner just about any night of the week."

It was true—my mom was almost as good at providing food to the ravening hordes as Bernice was.

I told Mom how sorry I was they couldn't come, and that I was going to dress up as Madam Lasagna and read Tarot cards for people.

"Oh, sweetie," she said, "now I'm *really* sorry we won't be able to come. But you know, I've been trying to learn some Manx Gaelic, and one thing I wanted to tell you is that the Manx Gaelic word for 'psychic' is *sheekagh*. Now, isn't that fun? You can tell everybody you're a *sheekagh*."

"I can until Dad learns the Irish Gaelic term for 'psychic'." My mom and dad were constantly in a friendly battle about which of the Celtic groups was best since my dad was Irish and my mom was Manx.

When I hung up with my mom, I called Patricia to invite her family to the twins' party. She answered her phone on the third ring, sounding reasonably calm. When I'd explained about the party, and that I wanted to invite the Loo-Loo ladies and their families, she actually cooed at me.

"I'd love to bring my children, though I don't know if my husband will come. And I've always loved costume parties. For years, we four friends have been going to costume parties as Princess Leia. I mean as four Princess Leias. Or would that be Princesses Leia? Anyway, we love to dress up as four different types of Princess Leia. Actually, we used to date guys who would dress up as Princess Leia, too, and once there were eight Princess Leias at one party!" She sighed. "But I don't know if it'll be the same without Jessamine." Another sigh. Then clearly she had an idea. "Oh, Ariel, maybe I could get you Jessamine's costume, and you could go as Princess Leia, too!"

"Well, I'm planning to wear a Gypsy costume. I'm going to read cards at the party, so it fits the occupation."

"Oh, well," she sighed again, "I guess it'll have to be just the three of us." Then once more she was infused with a little energy. "But I'll tell you what I'll do. I'll save you some time and call Lorelei and Maggie for you and tell them to bring their families and friends to your party. Do we need to R.S.V.P. to anybody?"

"Oh, I think Bernice and the twins might want to know how many kids and how many adults to prepare for since they're going to have trick-or-treat bags and party food. But it's not like they'll have a sit-down dinner or anything."

"Well, okay, I'll call you or Bernice back after I talk to Maggie and Lorelei. Oh, this'll be fun!" And she clicked off.

As I closed up my phone, I heaved a deep sigh myself. Patricia sounded a little down today, and the initial lethargy of her delivery had left me feeling tired. I was glad the invitation to the party had perked her up a bit. I also had to admit the idea of all the Princesses Leia had tickled my

The Lawyer Who Died Trying

imagination. Then I thought about Patricia's invitation to me to join the group. Well, Jessamine would probably have been pleased if I'd accepted—since it was her costume I'd have been wearing. But I was hoping that by Friday, the mystery of who had killed her would be solved and I'd be able to go to the party by myself!

Just then my cell phone rang, and I saw by the caller I.D. subscript that it was Jessamine's lawyer. After the preliminary social niceties, he got to the point of his call.

"Jordan Steele's mother is currently taking care of Jeffrey Steele. Now that Jessamine is dead, it seems Jordan's mother is just as anxious to keep Jeffrey out of his father's hands as Jessamine was. So she's applying for custody. It will probably be a little more difficult for me to win the suit since the boy's father would normally take precedence over any other relative, unless a clear case can be made for his undesirable status. I mean, if it turns out he actually murdered his wife, then there'd be no problem—but otherwise, it may be difficult for Jordan's mother to get custody. So rather than using the deposition you gave me, I think I'd actually like to you come to court."

I thought for just a moment before answering. "I don't have a problem with coming to court, but what date are you talking about?"

"Well, as I think you know, we were scheduled to go to court next Monday, but now that Jessamine is dead, we've had to file amended paperwork, so the case will be heard on November 18th. And we'll subpoena you so you can get the time off work."

I glanced at the wall calendar I had over my desk and said, "That should work. I'm off that day anyway."

"Well, I like to cover all bases, since the court appearance might go more than a day."

"I understand," I agreed. "It's just that we're getting perilously close to Thanksgiving, and once that's past, we'll be near the end of the school term, and I won't want to leave my students without their instructor during the last week of school."

"Well, all I can promise is that you won't have to actually give testimony for more than one day. We can only hope it will be the first day we're in court. In fact, I'm hoping the hearing won't take more than one day. But that's up to the judge."

"I understand," I repeated, thinking that my experience with court appearances had so far in my life been limited to my current infatuation with episodes of *Law and Order* and a flirtation the year before with *Judging Amy*. One thing I was pretty sure of was that any real court case wouldn't be settled in just 45 minutes plus commercials, the way they were on TV.

"Now, there's one other thing I'd appreciate your doing if you have some time this afternoon. Jordan Steele's mother and his son Jeffrey will be coming to my office at 4 o'clock. Could you possibly drop by and meet with Mrs. Steele? Apparently Jessamine had told her a great deal about you and how fearless you were in your willingness to speak on her behalf.

Apparently a lot of her friends weren't willing to speak out against her husband because they were afraid of him."

I was a little puzzled by this statement. "Jessamine told me she hadn't been able to find anyone else to come to court on her behalf, but I didn't realize she'd asked her friends. Do you have any idea who she might have meant specifically?"

"I believe it was some of her friends who had been in Jordan Steele's classes early on in the marriage. People she'd known in college. I don't have any names in my file because she said they weren't willing to come to court out of fear. She said she had asked them, but no one wanted to incur Jordan's wrath or any possible repercussions. I don't necessarily believe he can actually do anything, but I've found in some similar cases that superstition often outweighs common sense. I'm sure in your extensive research on the subject of black magic that you've often seen the same thing. People afraid of the unknown and all that?"

"Actually," I countered, "what I've found is that certain cultures have a healthy respect for—and may want to keep a safe distance from—anyone whose objective is to control them with a misuse of power. Those who claim to use the dark arts may or may not really be able to manipulate energy. But I promise you I don't disrespect their efforts. My willingness to act for Jessamine was based on my belief that I can protect myself from those efforts. Whether I'm correct remains to be seen, but I have *actually* felt Jordan Steele's attempts to break through my shield. And last night he almost succeeded."

Jessamine's lawyer was silent for a few moments. Then he said slowly, "Well, perhaps I should take this situation a little more seriously."

"Perhaps you should," I agreed. "But we can talk about just how you might do that when I come by this afternoon. And it wouldn't hurt to check in with Jordan's mother and son to be sure they're properly protecting themselves, as well. Just in case."

"I'm certainly open to having you do that, if you think it's necessary."

"Why not err on the side of caution?" I asked, thinking about the warning I'd received concerning Jessamine that I hadn't acted on until too late.

As I hung up the phone, I could feel Jessamine's energy right behind me. I pulled a second chair up beside mine and said to her, "Jessamine, can we talk? I'd appreciate it if you'd come around and sit beside me, the way you did in your office two days ago. It's hard for me to talk to you while you're in back of me."

I felt her moving tentatively, and finally I could tell she was sitting beside me in the second chair.

"Okay, please," I asked, "can you tell me which of your friends you asked to testify on your behalf against Jordan?"

It took a few seconds as if she was searching her memory. Finally, the answer came, *"All of them. I asked all of them."*

"Do you mean Patricia, Lorelei, and Maggie? Are those the friends you mean?"

"*Yes. I asked all of them.*"

"And did they refuse to speak on your behalf?"

"*Yes. They all said they couldn't do it.*"

"Was it because they didn't know anything useful?"

"*No.*"

"Then why did they say they didn't want to do it?"

"*It was because they were afraid.*"

"I thought they didn't know about Jordan's dabbling in dark magic."

"*Oh, but I told them about that. So they knew. And they said they didn't want him to turn on them.*"

"How could he have harmed them?"

She was slow to answer, but finally it came. "*Lorelei said she was worried Jordan would find a way to stop her getting her judgeship. Patricia was afraid he might harm her children. Maggie wanted anonymity—she was afraid of having her lesbianism made too public and ruining her business.*"

"What about Ernie Redmond? Did you ask him to testify?"

"*No. By the time I got involved with Ernie and Aquavest, I wasn't married to Jordan anymore. Ernie never met Jordan.*"

"Is there anyone else you know that you might have asked to speak on your behalf?"

"*Only Jordan's mother. She doesn't trust him, so she was on my side.*"

"All right, then. Thanks for telling me." I sat for a few seconds, pondering what to do next. Then I looked at the clock beside my bed. "Okay, right now I have to grade some papers. But I need to be at your law office at two o'clock, and I'm going to ask you to come with me when I go. Then maybe we can get clear about who killed you."

Chapter 14

By the time I had to get ready for my appointment at Jessamine's law office, I'd had party R.S.V.P. calls from all three of the Loo-Loo Ladies—Patricia to tell me her husband had agreed to come after all, Maggie to let me know her partner was breaking a rule and coming with her, and Lorelei to say she'd be coming alone but had I thought about inviting that delicious detective fellow? I decided they were all hungry for something to take their minds off the Aquavest scandal and Jessamine's death.

It had occurred to me while I was talking to Lorelei that since I'd be meeting with Jeffrey's grandmother later that afternoon, I might invite her and Jeffrey to the party, too. But I was unsure about the appropriateness of such an invitation, so close in time to the child's loss of his mother. So I said, "Lorelei, you're Jeffrey's godmother, so I guess you know him pretty well."

"Ah should say so!" she agreed. "He's such a bright, sweet little boy. I feel so sorry for him, losin' his mama when he's so young."

"Well, I'm going to be meeting his grandmother this afternoon, and I was wondering if you thought it would be appropriate to invite her and Jeffrey to the twins' party?"

"Where are you goin' to be meetin' her?"

"At Jessamine's lawyer's office. I think she's going to be pursuing getting custody of Jeffrey."

"Now that's really interestin'," said Lorelei. "Is this because of what you were tellin' me about this course Jordan Steele's supposed to be teachin'?"

"I'm assuming so at this point, but I'll know more after I've talked with her and Jessamine's lawyer. But what do you think about inviting Jessamine's mother-in-law and son to the Halloween party."

"Why, Ah think it would be jus' fine, Honey. Ah'm sure the little guy would be happy to have a chance to do somethin' normal and cheerful."

"Okay, then, I'll do it. And thanks!"

By the time I'd hung up with Lorelei, I realized I'd spent practically the whole morning on the phone. I looked ruefully at the stacks of student

The Lawyer Who Died Trying

papers and realized how little I'd accomplished, but there was nothing I could do about it—the rest of my day was spoken for.

At two minutes to two o'clock, I parked outside Jessamine's law office building. There was an empty patrol car on the street, so I went to the front door of the office building and rang the bell. In less than three seconds, I heard a buzzer and pushed open the door. At the top of the stairs, a policewoman I hadn't met but whose badge said Trousdale was waiting for me in the hall just outside of Jessamine's office. I introduced myself, and as she turned and went in, I started to follow her. But there was a tug, and I felt myself being pulled backwards energetically.

Behind me, I felt Jessamine get excited and say, *"I can't go in!"*

I was perplexed and mightily disturbed because I thought Jessamine was keeping me from entering.

"Excuse me," I called out to the policewoman, "but I need to use the restroom. Is there one on this floor?"

"Yes, there's one down at the other end."

"Thanks. I'll be right back."

I went down the hall to a restroom that had a unisex sign on the door. Fortunately, it had only one stall, so I was able to lock the outside door and be sure I wouldn't be heard by anyone else in the building. Then I whispered to Jessamine, "Why can't you go into your office? And why are you stopping me from going in?"

"I'm not," said Jessamine. *"I think it's Jordan."*

"What do you mean?"

"It's an energy field. And I'm not strong enough to push into it."

I thought for a minute. Why would Jordan be blocking Jessamine's office, and what was he using to do it? It wasn't *his* office, so he shouldn't be able to invade Jessamine's space without some kind of assistance from her. Well, I didn't know that for certain, but since he'd sent crows to scare her at her apartment, it was unlikely he could conjure up anything more powerful than that at her office. So how could he have enough power to put up a force field that would reject the spirit of his dead wife?

Then I remembered I'd read about black magicians who could use objects they'd once owned to create force fields. But I knew the knife he'd given her that had been used to kill her was now in police possession. So it would have to be some other object.

"Jessamine," I whispered, "did Jordan give you anything else that you keep in your office? Anything besides the knife you used as a letter opener?"

She was silent for a few moments. Finally, she said, *"Lakshmi."*

For a minute I didn't understand what she'd said. Then I realized she had spoken the name of the goddess of wealth and beauty in Hindu religion. "Do you mean a picture or statue of Lakshmi?"

"Yes," came the answer. *"It's in my outer office on a tall, wooden stand. People who know who she is touch the base of her statue for luck. And maybe also for money and good looks."*

"Ah-ha!" I said. "Okay, stay out of my energy field for a few minutes while I try to go through the door." And I hurried back to her office. She stayed about ten feet behind me. And sure enough, this time I was able to go through the outer door.

As I went in, I saw the statue of Lakshmi Jessamine had referred to—it was tall and white, with a wide, oval base, and it stood on a wooden stand. The statue and stand together were about five and a half feet high. The statue was of a beautiful woman, even though she did have four arms. She also had long flowing hair and a radiant crown on her head, she was dressed in what appeared to be a somewhat revealing robe, and she stood in what looked to me like an open, multi-petaled lotus flower. And it was floating on stylized ocean waves. I thought she looked a lot like Botticelli's Venus—except of course, for the extra arms, the crown, and the lotus.

Officer Trousdale was sitting in a chair near the door to the inner office. She had glanced up as I came through the door.

"I'm sorry," I said, "That was a bit of an emergency. Thanks for being patient with me."

"It's okay," she responded with a little smile. "You're the one who's dating Sergeant Mason, aren't you?"

"Yes," I nodded.

"So," she said, "is this some kind of psychic thing you're doing? I mean, everybody in the department knows about what you did with that case last month with the dead chef. So are you here to get psychic impressions?"

"Sort of," I nodded again. "And the first impression I'm getting is that this statue is blocking the energy in this office. Is there a way we could remove it temporarily? Like take it down the hall or something? Just until I can get my bearings? I know this must sound crazy, but it wouldn't do any harm to move it, would it?"

Trousdale looked skeptical, then laughed. "I don't know what good it will do you, but I guess I could take it into custody for obstruction of justice," she joked, and she reached to lift it off its base.

"Actually, before you move it, do you know if it was dusted for fingerprints?" I glanced around and noticed that a lot of the surfaces in the office seemed to still have the residue of the fingerprinting dust on them, but the base of the statue was clean. "Ms. Steele told me it's the goddess of wealth and beauty in the Hindu religion, and that when people would come into the office, they might touch its base for good luck."

"I can check that," she said and took out her cell phone. I listened while she made a quick call to the station to check with Flanagan. After a brief exchange, she closed her phone. "He says it isn't listed as having been checked for prints. Kind of puzzling, considering all the other surfaces in the office were dusted. But he says I should bring it in."

I wondered if Jordan had put a sort of "glamour" over it so the police didn't notice it when they were dusting the office. I thought he might have done so to keep his force field intact.

The Lawyer Who Died Trying

Officer Trousdale put on a pair of rubber gloves before taking custody of the statue. Then she said, "I'll take this down to the cruiser, but I'll have to lock up the office until I can come back up. So you'll need either to step out into the hall while I do it or come with me."

"I'll just wait in the hall. Maybe I can get some other impressions while I wait." And I stepped out of the office.

As Officer Trousdale took the statue carefully in her arms, closed and locked up the office, and began to descend the stairs, I suddenly heard a popping noise and felt a surge, almost as palpable as a slap, of something that felt like anger being directed toward me. I realized Jessamine had been right, and the force field had collapsed. And somebody wasn't happy about it!

And then Jessamine giggled. *"That did it! I'm sure I can go in now."*

When Trousdale came back and unlocked the door to Jessamine's office, there was no problem bringing Jessamine in with me.

"I'm feeling I need to go into the inner office," I said, so Officer Trousdale led the way. And then I added, "I'm going to be talking a bit here, but unless I address you, I'm not expecting an answer. It's the...um...spirit of Ms. Steele I'll be talking to." I said this almost apologetically because I still wasn't used to telling uninvolved strangers about how I connected with the spirits I worked with.

Trousdale nodded with an amused smile and folded her arms while she watched me.

I looked around the office for a few moments. One thing I noticed was a line of salt on all the outside windows in this office. Obviously, Jessamine had taken my advice and tried to protect her space from negative influences with salt. But I supposed that wouldn't have done much good if Jordan had already set up a force field of some kind with the statue in the outer office.

There was an outline of Jessamine's body still on the floor in front of the filing cabinet. I stopped before I got that far and said, "Okay, try to remember what you were doing at the filing cabinet. Just go through it all, if you can." And I closed my eyes and tried to clear my mind, allowing Jessamine to take over the action and re-experience what had happened to her on Sunday.

"I was trying to find all the Aquavest files," she said. *"I had emailed Ernie and all of my friends, including you, from home, to tell everyone what I'd found out about Cristien and the company accounts. And I came to the office looking for all the company files because I thought if I could read them again, I might get some clues as to what had happened and how Cristien had duped us all. So I was at the file cabinet. Oh, now I remember. Something slammed into me from behind and pushed me down on the floor. There was a sharp pain in my back and chest. I felt someone turn my head toward the filing cabinet. And then I heard whoever it was leaving the office."*

"When you..." I stopped for a moment, thinking I should try to be delicate, but I couldn't figure out how so I just went on. "When you died, did your spirit depart the body, and did you see anything?"

There was a long pause. *"I don't think I died right away,"* she said finally. *"I remember lying there on the floor, thinking, 'I can't just lie here. I have to sort out the files. I have to find out what happened to Aquavest.' Then I got up, and tried to look in the files again, but I couldn't move anything, so I called you. And you came."* She said the last three words with a kind of gratitude. *"But I didn't know I was in spirit. I just needed to call you, because I thought you could use your psychic ability to help me to figure out what was wrong with the files."*

"I've been wondering about that," I said. "How did you call me if you were in spirit?"

"I...I don't know. I just remember thinking that if anyone would know how to make things right, it would be you. So I went over to my phone, and I tried to pick it up. But I couldn't do it. That confused me. Finally, I thought, 'I don't need the phone,' and I gave up trying to pick it up, and I just focused my whole consciousness on calling you through it, so you'd know I needed you to come here and help me find out what had happened. But it was sort of strange—because I was still walking around, I wasn't sure I was really dead. So I honestly thought I could still call you."

"Well, somehow it worked. But there are a couple of other questions I'd like you to think about now that we're here. First of all, how long were you in the office before you were stabbed?"

"Oh, not long. I got to the office about 10:10. I remember thinking about the repeated numbers when I glanced at the car clock as I was parking downstairs. When I got up here, I checked my email to see if any of you had gotten back to me yet. And then I came over to the file cabinet. So I was in the office—oh, maybe twenty minutes."

"Then where did the person who stabbed you come from? Was that person outside? Did he or she come in from the outer office, do you think?"

"I wouldn't think so. I locked the outer office door when I came in. When I'm here on the weekends, I always do that."

"So nobody rang to get in? You didn't buzz anybody up?"

"No," she said, *"I'm sure I didn't."*

"Then that must mean whoever stabbed you somehow had a means of getting into the office without your help or assistance. Maybe that person came up without your realizing it."

I thought about the interview the police had done with someone in a nearby building, who had seen a woman in a coat and hat like Jessamine's entering the building at about 10 o'clock.

"Jessamine, did you wear your black leather coat and hat to the office on Sunday?"

"No, I didn't. I wore the wool coat I'd gone to New York with. But I was warm when I got here, so I left it in the car."

That meant Jessamine wasn't the woman the neighbor had seen. And she had come in a little after 10 o'clock anyway. Then some of the pieces fell together for me.

I turned and looked behind me and realized there was actually a door in the opposite wall. It appeared to lead to another room or perhaps a closet. I hadn't remembered it was there because its depth extended into the outer

The Lawyer Who Died Trying

office. It had clearly been an addition to the offices rather than a part of the original building plan.

"What does that door lead to?"

"It's a powder room," said Jessamine. *"I had it added with the building owner's permission so I wouldn't have to go down the hall to the common restroom."*

"Did you hear anyone coming up behind you just before you were stabbed?"

Again she was silent for a moment. Then she said, *"No, I don't remember hearing anyone."*

"Then maybe the person was already here in your office when you got here. Hiding in the powder room. And wearing a hat and coat very like your own!"

I had both a picture and a time sequence in my mind now of what had taken place in the office that morning. But as hard as I tried, I couldn't get a lock on who had been in the office or even whether it had been a man or a woman. And apparently neither could Jessamine. And I wondered again if there was still some kind of glamour blocking my inner vision. If so, then the most likely suspect was Jordan Steele.

I looked at Officer Trousdale and said, "Officer, would you mind dialing up Detective Flanagan for me and letting me use your phone to talk with him? I'd like to share what Ms. Steele has told me with him."

I'd brought some of the Locke and Hobbes papers with me to work on while I waited in the parking lot outside Jessamine's lawyer's office. But at a few minutes to 4 o'clock, I packed everything away, got out of my car, and started across the lot to the building's back entrance. As I was nearing the door, Jordan Steele suddenly came around the side of the building. The moment I saw him, I automatically increased my own protective energy field. He reached the door before I did and leaned against it for a moment to keep me from opening it.

I wasn't afraid of the man, but his interference did make me a little angry.

"I have an appointment upstairs," I said. "If you don't mind, I'd like to go inside the building. Now."

"I know you have an appointment. I also know you're planning to help my mother get custody of my child. And I just want to let you know that if you don't stop interfering, you *will* be sorry." This last line, right out of a bad movie script, was delivered with a piercing look and a tight smile, and I thought Jordan Steele would have made an excellent Grade B actor.

One thing he hadn't mentioned was that he was aware Jessamine was still hanging out on this plane as my shadow. At least, I was pretty sure he knew that, too, since there'd been such a surge of anger when the force field in her office had collapsed.

"That sounds perilously like a threat," I said. "Should I report it to the police?"

"It's just a friendly warning," he said, though his tight smile didn't change. "But I don't intend to let anyone else have custody of my child. He should be with his father."

"Well, thank you for the warning." I thought I said it calmly, though I was feeling quite a bit of anger by this time. "Now, please let me into the building. I don't want to be late."

He stepped aside, shaking his head a little as if I were a hopeless case, and I went inside. I did my best to release the anger while I was going up the elevator to Frederick Dowling's law office, and by the time I reached his reception room, I was pretty much back to normal. But I nevertheless kept the mental force field around myself.

As soon as his secretary let him know I'd arrived, Dowling came out to the reception room to greet me and lead me to his office.

Mrs. Steele was already sitting in his office, and when she took my hand during our introduction, she said, "Please call me Althea. Jessamine told me so much about you that I feel I already know you. And she assured me you're quite courageous, so I'm confident you won't let my son run over you in the hearing."

Dowling and I took seats as well. Then I looked from her to Dowling and said, "I just encountered Jordan outside this building. He was warning me off from getting any further involved in this case."

"What did he say?" asked Dowling.

"He said if I continued to help you get custody, Mrs. Steele, I'd be sorry."

At this, Althea looked pained, and Dowling was clearly incensed.

"That should be reported to the police," Dowling urged. "A murder has been committed, and I gather Steele is a prime suspect because of the custody battle. So if he's threatening you, you should be sure to let the police know."

"I plan to call the detective who's working the case just as soon as we're finished here." Then I turned to Jordan's mother. "But if you don't mind, Althea, I'd really like to get your take on your son. What is it about him that causes you to want to keep your grandson from him?"

She looked serious and perhaps a little anxious. Finally she said, "My son is very cold. He's very hard. I think perhaps he has no remorse over the things he does. When he was a child, if I were to reprimand him for doing something wrong, he would just glare at me without answering, as if I were the one at fault. Now, mind you, he could put on a pleasant enough face if he wanted to get people to do things his way. But if they didn't, he was very good at getting even with them—and usually in devious ways. I wasn't at all surprised when Jessamine divorced him, and I'd hate to see my only grandson under the control of someone who is so hard and remorseless."

I nodded, thinking her assessment of Jordan Steele aptly fit the picture Bernice had drawn of a sociopathic personality.

She continued, "Now, I've berated myself for years, wondering if I did anything to contribute to my son's cold nature, or if there was anything I could have done to change it. My marriage to his father was strained from the beginning, and when Jordan was born, my husband was hard on him, even from babyhood. And unfortunately, I think he was extreme in his punishments when Jordan got a little older. And maybe I didn't run interference enough, because I was afraid of my husband, too. He was a very mean man. Eventually, his cruelty to me and to Jordan caused me to divorce him, but I've often worried that my divorce came too late to do Jordan any good—he was already a warped personality. Anyway, my taking Jeffrey would be an act of contrition for my having failed with Jordan. Perhaps I could make up for my earlier mistakes by protecting my grandson from a similar kind of abuse."

"We do find that abused children often grow up to be abusive parents," agreed Dowling.

"I've heard that," Althea nodded. "My primary fear, though, is that Jordan may try to run you off somehow. I know Jessamine was worried that he'd become involved in some sort of cult. From what she described, it sounded Satanic to me."

"Actually, what he appears to be involved in isn't Satanic, per se, although there may be some similarities. But it's a form of Hindu ritual, rather than from Western culture. Nevertheless, I think it could be equally dark and negative in its results if it's practiced with evil intent. And I think Jordan does have a certain amount of power he's able to wield. I've felt the force of it a couple of times, and I intend to keep my own protective shield up as a result."

"You were saying something about that on the phone," said Dowling. "So you really believe in this magic stuff? I mean, you don't think it's just superstition?"

I looked at him steadily for a couple of moments before answering, "I believe there is power in intention. And I believe that the power of intention can build through the channel of a focused mind. It's my belief that when magic works, this is why it works—intention channeled through a focused mind. And it doesn't matter whether the intention is what we would call good or evil, it's the intention combined with the focus that gets results."

Dowling nodded thoughtfully, and I glanced at Althea, who also nodded. So I continued.

"Now, much magic is supposed to operate through the interaction of human intention and some sort of other dimensional spirit that the magical practitioner has invoked—be it the spirit of a dead person, an angelic being, an earth spirit, a demon, or what have you. Many modern scientists would like us to believe that these spirit entities don't really exist and that those who believe they do are just superstitious and perhaps uneducated. But as one who has had a lot of traffic with one form of other dimensional consciousnesses—namely ghosts—I can't deny the possibility that various others of these traditional kinds of spirits may also exist. And if they exist, there's always the possibility somebody may invoke them. And if they're invoked, there's always the possibility they may have some sort of influence on the physical plane. And of course, sometimes that influence may be harmful. And denying their existence isn't going to stop any part of this sequence. Hence, as I told you this morning, I have a healthy respect for—and usually try to stay a safe distance from—magical practitioners whose intention is to do harm."

"And you think Jordan might be one of those?" asked Dowling.

"I can't say for certain. But Jessamine did. And she said she had hard copies of some of the materials he was teaching in his workshops that would prove he was including Kali worship as a part of his teachings."

"I have the original of those files under lock and key here in my office," admitted Dowling.

"Good," I said. "And just this morning, I got word that I may be able to access at least a portion of Jordan's materials that are in the part of his teachings that include Kali worship. Now, in my original deposition, I was only addressing the idea that Kali worship can be corrupted—just as any religion can—by practitioners with negative intentions. But it's possible that by the time we go into court, I'll have had a chance to look at more of the materials Jordan is teaching and I'll have more clarity on exactly what he's teaching, especially with respect to this alleged distortion of the worship of Kali."

"That would be very helpful," said Dowling. "And I hope you'll keep me posted on what you find out."

I agreed to do so, and feeling the interview was over, I stood up.

But before I could leave, Althea said, "I just want you to know how grateful I am that you're willing to continue working to keep Jeffrey safe from harm, especially now that Jessamine is...is gone."

"How is Jeffrey holding up?" I asked.

She shook her head. "He's sad, but not inconsolable. At first he cried a lot, but then he calmed down, and he's been able to play a bit without suddenly bursting into tears. Of course, since we haven't had the body released yet, we haven't had a funeral for Jessamine, though I've tried to make some preparations for it. But I think we'll all have more closure once the funeral is behind us. And of course, if we find out who was responsible for killing her and why, we'll be able to put her death behind us and move on."

"You don't have to hurry the grieving process," I said. "I'm sure Jeffrey is going to miss his mother for a long time. But it does occur to me you might want to distract him from time to time so he doesn't focus too much energy on missing her."

She nodded, and I went on. "Speaking of distractions, have you made any plans for Halloween?"

"No, we haven't."

"Then perhaps you'd like to bring Jeffrey to a party that's being held at my place on Friday. It isn't my party, although I'll be there reading Tarot cards. But it will have a lot of activities for children, including a magician, games, special cupcakes, and candy for the kids' trick-or-treat bags. If you'd like to come, I'll give you the address and a phone number to which you can R.S.V.P."

"That would be very nice!" said Althea, so I got out one of my cards and added Bernice's telephone number to it.

"When you call just let whoever answers know that I invited you. And you're welcome to come, too, if you like," I added to Dowling.

"Thanks, but I have plans for Friday."

I smiled, shook their hands, said my goodbyes, and headed out of his office. It was quitting time in the D.C. area, and all the highways both in and out of Alexandria were going to be hairy to travel on for the next couple of hours. I decided to head back to Bernice's and make a stop at a local market on the way for the steaks I'd promised Greg.

As I pulled into traffic and began to make my slow way toward the market and then home, my mind went back to what I'd said to Frederick Dowling and Althea Steele about magic working as intention focused through mind.

I was reminded of what Bernice had said that morning about Michelle overcoming her dyslexia and raising her I.Q. when she finally had both hemispheres of her brain stimulated through the proper course work.

Then I thought about Jessamine, who, though dead, was able to focus all her consciousness on getting through to me by telephone and—while it may not have registered on the phone records themselves either at her end or at mine—she succeeded, and I heard her call for help.

And then I thought about what must be involved for me to be able to tune in to people's motives and desires through Tarot symbolism. I decided that as soon as I had dropped by a grocery store and had my steaks in hand, I'd go discuss all of these ideas with Bernice.

Bernice and I were sipping tea, and I'd allowed myself one coconut and macadamia nut cookie, which I was nibbling while we talked about the significance of the workings of mind and brain power that I'd been considering all day.

"One educational psychologist of my acquaintance," mused Bernice, "thinks the right brain of the human being is what has access to the past, present, and future. It's what can tap into everything that's beyond time and space.

"Our left brain is just what we access in making our way through our word-and number-based, waking, walking-around, verbally-thinking, time-based reality. But the right brain is the portal to what I think of as the 'Star Gate of Everything Else That Is, Was, or Ever Will Be,' otherwise known in Jungian psychological terms as the universal or collective unconscious. In its all-knowingness, it's not constrained by language, or time, or space. And it's our right brains we tap into when we put our left brains to sleep."

"So it's my right brain I'm using when I have precognitive dreams, then."

"That's what current psychology and brain science suggests. We dream primarily in pictures or images. When words are used, they're very often puns, or plays on words. I remember having a dream once in which my family was living in tents—or more specifically in little pup tents. Later, I realized that was a message to me that because of some significant changes we were about to make, our lives were going to become 'intense.' I've always thought that was one of the funnier messages from my subconscious."

"Well," I mused, "if we empty the mind, as we do in meditation, then we're really quieting the left brain."

"That's true."

"And if we focus the mind on a specific goal, we have a pretty good chance of manifesting that goal."

"That also seems to be true. There was a study done at one of the Ivy League schools where some business majors were encouraged to write down their goals for the next twenty years, and others were discouraged from writing down their goals. Twenty years later, the researchers checked in with the grads and found the ones who'd written down their goals had all achieved everything they'd written and more, while those who'd stayed unfocused hadn't achieved much at all but had spent their careers floundering."

"Did the researchers consider that they'd probably ruined the careers of those they'd discouraged from focusing?"

Bernice laughed. "So far as I know, there were no moral judgments made on the study, but I get your point. Nonetheless, it does seem that the more one is able to focus, especially on a goal that one can visualize with sensory experiences, the more likely it is that the goal will be realized."

"Then what do you think about the idea from magical ritual of invoking a denizen of the spirit world to assist in fulfilling a magical outcome?"

"I'd say that as long as the practitioner is able to visualize the spirit he's calling on or visualize the outcome he's seeking, there's a good chance his magic will work."

"So...how does this fit in with Jordan's being able to create an energy field at a distance? How do you think he's doing it?"

"Probably the same way body builders build big muscles. Start small and keep working. Take small steps, stretching each day until you can take longer steps. Jordan is working with energy, and he may be calling on the goddess Kali to help send his mental energy, but this doesn't mean he was able to do what he does when he first started. He's been working at it for years. And the more success he has with transmitting energy, the bigger the energy field he'll be able to transmit the next time."

I nodded, still thinking about how all the powers of the mind might fit together. Then I asked, "Do you think I'm being foolish to believe the little force field I put around myself can protect me from Jordan Steele?"

The Lawyer Who Died Trying

Bernice looked at me and blinked a few times. Finally, she said, "I hope not. I like you, and I don't want you to get hurt." She stirred her tea for a moment, then added. "But how long have you been arming yourself with a personal force field?"

"Since I was about 12," I said. "That's when I first read about how to do it. And during Desert Shield and Desert Storm, I never went out of my tent without surrounding myself with protection."

"Well," she smiled, "I don't know if that's proof that it works, but it sounds like maybe it is."

Just then the phone rang. Bernice went to pick it up, but it turned out it was Ernie Redmond for me.

"I've got some news I think you may want to add to your information pile with respect to Jessamine Steele's killing and the future of the Aquavest company. We're going to hold a special meeting this Thursday evening at seven p.m. to talk about it." He paused for a moment before continuing, "I was informed earlier this evening by the New York City Police that Cristien Frandsen, our erstwhile inventor, has been murdered!"

Chapter 15

"What happened to Cristien, Ernie?"

"I don't have a lot of details, but it appears to have been a murder that was intended to look like a mugging."

Bernice looked alarmed when she heard me ask the question.

"It's about Cristien Frandsen," I said to her, putting my hand over the receiver for a moment. "He's been found dead in New York!" Then to Ernie I said, "Do they have any idea who killed him?"

"No one has told me anything directly. I was contacted because the NYPD found my business card in Cristien's wallet. I immediately connected them with the Alexandria police, because of the relationship between Cristien and Jessamine, and the proximity in time of the two murders. Of course, there's a lot of speculation now that whoever killed Cristien may also have killed Jessamine. And one other little piece of information I managed to pick up was that by the decomposition of Cristien's body, there's also speculation that he was already dead by the time Jessamine went looking for him in New York."

I thought about this for a couple of beats, then said, "Jessamine told me Cristien was really tight with his lawyer. That's one of the reasons she went to New York, wasn't it? And her email suggested she suspected Cristien's lawyer of helping embezzle the company money. So...doesn't that suggest that the lawyer might have killed Cristien? We all saw Cristien alive on Thursday night. Then he checked out of the hotel, went back to New York, and was killed before Jessamine went looking for him on Friday. It seems to me the most logical suspect would have been the person he was working with in New York."

"I agree, and I made that suggestion to the police. Of course, they want to find him, whoever he really is, because the Alexandria Police also want to question him about Jessamine's murder." He paused for a moment, then continued, "There was also a hint of a suggestion that Jessamine might have killed Cristien when she went to New York. Personally, I think that's nonsense, but she *was* there on Friday, at least by mid-day, and he was killed probably by mid-day."

The Lawyer Who Died Trying

Jessamine was suddenly right behind me. *"I can hear what he's saying,"* she practically shouted. *"I didn't do any such thing!"* It felt as if she was pounding me on the back to be sure I got her point.

"Just a second Ernie," I said and set the phone down. I walked a few steps away and spoke reassuringly to Jessamine. "I know you didn't do it, so please be calm. I'll find a way to assure the police that they need to look for somebody passing himself off as William Love." When I felt she was calm, I went back to the phone.

"Is there anything else going on that I should know about, Ernie? For example, is there any way the police will be able to identify Cristien's lawyer?"

"Funny you should ask that. There was a meeting several months ago of the corporate officials, and Cristien brought his lawyer. He introduced him as William Love, who was a partner with a firm up in New York. But the fellow made an issue about not wanting to be photographed, so he wouldn't stand with us in the 'grip and grin' photos we had taken. Later, though, at a little party, our hired photographer got a shot of him scarfing down canapés, and I've got that shot in an album our company secretary put together for me. So I'm passing it on to the police in hopes they'll be able to identify him."

"It occurs to me also that someone ought to be watching the banks in the Cayman Islands and on Jersey where the company funds were switched to."

"That, too, is already covered. We've notified the banks that the transfers were made with embezzled funds and that the person who may try to access them is a murder suspect. We've asked them to put holds on the accounts, pending our proof that at least one of the signatures that was used to transfer funds was forged. So, in the terminology of my profession, maybe we're not in as deep a cavity as we thought at first!"

"I'm glad to hear it, Ernie, and to know that you're making some progress."

"Anyway, I just wanted to let you know we'll be having a little meeting of the shareholders on Thursday. It will be at the Hyatt again, and I wanted to be sure you and Dr. Wise were apprised of it. I know she's not a shareholder, but she has a level head, and that's always valuable when we're dealing with people who may be emotional."

"Well, thanks for the invitation. I'll extend it to Bernice and see if she's available." And I rang off, thinking that if I did pay her a month's rent with some of my stock, she would be a shareholder before long.

I told Bernice all the details that Ernie had shared, plus about the invitation he'd made to both of us to attend the Aquavest meeting on Thursday. When I mentioned the part about his feeling her being on hand would be valuable in case anybody became emotional, she laughed.

"That sounds like Ernie," she said, "covering all his bases. He'd like to have me on hand for free psychotherapy, just in case its needed!"

"Oh, my gosh!" I gasped. "I've had a brain warp all day long! Too much going on in my life, I guess, but I totally forgot to make the description sheets Mike and Michelle asked me to edit and print for the light boxes they're going to use at the Halloween party. Your mentioning covering all the bases reminded me of it. And now I don't have time to do it before I go over to Greg's for dinner."

"Do you think you can work on them between classes tomorrow at school?"

"Probably. I'll try to remember to take the disk with me. At least I can do any editing at school, then print them up when I get home tomorrow."

"Well," said Bernice, "I'll make a note on my calendar to save a couple of hours to help you tomorrow evening. The displays won't be set up until Thursday anyway, so we'll still have time to get the light boxes ready before they're needed."

"Thank you so much!" I said, pulling the steaks out of Bernice's refrigerator that I'd bought to take to Greg's and dashing for the back door.

"And maybe," she added, "once you've lulled that hunky cop you're dating with steaks and a little romance, you can find out if the police know any more than Ernie did about Cristien's and Jessamine's murders."

As it turned out Greg didn't know much more than Ernie did about what had happened to Cristien, but he did know how to toss a salad, bake a potato, and smother a steak.

Over an after-dinner liquer, he returned to the question of Cristien. He did know that Cristien's death was the reason Flanagan had hung on to Jessamine's crime scene until this afternoon.

"Our department got the word from the NYPD that Cristien's body had been found just before Flanagan was going to release the scene on Monday. So he held it over for a day so he could make sure our department had copies of all the Aquavest files. I didn't tell you about it this morning when we talked because I'd only just heard about it myself. And remember, I'm not working this case, so it's not my place to say anything until it's become more widely known. Of course, Frandsen's murder makes it all the more important that the police have information on the principals involved in the Aquavest company."

"By which I assume you mean anybody who might be a suspect—people with motive, means, and opportunity."

"Right," he grinned, "you remembered that!"

"Hey, I've learned a few things from hanging out with you. I'm not just here for food and sex."

"Maybe not, but you have to admit those are two very good reasons for dropping by," he said as he leaned over to kiss me.

"Very good reasons," I agreed, "but before we move on to a main course of either one, I have a few things I'd like to discuss."

"For example?"

"Like, are the police in either Alexandria or New York speculating that Jessamine might have killed Cristien?"

"That's one scenario, though if she did, it doesn't get us any closer to finding out who murdered *her*."

"Well, I just wanted you to know that she says she didn't do it. Should I tell that to Flanagan? Might a ghostly denial be in the same category as a deathbed confession?"

He laughed. "That's an interesting thought! But do tell Flanagan. Though it's really the NYPD who would be looking into that possibility—Frandsen's death is not in our jurisdiction. But speculation about her possibly being his killer could hold up the release of Jessamine's body for a while longer, just in case they have specific questions they want answered that haven't been answered already by our autopsy."

"I understand that, but I really don't believe she did it because in her present state, she has no reason not to tell the truth."

"Good point," he grinned. "So did you learn anything useful while you were in Jessamine's office today?"

"Not a whole lot, except that I'm pretty sure the person who killed her was hiding in the little bathroom in her inner office when she came in on Sunday. She still doesn't know who it was. She didn't see who was behind her when she was stabbed—she really didn't know that she was stabbed, just that she was on the floor and needed to get up—and when she did get up, there was nobody else there.

"You mean whoever it was didn't hang around to see whether the job had been effective?"

"It seems that way."

He nodded thoughtfully. Then he smiled a little. "The only other thing I heard was that you had Trousdale take a statue into custody for obstructing justice. What was that about?"

"That, I think, was Jordan Steele, getting in the way of our inspection of the crime scene."

I explained how Jessamine had been blocked from going into the office because of some kind of energy field emanating from the statue, how I couldn't go in either while she was in my auric field, and how the blockage seemed to collapse once the statue had been removed.

"My only explanation for it is that Jordan Steele somehow set up the block to keep Jessamine from assisting anyone who might be susceptible to her influence from learning any details about the murder. That's why right now he's my biggest suspect. That and the fact that he threatened me this afternoon."

"He *what?*" Greg was obviously upset by this disclosure.

"Yeah. That's another little detail I forgot about—I don't know where my mind is these days—too much stress I guess."

"So how did he threaten you? Did he call you?"

"No. After I talked to you this morning, I got a call from Jessamine's lawyer, Frederick Dowling. Now that Jessamine is dead, Jordan's mother is seeking custody of Jeffrey Steele. Anyway, after I went to Jessamine's office, I went over to her lawyer's office. And Jordan Steele was outside."

Suddenly, as I was explaining the chronology of my day to Greg, I began to feel very spacey, like somebody had given me a shot of codeine. I closed my eyes and put my hand to my head.

"What's wrong?" asked Greg, putting his hand on my shoulder.

"I don't know, but I think it has to do with what I'm talking about. Give me a minute to see if I can clear it."

I sat forward on the couch, closed my eyes, and visualized myself being surrounded by white light. When I felt totally immersed in the protective shield, I began to visualize expanding it, moving it out further and further so that it extended several yards from me in all directions. And then, as an added protection, I visualized placing mirrors around the outside of the field, so that anything being directed at me would bounce back on whoever was sending it. Once I felt my protection was stable, I relaxed again and opened my eyes.

"Okay, that feels better. I think somebody was messing with my mind and trying to scramble my thoughts—making me feel drunk or drugged. But I think I'm okay now."

Greg looked really concerned. "Can you tell me more about what you were talking about before?"

"Yeah, I think so. Where was I?"

"You were saying he had been waiting for you outside Jessamine's lawyer's office this afternoon."

"That's right. Okay, he told me he didn't want me staying involved in the custody suit, and that if I didn't back off, I'd be sorry. I was intending to call Flanagan and let him know about the encounter, but...I seem to have forgotten to do that."

I rubbed my forehead, thinking how the spacey spell had come on all of a sudden. Then I remembered how I'd felt the blow to the top of my head the night before while I was reading Jordan's cards. But my mind seemed clear now. So I recounted to Greg all the times that I'd felt what I was pretty sure was Jordan's energy from a distance—last night while reading the cards, in Jessamine's office this afternoon, and just now in Greg's living room.

"I don't know how he's doing it," I said. "I don't know how he knew I was reading his cards last night. And I don't know how he knew I'd be at Jessamine's lawyer's office this afternoon. But one thing is pretty clear to me now. He's got a lot more power than I was giving him credit for, which says that he's into some really heavy magic. And until all this is settled, I'm going to have to keep up a bigger shield than I've ever needed before!"

Chapter 16
Wednesday, October 29th

While I was on campus between my first and second classes, I popped the disk Mike had given me at breakfast the day before into my computer and looked at the descriptions of the displays the twins and their friends would be setting up for their Halloween haunted backyard. The text was really more story-like than descriptive, offering some of the spookier aspects of some of the world's most famous ghosts.

Included were some that had pop-culture appeal—like ghosts of Blackbeard the pirate, who was still protecting his buried treasure, and of Ann Boleyn, Henry the VIII's beheaded second wife, with her head tucked underneath her arm. Also included was Abraham Lincoln, whose ghost I was surprised to find had been sighted over time in at least four different places.

There were lots of literary ghosts—that of Marley and all the ghosts of Christmas from Dickens' *A Christmas Carol*, Banquo's ghost from *Macbeth*, the ghost of Hamlet's father from *Hamlet*, and "Great Caesar's ghost." And there was the "ghost" or specter of the Headless Horseman that chased poor Icabod Crane in *The Legend of Sleepy Hollow*.

There were a variety of ghosts from the infamous Louisiana plantation The Myrtles, known as "the most haunted house" in America. And there was the Mummy, which, while not strictly a ghost, was nevertheless a returnee from the dead, otherwise known as a revenant, whose story had grown out of the discovery of King Tut's Tomb early in the 20th century.

And there was Annie Grace, the ghost of the pre-Civil War slave who had died on the property now owned by Bernice where the Halloween party would take place. I noticed the twins were going to put this station near the little garden house that had once served as Annie Grace's kitchen, where she'd been murdered with one of her own iron skillets. I felt a little touch of pride when I read what the twins had written about Annie Grace, since I'd been the one who had helped bring through the truth about her death, after which she'd been willing to move on to higher realms.

Finally—and I thought this might have been planned to give a cheerful conclusion to the spooky show—there was going to be a station for Casper, the Friendly Ghost.

Honora Finkelstein & Susan Smily

I had no clue what kinds of displays the twins and their friends would set up for the party, but I was pretty sure that with the art and theater departments involved, it was going to be a pretty good show.

I copy-edited the text of the stories, then selected a nice script that would be large enough to read from a couple of feet away. Finally, I tried to make the text fit into the six–and-a-half by ten inch rectangular space the twins had specified as the needed dimensions for the light boxes.

Just as I was finishing up, I heard a little knock, and looking up, I saw Michelle standing at the opening to my cubicle. She had a box in her arms that looked as if it could hold about three reams of paper.

"Hey, you," I said with a grin, "I have your light-box texts all finished."

"And I have a printout of all the stuff we got off Jordan Steele's website. I was reading a little more of the advanced stuff, and I'm kinda creeped out. I think I don't want to be his best friend."

"I'm not sure he wants friends," I said. "Maybe worshippers or devout subjects or possibly slaves. But probably not friends."

"Well, brace yourself while you read it. There's a very subtle undercurrent in it that seems to sneer at sympathy, empathy, morality, and ethics. Strength, power, and winning are considered virtues—but none of the softer feelings are permitted."

"Thanks for the warning, sweetie. I'm now forewarned and forearmed!"

When I got home that afternoon, Bernice was waiting for me as she'd promised. I went upstairs and ran off the copies of the light-box stories, then changed clothes and headed back downstairs, where she had tea in travel mugs and freshly made lemon cookies, "To fortify us while we work," she said.

She led me out to the garage where all the Halloween paraphernalia were stored. The light boxes were on wooden stands about five and a half feet high. The boxes themselves were open at the top, with the front side open, and just slightly smaller than a standard sheet of paper. I examined one of the boxes and saw the light inside was a night-light size bulb. Each of the stands had a wire and plug running out of the bottom that presumably would plug into an electrical line when the time came to light everything up.

"Very elaborate!" I said to Bernice.

"Oh, you don't know the half of it," she replied resignedly. "Mike likes Halloween better than Christmas, I think. We've been doing these parties for years, and since the twins got to college and involved their friends, the productions have become bigger and more outrageous every year. But the displays are easier to set up now than they used to be—at least we keep the light-boxes from year to year, and we probably have enough electrical cords to wire Disneyland."

"So what do we have to do?"

"First we have to test all the lines to make sure they still work—sort of like testing Christmas tree lights before you put them on a tree. Just plug them into the line over there on the wall. If any of the bulbs needs changing, it's easier to do it before we put the text into the boxes."

Once we'd tested all the lines and bulbs, she handed me a roll of silver duct tape and we began taping the text pages carefully into the boxes. Since there were only a dozen boxes, we were through with the project in about half an hour.

Just as we were closing the garage door and turning back toward the house, I had one of those moments of *déjà vu* as I saw a woman in black slacks, a black leather coat, and a matching slouch hat coming toward us from the side of the house. Then I realized it was Maggie, because in her hand she held a heavy-looking book that had to be the promised coursework for Jordan Steele's self-improvement course.

"Hi, ladies," she said brightly when she came up to us. "I saw you from the driveway." Handing me the massive tome, she added, "Here's the course workbook. You can keep it as long as you really need it, but I do want it back because I review some of the principles every few weeks. But just give me a call when you're finished with it, and I'll drop back by and pick it up."

"Thanks so much, Maggie," said Bernice. "Would you like to come in for a cup of tea and some lemon cookies?"

"Oh, I can't stay. I have a showing of one of those wonderful old houses down in Old Town in just a little while."

"One of the haunted ones?" asked Bernice, raising an eyebrow.

"Hey, just among the three of us, all those old houses are haunted," said Maggie laughing. "But oddly that's what most of my clients want. There's some weird sort of prestige about having a ghost in your house in that part of town."

"It's strange what things people find necessary in order to feel they're keeping up with the Joneses, isn't it?" I said, grinning at Maggie.

She nodded and laughed. Then looking a little more serious, she asked, "Oh, will we see you ladies tomorrow night at the Hyatt?"

"Yes, I think so," I agreed.

Bernice nodded and said, "Probably. News seems to be breaking daily, and we don't want to miss the next installment."

When Maggie had made her departure, Bernice and I went back into the kitchen to finish our tea and look over the massive book Maggie had brought. Glancing over the chapter headings, Bernice said, "This does look very much like any normal self-improvement course from the human potential movement—and there have been dozens over the last thirty-five years."

"Well, let me go grab the stuff Michelle ran off from Jordan's web site. I left it in my car when I came in because there was so much of it. We should probably compare the texts side-by-side to see if there are any differences."

When I'd retrieved the box of printouts, I lifted the whole stack out and put it on the table. Michelle had separated the different parts with green sheets of paper, so I put the three sections in three different piles. The first one was about the same size as the book Maggie had brought. The second was a little bit thicker. And the third was much smaller.

"Why don't I take Maggie's book and this first pile, which should be similar, and see if there are any differences between them? I've had years of comparing student papers with their sources, so I'm used to matching somewhat parallel texts. And while I'm doing that and getting a sense of what Jordan teaches to beginners, you take a look at the second level of the course and see what you think of it. And since we don't have to give back the set of papers Michelle brought me, feel free to write in the margins if you have any thoughts or comments. And fold down the corners of any pages you write on so I'll know to look at them."

"That works for me," she agreed, getting a mug of writing implements from the telephone table and pulling the cookie plate toward her as she sat down.

We read in relative silence for nearly an hour, each engrossed in our tasks and both clearly assessing what we were reading with a critical eye. Every once in a while, I'd hear Bernice snort at something she was reading, pick up her pencil, and scribble furiously in the margin of the paper. Then silence would prevail again until the next snort.

For my part, I had to agree that what I was reading was straight-line human potential and self-development rhetoric, as for example, the following:

"There has never been and never will be another person exactly like you, with your unique talents and gifts."

"You have not just the possibility but the responsibility of becoming the very best you can be."

"What the mind can conceive, and the heart can believe, you can achieve."

And of course, the ever-popular and often quoted translation from the poet Goethe,

> "Whatever you can do, or dream you can, begin it.
> Boldness has genius, power, and magic in it."

Okay, these kinds of things were all good, valuable, positive-thinking insights, intended to get people feeling good about themselves and their abilities. Nothing I was reading seemed the least bit harmful, and if some of these ideas were used as personal mantras, they probably would help people see themselves as beautiful, capable winners.

Bernice looked up and said, "We're sitting here practically in the dark," and she got up and flipped switches so the overhead lights came on. When she did, I noticed that Freud the Cat had inched close to me on the bench I was sitting on and practically had her nose in my lap.

The Lawyer Who Died Trying

"I don't know about you," I said, "but I get a little obsessive when I have a task like this to do. I didn't notice it was getting dark, and I didn't notice Freud had come for a visit." To make up for of my obsessiveness, I gave Freud a few strokes to get her purring.

"Well, for my money, it's time for some supper. Maybe followed by a large dish of something with lots of chocolate on it."

"In need of endorphins, perhaps?" I asked.

She sighed with some irritation. "It's not bad material, but I've read it all before."

"Do you mean figuratively or literally?"

"Oh, literally! There's material from Carl Jung, Fritz Perls, Werner Erhardt—you name the psychotherapist or pop culture guru, and there's a good chance his works have been lifted by Jordan Steele. Hey, you can't really go wrong if you've plagiarized from the best, now can you?"

"I was pretty sure I'd read most of what was in my portion in Napoleon Hill, Anthony Robbins, Wayne Dyer, and Deepak Chopra."

"Well, there you go. I bet he built the basis of this course from the shelves of the public library. Or maybe the New Age section of one of the local bookstores."

I nodded, then countered, "But there's nothing to stop him for selling psychological retreads, is there? I mean unless he gets really famous and the people who originally wrote this material sue him for plagiarizing their material?"

She shrugged. "He seems to have gotten away with it so far."

We looked at each other in silence for a few moments. Then I said, "But that's not the point is it?"

"No. The point is that he pulls people in with tried and true materials, guaranteed to get them moving, breaking old habit patterns, giving their personal best, setting and achieving goals, and getting in touch with their inner power. Then, if Jessamine is to be believed, somewhere along the line he moves them beyond just their personal best and their power to achieve whatever they can imagine for themselves to another level altogether—where they become involved in power *over* others. So far I haven't seen any of that material in what I'm reading in this portion, but given what Mike said about a psychological test that divides those who will conclude their training from those who'll be given further options, I'd bet the end of this book will point the way to it." And she flipped to the back of the text.

We found the test, then we found two versions of where a congratulatory letter to the student would go next, based on which category his final exam would place him in.

Bernice scanned the text in silence for a few lines, then said, "Okay, here we go. This seems to be the letter that will go to those students who are being given the option of continuing the course." And she began to read.

"*Congratulations on completing this portion of the course. You have accomplished many goals in the last few months, broken many barriers, and have reached the level that many people would define as self mastery. Would you be surprised to learn that you are now in the top five percent of the population? Well, you are, and you should be proud of yourself.*

"That's why I'd like to invite you to take the next step—a step that will allow you to achieve at a level only a handful of people have ever dreamed possible. I'd like you to consider an initiation into a course of study so profound, so powerful, that until now only one or two human beings in any generation ever even attempt it. But its accomplishment would mean mastery over virtually anyone or anything on the planet.

"Only those who have completed the second level of this self-development course and have shown exceptional ability, strength of will, and mental power are invited to participate. And only a rare few of those will complete the final course.

"Should you feel an interest in pursuing this ultimate level of life mastery, please do not undertake it lightly. It will require your placing complete and total trust in your spiritual master. It will require that you give up everything you have ever thought or believed about the nature of the world around you. Like the initiates into the mystery schools of old or the secret brotherhoods throughout the ages, you will undertake quests that will profoundly change you and what you understand about the nature of reality. Are you up to the task? If you are, then the end result will be total and complete mastery."

She looked at me. "Then there's a post office box number people need to write to in order to get the access code to the next computer level of the course."

"But we have some of the next computer level of the course because Mike's friend hacked into it."

"I know," she said, nodding. "But I'm not up to tackling *that* on an empty stomach!"

After each of us had consumed a plate of shrimp and sausage jambalaya and a double hot fudge sundae, we moved into Bernice's living room where we could sit side by side and pore over the portion we had of the third and final section of Jordan's self-development course.

It didn't take long for us to begin to see the path the course was taking. "Do what thou wilt shall be the whole law," quoted from Aleister Crowley, was the primary topic of the first part of the lesson, with a discussion of exactly what this meant.

This portion explained that Kali, like certain other mother goddesses, was worshipped both as giver of life and bringer of death. The feminine aspect of god, so the text ran, was always seen as dark and negative, because though it brings life into the world, that very act is the beginning of entropy, for it places the being into physical form, which by its nature is constrained by space and time and must eventually become subject to the ravages of growing old and dying.

"I think you said that last week, didn't you?" asked Bernice. "It's a way of looking at the mixed blessing of living in the third dimension."

The Lawyer Who Died Trying

A little further down, however, Jordan indicated the student would be learning how to invoke this dark-natured goddess for the purpose of manifesting whatever the practitioner might desire.

"Desire is good," said the text. "It motivates the practitioner to achieve goals through focused attention and conscious action. Having strong desires that you can visualize tasting, touching, smelling, hearing, and seeing in as much sensual depth as possible will assist you in making those desires manifest.

"For when we say, 'Do what thou wilt,' it implies the use of *willpower*. Your personal willpower can control your local field of time and space. And you *will* do it with the assistance of the most powerful force for manifestation on the planet, the force that is the overseer of life and death—the goddess Kali."

By the end of the first part, the text was describing the uses of sex magic as a path to power and how to use sex to bring the energy of the kundalini—the body's flow of energy up the spine—under control of one's conscious desires. Like Michelle, I was a little bit creeped out by the rhetoric Jordan was using—too many words and phrases suggestive of self gratification, and too little concern for personal responsibility.

"You know," I said to Bernice, "I didn't get any hint in the language of the earlier parts of his course as to just how much Jordan was teaching the exercising of power over others."

"Well, of course not!" she exclaimed. "The earlier parts of the course were all lifted from good, healthy, personal growth workshops and texts that have helped people in the last few decades to grow beyond their pain of being frail and human and to learn to lead productive, responsible lives.

"But just because he plagiarized all of that material from positive places doesn't mean he was really interested in teaching positive personal growth. I think this new material shows that his introductory courses were probably used to cull out the people who wouldn't be willing to move into the black arts. He's very charismatic, so I'm sure he'd draw a lot of people to his courses who would tend to see him as a guru. They'd open up to him, at which point he could use his skills to discover who he might take on as acolytes—and he'd probably choose people who were already in a position of power or who might become powerful in some way so that he could expand his field of influence. I'd venture to guess that the more we read, the more we'll find the 'elite' crowd he's pulled into this course would have no compunction about harming others. In fact, learning to inflict pain without guilt is probably going to be a part of what he teaches in the course."

And sure enough, in the next section, that was exactly what we encountered.

"Okay, here he argues that what people label as 'sin' is really just the guilt we feel for our repressed desires," said Bernice. "And in a sense, this is true. Then he moves on to saying that repression is unhealthy, and that it's important to get in touch with those desires—to bring one's shadow side out into the open. Now this is also true from a psychological perspective, and it's one of the purposes of psychotherapy to help people get in touch with repressed desires and negativity and figure out how to channel it off in positive ways. However, *his* next step is to suggest that the only course of action after getting in touch with these desires is to act them out, whatever they may be. He says that what we call 'conscience' breeds weakness and feebleness of action. So he's using the steps of his argument to bring the student to a place where he or she can more comfortably disavow conscience and moral judgment. And lack of conscience is tantamount to sociopathy, in my opinion. So he's really giving his students permission to do exactly what their darkest desires might lead them to if conscience didn't stop them."

"And what do you think that means?"

"It means, in the most extreme cases, abuse, rape, acts of brutal cruelty, physical and emotional sadism—and of course, murder."

I already knew Jordan was capable of murder since Jessamine had told me he was a trained killer—and also since I had tasted blood in my mouth the one time I'd held the knife that had killed Jessamine.

"I think we can assume Jordan wouldn't have minded if Jessamine was killed. But do you think he actually did it?"

"I certainly wouldn't put it past him," said Bernice. "But he might not have had to do it himself if he'd had any students who were devotees of his teachings. He could have just suggested that his wife needed killing, and one of his disciples might have done the job for him."

I nodded thoughtfully. "Of the people we know, there's at least one who admits to following some of Jordan's principles—and who also has a black leather trench coat and hat."

"Yes," she agreed, "Maggie still looks like a pretty good suspect!"

Chapter 17
Thursday, October 30th

After a quick jog around the neighborhood and a shower, I donned some clean sweat pants and a matching sweatshirt and settled down with a hot cup of tea and a stack of Locke and Hobbes papers, determined to conquer the remains of this assignment so I could return them to my classes the next day. I was still working away when I began to hear hammering, sawing, and lots of voices down in the backyard.

Glancing at the clock, I saw I'd been working for nearly four hours, and it was now noon. I went to the window to look into the yard and saw Mike and Michelle plus about seven other young men and women beginning to put together what looked like several small cottages—or maybe large outhouses would be more apt. They were all open on one side so that the inside would be visible to the people coming to see the displays. Curiosity got the best of me, so I went down to the kitchen to see what was going on.

Bernice was standing at the center island setting out sandwich makings. "Egg salad, ham salad, or tuna?" she asked when I appeared.

"Um, ham salad sounds good. And I came down to see what's taking shape in the backyard."

"You don't want to go out there," she warned. "The twins will press you into service and your life will be forfeit for the next two days. Have a sandwich instead and then go back upstairs and hide."

"But by the sound of it, everybody is having fun."

"Fun, yes, but the Dynamic Duo will be working the bunnies off everybody who's volunteered to help put this show together. Please take my advice—I've lived through many of these mutated Disney development projects. Take a sandwich and hide! Or take two and hide twice as long!"

I laughed and started making a ham salad sandwich on rye, with lots of chopped veggies and mini carrots on the side.

Just as I was slicing the finished sandwich, Michelle popped her head in the door. "Hi, Ariel! Hi, Mom."

"Oh," moaned Bernice, "you've been seen! Well, don't say I didn't warn you." And she took her own sandwich into her office and closed the door.

"Thanks for putting out sandwich makings, Mom," Michelle called out toward the closed door. "I'll let everybody know they can forage."

"You're welcome," came Bernice's resigned voice through the closed door.

"So Ariel, would you like to help?" Michelle asked brightly. "We're having such a good time already!"

"I've been hearing the noise from upstairs. I wasn't expecting you to start assembling everything quite this early."

"Well, we only have about thirty hours until party time, so all the kids who are going to set up displays have to start early. We're skipping classes this afternoon and tomorrow—though some of our professors are letting us off because the projects fit in with work we're doing in class. Like for instance, Mike talked some of the art profs into letting their students get extra credit for participating, and my theater teacher is letting me and four others in the department get credit for the acting we'll do in some of the live displays. But I thought you might want to get involved."

"You know, I really would," I said, thinking that her enthusiasm was contagious and I was almost being truthful, "but I've got to finish grading papers before suppertime because I have to go to a meeting tonight. So I'll have to beg off today."

"Oh, too bad. I understand, though. But if you'll leave your door unlocked this evening while you're out, I'll bring by some Gypsy fortune teller clothes for you to wear tomorrow night. I've got a couple of outfits you can choose from, plus a scarf with spangles, and some loopy earrings and beads—a bunch of stuff. I'll just put everything on your bed, and you can decide what you like best."

"I'd appreciate that," I said.

She was about to close the door when she popped back in again. "I almost forgot!" she said and came over to me.

"I got a call from Channel 10 asking me to pass on a message to you." She reached in her jeans pocket and pulled out a folded slip of paper. "They don't give out staff or guests' phone numbers, but they do try to get messages to people when viewers want to get in touch. Anyhow, this is from a woman in Old Town Alexandria named Galloway, who is beset by a ghost in her house that she thinks may be harming her daughter, Angela. She'd like you to call her as soon as possible."

I took the message and unfolded it, thinking I might want to call as soon as I got upstairs.

"You know," Michelle continued thoughtfully, "I bet these are the same Galloways Mom knows from some arts club or other. They went through an awful tragedy a couple of years ago. Angela's about my age, maybe a little older. She had a twin sister who had been going somewhere with her dad, and they were hit by a drunk driver and killed. It's bad enough losing a sibling and a parent, but I bet the loss was even greater with it being an identical twin. Kind of like losing a part of yourself. Being a twin myself, I could really empathize with her when I heard about the accident."

The Lawyer Who Died Trying

"This sounds like it could be a much more serious situation than most of the other stories I've read on email. I'll give her a call right away."

"Okey-dokey," she said, "see ya later."

I took my sandwich plate upstairs and made the call from my apartment. The sad female voice that answered brightened considerably when I gave my name.

"Oh, thank you so much for calling me back!" said the woman effusively. "I've been at my wits' end."

"What seems to be the problem?" I asked and thought how cheesy it sounded after it was out of my mouth.

"We have a ghost, that's the problem! When we moved in here, I thought it was really—well, titillating to have a ghost in the house. I guess I was expecting it to be like in the movies, with occasional midnight apparitions and maybe a little poltergeist activity. My daughter, well, she doesn't get out much, and I thought it would be fun to have séances, or maybe work the Ouija board."

"So you knew the house was haunted when you moved in?"

"Oh, yes. You know, everybody in Old Town has a resident ghost. But it's not like we thought it would be. There's no reasoning with this ghost. It shows up every night, and it's sort of attached itself to my daughter. Very clingy."

How like my own problem with Jessamine, I thought. To Mrs. Galloway, I said, "Is the ghost male or female?"

"It's a young woman."

"Do you have any idea what this ghost's story is? Why she's still staying around on this plane?"

"We get the sense she died young, but not through disease."

"I'm not surprised. Many people who study this area believe one of the strongest reasons why the spirits of the dead stick around is that they didn't get to play out enough of their lives to feel satisfied."

"Well, I wouldn't mind having her in the house, except for the clinging to my daughter. Angela hasn't been well lately, and I think it's because of this ghost who won't let her alone. So I was hoping you might be able to come and communicate with the ghost and explain she needs to move on."

"All right. I have some time on Saturday," I said. We agreed to a noon meeting, and, after letting her know I was open to donations, I hung up.

Settling back down in my chair, I took a bite of sandwich and listened to the voices from the yard below. Picking up yet another stack of papers, I said, "Mr. Locke and Mr. Hobbes, I'm finding your arguments less and less entertaining the more I have to read about them. I hope you won't be offended, but I'm really glad I'm not scheduled to teach this half of the world cultures course again next term."

I still hadn't finished the final batch of student papers, but I reluctantly put them away at about six p.m. and got ready for the Aquavest meeting.

Bernice had begged off from going to the meeting, saying she had food and trick-or-treat bags to prepare for the party, and that if she ran away to a meeting, her children would consider it an audacious breach of family trust. So I was alone when I parked my car in the Hyatt Regency parking garage in Crystal City and went looking for the Aquavest meeting room. The fact that I was alone was surprising to me and even a little strange—I'd had Jessamine with me practically every waking moment since the previous Sunday. I decided maybe she'd gotten bored with Locke and Hobbes and had gone to visit someone else for a change.

Many of the people attending the meeting were quite upset and even angry, but Ernie did a superlative job of calming everybody down. Primarily, he said he wanted to update the investors on the status of their money and on what progress was being made in solving the recent murders of the company lawyer and the inventor of the Aquavest device. He made it clear that he and the other Aquavest directors were working hard to find a way to retrieve the company's funds and bring whoever was responsible for the killings to justice.

He assured everyone that progress was being made in identifying and finding Cristien's bogus lawyer, and that the police in both New York and Alexandria wanted him for questioning in the murders of two of the company's principal officers. Finally, he explained to the investors at large what he had explained to the small group of us on Monday night—the technology Cristien had been planning would not have worked where he was proposing to use it, but this didn't mean the device wouldn't work somewhere else in a slightly different configuration. Once he had promised that he had a team of engineers working on reconfiguring the device and that he might have new information within the month, he opened the floor to questions, giving the investors an opportunity to ask what most concerned each of them.

Very little went on in the meeting that I wasn't already aware of, but I was impressed with Ernie's masterful handling of the situation. And when I realized at the end of the meeting that Jessamine was still not tailing me, I felt so free and light I was practically euphoric.

"Anybody want to go to the bar for a drink before we head for home?" asked Maggie.

Lorelei and Patricia agreed and insisted I was included in the "anybody," so I said I could probably tolerate the expense of a glass of wine, though I was pretty sure—but didn't say it—that at this hotel a single glass of house wine would cost what a bottle of the same vintage would run at the nearby Giant grocery store.

Once we'd ordered our respective libations, Patricia turned to me.

"Ariel, I forgot to ask you when we chatted on Tuesday. Did you have a chance to finish our Tarot readings? I'm dying to know what you found out about each of us."

The Lawyer Who Died Trying

I felt a little embarrassed. Thanks to everything else that was happening in my life, I'd totally forgotten to look at the list of cards I'd pulled on Monday night.

"I apologize to all of you. I know I promised to get an analysis out to you right away. But I'll tell you what, I'll do my best to have it ready in time for the party tomorrow night. Only when I give it to each of you, you'll have to hide it right away, or everybody at the party will be expecting the Gypsy fortune teller to give them a full reading!"

I knew from experience that everybody's most important concern was with self, and that everybody wanted to get exactly what everybody else got, no matter what.

"But I promise," I went on, "the reading will be fuller and more perceptive after tonight, because now that I'm with you, I can tap your energy again right here and make sure my interpretations are accurate. So if you don't mind, let me take each of your hands in turn, and I'll just let the vibes settle in."

They all nodded at this suggestion, so I started with Lorelei. But when I took her hand, I drew an absolute blank. It was as if my mind was truly a blank slate. I tried for several seconds, but still I was drawing a blank. But to save face, I smiled and said thanks and went on to Patricia. And the same thing happened—totally blank mind, totally blank emotions. Again, I thanked her and moved on to Maggie. And once more, my mind and all my sensitivities were totally blank. It was like running into a brick wall—three times! Failure to achieve a connection was a remarkable event—somebody was definitely blocking me, and I thought it had to be either Jordan or one of the women I was sitting with.

Hoping my ability to act nonchalant was intact, I smiled and thanked them all. In a way, I was sorry Jessamine wasn't with me at the moment—I could have gone to the ladies' room and asked her what she thought of the blockage I was experiencing.

"Sugar, I was wonderin', did you have a chance to invite Jeffrey and his grandmamma to the Halloween party tomorrow night?" asked Lorelei. "Ah've been feelin' so bad for the poor little guy, I wanted to get him a present. An' Ah thought if he was goin' to be at the party, Ah'd bring it along."

"Yes, they agreed to come, so you can bring the present along with you."

"Where did you meet Jeffrey's grandmother?" asked Maggie.

"At Frederick Dowling's office—he was Jessamine's lawyer for the custody suit she was in with Jordan."

"I was wondering whether anything was going to happen with that suit," said Maggie. "I just figured now that Jessamine was gone, Jordan would automatically get custody."

"That's certainly what he wants," I said. "But his mother is seeking custody on the basis of his being unfit as the custodial parent. And she'll be using the same arguments Jessamine was going to use, so I'm going to have a day in court after all."

Everyone was quiet for a moment; then Lorelei said, "Are you sure you want to be involved? I mean, Jordan Steele can be a pretty tough character."

I sat there thinking through what I wanted to say to this group of women. According to Jessamine, they had all refused to stand up for her in court, presumably out of fear of repercussions from Jordan. But was there anything else involved? Having just been blockaded from tapping into any of their psyches, I wondered who I could trust and who I couldn't. It occurred to me suddenly that I might be sitting with a mini-coven of Kali worshippers—perhaps they were all three in Jordan's pocket. And in that case, any one of them, or perhaps all of them together, might be responsible for Jessamine's death!

Then I realized there were a couple of things I could say that might jar something loose and give me a clue about who was false and who was true. So I decided to tell both things and see what would happen.

"I do know that Jordan is pretty tough. He made that perfectly clear when he approached me on Tuesday afternoon outside Frederick Dowling's office."

All three of the women looked properly shocked, but nobody said anything, so I continued.

"He told me if I didn't extricate myself from the custody case, I'd be sorry."

Patricia seemed terribly stressed at this news. "Oh, my dear, you need to be very careful. That man has a lot of power, and I'm pretty sure he wouldn't hesitate to use it—in nasty ways."

Both Lorelei and Maggie nodded vigorously.

"You don't want to cross him personally," said Maggie.

"Oh, I think I can protect myself," I said. And then I dropped the second bomb. "And besides, I have Jessamine on my side."

"What do you mean?" asked Maggie.

"Besides being able to read Tarot cards and people's energy fields, and besides knowing a little bit about the uses and abuses of magic, I have another hidden talent—though thanks to a recent television appearance, it's becoming not so hidden. I talk to ghosts. I've done it ever since I was a child. And Jessamine's ghost has been with me since the day she was murdered."

A chorus of clichéd phrases erupted from the three of them: "You're kidding!" "I don't believe it!" "Oh, my goodness!" and so forth.

Lorelei put a gentle hand on my arm. "Is she here now?" she asked.

"Oddly, no. It's just about the only time I've been free of her since she was killed—it's like having a rather heavy shadow in my auric field—albeit one that talks. A lot."

"You're really serious, aren't you?" said Patricia with lingering disbelief.

The Lawyer Who Died Trying

And then from Maggie the question I'd been waiting for someone to ask. "Does she know who killed her?"

I paused a couple of beats for effect, then said, "Not yet. But I'm expecting the answer to come back to her any day now because I've been working with her to help jog her memory." This wasn't strictly true. I had been working with her, but I really didn't have any hope she'd come up with an answer. Nevertheless, these ladies didn't need to know that.

"I...find this pretty hard to believe," said Patricia. "I've never really believed in ghosts."

"Oh, they're real enough," said Maggie. "In real estate, we have to let people know if a house has a reputation for being haunted, or if someone has died or been killed on the property."

"Really?" said Lorelei. "Ah didn't realize that. But then, real estate law isn't my field. But Ariel, honey, what in the world is goin' on with Jessamine? What's she doin' hauntin' *you*?"

"Mostly driving me crazy!" I said. "I can't tell you how hard it is to be followed day and night by a disembodied spirit. But maybe if we can figure out who killed her, she'll be satisfied and leave me in peace."

"So you don't think, like the police do, that the person who murdered Cristien also murdered Jessamine?" asked Patricia.

"I'm pretty sure it wasn't the same person. I'm satisfied that I've managed to narrow the field to a handful of people. And I'm in touch with the police every time I learn something new that may bear any fruit." Again, this wasn't all strictly true, but it was in the near ball park of truth. And then I thought to myself, I've been around Ernie too much this last week—I'm mixing way too many metaphors!

I looked around the table to see what effect my last statements had had on the ladies and saw that they all looked pretty grim.

Finally, Maggie asked, "Do you think the murderer is Jordan, or do you suspect someone from the Aquavest company?"

I realized I didn't want to implicate any of them, so I told another little white lie, "I'd rather not speculate here and now. Look, I'll keep you posted on any breakthroughs I find out, either from the police or from Jessamine. And if any of you come up with any additional clues or information, I hope you'll do the same for me. It would be a great service to me because if this case isn't solved soon, Jessamine is going to drive me nuts!"

The little party with the Loo-Loo ladies broke up by the time we'd finished one drink, and I came home to discover a pile of clothing and costume jewelry suitable for a Gypsy fortune teller on my bed. I sorted through it, and just for fun tried some of it on, settling for a long-sleeve purple silk blouse, a rayon skirt of black, red, purple, and gold paisley, an open black vest with gold and red trim, and a triangular red and purple head scarf with large gold sequins sewn around the edges. I chose the skirt because it had large pockets, suitable for me to put my Tarot cards in, and I picked the rest of the outfit to go with the skirt. Then I remembered I had a pair of purple suede boots in my closet, so I retrieved them and put them with the outfit. I was pleased to see they were a pretty good match for the blouse. I decided I might just have to make Michelle an offer she couldn't refuse for these clothes so I could keep them in my own costume repertoire after the party.

Just as I finished clearing off my bed and making piles of the clothing I would wear and the items I would give back to Michelle, Jessamine suddenly appeared again. Except this time she wasn't right behind me but rather standing in front of me.

"Where have you been?" I asked, curious because I recognized that something had definitely changed.

"Did you miss me?" she asked.

Since I really hadn't, I avoided answering and simply said, "I went to the Aquavest meeting this evening and just wondered why you weren't with me."

"I went looking for Cristien. At first when I heard he was dead, too, I didn't think of trying to find out what had happened to him. But this afternoon, while you were so busy with all your paperwork, I had this little niggling feeling that I could perhaps get something done from this side that you couldn't do from your side. So I went looking to see if he was still here the way I am, or if he had crossed over."

"And what did you find out?"

"It took me a while to get the hang of how to do it, but I finally figured out how to cross distance very rapidly. All it takes is the desire to do it and then the conscious willingness to actually move, and without the limitation of a physical body, you can go anywhere you want just by thinking about it. Well, no, you can't since you still have a body, but I can."

"I understood what you meant. So did you find Cristien."

"Yes, I did. He was still hanging out in the alley where he'd died, saying, 'What happened? What happened?' over and over again."

I thought how this sounded very much like Jessamine herself had been right after she'd died.

"Did you tell him he was dead?"

"I tried to. But somehow I couldn't convince him of it. He didn't believe I was dead either. But when I confronted him about the missing money, I did get him to admit he'd embezzled it. It was a simple plan, and similar to what you had deduced—he had his lawyer, who is a really slick con man, forge Ernie Redmond's signature on a company check. He was supposed to transfer the money to an offshore bank in the Cayman Islands—that was his lawyer's idea—and they had set up an account there together. But he didn't especially trust his lawyer—because who would trust a con man, right? So he opened another offshore account in his own name in the Channel Islands, specifically on the Isle of Jersey. He thought of that because he's Canadian, and many of the British people use the Channel Islands for their offshore banking. So he put a small amount in the Cayman account, and a lot in the Jersey account."

This was new information, and it crossed my mind that before I went to sleep tonight, I needed to get this information to both Detective Flanagan and Ernie Redmond

"So how did he die?"

"His con artist lawyer killed him. Stuck him with a large switchblade in a bunch of strategic places, then took everything of value—wallet, watch, cuff links—so the killing would look like a mugging."

"Jessamine, the police think Cristien's lawyer might have killed you, too. Did he?"

The question seemed to astonish her. Finally, she said, *"Somehow I feel my murderer was a lot closer to home!"*

And she disappeared.

Chapter 18
Friday, October 31st, Halloween

I had called Detective Flanagan immediately after talking to Jessamine and told him about the two items I hadn't been aware of before—the information about how the second account on the Isle of Jersey had the bulk of the company money and the description of exactly how Cristien had been killed.

When I'd mentioned the stab wounds in lots of strategic places and what had been taken from Cristien's body, Flanagan had been silent for a few moments before saying, "That's exactly right. But that's unpublicized information."

I'd said, "I can't take credit for being psychic here. Jessamine just told me what she'd seen."

He'd given a snorting little laugh and joked, "You're too modest!" and I'd wondered if he was being facetious. Then I realized that getting information from a ghost was actually being very psychic!

I'd also called Ernie Redmond, but I got his answer machine, and rather than leaving a detailed message, I'd just asked him to call me back.

I didn't sleep well that night, so I was pretty groggy when my alarm went off and I had to climb out of bed and stumble to the shower. But I gradually picked up a little energy as the day wore on. Perhaps it was the excitement of the upcoming party, or perhaps it was being without Jessamine's clinging tight to my energy field, but by the time afternoon had rolled around, I was practically dancing down the halls of the university.

I'd cancelled my afternoon office hours so I could go home and get ready for my gig as a Gypsy fortune teller, and I'd told all of my students about the party, just in case any of them would want to drive to Alexandria and see what some of their fellow students had put together for the evening's entertainment. I suggested that if any of them wanted to come, it was free, but that donations of bags of chips or cookies or six packs of soda would be appreciated. I figured if they came and brought snacks Bernice wouldn't run out of food or drink for the masses.

As I arrived home about 4:30 and pulled into the driveway, I saw Mike coming around the side of the house with large sign. He waved to me, so I rolled down the window.

The Lawyer Who Died Trying

"I'm glad you're home. If you don't mind, we're all doing parallel parking along the edge of the drive so that if people need to get out and go for supplies, they won't be blocked in by a bunch of cars behind them. Also, it makes it easier for walkers to get up the driveway to the backyard. I'm about to go set up this sign so people will know this is a private party for invited guests, GMU students, and neighborhood trick-or-treaters. We may get a few people we don't know, and as long as they behave themselves, they're welcome to come see the haunted backyard displays, but I'm about to chain off the drive to discourage the general masses from party crashing. Also, people who don't live here or who aren't part of the presentation crew will have to find street parking. Anyway, if you need to go out later, you'll have to remove the chain."

"Okay," I said, "thanks for giving me the party rules and regs."

I parallel parked behind the last car on the side of the driveway and walked around the house to the back door. Bernice was bustling around the kitchen with piles of foodstuffs already prepared to go on serving tables, so she commandeered my assistance. Stowing my school gear behind the trestle table in the kitchen, I went outside with her to put up folding tables at the top of the driveway. Then we set out trays of assorted Halloween cookies along with bowls of dips, all of which were covered with foil, plus empty bowls of various sizes for the chips and snacks that would be opened later. Real food would be served from the kitchen at about 8:00. I was a bit surprised when Bernice told me that Mike had prepared a spicy chicken casserole for the event.

"Oh, yes, they both *can* cook. They'd just rather that Mom do it for them! Mike calls this one of his Coach House Specialties."

Bernice also hooked up some warming trays to electrical cords that were plugged into outlets at the house. I realized then there were dozens of cords running off in all directions, many of them meandering toward the displays around the backyard that looked as if they were finally complete. Then she had me stock four coolers with ice and various kinds of canned drinks.

Just when I thought we were finished, she hauled me out to the garage to set up a second set of smaller tables for the kids' area. We put covered trays with more Halloween cookies and strange treats from the kitchen on one of them. There were cookies that looked like spiders, ghosts, mummies, and bats. There was a dirt and worm pie, a plate of witches' fingers, and a cupcake graveyard. On the other table she had me scatter about fifty small orange and black trick-or-treat bags and a regimental-sized bowl of wrapped candies.

"There's more inside, if it's needed. We have about twenty kids coming whose families have sent R.S.V.P.s, but we may draw some neighbor kids along with those passersby who'll just want to see the Haunted Backyard. We'll take orders for hotdogs and chips later from those kids who might get hungry before the party's over."

Honora Finkelstein & Susan Smily

When she told me my services were no longer needed and I could go get dressed in my Gypsy finery, I took the opportunity to wander around the yard and get a pre-party glimpse of some of the displays. And I was quite impressed. The Tree of Life that Michelle had laid out the month before was decorated with 10 different lighted jack-o-lanterns, one in the middle of each sephirot. A path had been set up from station to station with little garden lights—the kind that come on automatically when it gets dark—staked into the ground on both sides of the path. All of the little three-sided cottages, though portable, now appeared to be fairly sturdy.

In addition to the light boxes that stood just to the left of the front of each display, there were at least a couple of spotlights strategically placed so as to make the dioramas in each of the cottages perfectly visible, though some were covered with colored gels, so I figured they'd be pretty eerie when they were turned on.

Eight of the cottages already had some kind of display inside—I figured the ones that didn't would probably be used by the live actors Michelle had talked into participating. I couldn't resist punching a couple of buttons marked "Push," and I was impressed when Anne Boleyn, who seemed just slightly under life size, took her head out from under her arm and held it out for inspection and when the Mummy pushed open his sarcophagus and sat up. Good animatronics for college kids, I thought.

When I'd satisfied my curiosity about the displays, I went upstairs to my apartment and changed into the Gypsy clothes, putting on enough eyeliner, mascara, rouge, and lipstick to look pretty theatrical myself. Then I switched on my computer, got the notes I'd made the previous Monday for my Tarot readings for the Loo-Loo Ladies, and typed them up, each lady's on a separate sheet.

Since I literally hadn't picked up anything new the previous evening from any of them, I made my interpretations strictly by the book, without including any of the personal comments I might have shared with them had they come to me privately—assuming, of course, that they wouldn't have blocked my intuitive abilities.

"Just the facts, ma'am," I said as I hit the printer button, and the three sheets began to print out. I folded each one to letter size, put it in an envelope, and marked the appropriate lady's name on the outside. Then I tucked the three envelopes and my Tarot cards into the pocket of my borrowed skirt, locked both my door to the back stairwell and the one to the front hall, and went downstairs.

So far today Jessamine hadn't shown up, but I figured she would when she had something else to say or something for me to do. Then it occurred to me I hadn't heard from Ernie all day either. I stopped at the phone in the kitchen and dialed his number, but I got an answer machine again, so I didn't bother to leave a second message.

It had been a day of Indian summer, and though the sun was setting, it was still pleasantly warm. As I went out into the back of the house, some of the garden lights on the path around the displays, especially those that were the furthest back in the trees, were already coming on. Bernice had placed a couple of lighted jack-o-lanterns on the serving tables, and Mike and some other members of his display crew, who were all now dressed in black shirts and pants, were beginning to turn on all the spotlights and light boxes associated with the displays.

I could also hear strange noises coming from various places around the yard, so I figured each of the displays now had its own appropriate scary music, eerie moaning, or evil laughter. And barely audible, just beyond the garden house, I could make out a sort of music box tinkle of the tune to "Casper, the friendly ghost, the friendliest ghost you know...."

Then Bernice came out the back door in a long black dress with a witch's pointed hat and a broom.

"Is Alan coming?" I asked. I figured her divorced but often-visiting husband wouldn't want to miss the annual Halloween party

"He's already here," she said. "He's upstairs getting into his Dumbledore outfit."

People were beginning to straggle up the driveway, so I decided to go see how well my fortune-telling powers were working, and I pulled my cards out of my pocket, giving every interested person a one-minute *"carte de jour"* reading.

My readings were going along pretty successfully when the Loo-Loo Ladies showed up in their Princess Leia costumes. There were actually five princesses, two of whom I didn't know. A very small one was Patricia's five-year-old daughter, and another adult one turned out to be Maggie's partner Andrea. Patricia's husband wasn't dressed as Princess Leia, though Lorelei had apparently tried to talk him into it. Instead he came as Han Solo, and Patricia's two sons appeared to be young Luke Skywalkers at various ages.

While I was admiring the Star Wars crowd, my sister Bibi arrived with her husband, Victor, and her three young sons, Harrison, who was 5 years old, and the twins, Max and Alex, who were 4. She handed me a large plastic container. "Here," she said, "I brought a pecan pie for the food table."

Bibi and Victor were dressed as Mickey and Minnie Mouse. Harrison, with his hard hat, overalls, and trick-or-treat toolbox, was obviously Bob the Builder. Alex appeared to be some kind of alien, all in green with little bobbling antennae on his head. And Max, the one grandchild so far in our family who also talked to ghosts, was dressed as one in a little white outfit, with a separate covering for his head with eyeholes cut out.

In a *sotto voce* aside, Bibi said, "Max wanted me to make the head covering pointed, like some of the ghosts in the Casper cartoons, but I was afraid he'd look like a little Klansman, so I talked him out of it."

"I'm glad you did!" I laughed. "I don't think that would go over very well around here."

"Auntie Ariel," said Max, lifting up his head covering, "are the twins here?" Max had met Mike the month before, but he had yet to meet

Michelle, and the novelty of seeing a pair of adult twins was something that piqued his interest.

"Yes, Max, they're here, but they're really busy right now, making sure that the Haunted Backyard displays are all working, and that the entertainment is happening. But I'll try to make sure you get to meet them before the party's over."

He smiled up at me with a cherubic little face and added, "Irene says to tell you 'Happy Halloween.'"

This didn't surprise me, as Irene was the resident ghost at Bibi's old farmhouse out in Leesburg, and Max had given me messages from her on previous occasions. Though I'd felt her presence on occasion and had sometimes smelled her perfume when I'd lived with Bibi's family earlier in the year, I'd personally never seen Irene.

"Did Irene come with you?" I asked Max.

"No, I asked her if she wanted to, but she said she didn't. But it's okay, because I know there are going to be lots of other ghosts here tonight."

"Well, you go enjoy all the ghosts, and later there's supposed to be a magic show and hotdogs and cupcakes and trick-or-treat candy."

As Bibi's family went to check out the Haunted Backyard, Greg and Brandon arrived. Brandon was dressed as a dragon with a shiny green suit and a wonderful headpiece that trailed spiky scales down his back, and Greg was a knight, though with only a sword and shield, so he jokingly said he couldn't be my knight in shining armor until his armor came back from the cleaners.

"I'm just as glad you decided to keep it simple," I said. "It's too warm a night for heavy armor."

"It's also too hard to get close when you have to wear a layer of armor," he said, putting an arm around my shoulders and giving me a hug.

Brandon tugged on his other arm and said, "Roar!"

"Oh, yeah, Brandon's been practicing his roar on the way over so if he encounters anything scary, he can scare it right back."

"Very wise of you, Brandon. Feel free to scare anything or anybody that isn't smaller than you are."

"Can we go see the Haunted Backyard, Dad? Roar?"

Greg looked at me with raised eyebrows. "Can you join us for a walk or do you have other duties at the moment?"

"I sort of seem to be a semi-official greeter, but I hope that status will change pretty shortly. I'd like to be here when Althea and Jeffrey Steele show up, though, so they won't feel too out of place."

"I understand," said Greg. "Why don't I go through the backyard with Brandon and then maybe later we can take a walk in the dark together?"

"I'd love it," I said, regretfully letting the two of them go through the displays without me. Hearing music, laughter, and occasional applause coming from a couple of spots in the yard, I was sure Michelle's fellow actors were in full swing.

The Lawyer Who Died Trying

I had done several more one-minute card readings for arriving guests before I finally saw Althea Steele coming up the drive with Jeffrey. She hadn't dressed in costume, but he was in a cowboy outfit that made him look like Woody from *Toy Story*. He seemed a bit subdued, so I introduced myself and told him there were cupcakes and drinks in the garage area and that a magic show would be starting in just a little while. I said if he wanted to see some displays that weren't really terribly scary, he and his grandmother could go through the backyard down the lighted path. He gave me a tentative little smile, though still holding tightly to his grandmother's hand.

"I'll let him decide what he wants to do," said Althea, "and thank you for inviting us. This is the first time all week that he's been willing to leave the house."

Just then Michelle came bounding out with a bullhorn and announced there would be a magic show in the garage area in five minutes for all the children who were on the grounds. Though more people were arriving all the time, there were only about a dozen kids gathering for the magic show, as most of the party's attendees were college-age students. I did a couple more readings, then as Michelle on her bullhorn announced the start of the magic show, I glanced at my watch and was surprised to see it was already 8 p.m. I decided I'd been the unofficial greeter long enough, so I tucked my cards in my pocket and went to see what kind of magic Bryan Corcoran might be able to perform.

As it turned out, he was excellent with sleight of hand. Brandon had joined the kids who were sitting on folding chairs in a semi-circle around Bryan, and he was quite pleased when Bryan pulled a quarter out from behind Brandon's ear and then let him keep the quarter. I looked for Greg and saw him leaning against the wall on the right side of the garage near the door, so I went over and took his hand.

He smiled down at me and whispered, "How long will this performance last?"

"I don't have a clue," I whispered back. "But probably not long enough for us to take a walk in the dark."

He tugged my hand and led me out into a part of the yard where our talking wouldn't disturb the magic show audience.

"I'm probably going to have to take Brandon for a little trick-or-treating shortly. He was agitating for it just before the magic show started, and I don't think I can talk him out of it."

I was a bit disappointed, since I'd been hoping to spend some time with Greg this evening.

"Why don't you go trick-or-treating through the neighborhood around here and then swing back by a little later? I could make us some hot cider, and I understand that for those who hang out late, there'll be horror movies up in the twins' apartment until midnight or maybe even later."

"You can make cider?" he asked in mock astonishment.

"Are you looking for a Gypsy curse, mister?" I said in rebuttal and smacked him on the arm.

"Watch it, lady," he said laughing. "That's my sword arm you just walloped, and if you mistreat your knight in shining armor, he won't be able to protect you!"

Just then there was a piercing scream that I was pretty sure wasn't a part of the intended action in the Haunted Backyard. Greg and I both turned and hurried down the path toward the sound. About halfway around the walkway, in front of the display dedicated to the four ghosts from *A Christmas Carol*, we found a group huddled around Lorelei, who was cradling Jeffrey in her arms and loudly proclaiming anguish and distress.

"I'm all right, Auntie Lee, I'm all right," Jeffrey kept protesting, but to no avail, as Lorelei just kept wailing.

"You could have been really hurt! You have to take care!"

As Greg and I came up to the group, she looked at me accusatorily. "He was running down the path and he fell. It's too dark here—he could have hurt himself very badly."

"Let's take a look," Greg said, expecting that his voice of authority would help calm Lorelei. He knelt down by the two of them and tried to encourage Lorelei to release her vise grip on Jeffrey, but she actually pushed him away.

"No!" she almost shouted. "Don't touch him!"

For some reason she was near hysteria, and I wasn't sure what would calm her down. This seemed so uncharacteristic of Lorelei that I thought something else must be going on with her.

All at once, Jeffrey broke out of her grip and scrambled off her lap.

"Let me go, Auntie Lee, let me go. I'm okay, I'm not hurt. I just wanted to talk to my mother."

"What are you talking about, baby?" wailed Lorelei. "Your mama is *dead*!"

At the word "dead," a sort of hush fell over the yard.

Then Jeffrey said quietly, "I know she is. But that little ghost boy told me he'd seen my mom and my mom had talked to him and told him to tell me she was here and wanted to talk to me, too."

Uh-oh, I thought, Jessamine's back. But the part about the little ghost boy confused me, so I asked Jeffrey, "What little ghost boy are you talking about?"

He looked around and spotted Max, who was near the edge of the display wall, his ghost headdress up and hanging down on both sides of his face like a pair of droopy rabbit ears. I held out my hand and motioned for Max to come to me, and he did.

"Hey, Maxie, what's this about Jeffrey's mom talking to you?"

He gazed at me with his angelic smile. "She did, Aunt Ariel. I told you there'd be lots of ghosts at this party, and I knew she was one of them because I could see through her. And she told me to find Jeffrey for her and tell him she was looking for him. She said he'd be in a cowboy outfit, so he was easy to find."

"The child is making it up," said Lorelei, still sounding as if she was on the verge of hysteria.

"No!" said Jeffrey, "He's not. When he told me he'd seen my mom, I looked to where he was pointing, and I could see her, too. That's why I was running—I was following her." He looked down the path. "But she's not there now," he concluded sadly. He reached out for his grandmother and pushed his face against her skirt.

Max pulled away from me to touch Jeffrey on the shoulder. "It's okay. She'll be back."

"How do you know?" asked Jeffrey.

"Because," said Max, "she told me. She's friends with Auntie Ariel. And she said she was going to stay around to make sure Auntie Ariel was safe. She doesn't want anything to happen to her. So she'll be back!" And he patted Jeffrey on the shoulder.

Lorelei looked at the two little boys, the one comforting and trying to convince the other, and she finally seemed to calm down.

"Ah'm sorry," she said. "Ah guess Ah over-reacted. Ah apologize for makin' a scene. Ah was just so upset when I thought Jeffrey might have been hurt. But Ah see he's all right now."

She started to stand up, and Greg gave her a hand. Once she was standing, she began brushing herself off. When she thought she was presentable, she turned to Althea and Jeffrey and said, "Ah'm sorry, Jeffrey, Ally. Ah do apologize to you for overdoin' it. All Ah can say is Ah was so startled to see him fall, knowin' what he has to have been goin' through this week...well, Ah got upset too quickly, Ah guess. Ah hope you'll forgive me. Oh, an' Ah have somethin' for Jeffrey!"

At that, she reached into the folds of her skirt and pulled out a little package. "It's for you, honey," she said to Jeffrey as she pressed it into his hand.

I decided things were back to normal—or at least as normal as they ever were in my spook-experiencing family—and that Greg and Max and I could probably leave the scene, so I took my nephew's hand and said, "Let's go find *your* mom."

When we got back to the garage area, the magic show had just wound down, and Brandon came out with a big grin on his face.

"That was fun! Hey, can we go trick-or-treating now, Dad?" he asked. "You can come, too, Ariel. And I'll share anything chocolate with you."

"Are you trying to steal my girl?" asked Greg.

"I just know she likes chocolate!"

"'Loves' is more like it," I said. "Thank you so much for your offer—it's very generous. But I'm sort of committed to stay here until the party winds down, or at least until the people I've invited go home. But you could come back later if you like. I think there's going to be a showing of the musical *Little Shop of Horrors* for all the party guests starting about 10 o'clock!"

I was trying to make it sound really attractive, because I wanted to sit in the dark with Greg and have him cuddle me close while the movie was going on.

"Could we do that, Dad?" asked Brandon, as if he really wanted to.

Greg shrugged. "Okay, pal, if that's what you want to do." And he gave me a wink, adding, "I guess we'll be back."

"Oh, boy," said Brandon. "That means I'll get to stay up 'til midnight!"

"I want to stay up 'til midnight, Aunt Ariel!" said Max, tugging on my hand.

"Well, let's go find your mother, and then we'll see," I said, hoping everybody *I'd* invited to the party would go home very soon.

In my dream, I was in a nun's habit, and I seemed to be living in a convent. I knew I was a sort of librarian. I also knew there were many other nuns at this convent, with many other talents and efforts to share with the group. I saw myself lecturing them, telling them that women should have rights like those of men, and that they should strive to educate themselves.

I turned and saw I was being watched by a seated man dressed in the robes of the Tarot's High Priest, with a bishop's mitre on his head. He had only one acolyte serving him, but that one held up both gold and silver keys that glittered in the dim light. And by the look of it, the acolyte was female.

Then the High priest stood, took off his robes and mitre, and put on a black nun's habit. He walked to where I was lecturing and shook his head.

"Don't talk," he said, and though he looked like a nun, he was commanding me in a booming male voice. "Don't study, don't read, don't teach, don't think!"

He took my lecture notes, tore them into pieces, and threw them into the air—and they blew out the windows, scattering all over the world.

Then he changed again, taking off the nun's habit and donning the robes of the Magician, but the colors of his robes were black and red instead of red and white. The keys he had held as the High Priest morphed into the four implements of the Tarot deck—a coin, a cup, a sword, and a wand, representing earth, water, air, and fire.

"I control all things," he said, "and you will do as I say."

He put the four elemental implements on the table in front of me, except that he put them upside down—the coin balanced on its edge so that one of the points of the star on it was downward, the cup empty and its mouth down on the table, the sword with its point in the wooden table top, and the wand balancing on its broad end.

He opened his palm to the earth and lifted his left hand to heaven—and I realized he was actually backward from the Magician in the Tarot deck—he was mirroring and mocking the empowerment implied by the symbols on the card. Then he slowly brought his hand down and pointed his finger directly at me, and with a whooshing sound I was flying up some stairs to a tower room. When I looked out the window, I realized I was at the top of the Washington Monument, and a huge black crow was behind me, cawing loudly, rushing at me and trying to push me off.

The Lawyer Who Died Trying

All of a sudden, the Fat Man stepped between me and the other nun, grabbed my shoulders, handed me a duck, and pushed me into a crouch, and I watched the crow fly over the edge of the railing. Then there was a crack of thunder and a bolt of lightning.

And I woke with a little shriek!

Chapter 19
Saturday, November 1ˢᵗ, All Saints' Day

I was actually trembling from the dream, and I could feel myself pumping adrenalin for at least five minutes after I woke up. I switched on the bed lamp and grabbed my dream journal, jotting down the symbols, images, colors, sounds, and feelings. I couldn't get back to sleep and could hardly wait until breakfast to discuss the dream with my resident psychotherapist, so I took the last batch of Locke and Hobbes papers and my dream journal, went down to the kitchen, and made a pot of coffee that I was still drinking from when Bernice wandered in from her bedroom a little after 7 a.m.

"Hey, Bright-eyes, what are you doing up so early?" she asked as she poured out the dregs from the coffeepot and started a new batch.

"I had a truly horrible dream, and I'd like you to work through it with me." And I read the dream in all its vivid detail.

When I finished, Bernice said, "Clearly you're afraid of some very strong, negative, masculine energy that's trying to disempower you. I'll let you say who you think it is."

"Oh, no question. It's Jordan Steele—he's playing the Magician from the Tarot, and he's turning all the implements of earth, air, fire, and water upside down with his distorted magic. But he's also playing the High Priest—putting on the bishop's robes and hat to show he's following the external rituals that hold together the institutions of society and religion, and by so doing he's gaining the 'keys to the kingdom.' But he has only one acolyte, which is a little strange."

"Unless Jordan needs only one other person to help him hold his force field together," Bernice suggested.

I thought about that for a second, then agreed. "I guess that could be. He'd only need one other person to help him sustain his power, especially if that person was female and there was sex magic involved." I thought of Patricia then—the Queen of Cups with her extreme sexuality and attraction. After my drink with the Loo-Loo Ladies two nights before, I didn't think I could rule out anybody as a foil for Jordan.

"What's this business with the nun's habit, though?" asked Bernice. "I don't remember any nuns in the Tarot deck."

The Lawyer Who Died Trying

"Oh, that's probably a carryover from something I was teaching a couple of weeks ago. Actually, I was teaching it on the day I was first introduced to Jessamine. Sor Juana Inez de la Cruz was a 17th-century nun in Mexico who wanted to study. She assembled a huge library in her convent and was teaching other nuns the benefits of learning. But she ran afoul of her bishop one day when she was declaiming against some things a famous male writer of the time had written. The bishop asked her to send him a copy of her discussion, and she agreed when he promised it would be for his eyes only.

"Then he not only circulated it, he published it. There was a huge furor, especially from high church officials, and the bishop then wrote to the sister, pretending to be another nun named Filotea, who was giving her advice on how a woman in the church should behave.

"Sor Juana responded with *La Respuesta a Sor Filotea*, which translates as *The Answer to Sister Filotea*, in which she attempts to show not only that her side of the argument was correct but that there was historical precedence for women needing to become educated."

"And that went over *how*?" asked Bernice.

"Not very well. She was told she'd need to stop teaching and give away her library, or the Inquisition would come and take her away."

"I guess it didn't pay to mess with church authorities back then. So what happened to the good sister?"

"She died about a year later of some widespread plague that hit the convent."

"Too bad."

"Yeah, but she's been rediscovered in recent years as an early voice for feminism. So I sort of identify with her."

"Well, your high priest in the dream certainly doesn't like what you're teaching or thinking. Sounds like the Inquisition all over again."

"Jordan definitely wants me out of his custody battle. I think he does want that badly enough to try to kill me if he can. Oh, and the crow in the dream also comes from something Jessamine told me the evening we went to Tyson's Corner for dinner with the Loo-Loo Ladies. She said Jordan had sent a flock of crows to her apartment that morning, and that they were rising and settling, rising and settling on her balcony, and cawing and pecking at the glass to try to get in."

"That would be disconcerting. So the crow in the dream is a reference to Jordan's power to control natural forces and make them do his bidding?"

"I think so. And of course, the Washington Monument in the dream is a variation on the Tower struck by lightning in the Tarot deck, with people falling off. I even heard the thunder and saw the lightning flash. Really creepy and scary!"

"I agree!" said Bernice.

"So what do you think I should do?"

She took a slow deep breath before asking, "You don't intend to back off from giving your testimony, do you?"

"Not really. I think Jordan is a pretty scary guy, but I wouldn't be able to look at myself in the mirror if I let him scare me off."

"That's what I figured. So in that case, keep surrounding yourself with light as often as you think of it between now and the time you have to go to court. Also, stay out of Jordan's line of fire between now and then if you can. And finally, I wouldn't go visiting the Washington Monument if I were you."

"It wasn't exactly on my to-do list for the next few weeks."

"Well, if somebody lures you up there, just remember to duck!"

I was really restless after talking the dream over with Bernice. Plus, I'd nearly finished my paper grading while I was waiting for her to get up, and I figured I could polish off the last of them later in the afternoon. I wanted badly to talk to Greg, but he had planned to be out with Brandon all day, so I finally got on my jogging gear and went out for a run, just to work off some of the negative energy the dream had generated.

As my running shoes slapped the pavement in the quiet early morning neighborhood, I kept replaying the dream in my head. Over and over, I would see myself, looking over the railing of the Washington Monument, hearing the flapping of the giant crow's wings, and ducking down quickly so the crow would miss me as it flew by.

I remembered having read somewhere that if we have nightmares they usually portend something bad about to happen in our real-world lives. The recommended way to avert the real-world situation was to go into an altered state, go back into the dream, visualize the scary part, and somehow change the outcome. I wasn't sure I really wanted to change the outcome, but I did want to be sure I didn't fail to duck. So I replayed the ending of the dream over and over as I jogged. It was sort of like doing drills in the Army, I thought—get the troops ready to act on reflex should an emergency situation arise.

By the time I got back home, I felt better. My adrenaline was up, but this time I was experiencing eustress and enjoying the high that comes with a sufficient amount of aerobic exercise.

I was just beginning to strip off my things and jump into the shower when the phone rang. It was Ernie Redmond, finally calling me back.

After we'd exchanged preliminary niceties, I told him what Jessamine had told me, without telling him my source of information.

"I've had a psychic hit," I said. "Cristien didn't split the company money in the two offshore accounts. He didn't trust his lawyer, so he decided to put only a small portion of the money into the Cayman Islands bank account. The rest he put into an account in the Channel Islands that only he could access."

Ernie was silent for a few moments. Finally, he said, "You're good! And you're absolutely right. I learned yesterday that he put the bulk of the money into the account on the Isle of Jersey. And that may be our saving grace. The Cayman banks don't accept much in the way of interference with their accounts, and they don't offer much help if money has been put there illegally. That's why so many crooks prefer the Caymans. But on Jersey, the banks can be real sticklers for proper identification. They want all the 'i's' dotted and 't's' crossed, and proof that people really are who they say they are.

"Anyway, when we notified the Jersey bank that Cristien and a crooked partner had embezzled the money they were holding, and that Cristien had been murdered, the Jersey bank froze the account. There's a good chance we can file appropriate paperwork and proof of Aquavest's claim to the money. The money will be held in what the English call a 'constructive trust.' And probably we *will* have to operate through the courts on Jersey. But once we prove that the money was embezzled, and the court authorizes release of the funds, the money will be back in our company account before you know it! And we can surely demonstrate a paper trail of the embezzlement."

"That's happy news!" I said.

"And that's not all," he continued enthusiastically. "The engineering firm I contacted with information about Cristien's device has already said they think there's a viable way to change some of the specs on the device so they can secure it differently to the ocean floor. And then they might simply move it to other locations. There's another piece of information I wasn't aware of while I was working with Cristien's materials, but one of the strongest ocean currents in the world actually is at the mouth of the Gulf of Mexico, between Bermuda and Florida. Maybe we'll be able to do something with that information when we get the device reconfigured!"

"Well, good for you!" I said.

"I hope it'll be good for all of us!" he responded jovially, and we congratulated each other before hanging up.

Just at that moment Jessamine appeared. *"I heard you talking about Aquavest—it was to Ernie, wasn't it?"*

"Yes. I thought he should know what you'd learned. I also talked to Detective Flanagan on Thursday night to tell him you'd talked to Cristien about both what he'd done with the company money and who his murderer was. I thought Flanagan ought to know that what they suspected in that murder was correct, but that they were wasting time trying to pin your murder on Cristien's lawyer."

"Good. There's no point spending more energy on something that won't pay off."

"So do you have any more information about who killed you?"

"No, though I think Jordan was behind it, even if he isn't the one who used the knife."

"I agree with that. But what have you been doing?"

"I've been talking to Jeffrey. Sometimes he can see me and sometimes he can't, but I keep trying. And then, I've been trying to follow my so-called friends. Somehow, I think one of them might have been responsible for my death, but I don't seem to be

able to get close, or bring them into focus unless I'm attached to you and you're talking to them."

"You think one of them killed you? But which one?"

"That's the big question, isn't it?" And she popped out of sight.

"Wait! Don't go!" I said, surprised at my reversal of interest in having her with me.

"What?" she said as she popped back into view.

"I have to go talk to another ghost today at noon down in Old Town. There's a woman whose daughter is being beset by one who's a real clinging vine. It's sapping her energy and making her sick. I just thought that maybe you'd be willing to go with me, just in case I have trouble making contact, or in case she doesn't want to listen."

She looked at me as if thinking about it. Finally, she said, *"Okay. But isn't this an interesting reversal of your attitude? First you're sympathetic toward me. Then you're annoyed because I'm staying so close to you—while I was getting my bearings on the other side, I might add! And then you tell people I'm driving you crazy and you may go nuts! And now, you want me along for the ride, in case you need help communicating."* She actually laughed. *"That's a lot of different feelings you've had about me, all in less than a week!"*

I was chagrined and immediately apologized profusely. "I'm so, so sorry, Jessamine. I didn't realize you were picking up on my irritation."

"Hey," she said. *"I may be dead, but I'm not stupid!"*

And she popped out of view again with a drawn out, *"I'l-l-l be-e-e ba-a-a-ck!"*

At exactly noon, I pulled up in front of the address Mrs. Galloway had given me in Old Town. The house was a beautifully restored Georgian town home—dusty blue with dark burgundy and tan trim. But I knew there was a serious problem with the inhabitants—all the flowers in all the window boxes were dry and dead and looked to have been that way for a long, long time.

Jessamine wasn't with me—at least not yet. But she'd promised to come, so I figured if she didn't show up on her own soon, I could try calling on her. And if she didn't show at all to assist me in talking to the ghost, I'd give it a go myself. After all, I'd been talking to ghosts for years, with mostly decent results.

"It's show time!" I said to myself as I rang the bell.

The woman who answered the door was short and thin with gray hair, sallow complexion, and large, deep-sunken eyes. She looked sad and withdrawn, but when I told her my name, she brightened and beckoned me inside, where she took my hand in sincere gratitude before she closed the door.

"I'm Madeleine Galloway," she said. "Please come into the parlor. I have everything ready for tea, so we can sit and relax and talk a bit about the... the problem."

The Lawyer Who Died Trying

She led me into a room that was probably darker than necessary—the curtains were drawn, and the furniture in the room, though it all looked quite expensive in the way good antiques always do, contributed to the general gloom with dark mahogany woods and dark solid upholstery colors in midnight blue and burgundy. The pictures on the walls, all of which I decided were probably real oil paintings by very good artists, were also mostly dark in tone.

Once Mrs. Galloway had seated me, she excused herself and left me alone for a couple of minutes. The house was quiet, and I noticed that besides my own breathing, all I could hear was the ticking of a grandmother clock on the mantel. I glanced at my watch and compared it to the clock. Yup, both of them said 12:03.

Moments later, Mrs. Galloway came back in with a large tray of tea things—what smelled like Earl Grey tea in a white porcelain pot, two dainty cups and saucers that matched the pot, some little side plates and forks, napkins, sugar, creamer, and a bowl of lemon slices, plus a large platter piled with muffins, scones, tarts, and what might have been sliced pumpkin bread. She set the tray on the coffee table in front of me, then handed me a napkin and began pouring out the tea.

"Lemon or cream?"

"Cream, please, and some sugar."

"One lump or two?"

"Three, please. I like it very sweet." Okay, so it wasn't a health drink, but that's the way I liked it.

She doctored my cup of tea and handed it to me, and I set it on the table, wondering where her daughter was.

"Please," she said, "have some of the goodies. I so seldom have an opportunity to entertain anymore..." She choked emotionally at the end of the sentence.

"Mrs. Galloway," I said, "I'm very grateful for your hospitality, but I need for you to tell me what's going on in this house."

She looked at me at length, then put her face in her hands. Her shoulders began to shake. "I just don't know what to think!" she moaned.

"Where is your daughter? Why isn't she down here with you?"

Mrs. Galloway started to shake as if she were soundlessly crying, then softly she began to keen along with the shaking. I waited patiently, wondering if I should have invited Bernice along instead of Jessamine. I could use a psychotherapist for a sidekick!

Finally, Mrs. Galloway got hold of herself. "You must excuse me," she said. "I haven't known what to do, and I just sort of fell over the emotional edge." She looked up at me, grabbed a tissue from a box on the end table, wiped her eyes, and blew her nose. Then she said, "My daughter has become very ill. As I was telling you over the phone, we bought this house thinking it would be fun to interact with a ghost, to have séances and find out all about what happened to the dead person and why he or she decided to stay in the house."

She blew her nose again and continued. "But it turned out that after the first couple of weeks, when we were jokingly calling the ghost our 'friendly housemate,' something started happening to my daughter. Every morning she'd wake up with a headache, or a sinus infection, or an ear infection, or a cold. She was constantly having to go to the doctor and take antibiotics or some other kind of medication. The doctor didn't have an answer for it, but he suggested that with all the problems maybe she had some kind of parasite." She shook her head sadly. "If he only knew."

"All right then, so you think the ghost in this house has attached to your daughter in some way?"

"Yes, of course, what else could it be?"

"Well, it could *actually* be some kind of parasite. Did the doctor ever have your daughter tested?"

"He did, but there was never anything really definitive. But my daughter—Angela is her name—started having weird dreams every night, in which she was a woman in the 1800s who was in love with her best friend's husband. There seemed to be a lot of wish fulfillment in the dreams—sometimes she would actually dream that the friend's husband was making love to her, and Angela would wake up all in a sweat." She looked at me startled, as if she had only just realized how much she was telling me.

"Don't worry," I tried to reassure her. "Ghosts often have very lurid stories associated with why they're haunting people or places."

"Well, then, I guess the thing is, Angela began to think that this...spirit..., or whatever it is, wanted to take her over—like that evil demon in the *Exorcist*. Now, I don't think it's a demon, or I'd have called a Catholic priest a long time ago. But...it does seem to want to cling to her like a leech. It's almost as if it wants to re-experience life *through* her, since it doesn't have a body of its own anymore."

"Mrs. Galloway, there really is a vast amount of literature in the field of ghosts suggesting that some of these entities are so angry at having left their bodies before they finished their lives that they want to keep on experiencing life through the body of someone else. One of the terms for these attached entities is 'hitchhiker spirits.'"

"Hitchhiker spirits," said Mrs. Galloway. "Hitchhikers! Yes, that makes a lot of sense and would seem to be exactly what's been going on with Angela."

"Now tell me, is Angela capable of talking to me?"

"Oh, I hope so. Some days she just throws tantrums. Other days, she lies in her bed crying. And sometimes she's perfectly okay, and almost back to her normal self. Except that she's usually feeling sick, so she stays in bed a lot."

"Can she come downstairs, do you think? Or would that be too taxing for her?"

"Well, it might be best if I just go up and check on her. Maybe she'll be able to come down—she did seem more like her old self this morning, and not so much like a...like somebody else."

The Lawyer Who Died Trying

She stood up and straightened her shoulders. "Why don't you try some of the treats while I go upstairs and check on her?" And she made her way out of the room and to the staircase in the hall, ascending it somewhat haltingly but with decided determination.

I looked at the pile of sweet baked goods, thinking how hard it was in polite society to refuse things we know we probably shouldn't eat because the people who press them on us have provided them with love and have an investment in making sure we love eating them. I resignedly took a plate and put a piece of the pumpkin bread on it, then took a tiny taste from one corner. It was quite good, with just the right hint of cinnamon, cloves, and nutmeg, so I had another small bite.

I looked around the room, wondering what I was going to do when confronting Mrs. Galloway's daughter. Thinking I could use some backup, I said softly, "Jessamine? Where are you?"

And she popped into view in front of me. *"You called, master?"* she said, and did a sort of salaam like a genii from a bottle.

"Very cute!" I said, though I wasn't sure I meant it. "I thought you were going to come with me."

She smiled. *"I did come with you. I just didn't make myself known."*

"Okay, so you know what's going on in this house?"

"Yes. The girl upstairs is in her late 20s, and she suffered a terrible loss two years ago. Her twin sister, who was her closest friend and confidante, was killed in an automobile accident. And then she and her mother moved here. They bought the house because they thought it would be fun to have a friendly ghost on the premises. But from what I'm learning being on this side of life, there aren't very many ghosts like Casper."

"Well, I guess some are bad and some are good. There's a ghost in one of the historic houses in D.C. who's a bit of a misogynist—they say he likes to try to push ladies downstairs." But then I thought about Irene and the Fat Man and added, "However, in my experience, there are some ghosts who function almost like guides or guardians."

"Maybe that's true, but the one in this house certainly isn't very nice—at least to the young lady she's draining energy from."

I considered the situation. "So, Angela thought this ghost could be a friend, and she invited her to become a part of her life. And that made her open to possession?"

"That's pretty much it in a nutshell," said Jessamine.

Just then I heard Mrs. Galloway coming downstairs again. "Don't go away, please," I said to Jessamine. "In case I can't make contact, I'd appreciate your speaking to the ghost for me."

"All right," said Jessamine teasingly, *"I suppose I can spare a few more minutes from my busy schedule to help you out."*

Mrs. Galloway entered the room again, and I quickly put another tiny bite of the pumpkin bread in my mouth and made a show of chewing it up.

"Angela says you can come up if you like."

"How is she doing?"

"She's...been better, but at least I know it's my Angela who's talking to me."

I stood up and followed her as she turned back toward the stairs. We went up two flights to a landing, where a door stood partly open straight ahead of us. As we approached it, it slammed shut. Mrs. Galloway turned the knob and tried to open the door, but to no avail.

"Angela," she called, "can you open the door, dear?"

I heard soft footsteps, as of someone walking in bare feet, approaching the door from the other side. Then the knob twisted back and forth. Finally, a voice said, "It won't open for me, Mother."

"Jessamine, can you do anything?" I asked softly.

And the next thing I knew, the door was slowly swinging open. "Thank you," I said.

Once Mrs. Galloway had introduced me to her daughter, I suggested the young woman get back into bed. I also asked Mrs. Galloway to sit down and wait.

"Jessamine, is the ghost that's been haunting Angela Galloway in the room right now?"

"Yes, she's here, and she's very much attached to Angela," said Jessamine. *"Her name is Emily Manning. And she's also pretty annoyed that you've come to try to remove her."*

"Well, before we do any actual removing, would you ask her, please, if she'd be willing to talk to me?"

I saw Jessamine practically step inside Angela to communicate with Emily. Then she stepped out again, and I got the impression of another shape beside her, which was in all probability female. But beyond that I had no real perception of the woman who was causing all the trouble.

"She'll talk to you, but she doesn't really want to leave Angela."

"Emily, if you can hear me, can you tell me why you want to stay here and attach yourself to this young woman? Why don't you want to cross over to the other side, where there's light, and love, and more joy than you've ever experienced on this side of the veil?"

There was quiet for a moment. Then the figure said softly, *"I know there's another side, a good side, I've seen it. But I'm not going to be welcome there. I killed my best friend, and before that I lay with her husband, Joshua. And even before that, I was jealous of her life and begrudged her any happiness.*

"I know now I was a fool. I was so in love with her Joshua, although it was from a distance, that when he finally realized I was an easy mark, he drew me into an affair. After a time, he convinced me to kill his wife so we could marry. So I did, with oleander—in my day, it was almost impossible to detect oleander as the poison. But somehow, I was careless—I may have talked about it to someone else, and I was caught and hanged. Joshua went free, of course, because he was the poor, aggrieved husband, and nobody believed my story when I told them he'd begged me to commit the murder.

The Lawyer Who Died Trying

"I really can't forgive myself for these bad things, and I don't believe God will forgive me either. If I leave here, I won't go to the good side, I'll go to hell. And if that's the case, I'm better off staying here. And Angela said she'd like me for a friend."

"Emily, there is no heaven or hell in the sense you believe in it. The only judgment we'll have to face is from within ourselves. We carry judgment around inside ourselves for the good or bad things we've done. That's all you'll have to face."

There was silence for a while. I sensed Jessamine having a conversation with Emily that I couldn't hear.

When Jessamine came back again, I asked, "What happened?"

"I practically had to go through her whole life story again with her. But she's agreed to let go if Angela wants her to."

I turned to Angela. "Emily Manning is the name of the ghost that's been sapping your energy. If you can bring yourself to tell her to go away, that you don't want her to be attached, that she doesn't own you and has no right to use your body, you'll be declaring your autonomy and cutting off access from her. But you have to really mean it."

Angela looked startled but didn't say anything.

Finally, I said again, "Angela, do you really want to get well?"

Slowly, she nodded.

"Even if it means you will no longer have this friend?"

Again, she nodded slowly. Then she started to cry. "I miss Sarah so much," she said. "I really don't feel like a complete person without her."

Mrs. Galloway moved to her daughter and stroked her cheek. She took her hand and said, "Angela, darling, anything you want or need, I'll try to help you have. I just want you well again, sweetheart. We'll get you some help, and we'll work through this together."

Angela nodded, closed her eyes, and spoke the necessary words, "Then I want you to go, you ghost of Emily Manning. I want you to leave my body alone and go to the other side of life. My body belongs to me, and you can't use it anymore. So go away, and leave me alone! And I really mean it!"

In a few moments, she gave a little shudder, and I thought the ghost had detached from her. But I checked in with Jessamine just to be sure.

"Yes," agreed Jessamine.

"All right," I said to the two women. "The ghost has detached."

Angela cried on her mother's shoulder for a few moments. When she stopped and blew her nose, I said, "I know it's going to sound preachy of me, but it's really important for people to realize that playing with ghosts isn't just a game. A lot of people here in Old Town think it's a sort of status symbol to have a resident ghost. But if they have one, then it means that soul hasn't moved on. Now I'll admit there are some good-hearted ghosts who want to act as guardians for the people they share space with. But there are also plenty of ghosts who want to live *through* the people they share space with, and that's what you had here. Emily Manning thought she'd had a raw deal from life, and after she was hanged, she wanted to live again.

Maybe she's sapped other people before, and when Angela invited her to be a friend, she just moved right in!"

I smiled reassuringly at both of them. "I think there's a good chance Emily will move on now. She's agreed to do so, and if you don't call her back, I think she'll stick to her agreement. And Angela, I think I can help you with your depression over Sarah's death. Mrs. Galloway, I understand you know Bernice Wise?"

"That's correct," she said. "She's a psychotherapist I've met on a few occasions. How do you know her?"

"I'm her housemate at the moment, and she's said that she'd be willing to take Angela as a client. So, if you'd like to give her a call, I'm sure she'd be happy to set something up as soon as possible."

Mrs. Galloway looked at Angela, who gave a little nod. "That would be wonderful," she said. "And Ariel, I just want you to know that what you're doing is wonderful, too! We can't thank you enough for helping Angela—I really was afraid for her life. And please let me know if there's ever anything I can do for you."

I grinned a little ruefully. "Right now, my biggest concern with this work is how I'm going to help all the people who've contacted me because of the TV show. I've even had a couple of calls from out of state. I don't have the time or the money to travel, so I'll just have to do what I can by telephone."

"Speaking of telephones, I'm curious," said Mrs. Galloway. "You've been having *sotto voce* conversations with someone other than Emily while you've been working with us here. Do you have some kind of miniature cell phone attached to you? And if so, who were you talking to?"

"No, I don't have a phone like that. The person I've been conversing with is another ghost—one who still has some business to conclude on this side before she moves on."

"And are you helping her, too?"

"I'm working on it. Although I'll admit that this afternoon, things here wouldn't have gone nearly as smoothly without *her* helping *me*!"

After I left the Galloway residence, I was practically bursting with the need to talk to somebody who knew the details of Jessamine's case because the possibility that there might be parallels between the Galloway ghost and the person who had murdered Jessamine was really nagging me.

Jessamine herself didn't leave the Galloway house with me, and when I called her, she didn't come. When I got back home, Bernice and the twins were out, and Bernice had left me a message on the kitchen chalk board: "Alan and I are going out for dinner and a night on the town—don't wait up."

I tried calling Greg on both his land line and his cell, but I got shunted to a voice messaging system in both cases, so he and Brandon were probably still out having a terrifically fun father-son Saturday. I knew Brandon would be spending the night at Greg's, so I wouldn't see Greg again until the next evening.

Finally, I brewed myself a cup of tea, saw there were some cookies left from the previous night's party and put a few on my saucer, and sat down at the kitchen trestle table with a pad and pencil.

I thought about Jessamine's referring to the Loo-Loo Ladies as her "so-called" friends and thinking one of them might be responsible for her death. I had assumed she was using the "so-called" turn of phrase because they had refused to testify for her against Jordan in the custody case. She said they'd all been afraid. And yet I'd actually met them *after* they'd refused to help her, and she was still on very good terms with them. So why was she still counting them as her friends at that date? And why was she now suspicious of them?

It appeared that she was able to communicate with other ghosts, with people who could see ghosts, such as little Max, and with her son, and she could travel distances at will. And she could hear other people when they were talking to me. But she didn't seem to be able to visit or hear other living people, in order to learn more about her own death.

Her emotional entwinement with her friends was convoluted and of long duration. She'd involved them in Aquavest, and she felt some responsibility for that. Also, they'd all been chums for a very long time, so perhaps she'd decided that if *she* had reason to be afraid of Jordan, they certainly would, too, if they testified on her behalf. Heck, I had put *myself* in Jordan Steele's line of fire for agreeing to testify! So maybe she hadn't really held it against them that they wouldn't side with her.

I made a few notes about all these things. Then in big letters I wrote: WHY IS JESSAMINE SUSPICIOUS OF HER FRIENDS *NOW*?

I made a little star mark on the pad to indicate a thinking point. Jessamine had told all her friends there was a likelihood they had lost money in Aquavest on the morning she was killed. But from what we'd learned in our return trip to her law office, she'd been putting out the information on the problems with Aquavest while her murderer was lurking in her bathroom. So loss of money through Aquavest didn't seem to be the motive.

I made another star mark on the paper. Okay, they had all taken a course from Jordan Steele. But Lorelei had said she'd thrown her course notes away, and Patricia had said she'd put hers in the attic. Maggie was the only one who still admitted to using the principles from Jordan's course. And as Bernice and I kept noting to one another, Maggie owned a black leather coat and hat that made her a suspicious possibility for Jessamine's murderer. But then, Patricia was supposed to own such an outfit as well, though I hadn't yet seen her in it.

I still had the nagging feeling there was a parallel between Emily Manning and the person who had killed Jessamine, though I couldn't put my finger on anything specific. Was there any real reason to think any of the ladies would actually want to cause Jessamine physical harm, and if so, did it have to do with her ex-husband?

I made a third star on the paper for notes about Jordan. Clearly, he had a charisma that drew people in when he wanted to use it. So maybe he had somehow captured them all—or at least one of them—in his psychological, emotional web. If there was a link between Emily Manning and Jessamine's murderer, then it suggested someone had envied Jessamine for her husband and had wanted him herself. Could it possibly have been Patricia, Lorelei, or Maggie, or was it somebody else altogether?

Oh, really, I thought, this is silly. Maggie, the person who still uses Jordan's course and who might seem a likely suspect from that perspective, is a lesbian. So it isn't likely she'd kill Jessamine to get her husband.

Patricia was married and by all appearances happily so, with lots of offspring. Nevertheless, she was the Queen of Cups, the supremely sexual woman—and it wouldn't be the first time a seemingly happily married woman had fallen into an affair with a friend's husband. Was that the connection with Emily Manning? But would she murder one of her best friends? Especially since Jessamine and Jordan were now divorced? What would be the point since she could have an illicit affair with him if she wanted to without having to worry about Jessamine's feelings?

Finally, there was Lorelei. A strong woman and a single woman. This probably made her a better suspect for an illicit partner for Jordan than either Maggie or Patricia. But again, what would be the point? Jessamine and Jordan were already divorced. She and Jordan could have each other any time if they wanted each other. And if what she'd been telling me was correct, she was as fearful of Jordan and his dark powers as Jessamine had been.

So either I didn't have the right motives or I didn't have the right suspects. Or maybe I just didn't have all the clues yet. Still, the link between Emily Manning and Jessamine's case continued to nag me. I wondered if Jordan, like Joshua, had asked one of these women to kill his wife.

Finally, I gave up trying to puzzle it out and went upstairs, intending to conquer Locke and Hobbes once and for all and figuring if there was a clue connection I was missing, maybe my right brain would provide it while I wasn't looking!

Chapter 20
Sunday, November 2nd, All Souls' Day
~*Dia de los Muertos*~

The next morning dawned bright and clear, promising yet another beautiful Indian summer day. As I went down to start my jog around the neighborhood, I noticed Bernice's car was still not in the driveway, though the twins' vehicle was parked in its usual spot outside the furthest garage slot. Bernice and Alan hadn't spent this much time together in one extended period since I'd been living here. I decided I'd have tease her about her "boyfriend" the next time I saw her.

As I had done the day before during my run, I continued to rehearse my need to duck and roll should I be in a high place and sense danger. By the time I'd finished jogging, I'd probably rehearsed the scenario at least another fifty times.

When I got home, I was heading for the shower when my cell phone rang. It was Lorelei, with an invitation to brunch.

"Ah'm so sorry to be callin' you on such short notice, but Ah've been talkin' all weekend to the other ladies about Jeffrey and this custody suit thing. After Jeffrey's little accident on Friday night, an' his insistence that he was seeing his mama, Ah started feeling ashamed of myself for not testifyin' in the case. An' Patricia an' Maggie are also thinkin' maybe we made a terrible mistake not standin' up for Jessamine when we had the chance. Anyway, we were all hopin' you could come over this mornin' an', well, maybe just help us get the backbone we need to testify against Jordan ourselves. Would you be free to come by about 10 o'clock or so?"

Having finally prevailed over Locke and Hobbes, I had no other plans until evening, when I was supposed to see Greg for supper. So I said yes to brunch, thinking another block of time spent with the ladies would at the very least give me a further opportunity to figure out which of them was capable of blocking my psychic abilities. Lorelei gave me the address for her apartment building and told me I could park in any of the slots in the adjacent lot that were marked "visitor."

My car clock said it was 9:55 when I pulled down the long driveway that led to the Washington Arms Apartments. It was one of the few high-rise apartment buildings in Alexandria, with at least eight floors, on the northeast side of the city just before Washington Street turned into the George Washington Parkway heading north. I'd never been to this complex before and was impressed with the elaborate landscaping of fall mums in shades of orange, brown, yellow, and white. This was probably one of those really upscale places that changed out its flowers on a seasonal basis.

At the front door of the building, I rang the bell for the number Lorelei had given me for her apartment and waited a few moments until a buzzer sounded. I pushed open the door and found myself in a tastefully decorated lobby, with pecan wood furniture upholstered in sea greens and shades of pink and matching patterned pink and green carpet on both sides of the area—much like a very nice hotel lobby. The center span of floor, from the front door to the two elevators, was a nicely tiled mosaic, again in shades of pink and green, of various kinds of seashells and ocean life. I couldn't help admiring my surroundings as I pushed the button and waited for one of the elevators, and I thought that Lorelei, like Jessamine, must be doing very well in her chosen profession. Perhaps I should have gone to law school with my veterans' benefits—at least I'd have more than a part-time job if I'd gone in that direction.

I was still musing about life choices on my way up in the elevator, so I wasn't particularly focused on the upcoming meeting with the Loo-Loo Ladies. When the elevator stopped on the eighth floor, I got out and followed the signs to the appropriate apartment number, and when I buzzed, Lorelei was there in seconds to open the door.

"Let me take your coat," she offered, and helped me out of the black leather flight jacket I'd decided to wear in case the temperature dropped to something more seasonal for November. "Patricia and Maggie are goin' to be late," she said. "Patricia said she was takin' her family to a 9 o'clock mass, an' then she'd be right over, but she lives on the other side of Arlington, so it may take her a little while to get here. An' Maggie had a showing this mornin', also at about 9 o'clock, but it was near here—some house in Old Town. But she just called to say it was goin' to take her a little longer than she'd anticipated."

As I listened to her patter and watched her hang my jacket on a coat rack near the door, something gave me a mental nudge, but I wasn't quite clear as to exactly what was out of place.

"But let me get you some coffee while we wait for the others to arrive."

"That would be good. Cream, no sugar."

"Be right back!"

As she went into the apartment's kitchen, I took an opportunity to glance around the living room. There were several pictures of Jeffrey in the room—on bookshelves, end tables, and a desk. She really was a doting godmother, I thought.

I glanced down the long hall and saw four more doors—one at the end, two on the left, and one more on the right side—enough for perhaps three bedrooms and a bathroom. The apartment was quite spacious, with more than enough room for a single woman.

The Lawyer Who Died Trying

And there was a lovely little balcony off the living room, with a good view of the Potomac River. But there seemed to be a lot of white debris littering the balcony. I opened the door to get a closer look, and I saw that it was bird dung. I wondered if there were birds nesting on top of the building.

Lorelei came in with a cup of coffee just at that moment, and I took the opportunity to compliment her choice of apartments. "Nice view!" I said. "And this looks to be a very spacious apartment."

"Yes, it is," she agreed, handing me the coffee cup and saucer. "Though Ah can promise you all the amenities are somethin' Ah pay through the nose for when Ah sign my monthly rent check!"

Just then a big, fluffy, orange and white cat came gliding into the room.

"Oh," I said, "you have a cat!"

It rubbed up against my legs, so I bent over to scratch it behind the ears. And as I did, I noticed a trail of salt lining the carpet all the way along the doors that led out to the balcony. As I slowly stood up, I glanced to the windows that fronted the room. They also had a line of salt running along their ledges.

I'd told Jessamine to put salt inside all her doors and windows, to protect herself from Jordan's spells. She'd done it in her office. And she'd done it here. This wasn't Lorelei's apartment—it was Jessamine's.

And then I knew what had bothered me about the hall tree where Lorelei had hung my jacket—it also contained a black leather trench coat and matching slouch hat. Jessamine's coat and hat.

The bird dung on the balcony was from the crows that Jessamine had seen there the Monday before she'd been killed. The *murder* of crows.

An odd calm settled over me in the few seconds it took for me to put all the pieces of the puzzle together. Still holding the cup of hot coffee in my hand, I turned to face Lorelei and said, "This is Jessamine's cat, isn't it? The one you were feeding for her while she was in New York last weekend."

She looked at me with a somewhat startled expression. "Why... yes. Ah brought him over here to *mah* place when Ah realized she...wouldn't be comin' back."

I searched her face, trying to understand the lie.

"Why did you kill Jessamine, Lorelei?"

She tried her best to look wide-eyed and innocent. "Why, what do you mean? What makes you think that?"

"This is Jessamine's apartment, not yours. That's Jessamine's leather coat and hat on the hall tree. You said you didn't have them in black. But you wore hers, didn't you? Last Sunday, when you went to her office, you wore hers. A woman wearing a black leather coat and slouch hat was seen on the street outside her office. And all the Loo-Loo Ladies except you owned that outfit. It was an interesting tactic—and it did confuse everyone, including the police."

She sighed in annoyance. "Well, Ah reckoned you'd figure it out sooner or later—you bein' psychic an' all. Ah mean, Ah was sure after I read your assessment of mah Tarot cards that you were only a day or two

187

away from puttin' all the pieces of the puzzle together. It hasn't been easy to block you."

"I knew one of the three of you had put up a block to keep me from learning more about your motives. But I couldn't tell which of you it was. And I don't understand why you're tipping your hand now. There's really been no way for me to determine which of the three of you was the murderer."

"Oh, but Ah *knew* you just wouldn't stop tryin' until you finally figured it out. An' Ah'm not so much tippin' mah hand now as Ah'm jus' takin' action to eliminate you." Her voice was totally calm. "'Course, Ah should have known you'd figure out this was Jessamine's apartment. But that really doesn't change anything, except the timing of your suicide."

"My *suicide?*"

"Oh, yes, dear," she said, and pulled an extremely dangerous looking knife from behind her back, which she'd obviously had tucked in the back of her belt. "You've just been so troubled, seein' our dear, departed Jessamine so regularly that she's been drivin' you crazy. That's why you called me this mornin' an' asked to borrow the key to get in here. You said you wanted to bring her back to her own apartment, hopin' when she saw all her own stuff, you could convince her to leave you alone. An' as I will be tellin' the police, Ah just have to assume that you were so crazed, you must have believed Jessamine was refusing to comply, an' that must have driven you over the edge."

I didn't bother to argue with her or to tell her the police wouldn't believe her. At the moment, I was much more curious about her motivation for having killed Jessamine, since I still didn't understand it. Remembering her Tarot cards, I realized it somehow had to be about power and her fear of losing it. Then it finally hit me. "You're one of Jordan's advanced students, aren't you?"

Lorelei looked at me and gave a little shake to her head. "Mah dear, *Ah* am the most advanced student he has ever had."

I raised my eyebrows. "Sex magic and all?"

She smiled. "Sex magic and *all*."

"But Jessamine and Jordan were divorced. So why did you need Jessamine out of the way? You and Jordan could have had each other without any interference from his ex-wife." I was still thinking about my reasoning out the Loo-Loo Ladies' motives for murder the day before, and how I had felt there was some parallel with Emily Manning.

Lorelei just blinked at me, batting those long lashes. "Why, sugar, we were havin' an affair practically the whole time those two were married."

"So you've been in love with Jordan this whole time?"

She gave a little laugh. "Ah wouldn't call it *love*, exactly. He's got power, and Ah want to be around power. Ah certainly intend to be a judge myself—with all the power that goes with that job."

"So is that what Jordan offered you in return for killing Jessamine—the judgeship?" I was thinking her motive was a sort of locked-into-power craziness, and that perhaps she was as sociopathic as Jordan. Which was a pretty scary thought, considering she wanted to be a family court judge.

"Oh, Jordan really had nothin' to do with mah killin' Jessamine. It was just a little gift to him from his closest and most powerful partner. Jessamine really brought it on herself, by tryin' to insure that Jordan would never see Jeffrey again. An' Jordan taps into his power more fully through Jeffrey—through the offspring of his loins."

The revelations had suddenly taken a right-hand turn, and it took me a moment to catch up.

"So you did this for Jordan," I said, stating the obvious. "But not because he asked you to."

"That's right. Ah did it because he needs custody of that little boy."

"And that's why you were so afraid at the party about Jeffrey possibly being hurt?"

"Yes, of course. Jeffrey has to be with Jordan. With his son and with me to help him, there'll be nothin' he can't accomplish. An' Jordan needs all the power he can muster right now. It's just so *stupid*."

Now that Lorelei was talking, I didn't want her to stop. In assessing the situation, I was pretty sure I was talking to a madwoman and that she was planning to kill me if she could. But the longer I could keep her talking, the more the advantage shifted in my direction. Because she was talking about something deeply important to her, she was more emotionally involved and less aware of what I might do. I thought I was probably physically strong enough to take her down if I could stay out of the path of her knife. And I could see from watching her body language that she was becoming unfocused and brittle, so I figured even without a weapon, my chances of surviving were at least even.

"Okay," I said. "You've confused me. You say 'it' was stupid. But I don't understand what that pronoun refers to. *What* was stupid, your murdering Jessamine?"

Again she batted those long lashes at me. "You really don't have a clue, do you, sugah? But Jordan told me he was sure you knew about him. That's why he put a dead stop to your readin' his cards last Monday night."

The reference to the cards caught me by surprise. I thought back to the previous Monday night, when I'd been analyzing all the principals involved with Jessamine. And I'd been slammed on the top of the head just as I'd drawn an extra card for Jordan. That card had been the Nine of Swords—often considered the true death card in the deck.

"The Nine of Swords," I said softly. "Jordan is ill, isn't he? Very nearly sick to death. And he didn't want me to know it." Then I remembered again the taste of blood in my mouth when I'd handled the knife that had killed Jessamine. "Is it AIDS? Does Jordan have AIDS?"

Lorelei took a deep breath. "He's not gonna die—he can overcome even AIDS! But he has to have me and Jeffrey to do it. We need to hold the energy field together for him!"

And then I understood the Emily Manning connection. Lorelei, like Emily, was living vicariously through another person. Her sense of herself had become strongly associated with Jordan's need for her.

"How long has Jordan known about this? How long has he had the disease?"

She looked annoyed, clearly not wanting to talk about the disease or its ramifications. Finally, she said, "He found out just about six months ago. He had to take a physical for the military. And the doctors noticed some lesions on his back and ran a test." She sounded stressed but shook herself and added, "But he's got it under control."

Then a couple of other things occurred to me. "It was you who called Jordan last Monday night, wasn't it? You knew I'd be reading everybody's cards, so you called him as soon as you got away from the dinner party to let him know I was planning to read him as well."

"Yes, of course."

"And you also called him on Tuesday, didn't you, to let him know I was going to Frederick Dowling's office?"

"Right again," she said, with what I thought was a little bit of pride at how long it had taken me to figure out all the details of the puzzle.

Seeing her confidence growing, I asked, "So how long did the doctors give Jordan to live?"

She became rigid at the question. "Ah don't think we should be talkin' about this. Ah think it's time for you to commit suicide now," she said as she waved the knife at me. "Ah have your note all ready, an' as soon as you're dead, I'll just set it out an' leave."

"Lorelei, I don't think I'd kill myself with a knife."

"Oh, Ah'm not gonna kill you with a knife, you silly. You're gonna jump of the balcony."

And then, of course, I recognized that I was about to go out on a ledge on the Washington Monument.

"Now turn around, and go out onto the balcony," she ordered. "You're gonna climb up on that little stool out there and jump."

I pushed my protective shield out as far as I could and made the turn. Then I felt the point of the knife she was holding grazing my back.

"March!" she said.

With the knife at my back, I took the few steps required to get out to the balcony. But with the pattern of the dream firmly in my mind, as soon as we were both on the balcony, I dropped and rolled, tripping her up. I felt the tip of the knife scratch my back as I went down, and one of Lorelei's feet caught me in the ribs as I rolled into her.

Not surprisingly, she fell over me, and I heard her say, "Oof!" as her chest hit the balcony railing.

And then she was airborne, as the rusted railing gave way. I heard her scream as she went down, but by the time I could crawl to the edge of the balcony and look over, the sound had come to an abrupt stop. She was lying on the mosaic tile patio area behind the building.

The Lawyer Who Died Trying

As I sat up and scooted backwards through the bird dung on the balcony, I heard Jessamine's voice beside me.

"*Good job!*" she said. "*I wasn't sure whether you were going to need any help, but you handled that really well without me!*"

I looked up and saw her hovering near the edge of the balcony, as she looked down at Lorelei's prone form.

"What would you have done if I hadn't dropped and rolled?"

"*I might have had to give her a little shove, like that bad ghost you told me about who doesn't like women in his space. I was gearing up to focus my energy on that, just in case it was needed.*"

"You mean you would have pushed her over the edge?"

"*No,*" she laughed, "*she was already over the edge. Beyond the fringe. Past the point of no return. I would have just shoved her out of the way and given you a better chance at defending yourself.*" Still she hung there, looking over the edge of the balcony. "*Aren't we glad I never had a chance to call the super about getting this balcony railing repaired?*" Then suddenly she said, "*Oh, there, her spirit's separating from her body! I think I'll just go down and have a little chat with her!*" And she was gone.

Even before I stood up, I reached in my pocket, got out my cell phone, and dialed 9-1-1.

Epilogue
Tuesday, November 18th

Greg and I had just finished dinner from a picnic basket Bernice had prepared for us—a lovely vegetarian lasagna, some garlic bread, a salad of mixed greens, baby spinach, sliced red peppers, cherry tomatoes, black olives, and slivered almonds, with her homemade garlic, oil, and red wine vinaigrette dressing, plus a sizeable portion of tiramisu for dessert.

When I'd come home from court, she had pointed to the basket and said, "Dinner is ready—all Greg will need to do is warm it up."

When I'd thanked her appreciatively, she'd smiled and shrugged. "It's just a little comfort food I decided to whip up. If things had gone badly in court, I figured it would help pick you up. And if things had gone well, I thought you'd want to celebrate."

I had also picked up a nice bottle of cabernet sauvignon, which Greg and I were sipping as we finished off the last crumbs of the tiramisu.

Oddly, things had gone both badly and well—a sort of mixed blessing that made me believe even more firmly than I ever had before that the universe sometimes works to provide an equitable balance. I had delivered my testimony on Kali worship and its historic corruption when misused, and Dowling had submitted all the materials we had uncovered from Jordan's web course. Then I'd sat white knuckled, clenching my fists while Jordan delivered his plea to the judge for custody of his child, and I could almost see the shift his charisma made in the judge's attitude through the way it affected her body language. I wondered if he had more than one star student in his higher level magic class.

In short order, Jordan had officially won custody of Jeffrey. Then, to everybody's amazement, he had announced that his reserve unit had just been called up for service in Afghanistan, and that he was allowing his mother to keep Jeffrey for the time being.

When I'd told this to Bernice, she had said, "I think that fits his sociopathy. He wanted to win, he won, and now he can pass the child back to his grandmother."

"But I can't help wondering how his illness plays into this. He can't really be going to Afghanistan if the military doctors know about his AIDS, so that has to be a lie. I'm wondering if the energy field he was building to hold back his AIDS fell apart with Lorelei's death so that having custody of Jeffrey no longer makes any difference to him."

She'd raised an eyebrow and said, "That certainly could be the case, though I suppose it doesn't matter, does it, as long as he isn't taking over the care of that little boy? But what about Jessamine? Now that her son's future is settled, at least in the short term, is she still clinging to you?"

"No—and that's a double blessing of Jordan's decision. Jessamine told me she would spend a little more time on this plane saying her goodbyes to Jeffrey, and then she would move on."

"So you and Greg should have a lovely evening—with just the two of you!"

And that's what we were doing. Throughout the meal, I'd regaled him with all the details of my day, but now that dessert was finished and I was winding down, I said, "So how was *your* day?"

He had a tiny grin on his face as he answered. "Well, remember a few weeks ago when you suggested I should give myself a little message each night as I was going to sleep about getting information from my subconscious about some of the stolen cars we've been trying to recover? And how you told me to write down whatever I got? Well, I decided to try that. And over the next couple of weeks, I actually had the same dream about three times. And in this dream that kept repeating, I'd be walking over a covered bridge—like the rustic covered bridges they used to build a long time ago. Now, the bridge itself was a wooden bridge, and when I'd wake up, I'd be thinking, 'Wood bridge...wood bridge... wood bridge.' And then on the last morning I had the dream, I was brushing my teeth, and I thought Woodbridge, Virginia!"

"Eureka!" I said with a grin. "You got a clue!"

"Yeah! So then I went back to the dream and thought about other details of the bridge. And I remembered the cover on the bridge was red. And when I took a really good look at the sides of the bridge, they weren't wooden, but were a sort of corrugated metal in a kind of gunmetal gray. So I took a chance and called down to the police in the Woodbridge jurisdiction and asked them to check out any local warehouses with red roofs and gray corrugated siding for a possible chop shop for stolen cars."

"And?"

"And today I got a call that they had found a chop shop and busted a dozen people. So chalk up one for the good guys!"

"I'd say chalk up one for the good guy who's been developing his access to enhanced psychic abilities. The next thing you know, you'll be asking me to teach you to dowse!"

"I can't let you have all the fun," he grinned.

"Well, sometimes being a little psychic is fun, but other times it's just confusing. I mean, I can get some really good information in dreams, but the one I had about possibly being pushed off the Washington Monument was just plain scary, and it didn't really tell me who was the murderer. I think that with their combined energies, Jordan and Lorelei were somehow keeping a 'glamour' over themselves so I wouldn't know who the bad guy was. Of course, I suspected Jordan, but since we can't prove he was part of a conspiracy to eliminate his wife, I'm just glad things have worked out for a happier ending for Jeffrey and his grandmother—at least in the short term."

"You know, even if we can't legally bring him to justice, and even though he won the custody suit, you can be proud of yourself for a couple of things."

"Okay, stroke my ego a little," I said. "Tell me what I have to be proud of."

"First, you didn't get yourself killed, for which I'm really grateful. You surrounded yourself with protection, because it's something you've learned to do that gives you courage, so you were willing to stand up to Jordan. And with Lorelei, when push came to shove—if you'll excuse the expression!—you did what your dreams suggested and you ducked. So you protected yourself from Jordan *and* from Lorelei because you followed your own intuition. You trusted your power and didn't let anything they threatened you with cause you to dysfunction."

"That may be true, but I didn't best Jordan when it came down to the final battle in court."

"I don't think that matters. His son is going to stay with his grandmother, and Jordan will be out of the picture, at least for a while. And he has AIDS, so he isn't going to be around forever. In a way, he's defeated himself in the long run, hasn't he?"

"Yeah, I guess so. Eventually that will take its toll."

"We can only hope," he said. Then he glanced at his watch. "You have class tomorrow, don't you?"

"I do."

He stuck his lower lip out in mock disappointment. "I was hoping you could stay around a little longer. I mean, I really shouldn't let you drive just yet, since you've had some wine."

I leaned over and kissed his stuck out lip. "I brought a change of clothes for school tomorrow, just in case you should want some company tonight."

He grinned and reached up to stroke my cheek, whispering, "So...are you up for some *Law and Order?*"

"Sure," I said, "just as long as you don't bother to turn on the television!"

And I switched off the light.

Honora Finkelstein & Susan Smily

Honora Finkelstein has been an intelligence officer with the U. S. Navy, a small-press publisher, a technical writer, and a prize-winning features editor for Arundel Communications in Northern Virginia. She has been widely published in newspapers, magazines, and journals, has co-authored two nonfiction books, and has taught futurist and self-development workshops across the United States, in Canada, and in Europe. She is a member of Sisters in Crime and Romance Writers of America; she was also a workshop director for the International Women's Writing Guild for 15 years. She has a Ph.D. in English and is an adjunct associate professor in Western culture, literature, and writing at the University of Southern Indiana and the University of Evansville in Evansville, Indiana and the Union Institute & University in Cincinnati, Ohio.

Her interest in metaphysical subjects goes back to childhood when she had her first out-of-body experience while learning to tie her shoes. In the 1990s she produced and hosted a talk show on self-development and futurist topics called Kaleidoscope for Tomorrow on community cable television in Fairfax, Virginia, an experience that qualified her as an "agent provocateur." To the embarrassment of some of her more traditional friends and academic colleagues, but like her protagonist Ariel Quigley, she has precognitive dreams, does past life and Tarot card readings, and occasionally talks to ghosts.

Susan Smily, during her 25 years in the classroom, was an author, publisher, and workshop leader in elementary science education in Canada, Australia, and the United States (acquiring a gray hair for every student she taught). She created her own business for the development and production of a wide range of elementary education materials, worked as a writer, editor, and consultant with several educational programs, and made presentations at over 40 school and district professional development days. She was also once the Science Teacher of the Year (cover girl) for Boreal Science Supply Catalogue and as a result had coffee stains on her face in every high school in Canada.

She is the author of "Pianissimo," a one-act play that was presented off Broadway on April 13-15, 1998, at the Festival of Collective Voices, at the Harold Clurman Theatre in New York.

She has traveled extensively in North America, Europe, Australia, and the Far East. She developed an interest in metaphysical studies in the early 1990s and has since become involved in studying many areas of spirituality, including Native American, Vedanta, and Kabbalah. She is also an energy reader and "psychic diagnostician."

Finkelstein and Smily are both Reiki teacher-masters, interfaith ministers, certified hypnotherapists, and Hemi-Sync® outreach instructors for the Monroe Institute in Faber, Virginia. They are the co-authors of the Ariel Quigley mystery series and the accompanying Killer Cookbook series. Referring to themselves as the "Jewish-Irish comedy team" (Smily is Jewish and Finkelstein is Irish).

Printed in the United States
93791LV00003B/256-276/A